YES TRESPASSING

Stories by

ERIK †. JOHNSON

SO, I SUDDENLY REMEMBERED THIS PICTURE MY DAD TOOK OF MY SISTER AND I IN LIKE 1978 OR SOMETHING. WE'RE IN THE WOODS IN CONNECTICUT AND WE LOOK LIKE, SORT OF CREEPY. AND I WOULD LOVE IT IF WE COULD FIGURE OUT A WAY TO USE THIS AS A COVER, SOMEHOW, MAYBE EVEN A WRAPAROUND, THROWING OUT IDEAS, ETC. YOU KNOW. I CAN GET A VERY HIGH QUALITY VERSION OF IT, ALTHOUGH IT IS KIND OF COOL IN THIS 70'S GRAINY WAY. IT COULD BE ALTERED, I DON'T KNOW... BUT I ALSO THINK IT FITS THE IDEA OF YES TRESPASSING AND ISN'T EXCLUSIVELY HORROR-SUGGESTIVE OR FANTASY-SUGGESTIVE.

Erik Johnson Cover Idea with hand 2.13.15.

YES TRESPASSING

ERIK JOHNSON

WRITTEN ON THE PALM: YES TRESPASSING.

PALM PRESSED AGAINST THE COVER AS THOUGH FROM INSIDE BOOK.

SORRY → Hands are hard to DRAW.

YES TRESPASSING

Your Fantasy and &c!

ERIK JOHNSON

&c!

Sketch Cover Idea 2/13/15.

Note &c! symbol can be scrawled in red ink prominently on the cover.

Don't know what will go in middle — Doesn't have to be wing, maybe...

DO YOU MIND REACHING OUT TO JOHN TO SEE IF HE'D BE WILLING TO WRITE THE INTRO?

YES TRESPASSING

12/21/18

KRISTEN—

Can't express enough gratitude for your interest in my writing... So I'll just say, Thanks so much!

ERIK

NEED A BOOKMARK BEFORE GETTING STARTED?

FLIP TO PAGE $\sqrt{-1}$

Yes Trespassing

[HORROR. WONDER. MINDSCREWING.]

by Erk t.[*sic*] Johnson

Written Backwards

Cover and interior design by Michael Bailey
Scribbles and insanity by Erik T. Johnson
Introduction by John FD Taff

"A Few Leaves from the Travelogue of Doctor Julius Jonsson, Cryptobotanist and Hylesoprotolist: Bay Ridge, or, The Belief in the Undead Still Exists in New York" first appeared in *Trunk Stories #1*, Chizine (2003); "Water Buried" first appeared in the *British Fantasy Journal* (Winter 2010); "The Inconsolable Key Company" first appeared in *Pellucid Lunacy*, Written Backwards (2010); "The Invention of the Mask" first appeared in *Saucytooth's Webthology, Issue 2*; "The Black Tree's Box" first appeared in *Box of Delights*, Aeon Press (2011); "Blumenkrank" first appeared in *Golden Visions* (July 2010); "The Depopulation Syndrome" first appeared in *Dead But Dreaming 2*, Miskatonic River Press (2011); "The Invention of the Umbrella" first appeared in *Sein und Werden* (July 2011); "Labrusca Cognatus" first appeared in *Shimmer* (April 2011); "Things Found in a 4th Floor Room" first appeared in *Anthology of Ichor III: Gears of Damnation* (2011); "The Purple Word" first appeared in *Fictionwise eBooks* (January 2004); "Some Things Aren't Anything" first appeared in *Morpheus Tales #13* (2012); "The Apologies" first appeared in *Chiral Mad*, Written Backwards (2012); "Brain Scram" first appeared in *Space and Time Magazine #116* (2012); "The Leaf" first appeared in *Electric Velocipede #24* (2012); "Krug's Pen" first appeared in the *Mortis Operandi*, The Harrow Press (2012); "Martin Was Here" first appeared in *Strange Case Files*, Divertir Publishing (2013); "Welcome Home, All You Uninvited" first appeared in *Chiral Mad 2*, Written Backwards (2013); "The Angel Chaser" first appeared in *Qualia Nous*, Written Backwards (2014); "The Immigrants" first appeared in *You, Human*, Dark Regions Press (2016); *Scissors Seldom Come* first appeared as *The Chapman Delirium* in *The Chapman Books*, Uncanny Books (2014).

FIRST EDITION
ISBN: 978.0.9961493.9.6

HORROR & WONDER

SHOULD WE CUT THESE 2 STORIES? :(

IF ONLY TO KEEP THE BOOK AROUND 420–430 PAGES...

EDITOR'S NOTE: MAYBE WE CAN SECRETLY INCLUDE THE TWO CUT STORIES SOMEHOW. PERHAPS WE CAN HAVE A QR-CODE OR SOMETHING PRINTED ON THE PAGES AT THE VERY END OF THE BOOK, OR WHERE THESE STORIES SHOULD HAVE GONE IN THE COLLECTION IF THERE WERE UNLIMITED PAGES.

ANYONE WITH SMART PHONE (ARE THERE SUCH THINGS AS 'DUMB' PHONES?) COULD SCAN THE QR-CODE TO GET A FREE PDF 'BONUS STORY' OR TWO TO READ ON THE GO ...

JUST AN IDEA.

THIS IS WHAT I MEAN. MAYBE THIS IMAGE CAN LINK TO A BONUS 'PRE-STORY,' LIKE "THE ANGEL CHASER" SINCE THAT ONE MAY BE CUT, AND ANYONE COULD SCAN, DOWNLOAD THE BONUS_02 FILE FROM A NEW NO_TRESPASSING SECTION OF THE NETTIRW.COM WEBSITE, AND THEN READ AS A 'HERE'S WHAT YOU CAN EXPECT' KIND OF STORY BEFORE DIVING COMPLETELY INTO THE BOOK.

** I WONDER IF AMAZON'S 'LOOK INSIDE' FEATURE WILL ALLOW PREVIEWERS ACCESS TO THIS PAGE, WHICH WOULD BE COOL! **

MIND SCREWING

THIS IS WHAT INSANITY LOOKS LIKE...

EDITOR'S NOTE: YOU WOULD OF COURSE RETAIN <u>ALL</u> RIGHTS TO ANY SUCH WORKS LINKED THROUGH QR-CODES.

SCRATCH THAT. I PUT VERBIAGE IN YOUR CONTRACT STATING "ALL RIGHTS REVERT BACK TO AUTHOR IMMEDIATELY UPON PUBLICATION," FOR ALL WORKS INCLUDED IN THE COLLECTION, SO YOU SHOULD HAVE NOTHING TO WORRY ABOUT.

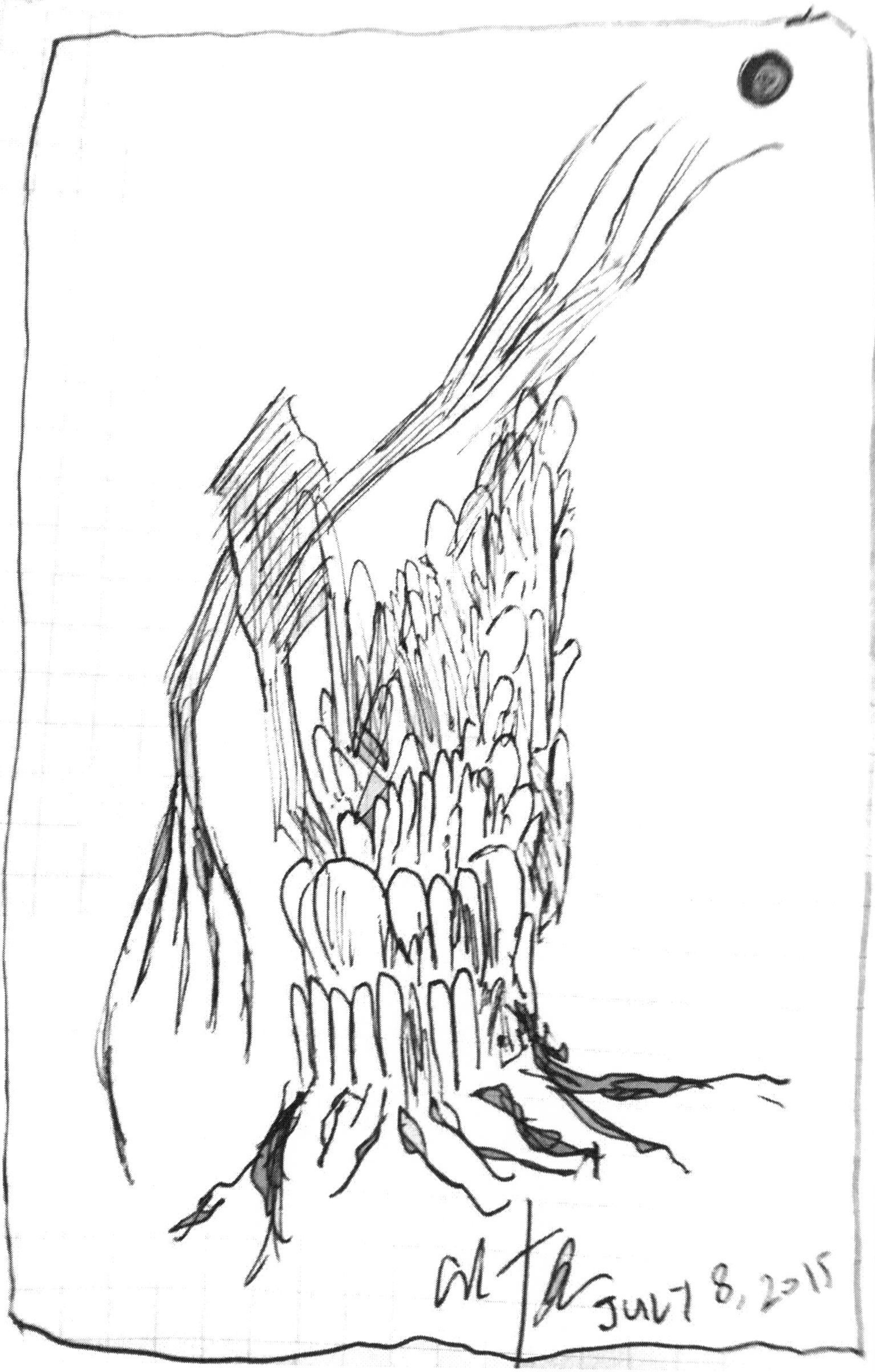

from page

JULY 8, 2015

John FD Taff's Introduction

Before we begin, let me just say that I have been an unabashed fan of Erik T. Johnson's writing far longer than you, unless, of course, you are his wife, his parents or in-laws, perhaps, his amazing son. Or some of his long-time friends. Okay, let me amend that. I have been an unabashed fan of Erik T. Johnson's writing far longer than most.

We met a decade or so ago, before social media ran rampant over the earth, in that quaint and curious age where there was only lowly e-mail for writers to converse with each other over the partially continental distances separating us. We'd both sold stories to some ephemeral, barely-here-then-gone anthology about—*yawn*—zombies. That book, if it did nothing else (and it certainly did nothing else), exposed me to his work for the first time, through a story entitled "The Purple Word," which appears herein.

I say the word *exposed*, and some are sure to frown at that word. I used this same word, in the past, to describe my attitude to unleashing organized religion into the lives of my children. "It's best, I suppose, that they're exposed to this at a young age," I'd opined. "So that when they're older, they can make up their own minds." I used the word *exposed* here to suggest baring my children against something dangerous and unpredictable, rather like a virus.

When I say *exposed* in reference to Erik's work, though, I mean it more in the sense of a bee exposing a flower to pollen eventually resulting in succulent fruit. Or perhaps exposing a log to spores which will result in a glorious crop of tasty mushrooms. Either way, I mean it in the best sense, with only the highest regards.

Certainly, my first exposure to Erik's writing resulted in the need for me to read more... and more... and more of his stuff. And besides the obvious lure of the profoundly (yet, curiously, plainly presented) weirdness of his stories, the intricate build of words he uses to convey the most absurd of ideas, and characters that skirt the very ragged edges of humanity, there is something that I come back to time and time again in his stuff.

I've said this before (because I speak about Erik often, to anyone who will listen), and I will take a few words here to say it again. No one writes a line like Erik T. Johnson. Oh, I know it takes more than a line to make a great story. I know that. He does that. Let's accept that as axiom here and move on to his brilliant use of individual, superbly crafted lines in his stories to make a point, highlight an eccentricity or nuance a character right into life.

His story in this collection, "Some Things Aren't Anything," is a good example, being as it's filled with what I love about Erik's work... namely his ability to turn a phrase that is so surreal and so lovely that it makes you want to go back and reread it. For example:

"And I thought a ship must be like this: everyone cooped up together, and to pass the time I'd imagine we had to eat each other like sailors lost at sea."

Yum. Or how about this from "The Black Tree's Box" (which, incidentally, appeared in a collection with a story of mine, "Box of Rocks." Coincidence? Perhaps.)?

"He settled on love, partly because it didn't demand the laborious planning and intense follow-through of revenge, and partly because it was really there."

Another story, "Krug's Pen," yields this. "She wore a gray raincoat. Her hair had the clean, shiny golden straightness of a Labrador's fur in an Alpo commercial. Her features were slightly asymmetrical like the plates on a table set in a hurry. But they were fine plates." Those kinds of lines make me smile.

Here's another thing that I like about Erik's writing. It demands something from you. It makes you work a little, think a little. His are not the stories that you're going to breeze through in fifteen minutes before you go to bed. No, his writing necessitates just a little more from you in terms of investment. But I'm not talking mainly of time here; I'm talking about neurons. Yes, actual firing neurons in your brain. And why shouldn't it? Yes, some writing is escapist, and there's absolutely nothing wrong about that. But some writing wants the reader to dig a little deeper, to set the bar of suspension of disbelief just a little lower (or dispense with it altogether).

Erik T. Johnson makes you work for the insights he's going to reveal in his stories, and that's an artistic choice that I can respect. He's noted before that one of his favorite novels is *Moby Dick*, a choice that sits well with me. Melville was an author, while not precisely cut from the same cloth as Johnson, still excelled at making his readers work.

But, as with Melville, the payoff for readers' investment in Johnson's stories? Oh, wow, the payoff is fantastic. The levels of grotesquerie and phantasmagoric splendor are thrown wide open, huge superbly weird landscapes of dizzying psychedelia are revealed. Characters of the most specious humanity, squamous and batrachian, are not just followed about their daily interactions, but connected to, sympathized with, even as they go about their various debauched and peccant business. (Didja see what I did there? Didja? *Didja?*)

You're going to find all sorts of high weirdness in this collection, from detectives working on improbable mysteries to a key shop where more than just locks are undone. Surely featured herein are enough acolytes to arcane traditions to fill a very, very bizarre church; enough grizzled, prophetic madman to glut an entire asylum.

I think you, dear reader, as I have, will thrill to the many conceits contained herein, marvel at the anoxic heights and the plutonian depths, become slightly queasy at the monstrous malformations of reality, and despair at a glimpse of universes less than a nudge removed from our own.

So, find your comfortable chair and set aside time to contemplate mysteries whose very existence you'd probably never even considered before. If your head swims, if your horizons are expanded somewhat beyond comfort, if you begin looking at the reality of your life as a thin veneer hastily glued over the particle board of something far, far weirder, well, then Erik T. Johnson has done his job.

John F.D. Taff
January 2017

AUTHOR'S INTRODUCTION

HI!

I can tell you the cover photo shows my sister and me holding hands, somewhere in green, black, and Connecticut woods, circa 1978. That our father was the photographer who snapped us in that space-time now beyond revisit or recall. Were we trespassing? It's easy enough in the wild: Demarcations of growth-mad kingdoms tangle, sign and break secret, restive treaties. The photo is much like a magic bear-trap. We willingly gave the meat of us over to the steel and sudden chomp of that moment, thinking we'd escape like pure ghost, unscathed. Why is the photographer, my father, so far away? How can we even be sure that it's still him over there? Look at the two children. We are vulnerable and objectified by the remoteness of the lens.

What happened earlier that day? Right after the shutter clicked? Each time I scry that pic, I see grotesque faces among the malnourished shadows and fallen trunks of sun. I study it far too often, see alterations in the monstrous grimaces have occurred between each of my morbid examinations. It seems like last minute preparations for mysterious rites, or 300-acre deep, unchancy practical jokes, are ever underfoot and way in that photo. Who else schemed, hid in the ribs of skeletal shadow, what waited? Is it the creature who set my imagination free only to squeeze itself into the crawl spaces of horror, go walkabout in the sparkling wonder of infinity, and accidentally release the mindscrewed from its long internment far below what I mistakenly thought was the most beneath? So that I could return and report on what I'd found. On that day in 1978, did we innocents escape unscathed? I don't know. I can't make out the vibe of my child-face. Did I glimpse this future me, a man compelled to flail in too many questions?

Such as:

Why *Yes Trespassing*?

Among these stories are both insolent warnings and warm invitations. Stories like the world as I've often thought it. Plays Trick-or-Trick daily. Hides your brain from your brain. Leers in beams of light. Salivates over the blueprints it's ever refining in the clouds, designing spaces to corner you. Puts unspeakable acts before your eyes that can't be unseen, and dares you to stare past them, making you feel—There's no word for it. But that's why there are these stories.

I hope you enjoy reading this labor of insomnia, grief, love, horror, anguish, humor, a beauty quest for color in the blinding blackness, born of hope and a need to communicate, and a rude, inexorable force of loathing, memories without number, real and imagined, and compulsive, grand spasms of "What If…" that nothing can undo. And I would also like to say that I tried my best.

I wish you a good time, or some other, weirder type, perhaps described herein.

I wish.

May you grant it.

Erik t. [*sic*] Johnson
Brooklyn, New York
February 2, 2017 at 3:26am

I dedicate this book to my mortality—Eat this, sonny!

WATER BURIED

i

Martin Box's asthma was at its worst on these humid summer afternoons, so he spent the day in a cool corner of his secret attic, waiting for his parents to come home from three days of some kind of counseling called EST. Under a rotten timber he found a piece of old paper burned on the edges by a fire that had died ages ago. Someone had written on them in a careful hand:

Water buried
Buried water
Drops fall down
Into the water
Which came first?
One or the other?

ii

It was hard to tell if the paper had been put to flame after the composition or if some distant relative had rescued a blank page from a fire and put the remnants to epistolary use. The words were either meant to be destroyed, or meant to remain. The difference was profound as it was ambiguous. But surely, the author was a relative, because the Boxes had lived in the house at 333 Spring Street for well over one hundred years, and the Boxes had rarely kept friends, and certainly never in the attic.

iii

333 Spring Street sat atop a hill at the highest point in Burtonsville, even higher than the clock tower. As a result, when the bells clanged the hours, time itself seemed to drift up to Martin in his attic roost, drift like something that could disappear. The attic had large, triangular windows on east and west sides, allowing Martin an asthmatic hawk's view of Burtonsville. From those windows he could catch the first raindrop of a storm in a spoon, and snowflakes with almost anything. In the west, Martin could see the principal features of Burtonsville strewn about the land like toys in a playroom. These were the clock tower, strangely mute of late, a fire house, two silver steeples, three green parks, seventeen red roofs, twenty-eight chimneys, seven roads, four statues of dead men, one set of train tracks, a muddy scrap of river, trees scattered like jacks, and one awful schoolhouse. On the eastern side of the attic, where he kept his yellowed books, a spyglass and lingerie advertisements, Martin could view a dense wall of swaying wilderness that always seemed about to fall, and to shout, but stood majestic and silent.

This then, was Martin's world, a lofty, comfy limbo bookended by wildly divergent lands to the east and west. The attic was not easily describable by sense of sight. One could call it dark as easily as sunny, cold as rightly as hot, muffled or echoing, spacious or claustrophobic as the mood struck you. Because the attic had no real purpose, or rather, no openly agreed upon purpose, Martin's eye did not look for one. In the attic, Martin looked out the windows or at his books, or poetry on singed paper. He did not, strictly speaking, look at the attic. In this world, part cavern, part peak, the environment was a haze of smells and their associations.

The attic smelled of timber cut with hand axes, tins of waxes and polishes with labels worn to gibberish, nearly empty oil cans, lubricants to whisk the cogwheels of forgotten machines, paper and ink, rusty window screens, piquant ghosts of books, ruined beehives full of dust, brittle colorless twine and lightning bolts, laundry left in the rain, paints made from milk, boxes of not sure what that is, rags that had wiped the hulls of wooden ships, that had wiped runny noses and bandaged bleeding hands cut hacking trees, stolen wishing-well pennies, bottles of traces of nothing, disintegrating rubber gloves, oozy umbrageous accretions, many-yawned air, dun and ochre garments, damp and sized too big for anyone Martin had ever met, and pervading everything, the urgent, brown scent of earth, earth stronger than drifting time, so strong it was able to pass through three stories to the high sunny attic from the depths of the largely unexplored cellar.

Two days ago, Martin noticed a new smell that corresponded with the day the old clock tower stopped floating the hours up to his asthmatic's hawk aerie. The smell was hard to describe. It was a sharp, new, musky, sweet, vanilla, sandalwood scent of not-the-attic. That same day, a shadowy thing moved in to share the attic with Martin. He did not get a good look at it. It stayed on the eastern side, by the forest standing fast and quiet, and Martin stayed in the west, closer to civilization. Until that day, the attic had been Martin's world alone. Even his parents never ventured up there. He was still not sure how he felt about the invader but he felt that he should not say anything, at least yet. Better to wait and see what happens. Probably it had lived in the top of the clock tower, and once the hands stopped turning and the men came to repair it, it sought another high place to hide in. Perhaps, Martin thought, once time begins again, it will leave.

IV

Martin's parents should have been home by now. They were due back from EST hours ago. He wanted to show them the burnt paper. More than once, the radio in the kitchen turned on for no reason and he thought they were home but it was nobody. He searched every room, even his own bedroom which he almost never slept in. Then he walked to the edge of the wilderness to the east. The trees grew densely and it would be easy to get lost in there. It was hard to imagine why his mother and father would have gone in that direction, but then they were hard to understand and didn't always do what was best for them. Martin felt a mosquito bite on his neck and something watching him. He knew who it was. As the day wore on to night he decided he had two realistic choices: ask the thing in the attic if it had any idea where they had gotten off to, or check the dreaded cellar. He did not want to go in the forest. He felt like he would not find his way out again.

V

The cellar had never really been built. It had been attempted. The walls were made of uneven stones piled atop the heavy, brown earth. Where a floor should have been, there was the dirt surface of an ancient world. The air was dark as soil. You only saw parts of what lived and crawled there, glossy, dirty body parts and millions of legs. You spied their webs and heard their rattling and scraping. You smelled the poisonous fungi and the endlessly rolling earth. It seemed impossible that there was a sturdy, dry house just above it.

Some Boxes from long ago had stored farming and other implements in the cellar. It was possible that Martin's parents had come looking for something they needed to bring to EST, and tripped over a wheelbarrow or butter-churner and were trapped. Martin's flashlight showed recent footprints in the deep, soft earth. He stepped forward, his smaller foot in the large boot-print, and heard a drop of buried water drip.

A rusty pipe, running along the low ceiling, was leaking into the curved blade of a rustier scythe. The footprints went past the scythe into a measureless gloom.

"Mom! Dad!" Martin yelled into the spongy inkiness.

He followed the bootprints further along their murky course. They stopped at a crate that had been dragged out of its old spot. Someone had rummaged through it. Martin held his flashlight in two shaking hands and forced himself onwards. The rarely inhaled air, thick with coal, mold and grime, choked him as he went. Asthma tightened his chest. The crate was full of ropes knotted into nooses, some more successfully executed than others.

Something with white leg joints and no head darted out from under a noose. Martin's skin gooseflesched and itched. The battery in the flashlight died. Martin turned and ran as fast as he could out into the night.

VI

Martin walked to the edge of the woods again and prevaricated awhile under the glimmering cross of Cygnus. He took a step between the trees and heard leaves making ocean sounds far overhead. A twig snapped underfoot, an owl hooted. The stars disappeared under the boughs.

The only thing to do was ask the thing in the attic if it had seen his parents. He slowly made his way through the rooms on his way upstairs, putting the lights on in each one. The television was on in the living room for no reason. He turned it off. In his mother's bedroom he thought he smelled the sweet, alien odor of the thing in the attic. But it was not there. In his father's bedroom he smelled traces of moldering earth. In the kitchen, rotting eggs. In the pantry off the kitchen Martin found another flashlight, and a sturdy old hammer.

The attic had no electric lights. Martin took the narrow flight of stairs up into his formerly secret world. He could sense the thing breathing there. Perhaps it was afraid of him. It was too quiet, repressed. He directed his flashlight towards the east and stopped the beam short of revealing the thing.

"Excuse me," Martin said. "Have you seen my parents?"

There was the slightest exhalation, and then the silence of tongue pressing into gums.

"Do you come from the clock tower?" Martin asked.

"*Yesss,*" a high but soft voice whispered artificially, like a Mel Blanc character.

"Did you stop time?"

"*Yesss.*"

"Can you tell me where my parents are?"

"Watch what... you *fish for.*"

"If you are going to keep up this nonsense, I am going to have to come closer," Martin said, lifting up the hammer.

The flashlight beam took a step forward with him and fell on a piece of paper with burned edges. Martin cautiously squatted down and extended the hammer out in front of him. He caught the paper with the back of the hammerhead and pulled it closer. It was covered in the same script as the poem he'd found earlier.

What does it mean?
What does it matter?
Water buried
Buried water.

"Did you write this?" Martin asked.

Before the thing from the clock tower could answer or not, the doorbell rang.

"Mom! Dad!" he yelled, running downstairs. "Are you locked out?"

With all the lights in the house on, it didn't take long to reach the front door. He opened it to nobody. So he went back inside, looked for the thing from the clock tower again. It was gone, but the radio was on in the kitchen.

"... and he took his wife up to the clock tower, Jim," the radio newsman was saying to his co-host. "And you know how the clock's been broken for a few days, right? Well, that's because he tied a noose around her neck and left just a little slack in it—like a leash. And then he fixed the rope to the clock mechanism, or whatever it's called—like an engine that makes the hands of the clock move around the face. And he bound her legs and arms to her body and he gagged her mouth with a rag doused in Channel No. 5. Then as the hands of the clock moved around, they pulled the rope up higher and tighter around the mechanism and she was slowly dragged off the floor, she was hung and then her neck snapped. And the clock stopped working. It's stuck at 10:11 PM, three days ago. That's how long the poor woman was hanging there, dead. And they can't get the clock working until they get her body down..."

Before Jim could express his shock, Martin turned off the radio.

VII

Martin watched the stars move a little more. Then he noticed the mailbox was overflowing and some letters had fallen on the gravel driveway. He picked one up. It was some junk mail, addressed to his mother, with her maiden name. Ms. Rosina Lake, it said.

VIII

Martin sat on the back steps all night, a cool summer breeze not making things worse. He knew better than to talk to the thing in the attic anymore. Instead he stayed awake and watched the dawn pull shadows from the sky and into the ground. And he waited until he heard time drifting up again from the clock tower, six clear bells ringing through the air. Then he got up and walked into the forest, to find his father.

6-19-16 (midnighty.)

I WAS GOING TO
WRITE SOMETHING ELSE RIGHT
(HERE) — In THIS Same physical
spot. BUT THIS KIND OF «PLACEHOLDER»
PLACE CANNOT SUBSTITUTE. OR
HAVE I JUST DONE
JUST THAT?

SOME THINGS AREN'T ANYTHING

THERE WAS A SPECIAL BREED of imaginary thing in that house, which could be touched. There was a piano, but my mother hated music, so none of us knew how to play it, so it was an imaginary piano. And there was a fireplace, but my father was too afraid of burning the house down to light a fire in it, so it was an imaginary fireplace. We were always so close to things that *could* be but weren't. Even Ship House itself was an example of this class of imaginary objects. It was a big, old, beautiful three-story Victorian with gabled roofs, top and lower-level wrap-around porches, and twenty acres of untampered wilderness in the Connecticut countryside.

To my young mind, that house should have been full of people laughing, dressed in lovely clothing, singing by gauzy candlelight. It should have been the place where all the far-flung members of a large happy family gathered to keep their great-great-great-grandparents' memories alive. They should have had a thousand-paged book which they treated like a priceless relic, full of family history, that they'd all read a hundred times and always wished there was more of it. If I shut my eyes, I heard music, I saw a fire glowing, and I sat on the lap of a colorful long-lost uncle.

Grandma's old house was like a ship because it was so isolated, perched atop an unmoving green wave, beneath a starry golden weathervane. And I thought a ship must be like this: everyone cooped up together, and to pass the time I'd imagine we had to eat each other like sailors lost at sea.

Of course, I would have had more fun at Ship House if I had permission to explore the bramble path near the house, which led off toward a river I heard but never saw. After all, the only reason we went to Ship House was to "get Charity away from other people for a while." But my parents forbid me from going down that way, saying it was dangerous, that some people had been reported missing on the bramble path years ago and were never found again. They said I should keep away altogether because I always went too far. But the bramble path kept growing closer to the house each year and soon it would be harder to resist.

The last time we went to Ship House, my father bought my mother a gold necklace that had Mom's name on a disc in the middle. She let me wear it in the car. My older brother Raymond sat next to me in the back. He was greasy and tall and sat with his scabby knees spread wide so I had no room and he'd make loud fart noises with his mouth and spit on me, by accident and on purpose, and he called me "Sicko" and "Creepy" and "Nutpot." He had a blue candy tongue and Dad's nose like he stole it right off his face. He was covered in freckles. Raymond was who I imagined people you hate must be like. He was their favorite child but I was sure he would taste sour.

During the ride from New York, my parents fighting and

steady movement lulled me asleep. When I opened my eyes the house was emerging from its isolated Connecticut hill. The summer sun was about to set and the grand golden weathervane was gleaming like something removed from the anus of a pervert in an emergency room.

Dad was gazing out the dining room window.

The phone rang. Mom got it.

"No, he's not here," she said, and hung up.

"Who was that?" Dad asked.

"That's what I'd like to know," she said.

"Why don't you go out and play," my father commanded. "But don't go far. You always go too far."

I stood at the edge of the bramble path. It was much closer to the house than I remembered it being last year. There was a slight breeze that brought a watery, metallic, woody, earthy smell like a clock dredged from a riverbank where the mud had stopped it long ago. I was just listening to the hidden river, since looking would not do much good and the bramble path was nothing but a small black tunnel made of thorny leaves and mottled with moonlight.

When I opened my eyes, I saw eyes like shadows cast by falling hailstones staring at me expectantly. It was hard to see who the eyes belonged to, except that he was covered in hair and was the light-and-dark color of white noise on Grandma's tube TV when the brightness control was set too low. I knew I should be scared but I was something else that I cannot name, that made my brain think and my heart pump and my skin goosefleshed and moved evening through my lungs. Sometimes I had the same feeling after I urinated in an empty beer bottle and left it for a bum to drink.

"Who are you?" I said.

"Some things aren't anything," he said, the voice muffled, as though there were someone hiding inside of him.

"I don't know what you want."

"When you are in the library, say *I hear something scratching upstairs.*"

"I don't really like the library much," I said.

"When you are in the hall, say *I want to stay with you and Dad.*"

He ambled a little closer. I stepped back. I saw a skeletal hand, and the big, black eyes moved quickly like beetles that had just righted themselves after a fall.

"When you are in the bedroom, *scream*. And when you are in the garden, say *Yes*," he said, moving still closer, and I saw his gaping mouth was horrible and huge as a point-blank shotgun blast.

My mother called me to dinner. I turned and ran without looking back, breath like wind at my neck.

At the dinner table, Raymond played with a claw-shaped stick and kept poking my back. I punched his shoulder. Mom yelled at him and then at me. We heard glass break in the library.

"Invaders!" Raymond shouted.

"What was that?" Dad demanded.

"How should I know?" Mom said.

"What the hell," he said, and got up.

Raymond ran to the library with his claw held high.

"Be careful," Mom said to him.

"Can I see?" I asked, even though I didn't like the library much.

"Stay here," she ordered me. She'd been reading a book with a bloody knife on the cover. "It's probably nothing."

Raymond yelled and something heavy toppled suddenly like a weightlifter fainting, and there was more glass cracking, and a gonging that made my toes hum.

"What the..." Dad growled.

Mom zoomed out. I followed.

Dad was lying on the floor of the library pressed under the

grandfather clock. He had tripped over a thorny vine that stretched across the doorway, about two inches off the ground. The vine appeared to have taken root in the old wood. When he reached out to stop his fall, his hand had grabbed the hands of the clock, and he pulled it down on top of him, tearing the minute and second hands off like a false moustache. The clock kept ticking, but as if we had entered another dimension, there was no way to know the time.

There was a decapitated head-sized hole in the window.

"The only damn thing in this house," he said, tossing off the broken clock with disgust, "that doesn't need work is the goddamn weathervane."

His face was covered in little Morse code cuts, all scratch-dashes and dot-bloodspots.

"Gerald, you are so stupid! That clock was an heirloom. And what about the window?" my mother said, uninterested in his wounds.

"Damn bird hit it, I think," Dad said without conviction, dabbing his face with a handkerchief.

Chaos excited Raymond. His eyes were wide, pale freckled skin flushed, breathing through his slack slobbery mouth. He was too everything.

"It's not a bird. It's some kind of monster," he shouted.

"Gerald," Mom said harshly. "Tell them monsters are not real."

Mom hated nonsense. My father said nothing.

"Some things aren't anything," she said to us.

"*I hear something scratching upstairs*," I said, and I did.

Dad took a metal-bulleted stick umbrella from a cherry coat-rack and held it like Raymond with his claw. It had a duck-headed handle.

"You watch that," Mom said. "It belonged to my mother."

"Everyone stay behind me," Dad said.

As we left the room, I noticed all the books were upside down on the shelves, like the library belonged to someone who walked on the ceiling.

C!

We went upstairs. It was dark and sleepwalky for us to be in the hallway, hunting, where we only ever passed through. I crouched down and looked through the legs of Mom, Raymond, and Dad. In the shadows at the end of the long hall, only I saw two eyes like the shadows of falling eyeballs, and a million, vague tiny movements like a puddle of kicking centipedes. The thing from the bramble patch hunched weirdly against the wall, back to us, face twisted around backwards leeringly, with a mouth that could not shut. There was a smile in him somewhere, but not on his face.

"Damn it, I can't remember where the light switch is, do you believe it?" Dad said.

"I believe it," Mom said. "You've really gone south."

I saw the switch, reached out and turned it on.

The thing was gone. I noticed all the sand in the hourglass on the hall table was collected in the top half. A thorn was stuck in the thin waist of the glass, blocking the grains from marking time.

"Charity, go downstairs," Mom blustered, because she thought of me as the baby.

"Yeah, get out of here, Psycho," Raymond said.

"*I want to stay with you and Dad,*" I said, because I didn't want them to treat me so small just because they hated each other so much and had to take it out on me.

"What was that in my bedroom?" Raymond said, darted down the hall, and ran into the room.

C!

We rushed after Raymond. Dad groped round the door for the switch and the yellow room jumped out like the page of a pop-up book.

But Raymond was nowhere to be seen.

As they searched the room for their favorite child, I looked at the pencil marks on the wall indicating the various heights Raymond had reached as he'd gotten older. There was a new mark there. It was right where the wall touched the floor, a single lead-gray hair affixed with a drop of blood. I tried to help my parents find Raymond.

I *screamed* because I saw him for a minute, in the non-reflective back of the mirror on the red rug.

I screamed because I remembered the rug used to be white.

That memory made my brain think and my heart pump and my skin goosefleshed and moved big sky through my lungs.

*C!

They told me to shut up and called after Raymond until Mom said: "Just forget it. He'll show up. He doesn't listen, like you."

"Where's the necklace I bought you?"

"You think that makes anything better? I donated it to Charity."

Dad looked at my neck. His frown had the same curve as the top of his balding head and the bulge of his paunch. He winced because the frown tore the Morse Code cuts on his face, and they began bleeding again, –.. . .– –..

"Don't break it," Dad barked, meaning the necklace.

"I don't break things, Raymond did," I said.

Something heavy fell outside, shattering pots in the garden.

"Raymond!" Mom yelled, and we ran downstairs.

*C!

I know Mom and Dad didn't see them lying down in the herb garden, hands over their eyes, peering through their twiggy fingers and sides rippling with suppressed giggling. They sort of looked like frosty scarecrow stuffing. Mom went around the back of the house. Dad tripped over one of their skinny, hairy foot-stumps, and his face smashed into the sharp and pointily-rayed weathervane, which had come off the roof. Mom came back, still looking for wonderful, glorious Raymond in the dark, forgetting my Dad existed. She stumbled over brambles that had not been there at sunset, and stepped on Dad's head, pushing the weathervane's South-point through his brain.

She fell to her knees and said "Oh my God" and then called my name, like an afterthought.

"I'm right here, Mom."

"Please, Charity, go call 911. Get help. Will you do that for me?" she asked.

"*Yes*," I said.

But I was tired of doing what my parents and those things from the bramble patch ordered me to do. So I lied; I didn't get help. I went my own way, walking as far as I wanted to go, maybe too far. The moon was bright as my necklace. The air was cool, and starless as a man tattooed in stars who'd had his skin ripped off. Hidden insects sang and an invisible river slithered.

After I got hungry I went back to Ship House. There was a new weathervane on the roof that looked like two people lashed together with brambles. I couldn't tell whether their struggling caused the arrows of their hands to move, rather than the wind, or whether the wind was causing them to look like two people locked in eternal struggle.

Lucky for my belly, there was a great feast being prepared in the kitchen. All the lights in the house were on, and figures were dancing in the parlor. The house was full of ghostly apish things laughing, dressed in bright clothing that made their moon-hairs shine like silver, singing by gauzy candlelight. It was as if all the far-flung members of a large happy family had gathered to keep their great-great-great-grandparents' memories alive. They handed me a thousand-paged book which they treated like a priceless relic, full of family history, that they'd all read a hundred times and always wished there was more of it. They showed me my name on the newest page, which was made of freckled skin. One of them played the piano and a fire was glowing, and I sat on the lap of a colorful thing who had a smile somewhere in him, but not on his face.

THE BLACK TREE'S BOX

GRIFFIN 1973

I am Griffin Gravel. This is my first diary entry ever. I am ten years old. Nearly eleven. I am only writing because I am bored. I found this book in the attic. Someone wrote 1956 on the first page and nothing else—see? I will cross it out and write 1973. This is what is happening:

It is summer and my aunt Sam is dying. My mom calls it wasting away. Can you waste closer? Mom is sort of nuts. She is afraid of telephones and washes her hands a lot and she thinks the house is too close to the river and it might flood and wash us away. But Aunt Sam is crazier. Dad calls her a real wackadoo. She never leaves the house. She says Jesus Christ is coming back one day, but I don't see how she could know someone that famous, let alone his travel plans. I only met her once. It was Thanksgiving when I was little. I can't remember what she looks like. I can't even imagine her.

So mom is visiting Aunt Sam until she dies. She's been gone a few days. Since she left dad has gotten weirder and weirder. He's never talked to me much. He doesn't listen. He always seems like he's reading a book even when he's not. He's usually super-careful and keeps everything neat. He even hates it when the welcome mat outside isn't totally straight. And we don't ever welcome anyone.

But now he isn't turning off the lights when he leaves rooms. And he's doing more horrible things. Twice he didn't flush the toilet after using it. All week he's been sleeping on the couch. He never did that before. And last night he was counting in his sleep, too, and then he suddenly shouted OPEN IT! *and then kept snoring.*

I don't know why he's acting so different, like something's wrong. He has many good things. I don't think it's my fault. I'm really well-behaved and they say I am precocious. My dad is even smarter than me and my grandfather was supposed to be a genius. Nobody says he's wasting away. He has a good job as the county librarian. Our house was built in 1823. Dad was born here. It's as big as a castle. I wonder if that's why his name is Royal.

Just in case mom is right about the river, I am going to rip these pages out and stick them in a bottle. Then if there is a flood and the house gets washed away, someone still might find it one day.

#C!

Griffin finished writing and put the diary down. He forgot about his bottle-idea and he hadn't noticed the passage written lightly in pencil on one of the last pages:

Nothing my father has explains him. No number or combination of details provides answers. Not his eyes blue as prize ribbons, absent-minded fingers worrying pocket-change, or painterly signature, bolder than his quiet personality. Taken together, the observable facts about him pile into a dense, private verticality through which I cannot look—like a stack of coins photographed from above so as to appear as just one, the quantity and value of the whole beyond guess.

#C!

The night Griffin wrote his first and last diary entry, he'd sat with his father at the dining room table, slurping Dinty Moore stew. It was a hot, uncomfortably still Sunday, made claustrophobic by his dad's immense silence. A balsa-wood, 1:72 scale Fokker sat beside his persimmon bowl.

Griffin had recently found the model triplane in the attic. It was once his Uncle Jay's favorite toy. He was long dead, as was Griffin's grandfather: both Jay and Josef Gravel had fallen down the unfinished well outside the house and cracked their skulls, Jay in 1947 and his grandfather sixteen years later, soon after Griffin's birth. To Griffin, the sum of either man's existence was little more than a line from Humpty Dumpty.

All day and during supper, Griffin and his dad hadn't talked or exchanged glances. The steam from Griffin's bowl assumed the shapes of mascots, blood clots, sandstorms. He wondered how it's possible to say things can be *like* other things, when Roy suddenly slammed a hairy-knuckled fist on the model plane, over and urgently over like he was trying to innervate a winding-down heart.

Griffin stiffened and stifled a cry at this unprovoked, uncharacteristic violence. He was afraid to move, yet trembling. He forced himself to look at his father's eyes. They were spooky, equally impenetrable and shallow, like shadows. His father had revealed a terrible power to make things real, transforming a toy, which pretended to be something it was not, into a splintered heap that could be nothing else than itself, exactly because it was unfixable and the real cannot be altered but is always real.

Maybe, Griffin thought, *that's wasting closer*.

Griffin left his father brooding over the table, Godzilla-huge-and-ridiculously-monstrous above the wreckage. He hid in the shadow-cluttered attic with the dusty atoms of countless broken things. He wished it were a fort, or a treehouse. He'd always wished for one but his dad was no good at building anything, and never asked him what he wanted anyway.

Griffin peered through a grimy window. A moony breeze threshed the woods. He tapped his chin, and a pain shot under his fingernail where a 1943 triplane splinter had punctured his skin. He extracted it with his teeth, recklessly biting into fingerprint.

Griffin dropped his head on old Farmer's Almanacs, pressed scrawny vertebrae into floorboards and propped his feet on the brass bones of a tattered lampshade. He stared at the chipped, wooden figure of a businessman with a clock for a head which rested in the corner, some dead relative's impulsive flea-market purchase. He loved his father, hated him, loved him, hated, and loved him in turn, one following the other as next murdered now.

He settled on love, partly because it didn't demand the laborious planning and intense follow-through of revenge, and partly because it was really there. But something was disconnected about the feeling, like the way an eye is removed from the objects it sees. The aptness of this simile was a problem. Each real feeling ought to be singular, incomparable, only what it is . . .

Griffin lifted his head as jarring, televised white noise drifted up from the living room. He crept downstairs; Roy was catatonic on the couch, face lathered in cathode rays. He was mouthing a regular series of numbers or words. Griffin stole into his parents' bedroom and searched for something to understand or destroy.

The top drawer of his father's dresser gaped like an idiot's mouth or a trap. Inside was a nest of indeterminately lucky, expired, important, valuable, useless, postponed objects unified by mere proximity, a schizophrenic's shopping list. Under soiled ochre handkerchiefs, graph paper covered in smutty doodles, kewpie doll plastic, dried-glue-backed photos of tight-lipped sepia strangers standing behind cakes and in front of fireplaces, a 1947 bone-handled pocket knife, oily and misshapen wax earplugs like thalidomide-child netsuke, New Old Stock condom packets, two ceiling light pull-chain segments, a thin book called *Logic & Philosophy: an Intractable Tract* by Josef Gravel, PhD, its spine broken in half, opened to the highlighted passage: *You must "read" a truth tree by examining its branches; however a truth tree differs from its real-world analogue in at least two ways: It grows upside-down; and we refer to this growth as decomposition* . . . pencils masticated to their lead guts, and errant Roman watch numerals, Griffin's fingers found the smooth black box.

He stood there several minutes, strenuously still, as if a physician were testing him to determine whether he'd live or die based on the results of a scan of his entire being performed through the sensitive, rectangular device. A tenebrous resin oozed out the tightly-grained wood, mixing with Griffin's sweat in the whorled sewers of his fingertips. It seeped into splinter-poked flesh.

ROY 1947

Roy's dad, Josef Gravel, was Chair of Ghostmoth University's Philosophy Department. He was an expert on symbolic logic. When he was not teaching or drafting award-winning monographs he appeared to occupy himself with carpentry, bricklaying, and other methods of practical construction. But Roy knew better. Take this June day for example: to the passerby, Josef was standing outside his rambling 1823 house, building a well with mortar and stones—but he was actually shitting on the world.

Josef would look at his handiwork and smile (a slightly less convex frown). He was pleased with his shit. Satisfied how he'd ruined another piece of the landscape and hidden his vandalism in the guise of a useful structure.

Roy was of no use to his father, who only spoke to him in commands, and watched him with detached expectancy, as if he'd built Roy as an experiment and was waiting to record the results. It made Roy ashamed.

Roy was sure he didn't have a knack for his father's building rituals, those precise, step-by-hundreds-of-steps techniques. He preferred to leave things alone, enjoy them as they were; and when obligated to alter the world, he had a dirty mind more interested in putting things in the wrong places than following directions. He'd once shoveled snow with a trumpet.

Jay was Josef's star pupil. They would shit together all the time, tricking people into seeing a new dining room table, a mended concrete walkway, a picket fence, a model Fokker triplane carefully carved from balsa wood for Jay's eleventh birthday.

Roy stood by the edge of the forest watching his dad and Jay constructing the well. He decided to wander. But Roy was tired of the old rusted haunts and the field of long grasses that looked the same whether you stood on your head or feet. He wanted the opposite of a well. He'd find something tall nobody built and climb to the top.

He explored woody terrain he'd avoided due to the many brambles, staying close to a stream shaped like the logical operator "Not" (~). After a long, thorny hour it dissipated into a swale delimited by another patch of dense trees. If Roy kept going, he might get lost. He would miss lunch and be punished. Roy would know he was punished without being told, without anything being different, in fact. It was a dizzying reverse-of-reverse-of-reverse-of-reverse feeling, like instead of waking up as himself in the morning, he woke up *as* himself. The punished world was the same as the you-did-nothing-wrong world; this was one of its most terrifying peculiarities.

Anyway, his father never beat him. He never did anything *to* him—no hug, no pat on the back—but for one exception. He'd been sweeping his parents' bedroom floor when sunlight speared the window and illuminated a slice of restless dust motes, pore-sized imploded zeroes. Roy stopped his choring to watch. Josef walked over and put his hand on Roy's shoulder. That peripheral touch, like the pressing of a remote button wired to TNT located a safe distance from the operator, set off a split second of hope in Roy's chest. Then his father walked away and stood before the window.

The bright sun filtered through the taut skin of Josef's ears and lit up the blood. So it *was* possible: when Roy, his father and the sun were in just the right positions, with Roy facing the back of Josef's head, Roy could see warmth circulating inside him. But such a moment was rare as an eclipse requiring worlds, stars, and inhabitants in precise alignment.

Now Roy heard the white noise of the forest growing and rotting and scrambled on into the woods. The trees grew closer together, high branches woven with blue sky slivers and trunks collapsing, the going difficult. The sun slinked west and Roy trudged east into the punished world.

After a few minutes he came upon a circular clearing, at the center of which an inverted tree declared itself. From top to bottom, it was benthic blackness. In place of roots, a countless variety of branches sprouted inky leaves. Hovering over the earth, each branch and leaf had a unique shape, dimensions, texture and attitude, as though the tree were made from the parts of many individual species torn from multiple moments in time, joined through demented arboreal/temporal taxidermy. The branches seemed to be randomly impaling the trunk rather than growing from it. Each leaf, too, grew from competing, fiercely black worlds and far-apart seasons. One was about to snap from a fragile stem but hung frozen in the second before autumn strikes. Another leaf was lashed by rain, the drops of dissimilar sizes and temperatures, falling from the skies of different days and nights; while the leaf adjacent shook in brumal gusts that didn't even graze its neighbors.

The myriad-limbed, wide trunk rose irrefutable as genocide smoke to the graying air, crowned with a root system about the size and shape of a school bus that drove off Rhymeshead Bridge in 1928.

Pinned to the earth beneath a ponderous branch was a rectangular black box large enough to be there and sufficiently compact to fit in a memory. He rapped on the smooth surface with his knuckles. It didn't answer as hollow or solid. Like a musical note rising through several carpeted stories, it didn't seem manmade or wholly natural.

Roy could see more such boxes growing along the limbs and trunk of the tree, too high to easily reach. He wanted to climb but had to get the fallen box before nightfall. He sawed at the branch with a bone-handled pocket knife. He listened to the splashy rhythm the rains from a thousand nowhere skies drummed on a who-knows-when leaf. It took muscle and many hours, and he cut himself once across a thumb-knuckle and twice on the back of his hand, inscribing a painful X. But by the time the sky turned the dusky, twilight hue of 1918 cyanosis, he'd removed enough branch to wrest the black tree's box from the ground.

It gloved his hand with a sticky, bituminous resin.

Griffin 1973

Griffin snuck out under a soft-white, two-dimensional moon, clutching the stolen box. He'd tried to open it but found no lid or hinge. It was disturbingly heavy as though crammed with the granite genitals of castrated monuments.

It was hard sliding the massive stone that sealed the well. It hadn't been moved since grandpa Josef died a decade ago. Griffin peered in, joining the millions who sought meaning in holes, be they bomb craters, birth canals, pupils, train tunnels, etc.

The box dropped down the empty shaft in slow motion, as though sinking through syrup. But it struck bottom with the brittle, glittering roar of a thousand guillotined clock-headed men. An astringent odor of overly scrubbed hands and a dusty, postcard-thin farewell scent flooded Griffin's nose and spread through head, lungs, and heart, and filled nameless, hidden places. His skin transformed into a flesh-colored gap between himself and the ground, sky, well, grassblades, and his surroundings, which retracted into memory objects like attics and soup-steam, even though Griffin could still see them.

Everything he saw turned into a species of remembrance. It was suddenly clear: lying in the attic, he'd mistaken the memory of loving his dad with the act of still loving him, and because memory and vision are similar, requiring space between us and their objects, he took this love to have a metaphorically visual quality. And it wasn't just his father. The only thing he'd really shared with anyone was distance, and the purity of this mutual experience had been marred by the very act of being shared with them.

The porch bulb clicked on and his father popped out of the house like an oversized exclamation point in a ransom note. Roy shambled groggily down the steps and onto the grass in his sweatpants, disheveled and shoeless.

"Who's there?" Roy said.

"I was."

"Griff? Thirteen words!"

This was an eccentricity Roy had passed on from his father, who, after exhaustive research, concluded that anyone articulate should be able to completely explain themselves in no more than thirteen words.

"1963 to 1973."

"Get over here," Roy said, walking closer.

Griffin tried to obey but his brain wouldn't follow externally delivered commands, as though his father were a remote control and Griffin a machine only responsive to manual use of its toggles and knobs. He stood there and remembered Roy glowering.

Storms of all kinds—wind, snow, sand, dust, fire and many types of shit—brewed in Griffin's atoms. They brought new tests, new boredoms, new deaths, new ways to try cheating them, new ways to fail. He didn't know how it would feel but he was sure it was coming—like when Mr. Mirsky told his gym class they'd need to start using deodorant soon.

"What's the matter with you?" Roy said.

"Theblackbox," Griffin slurred.

"Did it break?"

"Boxblackthe," Griffin said, as though the words were a paint color signifying the same thing whether brushed left to right or vice versa.

"I'm getting a flashlight and rope. You wait."

Griffin remembered Roy saying that, too. He stayed there as though it was taking place right now and he was following his father's orders.

ROY 1973

Roy tied the rope around the great rock that had capped the well for so long. He handed the Rayovac to Griffin. With empty eyes, his son fumbled for it as though there were no moon. He held the flashlight while Roy awkwardly clutched and slid down the rope, cursing middle-aged atrophy and tearing the lifelines of his librarian palms. The feeble light revealed fragments of the black box. Its six even planes had broken into eight vague shapes, each larger than the box itself as though the surfaces had unrolled on impact. The contours of each piece were entirely unrelated and appeared as incapable of reconnection as they were of having been disassembled from the same item.

Griffin inhaled and the rope gave way as though cut by his sharp breath. The box fragments altered before Roy's plummeting eyes. They formed spiky, serrated letters, words and numbers, rushing at him like bugs into a speeding car's windshield—IF . . . IN . . . 947 . . . US . . . 73 . . . LOSER—he didn't see them all clearly before his face, elbows, belly, and knees crashed into their toothy edges.

Roy breathed fetid earth, choked up rocks. His spine had come as close as possible to snapping without doing so. In the corner of his eye Griffin's hunched silhouette blotted the night. Griffin dropped the Rayovac and the beam flickered on and off at sixty beats-per-minute, the tempo at which Roy's fist had pounded the toy plane. Now Roy's hand throbbed in synchronicity with the flashlight signal . . .

He wanted to speak but literally couldn't find the words, like the man in that folktale, trapped in a room flooding with millions of keys, fumbling for the one needed to unlock the door before being smothered.

Griffin squatted, jutting his chin below the edge of the well head. His nerve-bitten lips dipped into the Rayovac's 6-volt light. The moon burned out. Griffin turned and disappeared into a night black as an inverted tree. Rain stuttered and then exploded through the air, like the coughing of concertgoers between symphonic movements. Every now and then Roy recognized drops of 1947 rain falling parallel to the 1973 shower. They were the ones that rolled down the curves of his ears into his head.

SUSAN 1973

Two days later Susan returned from Samantha's poorly attended funeral, almost too tired to be sad and too sad to know she was tired. She hadn't asked Roy to go because he was so selfish and easily bored, and he drifted into these embarrassing, trance-like states at inappropriate moments when he wouldn't answer when spoken to. It would've added anger to the already bewildering mix of emotions she was dealing with.

Standing at the graveside, two things had struck her: thank God she no longer had necrophobia; and she hadn't loved Roy since 1968, but having loved him once gave him a special status, Husband Emeritus. And who else would want her and her crazy fears anyway (not that Roy was a prize—*thirteen words*—what the hell kind of nuts was that?), and of course he got credit for helping make Griffin.

It was early afternoon when Susan found Roy embedded in the quagmire, more puppet than person. Because of her telephobia she decided to drive for help. But the Plymouth Valiant wouldn't start. She set off on foot, spending hours knocking on her few neighbor's doors, nobody home. She was hiking the uphill road when old, taciturn Carol Julius appeared unexpectedly, like a spirit summoned by an accidentally placed line in a hopscotch diagram. It scared her because he was shuffling out of 1963: it was Carol who'd found Josef Gravel in the unfinished well and hauled her father in-law's corpse out on his thin shoulders.

Carol wore a dapper pinstriped blue or gray suit (the color of two straight days of rain), a birdshit-white grin smeared into tanned wrinkles. She didn't even tell him what happened. She opened her mouth to explain and he seemed to know what to do by the spring-like way he nodded, the starting-up gesture of a machine built to retrieve bodies from well shafts.

His cold hand felt like a straw-stuffed glove but his grip was strong. As Susan led Carol to the well, she tried to remember what he'd done for a living or how he'd known the Gravels. All she could recall was he'd looked just as old as when she last saw him ten years ago.

Susan asked herself why, despite her fear of phones, she hadn't just forced herself to run into the house, wolf a few Valium, pick up the phone and dial 911. She'd found the courage to do that kind of thing before, when it was critical. And after all, this time, her husband's life was at stake.

But this was more than her usual phobic reaction. She felt in the grip of a mythic force: if she had *gone to* the phone and used the device for *her* purposes, as though it were an extension of her will, then the world of things wouldn't have been able to deliver its message through its agent, Carol Julius. Because that realm had come to make Susan recognize the *thing* in herself, the impending object she was becoming. If her sister's funeral had taught her anything, it was life and personality were just the first steps of an anonymous, step-by-hundreds-of-steps manufacturing process.

Carol looked down at Roy.

Am I finally going totally nuts? Susan thought. *Didn't his head incline exactly like that the last time?*

"Woman," he said at last, hacking up 1963 phlegm. "Do you have a ladder?"

Are these the same words again? Offending me the same way? Wasn't he wearing this very suit? Like a house that can't repaint itself? Where is Griffin? Where is Griffin?

Roy 1973

Roy woke from a dream where Carol Julius was saying "*Everything turns to dust—except dust...*" He was on their bed, wearing dirty boxers and sprinkled with cuts. Susan sat nearby in the rocker, looking out the window at the forest's edge. There were oily smears on the windowpane from where she'd pressed her face. It was early afternoon. The sky was brain-gray.

"Boxblackthe," he whispered, still half-dreaming, and then louder: "OPEN UP!"

Susan jumped.

"What? Roy, Griffin's missing. I need your help. What happened?"

Her voice was monotonally barbituated. He couldn't really blame her this time.

"The box broke," he said, sitting up with effort. "Did you get the pieces? I landed on them, they sliced me up."

"Our son's missing, did you hear me?"

"How long have I been asleep?"

"Two days. I didn't call anyone, not the police, nobody. You know I'm afraid to use the phone. But this was worse, it was like an omen. Remember when I wouldn't go near brass coat buttons, or baby robins that had fallen out of nests gave me panic attacks—"

"—There were no fragments of a black box, or any words or letters or numbers, the word LOSER, anything weird, at the bottom of the well?"

"No, what are you saying? Is it important?"

"I guess I was dreaming," he lied.

"What happened? Please, we have to find Griffin. You have to help."

"Of course ... right now everything's murky. My memory is screwed. Let me rest a little more. I could use some water, please. I'll figure it out."

Roy tried to look devastated but he was not. Susan was fooled. She smiled sympathetically. Her eyes closed, her forehead tilted into the window, and she fell asleep. What is the difference between emotions and opinions?

He told Susan he couldn't remember a thing. He must have amnesia. That night was purely between his son and himself. The events themselves—the rope failing, the father falling, the boy hunching and running away—had been frozen into hieroglyphics incapable of translation into wife/mother language.

He knew Susan was in pain and he should be there for her. Did he still love her? With a shrug, the way he once told Reverend Hawkins he believed in God: "*Uh yeah, I mean I uh, I believe there's something out there, you can call it God I guess . . .*"

He was dismissive about almost everything now. He'd always been a careful man, planning as much as he could well in advance, but he'd resolved to stop going to the library and had no plans to find another job. The abruptness of his mood change reminded him of when those empty baby carriages on sale outside the maternity store were blown down the street during that 1971 hurricane, and he knew there were no babies inside but kept wincing when one would flip or crash into a house, until the concern completely vanished in a moment that had the sudden illumination of a revelation and none of the profundity.

Still, at least one thing mattered. He had a terrible urge to see Griffin, to get to the point of all this, to determine the limits and possibilities of "this" once and for all. He didn't know why he'd broken the plane. He'd never been a violent man, and in that moment, Roy had felt anonymous, devoid of personality.

But Roy was also glad. Now he and Griffin shared something. They'd both found the black tree's box. They'd both wanted it and brought it to the well and thrown it. Whatever was next wasn't real yet, but when it came it belonged to them alone, would be incomparable.

The day after his *except dust* dream, Roy searched for the ~ gulch that led to the black tree, vaguely thinking it might take him closer to Griffin. For hours, he wandered the inextricable woods of his youth, unconsciously jangling pocket change. Nothing was familiar and the monotonous series of leaves, birdsong, and branches bored him. It was night when he returned.

Walking upstairs, he heard Susan scream.

In their bedroom, the night table lamp had been knocked over and the lampshade was horizontally askew. Susan's trembling leg fomented 1947 dust in a cone of 40-watt light. Her whole body shook under her nightgown. In one hand she gripped the receiver of their old black telephone, the cord stretched to the floor where the base had fallen. Blood ran from her shoulder and dripped off her wrist. Some drops pooled in the rotary phone's dial. The top drawer of Roy's dresser hung open, as it had the night Griffin stole the black tree's box.

Susan's face was colorless as the lamplight. She turned to Roy and then the handset, recognized it with horror and cast it on the bed. It left a red smear on the sheet before sliding to the carpet. She pointed at the large open window. The drapes concealing it rustled.

Roy yanked them aside, revealing a confusion of gray ear-tufts, an infant's twitchy finger and cerise lumps of acne. It took him a moment to see it was a single creature, a living collage of biographical stages, bonded by an inconceivable time-defying paste. A few beads of sweat leaked from a quarter-sized patch of young, summer-hot forehead pores, while elderly lips were chapped by winter wind. A drop of nowhere rain tapped a bulbous nose, one nostril bristled with hairs and the other was toddler-small and runny. The jaw was a skeletal U that reminded Roy of a gynecological stirrup. Its cracked rictus was studded with a few stainless baby teeth.

It was shirtless, emaciated torso and arms a patchwork of shriveled and smooth young skin that started and ended without design, suggesting a burn victim. A segment of umbilical cord, coiled like a pig's tail, squiggled from a hairy widower's paunch, resembling Roy's own gut. The neck was small and flimsy as a toilet paper tube. The heavy, adult-sized head was forced to permanently lean on one bony shoulder.

It was covering its eyes with hands sprouting fresh baby fingers, sticky schoolboy fingers, teenaged middle-fingers, middle-aged ring-fingers, diabetic grandpa fingers, dry corpse knuckles. Three nails were well over a foot long, ropy tips a brownish, industrial pollution hue. Others varied in length, chomped to cuticle or worse.

"Hey," Roy said.

The creature lowered its hands. Each eye was a damp pudding of pupils, irises, and sclera, milky cataracts glued to shiny, peek-a-boo glimpsings. One eyelid slid right to left and back like a haywire elevator door.

It shifted with ataxic gestures that made Roy nauseous. On its forehead was a crimson wound shaped like a hoof-mark where Susan had struck it with the phone's receiver. A globule of gleaming shoulder blood rolled out its mouth and spun like a mercury ball to Roy's shoe.

"I was asleep," Susan groaned. "I heard you rifling through your dresser but it wasn't you—it was that thing—and I hit it and it bit me."

She added, too mechanically:

"Get it out."

She gasped, fell to her knees and vomited. The thing didn't move. Pissy anti-maternal beverages flowed from its nipples, stinking of damning, inadmissible evidence.

Roy stepped back. The thing tracked him with sideways eye-moments, recalling, prognosticating. It wore trousers of insect flesh or rotten shanty-town roofing. Roy tore the sheets off the bed and spun them into a rope. He tread slowly into an expanding pond of icy nipple-urine. The creature barely resisted and may have been laughing. Roy easily pushed its face into the floor and pinioned the filthy, boy/baby/old/dead arms behind its back. It clutched something tightly in one palm. Roy couldn't see what.

He wrapped it in a blanket and brought it outside. Like a dream object, he didn't know if it was heavy or light, tall or short, wasn't sure if he carried it with his hands or hanging from his teeth. At the well, he untied the arms, wound the sheet-rope about its waist, and lowered it. Then Roy went to the kitchen, matter-of-factly fixed two bologna sandwiches, went back and dropped them into the pit. He dragged the heavy stone across the wellhead.

Roy envied this thing. He'd noticed most people rushed from the safety of one identifiable emotion to next—happy, bored, pissed, miserable, envious, the whole lot you could depict in a children's cartoon show. But the transition from one state to another could only be possible in conjunction with a series of murkier in-between feelings impossible to name, only identifiable as different from those common emotions that "make us human." Most people weren't aware of these interstitial states.

Roy was. Throughout his life, he'd spent unusually long periods of time in those liminal places: at the foot of the inverted tree, after he'd broken the balsa wood plane, when he fell and the rain rolled into his ears, watching Susan's head gently incline toward the greasy window. Each time he felt on the verge of solving a great mystery, but currents pulled him back to islands of intelligibility: his name, his house, his family, television, books, sleeping, eating, autobiography and the rest of it. It was hard to explain.

But the creature in the well must understand the secret times that hide in the cracks between the recognizable moments. It might even know how the punished-world could be distinguished from the you-did-nothing-wrong world. That was why Roy envied it. Plus, it got free bologna sandwiches.

He was prepared to keep it in the well in secret. Maybe it was a monster. But what if it was his son? If he waited long enough he might recognize him by some sign.

ROY 1947

Standing at the edge of the forest, Roy folded his arms and hugged the black tree's box against his chest. For a moment, he enjoyed spying on his dad and Jay putting their tools away, cleaning up after the day's work on the well. It was like forgetting himself to the point of actively becoming the forgetting, which was like being someone else who didn't want to forget. When they were almost done he approached with a skip in his step.

"What's that?" Jay asked Roy.

"I found it."

"Can I see it?"

"No, I didn't open it yet."

"That's nine words," his father said. "That leaves four to explain what's going on here."

All Roy wanted in the whole world was to get that box open. He skipped to the house. Josef went to grab the box from Roy's hands. He tripped over a taut wire strung between two bricks. Jay ran forward to help his dad up, but he slid on a wet patch of ground, lost balance and fell backwards, tumbling into the well.

After the accident, everyday sights transformed into dreadful things, the way a fly's significance waxes from repellent to ominous when it reposes on the head of an Ethiopian baby rather than a turd. A door Jay had helped paint, books marked with *Ex Libris* Jay Gravel stickers, his favorite spot on the couch, a cracked mug he refused to drink from, his model Fokker triplane. There was also temporal alteration: the truncated family lived under a scheme of time measured by units of Everything Just Out of Reach and Everything Entirely Out of Reach.

His father didn't finish the well. He sealed it with a big, flat rock. Roy thought it was shaped exactly like a giant toilet seat cover. Josef never shit again—or only did it in private.

Roy vowed to never open the black tree's box, to keep it safely hidden, and to never look for the ~ stream again. He didn't know why exactly. But then, who would?

ROY 1973

The day after the creature broke into house and skin, Susan was all kinds of almost dead. She guzzled whiskey for breakfast, gulping Valium, spitting feverish profundities ("what can't be forgotten doesn't need to be remembered") and a sepia bile Roy had never seen, the acrid secretion of a possessed 1842 photograph ("blecch"). She orbited the rooms with drowsy stomps, depositing shiny vomit on domestic objects. Whenever Roy wiped it up he'd see his face in it as though her system was purging itself of too much husband.

He cleaned out of habit, not because he cared. The things around him, even his wife, reminded him of empty baby carriages in a storm, mere suggestions of concern.

"I smell," she said, inclining her head, listening. "I think it's an omen."

"It's the throw-up."

"You know, a strong scent of nothing. Lots of omens lately."

"You better lie down. You look exhumed."

"You and Griffin," she said seriously. "You two are really connected. But you know what? You're both bonded as father and son only by the *longing* each of you has to be father and son. Which means you want to be what you are because you aren't. That doesn't make any sense."

"For once I agree with you."

He was hardly listening and wasn't really aware of his responses, as though reciting the Pledge of Allegiance.

"Will that thing come back?" she asked, careening into a wall (was it her cheek or the wallpaper peeling in pale strips?). "I can't lift my arm. How can I wave goodbye?"

"I killed it," Roy said. "Don't worry. Lie down. You're sick. I'm low on paper towels."

"Where is it?"

"I buried it in the forest. Go sleep."

"OK. Who is Carol Julius, anyway?"

"I don't really know him. He's been around here forever. He's just an old family friend."

"He can't be a family friend, because we're not a family, you know."

"Enough, please."

"We're . . . I'll tell you later. I have to think about it. There's a word . . ."

"Please, Susan, go lie down."

"OK, Husband Emeritus," she said, tottering away. It was her cheek. Roy scraped it off the wall and kicked it into a dustpan.

Roy went to the well. The toilet-seat cover stone had been moved. The creature was gone. A tenebrous liquid had risen almost to the brim of the shaft and scraps of bread and sodden sheets floated through Roy's surprised reflection on the dark, bright surface. Had the thing dug down and struck an underground stream? If so, the water would've lifted it high enough to escape. Roy dipped a finger into the freezing pool and sniffed it. Not water or urine. It smelled like the fearfully sanitized hands of the visitors to the ICU where Griffin spent his first month, and the dried glue which causes generations of family photographs to loosen and fall from their proper physical/chronological places on old album pages. This confirmed Roy's suspicion the thing was Griffin. The liquid was a bodily secretion that had filled the well and helped him rise. He'd lost a lot of it. Roy couldn't tell whether his son had bled or cried himself to freedom.

Dad, he thought.

When Roy returned, Susan lay mumbling on the bed, her wound red, crunchy-rimmed, rancid as hastily abandoned surgery. A thread of drool running from her mouth to the sweat-soaked sheet was gilt with sunlight and more alive than her eyes.

"Tenants," she said, brownish-red bubbles drifting out her nostrils, leaving the flimsy handprints of buried-alive infants where they popped on the ceiling. "That's the word..."

Instinctively, he grabbed the phone to call 911. Susan was watching him and for the first time, she didn't seem afraid of the object. Roy's finger slipped into the 9 (wxy) fingerwheel hole. The rotary dial wouldn't budge. He tried to spin it from 8 (tuv) and it worked. He hung up the receiver and tried to call starting with 9 again, without success. He fingered 0 (operator), and again the dial wouldn't turn, as though glued in place.

So, Susan was in on this too. She was not just a spectator, watching father and son engage in a puzzling mix of struggle and collaboration. Her blood was cunning; it had spoken, it condemned her. When it had dripped into the rotary fingerholes, it congealed in just the right way to make it impossible to reach the operator or emergency services. That was no accident. Hadn't Susan herself just been talking of omens?

Roy's hands shook and the phone slipped from his fingers, hitting the floor with a steel and Bakelite clatter. For a few minutes, he let the off-the-hook tone bleat on and on like a steering wheel horn depressed by the skull of a car crash victim. Roy recognized the sixty beats-per-minute tempo. It was a countdown to an explosion. Every now and then over the last few days, it had been obscured. But it kept reasserting itself through a fist, a flashlight, sky and vein liquids dripping at regular intervals . . .

It wasn't that he understood. But he saw it clearly: you drive through a tunnel, you don't know how a tunnel is made, but you know how to go through. It was like that. It was decided. There was no turning back.

Straddling Susan on the bed he gripped the handset and slammed it into her face. The transmitter struck her mouth and the earphone left a red, hoof-like mark on her forehead.

The design of that impression on her skin should be only what it is, not shaped like a hoof-mark, which is something else entirely, Roy thought.

"Help," she whispered into the mouthpiece, as though someone were listening.

She should have whispered exactly how you whisper when a phone's mouthpiece ruins your mouth . . .

Roy lifted the handset and again ground it as hard as he could into her face. An incisor broke loose. Sudsy blood-and-lipstick frothed over the delicate chin.

"Roy?" she said, like she was calling him to dinner.

She should have said "Roy" just as one says "Roy" when struck with a phone in the face, but instead she said his name *like* she was calling him to dinner.

It was just this way things had of being "like" other things that had to be destroyed, wasn't it? This flimsy "like" and "as if" and "as though," the wide spaces between things with room enough for infinite mistakes, misperceptions and confused feelings and thoughts. All these "likes" supposedly kept things together while maintaining enough distance between one thing, such as the phone-mark on the forehead, and that to which it was compared (the curved-shape of a hoof-mark), to suggest that each also existed on their own.

But this wasn't possible. It wasn't real. Reality was what couldn't be anything other than itself. It had to be certain. People, stones, dust, blood, noise, rain, years, words, holes, had been too many things for too long. Roy would escape this tangled state of affairs.

He pushed the receiver into the grotesquely emotionless expression with all his weight. She gurgled into the mouthpiece:

"Roy."

He lifted the phone. Once more and she'd be gone. But he didn't want her last word to be his name because she had said it like she was half-asleep, rather than dying. So he waited a minute while she breathed bright bubbles.

"Roy... I love you in 1968."

That was it. A few more pulverizing blows and he was finished. Out of habit, he hung up the phone and conscientiously placed it on the night table.

Exhausted, Roy dipped his face into the pulpy features, bathed open eyes in optic-socket mush and rested until he was about to drown in facial waste. He snapped his head back, coughing sick spit and last breath molecules, seeing red walls through stinging Susan blood. A thin layer of her lips sealed his mouth.

The phone began to ring.

WASTING CLOSER

What day was it? What time? How long had Roy's murderous explosion propelled him through the woods? When did the rain sluice Susan's face traces away? How had he located the inverted tree again? None of this mattered now.

But Roy was surprised to find someone had hacked neat steps into the trunk. They were cut around the tree like a spiral staircase, easier to climb than branches. Each time he reached a higher bough the air got darker and thicker until he wasn't sure if he were digging or ascending. Yet he could see each groove in the bark clearly, the way you don't need light to view memories.

Near the top he spied a loose black box lodged among a lattice of mismatched branches. It partially obstructed a chimney-sized opening to the sky. The crudely hewn steps seemed to have stopped. He dragged himself onto a bough slick with 1836 ice. Roy stretched out his hand to free the rectangular fruit. His foot slid, he was about to fall, but regained his balance just in time, clutching a nearby sun-dappled branch. He pushed the black box onto the top of the tree and hauled himself up behind it.

The floor area, about the size and shape of a school bus that drove off Rhymeshead Bridge in 1928, was surprisingly smooth and hard—where were the roots?

There was no light, nothing beyond the treetop, but Roy could see certain objects, as in a stylized drawing where many necessary things don't require representation. He saw countless black tree's boxes arranged in several neat piles. Next to one of them lay Roy's 1947 bone-handled knife, the blade bearded with bark and wood shavings. So Griffin had been here. He'd paved the entire top of the tree with black boxes, which he'd harvested using Roy's knife, forming the spiral staircase up the trunk; and had begun raising walls around the perimeter of the floor. The structure shared its proportions with the individual black tree's boxes, as though they were scale models made in preparation for this mysterious building. Roy was impressed by the work Griffin had put into this project even if he didn't get it. Until now, it had never occurred to him to do anything with the boxes than to try opening them. This desire had only grown after he saw the amazing thing Griffin had become, when he envied its indescribable insights.

But now he picked up a box and set it atop another on a low, incomplete wall. The resin oozed out and neatly mortared it to the box below. He looked at his contribution to the structure with satisfaction. It was gravely quiet. He wanted to say something banal, to prove he was safe, the tests passed, to show not every action and word had world-rending consequences. Something like: "It's very sturdy."

"Looks good," he said. "But what is this place?"

"A treehouse," Griffin answered, stepping from behind one of the larger stacks.

Even his speech was stitched together: kindergartener's vowels bookended by long-toothed consonants. He moved like a stop-motion figure of a thousand torn photographs, head lolling at a right angle to the puny neck.

Roy was proud of his son and even a little proud of himself, as if he could take credit for this accomplishment. He was very tired and foggy-headed, but that helped make him brave, and that was good because he'd also never been so terrified. He was about to take a great risk. Meekly, he offered up the only thing he had of value:

"Can I help you finish it?"

"Yes."

Roy grinned stupidly, relieved and strangely amused. He'd been seeking some incomparable state. He hadn't expected this typical conversation, moving briskly and clearly to a simple "Yes" even an idiot could understand. It was all so imaginable. It could've happened a million times before. Yet he also felt it was unique, perhaps the defining moment of his life.

YOU BELIEVE SOMETHING
WHEN YOU SAY YOU DO.
IF YOU THINK ABOUT
THAT SOMETHING, KEEP IT INSIDE
YOU HAVE WHAT IS CALLED FAITH.
WHEN THERE'S A MOMENT, NUMINOUS
BUT UNNOTICED, THAT'S REALLY IT.

MOST MEAT SPENDS MOST OF ITS
LIFE ALIVE.

THERE IS NO MEDICINE FOR AN ILL-WIND.

WHEN I AM ALONE IN A ROOM AND EXPECT
A PERSON TO SOON OR EVEN JUST POSSIBLY
ENTER MY ROOM, I OFTEN FIND MYSELF
POSING - NOT PERHAPS DRAMATICALLY, BUT
SO WHEN I AM SEEN, IT WILL BE ON MY
TERMS — ?

WHAT KIND OF CONSOLATION DOES
THE WORDS "THERE'S A REASON FOR EVERYTHING"
HAVE? IT'S LIKE SAYING: "THERE'S EVERYTHING."

POOL DAY

Synchronicity is no more baffling or mysterious than the discontinuities of physics. It is only the ingrained belief in the sovereign power of causality that creates intellectual difficulties and makes it appear unthinkable that causeless events exist or could ever exist. I find the floater I just left in the bowl appears unsinkable and unthinkable but I'm pretty sure I caused it. SHUT UP YOU PRETENTIOUS SHIT! HAHA GET IT? *No but yer mamma got it up the* ASS!!

– Carl G. Jung & Two Anonymous Commentators (as quoted & amended in graffiti, upon the bathroom wall of Vazac's Horseshoe Bar, NYC)

$234.38

A nose was sniffing the tip of Martin Box's pudgy tongue—It woke him up—He was lying face-down on an adamantine, smoothcold surface. He felt like a failed prototype of doctor Frankenstein's monster (More precisely, see, it was like the problem was the doctor couldn't get the stitches to hold and he'd butchered and reattached Martin in various configurations, but none took—*Except*—inexplicably but why not?—the nervous system of an eight-year-old girl). Martin practically needed forklifts to pry open his eyelids ... He was in an empty pool. His bruised, gaping mouth was dripping blood and steaming halitosis down a sulfurous drain.

Left for dead ...

Martin carefully lifted his head. The rat in the drain blinked its one eye and darted down.

He sat up. A great tiled, domed room. Big skylight with a big hole in it. His gun was gone. He shut his swollen eyes and struggled to remember:

Over the past two years there'd been an increase in homicides in New York, from the usual 500-something to about 800 annually—correlated with a disturbing decrease in the number of bodies recovered ... Yeah, whatever. Focus ... Statistics can be interesting, but there were more important numbers, these numbers led you to waking up in this horrid state ... think, Martin, think ... Oh yeah, man, he remembered: they were fiscal. Against his better judgment but in accordance with the voice in his pocket (which told him he'd only $234.38 in savings—and all of it in the talking pocket), he'd taken on several cases at once. His finances were looking like a reaper with one expression in its tired repertoire. He knew it was too many jobs to properly handle at once.

How many statisticians are just statistics in another statistician's statistical study?

But, c'mon, Some-Horrible-Icky-Thing—money, why's it so important? This despite the fact that *every* dollar bill is counterfeit. See, even supposing that In God We Can Trust, yet we still can't rely upon the paper that says so. See what they did there? Mixing, upsetting the essentials of humanity—you can't turn water into wine, but belief into currency, and cash into something holy, tasteless (in the *John* sense of both the Pope Paul *and* Waters), as unleavened wafer—

—Enough. All grumbling does is grumble ... Doesn't do Pool Day justice. It's good it started wrong, that's the point, it started wrong for Martin.

Now we'll start right, with the WHAT in WTF?!

Among the more promising cases in Martin's portfolio was the Pedestrian Blood Supply Case. The Local Blood Bank Association had hired him (Cash-On-Delivery basis, Damnit!) to find out about a phony, Mobile Blood Bank van that was driving around poor neighborhoods and claiming to be collecting for hospitals. It was an unusually normal gig for a private investigator who specialized in the strange and unworldly…

He was also working a missing person case. Hired by an eccentric, wealthy German couple, whose grown daughter had been reported missing a few weeks back. A cup'O-la-days ago, Charlotte's mother described her:

"She's unstable … *verrücht* … She goes around with tiny little skirts and no, well, not a thread of *Höchen.* If that doesn't make you blush, well… this is confidential right? Only between us? Because your name is Martin Box only—*Ja?* No middle name?"

"That's so."

"I sometimes think there is more to the *middle* name, or not having one, than having a middle name or not. Sometimes it seems people without middle names are missing something important. Less soul? Even more suspect, don't you think, is the use of a middle initial—those who *do* have a middle name, but represent it with *only* an initial *in der mittel* are… in possession of secret information, perhaps? General Ulysses S. Grant, for example, or Captain James T. Kirk…"

"I'm not sure how this jibes with your theory, but—interestingly enough—the man who'd been General and 18th President of the United States admitted the 'S' in his name stood for nothing. As for the Captain: 'T' is for Tiberius."

"And Clarence T. Tegreene?"

"Who?"

"He invented a particularly effective microwave oven, with an advanced control system. In 2009, in Tacoma. He's a distant relation, of an executed—I mean *ex-family* member. But that is not here … In any case, one single letter, standing alone that way, like a lone Christian between two much larger lions, can make a big difference. Think: Alpha, Omega, right? ... But this is just a quirk. I have no proof. Forgive me ..."

"Oh no, Frau Tarpit, actually, it's interesting: I have observed that when two strangers meet and discover they share either a first name or last name—but especially first name—they will inevitably show signs of bemusement, even laughter. It reminds me of watching two volunteers inspect a magician's empty top hat, only to have a rabbit pop out a second after. Whereas if it turned out they shared only a middle name, or initial even, well, there's no surprising magic in that. No playfulness ..."

She was going on 70 or so, and her face, masked with makeup, had the same effect on Martin's dick as a specially painted stealth bomber does on an enemy's radar—she was invisible to his, it was out cold the whole interview. She smelled like cigarettes and despair, though he didn't see any ashtrays in her enormous, *Bau-How-Hideous* Upper West Side aerie. It was record-breaking heat outside, but in here it was the *Cool Air* of Dr. Muñoz's West 14th Street apartment. She'd been pretty once upon a time. Martin kinda squirmed as she scrutinized him with eyes admittedly still beautiful blue—As if he was *vast*, she was taking in a scenic plot of land and considering where to build the dream house, the best location for the pond, the tennis-court, stables ...

"I'm sorry I went on like that just now. You were speaking of Charlotte, Frau Tarpit?"

"Ach, Charlotte, Charlotte. *Und* so she also slathers her groin with peanut butter and hangs around dog parks. The mutts, they lick her *Fotze*. Sometimes the owners join in. What a perverse city we live in, Herr Box ... To make herself more obvious she yodels *Ode an die Freude* or some of that *awful* Nina Hagen. She's been arrested before, but this time she's nowhere to be found ... I know this *ist ein ßischen* horrible, *Unheimlche* ..."

She handed him a photo with an albescent hand, glabrous, liver-spotted ivory ...

"Any distinguishing marks?"

"Hymn? Oh. No, not really. OK. I am ashamed to admit one thing. She has a tattoo ... *Ja.* A tattoo *on her wrist.* I know, *Tut mir leid!*—Very poor taste, putting it *there*, where . . . you know."

"You mean where they inked those millions for ovens, and unimaginably worse?"

She nodded, frowned her face lower.

"I mean the small of her back, the ankle where socks can hide it. Even the nape of her neck would be OK! But the *wrist*?"

"Please, it's OK. I understand and I am not here to judge . . . Could you describe it?"

"*Vielen dank*, Herr Box. Such a kind man, a good man. If only I were two years younger—or you two years older. But . . . describe *what* again, exactly?"

"The tatoo on Charlotte's wrist, Frau Tarpit. What does it depict? Flower? Tribal pattern?"

She laughed at her forgetfulness, then:

"Oh! Of course. It's a swastika. Even I must admit the rendering is beautiful. But, *Geezus Kyke!* The wrist, of all places . . ."

"*What the fuck*? I fucking *hate* Nazis! Shouldn't I shoot you? Report you to MOSSAD? Fuck! Even mere verbal bigotry pisses me off!" Martin did *not* express. Ever the very, very, very broke, broke professional:

"Don't worry, Frau Tarpit. I'll find her. Now, I don't mean to be crass, but about that retainer?"

He looked away so she could be embarrassed free of observation, if she did feel so. There were a few poetry collections atop a coffee table: Hölderlin, Goethe, and surprisingly, Yeats. A favorite of Martin's poetry-reading days. But who doesn't like Yeats?

Frau Tarpit wasn't embarrassed . . .

"Oh, *das Geld.* Honey, did I make you think that's how I felt that's how it works? *Nein.* This is Cash On Delivery. Abbreviated as C.O.D? It's the only way I do business. *Nein, nein* . . .

If you're so certain you can bring Charlotte *nach Haus*, then you've nothing to worry about. You're the pro, *wirklich*?"

Cold, fucking cold as David Letterman liked his *Late Show* studio.

"*Wirklich* and then some. I'll see you when you see Charlotte, then, Frau Tarpit," he mumbled, nodded, scrammed before the fuckin' Nazi could let out an *auf.*

Charlotte had obviously quite a pack of lovers across the city, only problem being that none of them could tell Martin anything, just bark, growl and whimper. Seems she didn't associate much with human beings. Fresh Direct for the peanut butter.

$2.38

Martin had finally located the Mobile Blood Bank—don't ask him how, he'd already forgotten, a good deal of transgressive red-light running, many the slim avoidances of traffic tickets and fatalities—and trailed the van all day, how? What's this, 20 Questions or something?

It was hot. A pool day if ever there was.

Reminding himself to keep in the present, focused, not mixing up unrelated cases, he was law-abidingly stopped at a red light in East New York. Someone hit him on the side of the head through his open window. He vaguely recalled being dragged into the back of the van before fists and boots faded the scene to black.

Now he pulled himself to his feet, spat out a tooth and looked around. Judging by the shadows, it was around 2post-morning. The empty pool was in a once-grand bathhouse, golden art-deco tiles gone greenish with neglect. There were a few small barred windows and a big metal door locked from the outside. Under a window was some kind of thin metal cross with a long chain connected to one end, a bit like an anchor. Next to this was a large, industrial fan set with the blades facing up. Besides the broken skylight, which was at least forty feet outta reach, Martin couldn't see a way out.

He looked out through the thick bars of a window and recognized three bad characters who wouldn't normally be congregating. God+Zero from the west side, Thylacine-Antichrist, the north, and from eastern ghettos stretching far as New Jersey, the much-feared Eggcream X. Inferno. Together they were likely responsible for the recent rise in murders and disappearances. They were smoking cigarettes and laughing next to the blood van. A herd of brainwashed pit bull slaves bowed down in a circle round their feet, facing defensively outwards. These guys *never* worked as a team, and their crimes, their interests, were so disparate as to make this meeting unlikely as, say, the rendezvous of two Boeing 757 hulls with the twin towers.

So not impossible.

Some pawns showed up, lugging huge gasoline cans from the back of the van. Thylacine-Antichrist signaled to them to go toward the big door to the bathhouse.

Nausea ... He felt just like both a craplogged toilet getting snaked, *and* the rusty snake violating the toilet at the same time ... to plumb further into the depths of this affective metaphorical state, to better understand Martin's experience, imagine also that both the toilet and the snake had regretted not having been born pretty flowers to begin with ...

Martin ran back into the pool and repositioned himself roughly the way he'd been when he woke, breathing through his mouth. In case someone came in, he didn't wanna look like he'd moved. He smelled the faint, out-of-place odor of fires burning somewhere far down the drain.

The door opened, heavy cans boomed, echoes of booms filled the air while the cans were dragged across tile. The guys were chewing some trendy new bubblegum by Wolvers Wonderproducts. It was called GOLDRUSH! and tasted like ass and was so gunky that it seriously affected the chewer's speech—BUT, it was handmade in Italy (*The Italy Factory* in China's *Guangdong province*), and looked exactly like solid, munchy gold.

"So dis vorks? Nobawdee evah findza boddeeze?"

"Thass what Telly sez, man. Nadduh strand a'nuddin."

"Telly?"

"You sez you doanno Telly? Man, heeze H.N.I.C."

"Whazyat?"

"Fugg! Sheet! I got you dis gig, man! I din-know you were a fugging dimwit. H.N.I.C.—Thass Telly. You know, Head-Nazi-In-Charge?"

WTF!? Martin knew the four gang-leaders involved here didn't even know what a Nazi was. What were the chances of that Lost-

Charlotte-Tarpit word popping up in relation to the Pedestrian Blood Supply Case? Carl G. Jung called it *synchronicity*. Oh yeah? Martin called it a *Load of Shit*. If you wanna say *Acausal Load of Shit*, that's fine too. He had to remember that so much of his job was about just that, and if you started to read meaning into every coincidence … Well, you get dyslexic. And then you can't read the *real signs*, the clues leading to solutions.

"Aw yeah! Right! Zorry," said the fellow who didn't know Telly. "Ha, the Head-Nasty-In-Charge…"

Whoever said two heads are better than one obviously never had one.

—A hand smacked a noggin. Martin heard them knock the barrels over and the gushing of liquid into the pool. The toadies hauled more cans into the room. One by one he heard each popping open and soon it was like lying at the bottom of Niagara Falls.

Don't move, he told himself, when it touches you… Does acid kill by burning or does the pain overwhelm, shut your body down?

With a lesser-evil relief he felt a warm liquid touch the tip of the middle-finger of his right hand first and then a whole tide came sweeping over him: It wasn't acid. He remained still, focusing on his drainy breath moving in and out. The one-eyed rat came back, sniffing at his tongue. It licked the tip slowly and purposefully. He hoped it didn't bite. The liquid rose around his face and he pressed it harder into the drain. If the pool filled entirely, it would be hard to stay like this.

The liquid stopped rising at the point just over his earlobes.

"Okay, drop 'em in," God+Zero ordered his mumbling goons.

Martin heard what he knew was the specific sound of dead bodies dropping into the pool all around him. Cadavers hit the ground uniquely unconcerned, clumsy as boulders yet with the ease of tightrope walkers pacing a gymnasium floor. Doesn't matter if the ground is dry or a little wet.

Remember this tip. You never know, the way our world is today… the horrors…

"Zat good?" was meechingly garbled.

"Get that fucking gum outta your cockholster, you douche."

A golden bubble floated in and out of view above the pool.

"Better. All right, now cut 'em."

He figured this was the end, but heard only the sound of fabric being ripped off of the bodies. When it was his turn he lay perfectly still and someone ripped a patch off his shirt-tail.

"Stitch the kite!"

Martin heard metal on tile clanging for a few moments, followed by the sound of the industrial fan turning on, and something hitting the glass skylight above.

"More to the right... that's it. Awright, scoot now if you wanna add a few entries to your diary."

The gang fuck'd off and the heavy metal door slammed shut. Martin lifted his head to find himself immersed in a pool full of the blood of unwitting do-gooders, blood-donors indeed, and corpse-islands, too. He recognized a few of the faces from people reported missing in the news—But no Charlotte...

A large red kite flew above the skylight, held aloft by the loud whirring of the industrial fan. The kite was made from pieces of blood-soaked fabric from each of the bodies in the pool, including his own.

Looking a bit like *Carrie* on prom night, Martin cased the room again. He nervously extended the casing to his pockets and discovered only $2.38 on his person. Suddenly the sky went darker than blinding light, and a giant, multi-patterned bird appeared over the kite. It had a different small flapping wing where each feather should be, and looked like it was made of every kind of bird imaginable, from sparrow to archaeopteryx. It opened a weirdly human beak and uttered a cry that started high and fell stuttering through a diminished scale. The bird-BIRD then walked down through the air as though there were invisible stairs above the pool. It began eating the bodies and drinking the blood with a prehensile beak.

It lifted its enormous beak in the air and sniffed in Martin's direction. It walked over to him in the corner. The bird-BIRD snorted at him once, decided he wasn't carrion and went back to finish what it had started. When there was no trace of anything left, it sang a terrible song that started with a low note and rose through ever higher chromatic pitches until Martin could barely hear it. Then it walked up through the air and out the hole in the skylight.

Bloody Martin heard voices outside the metal door. He took a gamble and ran back to the pool, went down the diving board and jumped as hard as he could. He sprang into the air and grabbed an invisible set of stairs the bird-BIRD had left behind, and bounded, guessing at the huge steps that were quickly disappearing beneath him as he struggled upward like a cartoon that's run off a cliff.

"Someone's up there!" he heard Eggcream X. Inferno roar.

A bullet whizzed like an unexpected ring at your midnight doorbell. Martin crouched close to the dome as another 9mm went past. There's nothing more coldly certain of itself than a bullet, even the ones that miss. Those are almost worst—like loudening footsteps announcing the metallic approach of your inescapable death. As if to say, you have one life but we have a thousand bullets... there's a *nyah-nyah, nanny-nanny-poo-poo* in every gunshot.

Something sniffed his hand. It was the one-eyed rat, who had hitched a ride. Like Martin, it was covered in pool-blood. As he looked at it, the eye grew larger and took up most of its face. It stuck out a long tongue.

Martin had worked many strange cases. He knew there was a logic to the bizarre. He knew there was some meaning in this gesture, which the rat had made before when it was in the drain. He stuck his tongue out and the rat touched its tongue to his.

"You are the only one who has greeted us in the proper way," it said, retracting its tongue. Not otherwise mouth moving.

O, bitches of impossibilities!

Martin withdrew his tongue, spat and rubbed his tongue on the back of his hand ,which was dry yet tasted *wrong.*

"I try to be polite," Martin answered, equally lip-sealed. "Mi baño es tu casa. How's it I can hear you?"

"I offered my tongue. It transfers tongue-speech from its tip, to yours—For a time, always difficult to measure. We, the *Rattus Rabelais Hydrostatrae*—more commonly the Otherwise Unclassified Rat, the OUR—are not the only species that speak this language, uses the tongue this way. In fact, many mammals converse this way, though not usually humans. Vowels and Consonants! What nonsense. Are you human? That was a joke, by the way, about OUR. Not one person exists to call us anything. That's why it was funny. Your Spanish needs improvement."

Another bullet, then two more, *very* close, twins in space and time, and ricocheting about the pool walls. Metallic death bearing down on target, sir.

"I need to get outta here."

"So do *we*," the rat said. "We can't keep having this bird-BIRD summoned here all the time, threatening our fiery under-kingdom, which is located right under this bathhouse."

"But it looks like it's after dead bodies, not you."

"What do you think a dead body is for? See, it's like this:

"There's one of us in each one. We wait until we are alone with the body and then we . . . it's hard to explain."

"All the better. So this bird-BIRD is ruining your trip?"

"It takes the bodies to the land beyond evidence, beyond proof or credibility. We're losing all our best to this thing. There's no coming back from where that bird goes, you know."

"Don't know much, what next?"

An effortless bullet rose through the hole in the skylight and pierced the kite, which waved majestically over Martin's head.

"Our only choice," the *Rattus Rabelais* said sadly, is to use the escape tunnel. Set in place generations before and not used since."

"OK, so how do we get there?"

"What do you mean *we*, *Homo Sappy*? It's beneath a manhole so old it says MADE IN INDIA on it, under a burned out Volkswagen Bus. It's buried out back among the carcasses of that no-man's car-land. We can get out that way, and split quickly where that bird-BIRD won't ever reach. Although, we are still preparing provisions—in a week or so we'll say our goodbyes to this bathhouse forever! I suppose we're a bit of a lazy bunch.

"But for you it would just be another way in—down to our fiery under-kingdom. That's not healthy. You see how this is of no help to you? Hymn, I see one more chance for you . . . maybe . . .

"You can get away on that kite."

"No way," Martin said. "It's too light."

"No, it's been purified with blood meant for the bird-BIRD. Such spiritual blood is sturdier than moons, yet lighter than a last breath. I have suddenly just recalled this lore!"

Seeing he had little choice, Martin grabbed the kite and swung off the roof.

"Sucker!" the rat cried—carried away by his malevolence—and Martin pulled an Icarus, straight into an enormous dumpster.

It was a shock, but Martin's an old hand at falling, often from great heights, and every 30 days or so it's into a dumpster. This was simply his time of the month—unpleasant but familiar, bloody, not ferocious nor irrecoverable … could be worse … although, as Scott "Engel" Walker says in "Cossacks Are":

It's hard to pick the worst moment.

This dumpster was unusually deep, enough to conceal an as-yet undiscovered species of insect, unknown toxins, fungi that could lead to medical breakthroughs, except no explorer would ever think to look, its ecosystem hidden like Prester John's Kingdom under the unbearable weight of deserts and mythologies.

The dumpster seemed to scan everything about Martin into itself, as though it wasn't for garbage, but a really big mind-reading device. Like the way, you know, possessed people strapped to their beds in movies know *all* your secrets, things no way they could without the help of a demon or the NSA … Or—almost the same thing—like the dumpster was his brain and, boy did he have a filthy mind. He felt disrobed by the innocent blood, as if it had stripped him naked rather than stained his garments through—adding, in fact, another layer around him.

Though filled with the usual contents of a proper dumpster (rotting food, used receptacles, cans, plastic bags of horrid unguessables, and other filthy matters that, when conglomerated into a repulsive yet soft bed, are an unwilling dumpster-diver's salvation), there was an aura of uncanniness in the thriving trash—Frau Tarpit's *Unheimlche*, upon which Freud had written a monograph with his not-always present acumen.

Typical urban and anodyne, yet it reminded Martin of a pile of disparate, indeterminate fragments of an antediluvian civilization, accidentally excavated by the play of abandoned children digging in abandoned dirt, pieces that don't fit together as such, but must represent an entire, vast way of life now lost to time ... Sorry, Ladies, Gents, *meine Dammen und Herren*, but *der Roman* has left the *Bildungsroman* ... hard to explain, it takes too much time, like a detailed, yet reasonable explanation of G.W.F. Hegel's *Wissenschaft der Logik*.

And it reminded him of other things that would occur to anyone. Martin groped about for an improvised weapon, touching objects with names that started with a single letter that could represent a person's middle-name ... And things that were like the *S.* in Ulysses S. Grant—standing for nothing, too absurd to explain and yet existent. Eyes tearing in reaction to who knows what toxic effluvia, sinking into deeper embranglement within the pit of guts and worse and things that Might-As-Well-Be-Guts-and-Worse. It's saliva-dark in here, with an occasional yawn of sunlight ... gold globs of masticated GOLDRUSH! stick to his forearms like hyperkeratotic exudations of a Kept-Under-The-Mattress-Life's-Savings ... To make matters worse, it's got to be so dinosaur-extinction hot ... A beach day, pool day if ever there were ... incongruously, a half-full container of bleach ... An oblong fishrotten can, bent so the red lettering on the side appeared to Martin like the name of a German/Asian gentleman—HERR ING ... Coincidence ... *Hymn* ... This used tampon would not make a useful weapon ... Nor this tangerine rind ... Is that grammatically correct? Who gives a shit! Does grammar even *exist* when you're about to die? On to more important things ... broken glass? Owtch! Cuts his hand and loses the Heineken in the debris ... A brown paper grocery-bag, loaded with what might be peanut, soy butter ... No way to identify anything by scent, as the midden overwhelms the nose ... This gun would make a useful weapon if it wasn't empty ...

A woman's outstretched hand. It seems desperate for Martin's intervention, as if only he'd the power to undrown her. Must belong to an old store mannequin. He clasps it as though it's human—

Very cold hand. Odd respite from the everywhere heat.

Sorta wucky, too. Or is it just his sweat sloshing in his palm trenches?

He broke up the four-way of flies from the wrist, and found the evil (but undeniably, exquisitely rendered—lines as though machine-cut)—swastika tattoo.

Redheaded Charlotte!

Consecrated Crackers!

I mean, *God*, you can't make this stuff up. It's so nuts.

The dogs are growling, closing in and they're two feet tall but they're such bad news they'd might as well be the 2011 Tōhoku tsunami.

Why's she here? What're the chances?

Don't ask Martin ... I mean, why's it whenever trees branch out, at any given height, the total cross-sectional area of the daughter branches approximate the area of the mother trunk or branch? And why'do prosperous young couples from Park Slope break simple etiquette rule #1—they yawn *without covering their mouths* when they ride the subway amid the blue- and entry-leveled collared—You'd think they were alone, taking their wake-up shit. Park Slopers oughta know better, what with all that private schooling, private nursery schools, private genetic testing, placenta with rice preparation and dinner reception, etcetera.

Look, what are the chances? They derived the word *office* from the Latin for Orifice—*ōrificium:* An opening, especially one leading into a body cavity or passage? (Hard to believe the powerful had chosen such a perfect yet ironic origin, for the word that represents the Total Asshole's executive corner-floor prize?) Why'd all those musicians die at 27—and, perhaps more mystifying—why did so many die at *other* ages?

What if, in this case, at least, the loads of shit *are* the clues?

What's this, 20 Questions?

Ever see anyone win that game? Even play it?

No. Don't go down that track. Best not to care why: The point of solving a mystery is solving it, not understanding. And once solved, he'd get his paycheck. He wouldn't normally have taken a case working for such moral slime, but at least he'd get to deliver the news to the Tarpits that their daughter was dog-food, so to speak... If he survived...

The dogs are growling, closing in, just dogs but they'd might as well be a Martin-Seeking missile, warhead loaded with TNT, RDX, HMX, PETN, TATB, HNS, and ETC.

Martin tugged at Charlotte's hand. She weighed less than his 1931, Remington 16 desktop typewriter, easy enough to dislodge her naked body from its entrapment between some contractor bags. Her eyes were vaselinated with near-translucent lamination, from behind which Martin almost glimpsed black holes struggling against the unbreakable freeze of death, to burst into existence, to suck up any populated galaxy, any place in the universe someone lived who didn't want to die. Inside Charlotte's dead, zoophiliac eyes was an inexpressible urge to destroy *home* in all its forms, from fairytale to front-page.

Was Charlotte's home Frau Tarpit's on the Upper West?

Then he understood the free-floating, generalized intention to decimate...

Besides the eyes that weren't even eyes but threats vague as they were vast, Martin never really saw Charlotte Tarpit. He didn't know where her skeletal torso ended and that oozing, Styrofoam container of mustard started... Charlotte was trash, now, and Martin in limbo between recyclable and rotting. He was still alive, but most meat spends most of its life alive.

The dogs are growling, closing in, just dogs but they'd might as well be the katabatic winds of the Cape Denison/Commonwealth Bay area, south of Australia—200 miles-per-hour of canine rage sweeping down toward his defenseless bucket.

Now the dogs were mere moments away. The grocery bag of peanut-or-whatever butter slid down plop on his shoulder. Martin plunged his hands into it and dove into obscure detritus, thickly spat, putty-hard GOLDRUSH! gum and wrappers, into wormfertile nakedness, locating her vaginal area, slathering what glop he could round the unspeakables. Thinking, this might be an okay substitute for peanut butter. Yeah, good idea, this is how she did it, transformed strange dogs into lovers ... Sinking into the shit both defecated and non-organic, everything slippery goin' slipperier, he accidentally fisted the corpse—All the more disgusting, because it was through an orifice he'd accidently punched into her abdomen. Wrenching out his hand, the peanut buttery substance flew across her face as well.

One hand on her head, the other *in* something viscid, dribbly of her, he launched himself up like a human-sized vomit and heaved her body out the dumpster. It landed a few feet away from the dumpster. The pack of dogs approached like gunslingers in John Wayne movies. Martin then immediately bent down, grabbed the bleach and poured what he could on himself, hoping the astringency would drive the dogs away from him.

He should've lickety-beat-cheex-split, but was momently enthralled when the pit bulls began lapping at the Charlotte's body. She had fallen on her back, thin arms thrown back over her head, lamellated eyes staring into the determined sun. Some of the pack stood back together, waiting their turn, while two Alphas went at her, gently. Martin imagined tears gathering at their eyes. In fact, it was Martin crying (just a *wee bit* from a *wee bit* of fear), and he'd mistook tenderness for canine caution.

One dog lapped her face and the other bit into her groin and moved his clamped jaws side-to-side, just like the alligator with baby Moses sent down the river—in the real version of the story. That was his client getting sexually devoured by dogs. Success most awful. He began to climb up a hill of anti-pure-snow as carefully as possible, hoping to dash off through a fenceless abandoned parking lot, that led to an overgrown patch of land. He scrambled quickly, looking over his shoulder more often than planned... You just hopefully don't see this every day, he was fascinated by the erotic nature of her body under Necrobestial orgy. As the pit bulls worked at Charlotte, her body arched up at the hips and the dog over her face lapped her upper lip into a sneer of abandon, then made them open and close as though uttering the dirtiest words of encouragement and command to the murderous quadruped. Screw needing forgiveness, it looked to Martin as though she reached climax just as there was nothing left of her face and the exenterated vagina, the body making a weird bloody jerk of Entering Heaven. It was sad that she was a Nazi, it was sad that she was dead, but this last funerary rite was probably just what she would've wanted, and a dead Nazi is a good thing, to boot... For what other bizarre rituals did Martin play the Priest without knowing it?

Okay, better get going now, for *real*...

Reality got diverted (but then, what else is new... Could Diverted not be a synonym for Reality?), when Martin dropped off the far side of the dumpster behind the bathhouse and, landing in a painful kinda kneeling position, found himself for the second time that day, eye-to-eye with an (eldritch?) beastie. It was the H.D.I.C. ... Martin shifts backwards, just an inch, thinking for some reason that he would resemble a fire hydrant the more. The pit bull just kept his yellow eyes on Martin's quivering browns.

Just as he had trusted in the logic of the bizarre with the *Rattus Rabelais Hydrostatrae* earlier, he now took the shortest-straw chance that the pit bulls were also tongue-speakers. That not beneficent *Rattus* had mentioned that other mammals used it... and what matters the difference between getting killed by a vicious animal with your tongue sticking out, or in?

So he stuck out his pudgy tongue. It was dry, his lips were dry. He had the impossible sensation of rubbing one of his bones against another.

The yellow-eyed hound took an easy step forward. The paw so regal. Martin closed his eyes. He had to drop some kids off at the pool, so to speak ... Don't die while crapping your pants. Think dignified thoughts... Poetic thoughts...

What about W.B. Yeats? Of course, a genius, moving as hell. Fires the blood with revelatory chills. Who can't quote *The Second Coming*—even covered in blood and crap and kneeling before a quadruped assassin. But only a few words of the classic poem came to Martin, most of whose energy was keeping his rectum sealed... He recalled only "The centre cannot hold" and "The blood-dimmed tide is loosed, and everywhere." He'd forgotten that stuff about *Où est Le falconer aujourd'hui? My tyre's expanded, falling apart... Sphinx headin' over to Bethlehem with a real bad posture*... Lord, Martin's centre simply *cannot* hold any longer…

Martin's in the dark of his head but it was the blackness of the pit, he keeps his solids together yet loses bladder domination, yoking back the stream only when he hears the dog shifting its paws in the warm pool. Then… Is it sky raining? His dry lips moisten, his chin, his dry tongue wet… his impossibly desiccant sensation deliquesces… "I never met a biped with tongue-speech before," the pit bull said, tongue 34% behind cheeks and jaw.

"Oh, I'm relieved," Martin said, opening his eyes, thinking he looked like something melted way down from its original form. And actually was that.

"I can see, hear, smell and taste *that.* It's good… speaking of which, am I correct in assuming that you smooshed that shit on Charlotte's twat because you assumed it was peanut butter, and that we dogs had a relationship with her based upon the exchange of the food, which we paid for by giving her pleasure?"

Nodded yes.

"Well we like stinky, dying things—even more than peanut butter, by the way. I guess you never had a dog…"

"So you're saying I shoulda spared myself making a PB mess and fisting a dead woman, that her ungarnished corpse would've been enough to distract your crew anyway, and that I've made myself messier than I needed to be? As if it makes any difference with this blood and trashy junk festooned all about me? And me sitting in my piss. About to shit! As if I should've made sure I'd been more appropriately tidy before you tear me to bits?"

"Your suppositions are reasonable given your limited point-of-view. But I'm saying a few other things. I'm saying it *wasn't* peanut butter you slathered on that dead girl. It was, in fact, literally shit. However, I'm agreeing with you that even if it *had* been peanut butter, it wouldn't have made a difference in our eagerness to gnosh.

"However, there is something rare and valuable in this specific shit you mistook for peanut butter. There's a particularly rare and delicious animal that we've sighted in this area, but haven't yet caught… Its big-eyed, rat-like body is great, but its shit is even more delectable than the rest of it. I suppose you could say that the cocky-doody of this creature is to us, uh, what you people call caviar. So another thing I am saying is that we're actually grateful that you mistook the glop for plop ... The unnecessary time you took in garnishing her carcass, made it an extraordinary meal. Unfortunately, our 'Masters' and the rest of my pack have got you cornered. I just wanted you to know you made a few dogs happy before you die. Obviously, you have no means of helping us find our favorite furballs—"

"—*Rattus Rabelais Hydrostatrae*?"

Baffled, the dog answered "What the Dickens! You know something?"

"Only if you swear to let me live ... and I've never had a dog's word before, so I don't know if it's good. How can I be sure after I show you their lair, you won't chew me up for the hell of it?"

"Oh, we have a way of proving the honesty of our intentions. One that I believe you will understand."

"Yeah, yeah, I wish I could hear it. And it was nice tongue-yapping ... But that's the sound of your human masters running this way, hymn? Looks like I'm dead meat either way, eh? God, just don't let Thylacine-Antichrist deliver the killing blow. I'd rather be snuffed by an eggcream ..."

The dog laughed as only a dog can, as can't be explained unless you were there to hear it, and now and then you remember it without meaning to, and should you recall at the wrong moment, it will scare your loved ones or lose you a job.

"You're about to find out just how good my word is."

All Martin could think of was the eleven hungry dogs coming to warm him up with bites, before the real torture began under human hands.

The Alpha called "We have a CODE NOTHING BETTER EVER NOT EVEN KILL FOREVER Situation here! I repeat CODE NOTHING BETTER EVER NOT EVEN KILL FOREVER! Turn around and target the Three Providers! NOW! This man's not to be harmed, he is now an ally. NBENEKF! DEVOUR THE THREE!"

A few yards away the pack stopped playing with their food, bloody foam and flesh dripping in synch from their eleven-headed angry face. At a nod of the Alpha, they ran the way they'd come tumbling ... Any second, the criminals would appear around the corner of the large bathhouse. Man was Martin screwed. But then men are screaming ... a gun goes off ... but it takes less than a minute for the pack to inflict what Martin assumes are extremely botched tracheotomies and brain surgeries on God+Zero, Thylacine-Antichrist, Eggcream X. Inferno, and whatever lackeys might have hung around. They didn't even make it into Martin's view.

"Wow. *That* is what I call an *Oath*," Martin said. "You've sold me."

"Anything for some Otherwise Unclassified. Now, your part of the deal, sir."

"Of course ..."

Martin explained what he'd learned from the *Rattus Rabelais Hydrostatrae* about their escape route being under a manhole concealed by a broken-down VW. The key then was to block the drain in the pool, open the manhole and set the dogs down. They would feast like kings! A pit bull checked and confirmed the existence of the escape route as described by Martin.

"I'll need something to pry the manhole cover with, first ..." he was saying, when one of the dogs dashed off to the dead criminals, brought back a heavy crowbar clenched between its undefeatable jaws.

It was a good, honest deal and, the most important thing, once it was concluded Martin limped away alive.

$25,659.49

And so, that's how Martin Box located the Nazizoophiliac Charlotte Tarpit, solved the Pedestrian Blood Supply Case, and helped reduce the incidence of murders in New York City to a tolerable 522 for the year. Certain statisticians—The Great Nameless God of Statistics, for one (probable Mesopotamian)—knows exactly how this figure—may even find it of interest—that this figure correlated with a 1,078,029.83% increase in Martin's savings account over the comparable, previous annual period.

EMOTION: A STATE OF LUCID CONFUSION

FUNNY TRUMPS FUN.

ALLOW ME TO UNDERSTAY MY WELCOME.

AS SOON AS YOU SAY "LIFE HAS NO MEANING" YOU CONTRADICT YOURSELF, HAVING MADE A MEANINGFUL STATEMENT.

ONLY A REAL DOWN-IN-THE-DUMPS PESSIMIST COULD BELIEVE IN LIFE AFTER DEATH.

LIFE IS ORGANIZED ARBITRARILY, WHICH IS TO SAY, IN CHRONOLOGICAL ORDERS.

OF COURSE I KNOW RIGHT FROM WRONG. THE "W" IS SILENT IN WRONG, AND THE WHOLE WORD'S SPELLED COMPLETELY DIFFERENT ANYWAY.

X: "She's a real cunt."

Y: "Now, now – It's more complicated than that... she's a fat, hairy, stupid cunt."

Sth. like

"X hung limp & still like an IV tube pulled from a vein."

Him

Mirror

THIS IS A PROBLEM

"The jagged spaces b/w the leaves were the holes in an unscalable fence through which you can see an escape."

THE IMMIGRANTS

IT'S ALMOST FOUR O'CLOCK IN THE MORNING when my guard-bones bark me awake (That's the best way I can describe this oddest of sensations. Old folks get lots of strange twinges and pains but this is new). I head for the bathroom. I glimpse myself in the medicine cabinet, just before it breaks along with the other mirrors in my place. Simultaneous. That's weird but not the real puzzle here. Look, shit breaks, weird happens, right?

What surpasses weird is the *way* they've broken. I go room to room, turning on lights (At least it's not a blackout). I try all eight mirrors. There's always a first time for all things to go wrong in unprecedented ways: I've never seen a mirror *malfunction* before.

Each time I look at the glass, there's no me, there's disparate *person-like non-people* there, watching for something a ways behind my back. Giving off a lost, worried vibe, waiting for a monumental appearance on the distant horizon…

Nothing there but the cramped walls of my tenement apartment, far as I can tell. And the black smudge of a squashed moth.

I return to seeking my seeking reflection.

Nope.

Two of them in my largest mirror. Can't tell if they're male, female, clay-mation automaton, nuclear vegetable, or what. But I was a door-to-door salesman my whole working life—which ended decades ago—and between the great variety of doors opening and closing in your face, the invites for a cuppa joe and the accusations of trespassing, you get good at reading people. Who woulda thunkd'it: Turns out you also catch the knack for reading aliens.

I see expressions above their necks that put me in mind of when a fish is taken out of water a few moments—not long enough to kill it—how in that time before it's thrown back into the lake—how that experience must be the closest that fish ever came to dreaming. This pair's giving a related impression. Or is it me feeling that way?.

Stop it already.

Know what I bet? Corporations run everything—and that's no crazy old-timer conspiracy ranting. I bet some business who secretly charges each American in limbs has blown a grid-load of fuses. Whatever clandestine company that provides you with this power: The power to pretend your face belongs to someone else—so you can look him in the eye and fix his hair—Well, that shadow conglomerate's had a damn awful outage I bet.

I've even lost the ability to objectively confirm I'm a fossil of a man who can't remember how long he's been living by himself. Or living (Can't be but a few years' difference between the two). A man who looks in the mirror to see an exile from an icy planet of pensioners . . . *Is that a biped? I don't recognize this creature of moley wrinkle and twitch, this "me"* . . .

A man who, a lifetime ago, misplaced a list of important things to do. Such as: stop travelling the road like Rosie asked you to; kick the booze; prove I'm man enough to take care of her; marry Rosie; get a steady job, a career with upward mobility; some kids to run round a sprinkler in a big, green yard in Long Island. Such as: don't let sixty years go by and wind up here with the dead moth-spotted walls. Don't misplace that list. Such as: stop fucking up, and die already. I'm late for being late.

Joy is careless. Misery couldn't care less. My reflections, be they in mirrors or brain, never helped me understand this World much.

There in the mirror I'm not reflected.

I'd have a hard time selling this crap back in the day.

Where my image should be, *some-almost-one* looks beyond me, not so much like I'm invisible as blocking a view, the guy in a 10-gallon hat who just sat down directly in front of you at the movies.

A nameless "X" is happening. What I mean is if the World's truly *spinning*—if that's the correct word—then no kid, drunk, dreidel, top or ballerina ever *spins*—They lack motive, have no Sun. We need another verb.

Better: Another verb is *here*.

The mirrors are *X-ing*.

How will I shave?

Here's a relief (I guess)—I'm not just losing it:

The radio is frantic with reports on this malfunctioning-mirror deal. It's a scourge. My reception is eroded, like the signals are wrestling with a mighty angel, yanking them back to Transmitter Desert before they can get close enough to gimme the skinny. Eventually, I can make out the most frequently iterated words and phrases:

Invasion ... Electromagnetic Attack ... Noted String-Theorist ... Unknown Quantum ... Tom Cruise issued this statement ... Visitors ... Dimensional Portal ... Terrorist ... So-called Bashing Parties ... Alien ... Impossible ... Reality as We Know It ... Bad Luck ... Knows No Borders ... Obama's Fault ... Apocalypse ... Calm ... Panic ... Trump calls for mass executions by guillotine ... Don't ... Do ... Stay Put ... Flee! Far Away! ... Tom Cruise has retracted ... Extraterrestrial Phenomenon ... Go-Bag Essentials ... Tesla's Revenge ... Is Obama an evil alien entity ... Global ... Guns ... Ghosts ...

(They can rule *that* one out. This "X" happening with the mirrors is nothing supernatural, there's no spirit world. When you're dead you're *dead*. I know because I died once. On an operating table. I was dead three minutes, and when the surgeons reeled me back, I remembered nothing of the experience, *and* I didn't forget a single detail, either. You get me? Because there is *nothing*. Even that word alone is *too much* to describe it.)

Detritus of interviews, mumbling heads, doctors with no degrees, comedians... Obnoxious jokes about vampires and bad luck beyond reckoning. They laugh, ha-ha. But laughter is like mist on a river—it might distract you from the water, but it cannot change its course, and the course is all a river is.

Were people always this stupid?

I shut that radio the fuck up, go through the rooms, visiting each of the formerly-known-as-mirrors. No, they certainly aren't humans, no discernible gender or ages, even. Who'da thunkdit: My Eisenhower-Era door-to-door toaster salesman skills could be today's cutting-edge forensic competencies. I register a new emotion on the "faces." It's difficult to explain. Let's call it a lost-coin look:

Whereas a coin toss has two possible outcomes, *losing* a coin is at least three kinds of loss. You lose a circular, metal object about the size of a 1947 pox-vaccination scar; you lose a bit of money; and you lose control (as with any loss). But these aliens, with their lost-coin looks haven't lost any coins... What gives?

I'm ashamed!

What arrogance. How do I know what they've lost? What wicked cosmos they fled? Do they keep their to-do lists on them at all times? Are they waiting for salvation? Have they suffered? Then again, they could be coming to destroy humanity, to ruin civilization itself, steal our oxygen—who knows?

They are looking *forward*, that's for sure. Which means when I see them, I'm looking backward.

At what, a *new past*?

This question brings an antique photograph to mind. It belonged to my mother. A picture of my great-grandparents on Ellis Island, having just arrived from Ruthenia. He was a laborer and she a laundress. They'd come here with great hopes, like many millions. They'd work their stinking birthplace skin off, grow a vibrant new American layer. Live well and start a family, the biggest, the most beautiful. The old story. The one you have to believe is true, if only for an hour or two each year. Or else you will go mad.

But now they've disembarked onto this land of no-turning-back-now. It's plain to see in the photograph: Whatever ordeals they endured to reach New York has drained any emotion from their eyes, leaving dark sepia spots.

It's obvious: All they want's to be left alone in the two-dimensional peace of that photograph. Because they quickly picked up how obscenely expensive cheerful eyes are over here. They'll never save enough. The question of housing. If only they could stay in that photograph! They swear they'll even wear those empty eyes forever, if that's the cost of settling down in that photo. On the back someone with a firm hand, my mother didn't know who, had written *Much luck!*

I'm tired of those peering mirrorific things and the memories they stir. If I try hard enough I can imagine they're eight weird, tacky posters not suited to my tastes. I like only Gauguin. And L.A. Spooner, I think. The one with the nudes.

#(!

I must sleep, it's late, dark.

I'm not sleeping for long. People outside, crude, loud city-racket. My eyes open but I don't feel like getting out of bed.

A mob gathering in the street. Shouting. Mad as hell, not going to take it anymore, sort of black-and-white-TV race-riot stuff, fascist acting-out ... The World outside my window counts down in remarkable solidarity: "Three ... Two ... One—Smash!" Sounds like the genocide of a million glass gypsies. Lynched with pissed-off collective WHACK!, baseball bats, crowbars, curtain-rods. After the shattering, lots of people screaming in burning-alive pain (I recognize the timbre of that particular dying-crying from the war). Must be one of those mirror-bashing parties that I think the radio's spluttering about. I remember when they burned books. That was bad. But much quieter. Thankfully the screaming stops all at once, as if at the push of a button. The death of a laugh-track.

I try the bedside lamp but it's kaput. I get up, fumble to the wall-switch: Nope, no light.

I open my window: Nope, no street. No people, nothing broken or burned. No stars. Which anyway are less loving than snakes, less than indifferent. Maybe they were just an omen of twinkling glass shards, extinguished now that of which they warned is come. It's always one thing after another and when it rains it pours and Murphy's Law. In other words, another grid has hit the fan. It's the classic New York City blackout I was so glad wasn't happening earlier. Lots of trouble tonight.

My frozen pirogues will stink like corpse farts.

Damn, I can't remember if I did my weekly shopping…

What will happen to those creatures in the mirrors? Looking expectant, lost-coin sad. These aliens who need their own verbs. These People of the Verbs. Will they find the right action words in time—There's urgent yearning on their side.

My God, am I *worried* about them? Remember, dumbass, you don't know their true intentions.

Don't lose your head. It's just a blackout. I can cope. The hell with Go-Bags. It is what it is and what're you gonna do? and it's a serious pain in the ass but whatever you do, stay calm. No problem.

In my calm I suddenly feel the need to talk to another person. Why? I don't know. It's harder to explain than it oughta be. It's not like me. I got to the telephone—a glorious landline, impervious to blackouts. Old ways aren't always outdated.

I have nobody to call.

But wait, there's always someone. There's billions of wrong numbers.

I sit on the edge of my bed. I find the fat candle on my nighttable. I hate candles. It smells like marzipan and I like marzipan. I open the drawer and take out the big box of safety matches.

I try lighting the candle, pick up the phone and wait for the dial-tone.

I want to hear another person say "hello." This isn't like me at all. At the same time, my heart is stirring as though obedient to a thread, yes, it hangs from a loose thread, which in its turn is submissive to a sort of inner wind now passing through, uneasing it from firm uprightness. What opening in me permits such an impossible breeze entrance? Oh, that's right. I can't believe I can remember how it feels: heartache...

I am obedient to the dizzy whims of the thinnest thread.

The safety matches are definitely not wet, so the whole box must be defective. Probably made in New Jersey. Not a single match works, do you believe it. There's no marzipan smoke from a flame in this room. I can't see a thing. My window is open and the street is awful mute. Silent as three minutes of operation-table, flat-line *nothing.*

There's no dial-tone, either. I'll hang on ... The dial-tone's probably just tired, taking its sweet time to reach me... It will arrive soon. Lame joke, old man. Please, stop lying. Something's very wrong tonight. I highly doubt there's a prowler running around cutting telephone wires, and barring that, I'm clueless as to why there's no dial-tone. There isn't even the *possibility* of hearing a person say "Hello, how can I help you?" or "I'm afraid you have the wrong number" or even "Don't you *ever* call here again, do you *hear me asshole*... DO YOU?" No chance for me to apologize to someone, say "I'm so sorry to trouble you, truly sorry..."

The crackling of mirrors begins throughout my apartment, a pizzicato crescendo. The eight mirrors are X-ing and other verbs, too, say, ZX-ing and XZ-ing ... It sounds traumatic as birth but what do I know, it could be joy, the immigrants are disembarking. Oh, I see. Shit in my pants. My old salesman senses are tingling ... I'm pretty sure they aren't friendly, I've got that *whatever-you're-selling we-don't-want-it-get-off-my-land* vibe. I hang up the phone, pick it up again. Is that a dial-tone? It's definitely something. Hope can impersonate anything from a dial-tone to the vision of future generations flourishing in a land of liberty... Still not a dial-tone.

A slight ringing? Nope, not that, either. It's a buzzing, an echo. No. You're imagining things. It's not the sound of a Coney Island conch in my ear. It's not Rosie saying *Can't you stay just a few more days... love?* But it's definitely something, that's for sure. It's not that I'm afraid to die alone, right now, what at my age and all. It's that I don't want to go *extinct* like this, here in my voiceless dark, and it's much luck to the immigrants, may at least a couple of their dreams come true.

Commander Bean flying after other things

B

?

Keep as B.

B

DO NOT EVEN LOOK AT THIS!

DO NOT PUSH BUTTON!

Change the base of the flag to suction cups

Keep but alter

maybe make it look like a phone? a [illegible] — Sth. shouldn't touch or [illegible]

Note to self

Note → This layout is bad!

ONE DAY BEAN FOUND SOMETHING STRANGE

THE APOLOGIES

EACH WEEKDAY, Lenore placed her mail in a wicker tray on the credenza in the violet hallway, just as Mother had done. She arranged envelopes in precise stacks, equidistant and inevitable as the numbered boxes of a calendar. On Saturday evenings she separated the bills from solicitations, charity appeals, political flyers, credit card offers, menus and other propaganda. These went into the chromium wastebin under the kitchen sink.

Sundays she woke at six. Sometimes she looked twice at her thin image in the bedroom's full-sized mirror, as if to confirm it wasn't a lost traveler who should be pointed in another direction. She then slipped into a scraggly suggestion of a robe. In the bathroom Lenore scrubbed her features in triplicate. She washed the soap into cleaner nothing. Her skin was smooth for a woman her age, but wasn't it constricted, tight as zipper-mouthed rubber?

She carefully wiped up the few sudsy splashes. She walked toward the violet hallway that adjoined the foyer, crossing a carmine shag carpet from which sewing needles lost during the Cuban Missile Crisis occasionally emerged, sharp and pointless.

Lenore gathered the week's bills from the wicker tray. From the credenza she extracted checkbook, pen, calculator, notepad, and magnifying glass. At the dining room table, she spread the bills before her in a broad, even grid with the unselfconsciously superstitious gravity of commuters lip-reading psalms in subway cars. Interpreted properly, the fine print foretold ruin, homeostasis, or mere nuisance—Thanks for All Your Hell and I Told You the First Time I'm Not Interested.

She took her time. Dates of service? Pro-rated amounts? Discrepancies: None. It went like that. When she finished she'd sit there a bit and just listen. She'd soon spend the rest of the day bustling about, cleaning and tidying things—even the clean and tidy things. But now the house was quiet. Lenore liked that. Best of all, there was no silence to break.

One Sunday in September—forty-one years since mother followed father (she by hospice, he through windshield)—Lenore was vexed to find an unaddressed, unsealed envelope hidden between bills and her Social Security check. A handwritten note slid out, paper rough and thin as FEMA toilet tissue. The cheap blue capitals shouted like vulgar welfare leeches:

> SORRY, I'M SO SORRY FOR WHAT I DID TO YOU. IT WAS SO MANY YEARS AGO BUT THAT ONLY MAKES IT WORSE. MORE TIME TO THINK ABOUT IT. YOU KNOW HOW A SKULL IS A MASK ON THE WRONG SIDE OF THE FACE? AND HOW THAT SEEMS CRAZY, BECAUSE WHAT POINT CAN THERE BE IN A HIDDEN MASK? WELL, I FINALLY FIGURED OUT THE ANSWER. BUT IT'S NO CONSOLATION. EVERYTHING ISN'T. I HAVE TRIED EVERYTHING TO REDEEM MYSELF IN SOME WAY, TO ATONE FOR WHAT I DID TO YOU, BUT THERE IS NO WORD FOR THE IDIOCY OF THOSE ATTEMPTS, IT IS

LESS THAN ABSURD, WHICH AT LEAST HAS A PLACE IN THE DICTIONARY. HOW I REGRET YOUR DOWNFALL EYES. I LOOK FOWARD TO

To what?

The handwriting was masculine. The letters were boxy cages, crafted slowly and certainly—built, erected. Yet the message ended mid-sentence, an overambitious edifice abandoned in sturdy pieces; and in the towers of each first-person "I", the pen had gouged inaccessibly minute peepholes through the paper.

No 800-Number, no manager to hear the complaint. Who had written it? Why had she received it? Surely it couldn't be meant for her. Nobody had done her a serious wrong. She tossed it in the kitchen wastebin.

Did he bite the pen that inked it?

To what?

Saturday, the gray sky swelled and foamed like the Atlantic, and the world outside Lenore's windows was rained into an educated guess. Another blank envelope arrived, damp as though washed through the mail-slot. There was nothing special about it, yet as Lenore's eyes traced its rectangular perimeter—

—a table-top white with hot light. A magician's beautiful assistant lies glimmering there in sequined still-life, engulfed by a rusted murk of sunken highway signs, the woody, brassy silt of drowned clocks. The magician hovers unseen in hushed, blindspot-blackness, waiting for the right moment to amaze. He is thunder in a top-hat—

—the vision had been quick and demanding as knife/flick/throat. Just as suddenly, the thing in her hand reverted to a typical, earthly envelope. The flap had been partially sealed, by rain she supposed. Lenore's index finger worked beneath an unglued spot, gently as though seeking evasive capers at molar recesses, then swiftly retracted—mail must be opened on Sunday, even refugee messages, daring enough to have fled the safety of their bottles. She shouldn't break protocol. Little things led to bigger, then too big; it was a short step from nailbiting to cannibalism. Change could be exponential but not inexorable, if you stayed … as you were. A distant church bell rang once, staccato, the resonance cut oddly short as though frozen by sudden embarrassment.

Between Saturday afternoon and Sunday morning, Lenore was unpleasantly impatient and vaguely expectant—somehow disembodiedly constipated. For distraction, she examined the floor in the violet hallway. Decades of coming-back and going-away had undone the boards. Nails bared their twisted, rusty heads. Naked eyesores of eroded polyurethane basked under the hallway light. The parquet inlays were loose; at a toe-tap, the floor emitted the disingenuous creak of thief-in-the-night opened doors. She pressed down on the parquet repeatedly to see if she could get used to it. No, it was worse than the inevitably bony flapping of interrupted pigeons. Reluctantly, she removed her orthopedic shoes, muffling the noise to tolerability.

On Sunday, she placed the note on the dining room table, adjacent to the bills but far enough away for a unique, quarantined status that rattled her concentration. She tried to conduct her usual routines, but the unopened envelope was a task that must be dealt with to be dismissed, a finger depressed on your doorbell with unyielding solicitous pressure—

You will go mad. You must open the door. Couldn't she break custom, just once? She tore it open and out tumbled familiar, willful shapes:

> I'M SENDING YOU ANOTHER. ONE ISN'T ENOUGH. THIS WAY I AM GIVING YOU MORE. MORE WHAT? MORE NOT ENOUGH, I GUESS. I HAVE SOLVED AN-

OTHER PUZZLE. I'LL SHARE: I WILL DO MORE FOR THE WORLD DEAD THAN ALIVE. I HAVE NEVER BEEN GENEROUS OR KIND. BUT DEATH IS CHARITY. I'LL GIVE A LITTLE EXTRA SPACE TO THE WORLD, AND LEAVE A FEW LESS LIES AND EXCUSES. AND I AM SO IDLE LATELY, BUT DEATH IS SO BUSY. I'VE NEVER SEEN AN UNEMPLOYED MAGGOT. I KNOW YOU CANNOT RIGHT A WRONG, BUT YOU CAN MAKE IT BIGGER, UNTIL THE WRONG IS SO TITANIC THAT NOBODY SEES IT AS ANYTHING ANYMORE, A SKY-LIKE WRONG. AFTER IT'S THROUGH I LOOK FORWARD TO DYING BECAUSE

Because what? Was this a joke? Lenore held the letter up to a light bulb without revelation. Under her magnifying glass, the letters were more gouged than written. She examined the blue trenches, so bold and frail. Faint STOP-sign red streaks had run deadended lanes down the uplifted arms of SORRY's emphatic Y. They were scentless, untraceable.

Things like this didn't happen to her.

Therefore, they must happen to someone else. And hadn't she once been such a Someone-Else, as a child—before Father died? She didn't recall much about that life. She didn't like looking back at it; she wished she couldn't… They didn't bury him like Father. They put him in the ground like nuclear waste. And then it was past/never vision, breaths she chose not to take, blood flew in diagonals, blotted out Lite Brite clowns when she pricked herself on sewing needles, and something worse, more terrible than the unexplained because it couldn't be described enough to lack explanation…

And then? She learned to mimic Mother's routines—face-washing, coupon-clipping, mail management, checkbook balancing, lists of lists without completion. And then? Well, everything was okay. Lenore had a gift for forging, then living Mother's life, day into day, silence after silence, as Father had excelled at wearing his 1951 nobody suit, the one he must be wearing still.

If she was someone else again, *then*... what?

This?

Because what?

That night, on schedule, Lenore went to bed at ten o'clock. No, she didn't like thinking back. It seemed unnatural; it was like grief or white teeth. Even so, she lay there for hours, eyes bared like exposed organs waiting for scalpels, thinking no, nobody owes me an apology.

She supposed maggots *were* industrious. She turned her head toward a far side of the room. Apparently—she had no memory of it—she'd placed the today's note atop her dresser. Why hadn't she thrown it away? The edges had curled inward; it had evolved into a new object that wouldn't fit inside an envelope. It would need a box—if you were to keep it.

Because what?

The next morning, Lenore sat in bed and stared at the note. The corners had unfurled slightly during the night. In the bathroom mirror, her skin seemed to cling to the hidden mask of her skull, a faceless abyss beneath her chin.

That week dragged damp gray minutes. By Friday, the house and all its hidden places were more than spotless, even inside radiator valves, vanity knob screwholes, and Metamucil bottles. But it was as though the mess had been inside her rather than the rooms, and when she thought she was cleaning it up, she was hollowing herself out. It was hard to explain.

Shopping made sense, so she went on several such expeditions.

She'd intended to visit a flooring specialist to get a quote on fixing the hallway, but kept forgetting to go through with it; instead, she bought more groceries than she needed. The people in the cereal and meat aisles looked fatally misguided as children smoking cigarettes; and she found herself looking for a top-hat among the irritably bored heads in the check-out line; and when she left the supermarket, the center of each barred apartment-building window quivered with clones—pale, sexless faces following her with disinterested, elderly voyeurism. Strangest of all was that Lenore had observed any of this. She didn't pay attention to people she didn't know, and she didn't know anyone anymore.

Had it really been rain? Or had he sealed the envelope with a tentative tongue?

She went through her routines in the usual manner on Saturday. She felt calm, transparent, practically absent, more like sight than eye—definitely there yet you can't touch it.

But as bedtime approached, Lenore glimpsed herself in the bedroom mirror and froze. She was startled to see a pale, lost traveler, and Lenore didn't have directions to offer. Transfixed, she had a thought she didn't understand: It was true that she knew no one, but that also meant everyone must know her. The mirror that held her provisional image was like a window facing a cement wall, compelling you to attempt spying through it, because somewhere, years back, you learned that's what windows are for, so…

She would not look back.

She refused.

Lenore needed a reason to step away from the mirror. Somehow, if she stayed there too long it would be too late. She began looking around her figure at the tidy objects reflected behind it. She noticed the note, past her shoulder. It was still on the dresser. Suddenly, she had not exactly an idea, and she reanimated. She retrieved a sheet of expensive, cream-colored paper and a fine, blue marker from the writing desk. In her painstakingly-looped cursive, she filled one page:

I forgive you. Let's talk about it.

Lenore sat at the dining room table and read it a few times. She believed in the words. She didn't know why. They must be addressed to someone. They struck her as true. It was the first time she'd felt sure of herself since the Sunday morning of the first apology. She neatly, firmly taped the sign on the front door. It was almost outrageously public beneath the porch light. She left the doors wide open. She put the shades up and lifted the windows high. At ten o'clock she turned off the lamps and got under the covers, and quick as knife/flick/throat, the answer came to her, and it tickled all over: BECAUSE YOU CAN'T LOOK BACK AT IT.

The clock struck eleven, then midnight. A shaft of moonlight bisected the blanket where it covered her waist, precisely where a magician's blade would saw his lovely assistant in two. She was trembling and happily confused when she heard him in the violet hallway, slipping off his boots so the floorboards wouldn't make too much noise.

KRUG'S PEN

1
NO CASE

The sound of gunfire a few blocks away made it hard for Martin Box, private investigator, to focus on the Lonely Hearts advertisements in the local paper. He'd never gone for this kind of thing before, but he was feeling alone lately. He didn't ask why. He did what a detective does—he investigated the possibilities. The problem was he wasn't sure why any woman would want him in particular. He was house-trained, sure, but that was no big prize.

The door to his office opened. He hoped it was an attractive woman. It was a desperate-looking middle-aged man. He clutched a small, black oblong box resembling a coffin. He was skinny and bald like a mendicant and his wild eyes roved behind small glasses. Martin was certain he was of a religious temperament. It was a sunny November day but you'd have thought he was fleeing a hailstorm in his long gray raincoat.

Martin wondered if this was another loony freaking out because the police were on strike, thinking a PI would help them with a car alarm that wouldn't stop or to report a missing wallet.

"I've heard no case is too strange for Martin Box," the man

said, peering over his shoulder at nothing.

"I don't mind crazy, as long as I can keep my head," Martin said. "I've worked for gods, monsters, fairy tale creatures, talking books, shady trans-dimensional corporations, you name it."

"I need you to find out if this pen exists."

"Let's see."

"Careful," the man said, as though it were a holy icon. "Careful!" He put the little box down on the table as though it were made of cards near toppling.

"May I?" Martin asked and didn't wait for an answer.

Inside was a black quill pen. "It looks like it exists."

"Yes, but does it? More importantly, can you prove it is Krug's pen?"

"That's a different question."

"No it isn't. I believe this is Krug's pen. Does Krug's pen exist? Only if it belongs to Krug. Does this pen belong to Krug? That's what I'm hiring you to find out."

Martin didn't bother to ask the man his motivation for confirming the owner of the pen.

He'd been around long enough to know it didn't matter.

With some relief, he put down the SWF ads and took the case.

II
MISSING IN PASSION

Telluros Krug lived in a once-fashionable mansion in the Weeds Hill neighborhood of Brooklyn. He was, according to Martin's client Jackson Flemosh, a man of letters who'd written widely and deeply on all subjects known to man, and some not known but nonetheless hidden in his books.

His last volume, like the others, was untitled and composed of loose pages of various sizes scattered throughout the gutters of Manhattan, each one written in a different hand and containing no discernable narrative.

Mr. Flemosh was Krug's greatest devotee. He claimed this last untitled book contained clues that led him to what he believed was

Krug's pen. He had found it under a graffiti-strewn overpass in Weeds Hill. It was pointing toward Mr. Krug's house. But he could not just second-guess destiny.

He approached, but stopped short of going up to the door. So he hired the kind of PI who didn't mind a few knocks.

Flemosh also told Martin that Krug hailed from Who Knows Where. He wouldn't let on anything else about his idol.

As the moon rose behind a water tower, Martin walked up Krug's crumbling steps. A pigeon pooped on his head. A paper fell out of the window above him. It said:

Missing in Passion.

He used the paper to wipe his hair and rang the bell. He waited a few moments and another, larger page floated down. In an entirely different script, it said:

Stillborn but Still Alive.

Martin realized the door had been recently forced open.

In the dim light filtering in from outside, Martin saw the house was covered in spineless books, floor to ceiling, resembling an overcrowded ossuary. There was no furniture at all on the first floor, just hallways made of paperbacks and hardcovers and journals. Martin got lost a few times before finding his way to the second floor, which at least had a bathroom of tile. A corridor made of different versions of the King James Bible led to a bedroom where Telluros Krug appeared to be hunched over his 18th century writing desk with a view of the lake in Weeds Hill Park.

"Mr. Krug?" Martin asked.

Krug didn't turn around but a pigeon coo answered Martin's question.

Martin walked over to the desk, littered with stacks of pages, some of which were randomly blowing out the window, which was how Krug published his works.

"Mr. Krug, is this your pen?" Martin asked, holding it aloft and noticing a family of pigeons living in the nest-sized hole in Mr. Krug's chest.

It was dark and Martin couldn't locate a lightswitch in the spineless book-lined room. He'd have to come back for further investigation. Besides, now the firemen and EMTs had joined the police on strike and reporting a body wouldn't do much good.

iii
LACK OF SLiDES

"This is a terrible omen," Mr. Flemosh said, "and complicates things immensely. If Krug is dead, is this Krug's pen? Be careful with that, it could be priceless."

"Do you know anyone who would want Krug dead?" Martin asked, putting the quill pen away in his blazer pocket.

They had met at a playground suggested by Flemosh. It was deserted due to the numerous crack vials and broken glass littering the astro-turf—and lack of slides.

"No," Flemosh said.

"There's someone watching us."

"What do you mean?"

"Up there—on top of that abandoned firehouse—don't ask me how he got there."

Flemosh turned his fanatical bouncing eyeballs to a figure standing on the roof.

"I don't see anyone," he said.

"Oh really? Hey! You! Come down here!" Martin yelled.

The man startled, ran away from them and appeared to jump off the five-story roof onto the next block over.

Martin raced through the playground to the other side and didn't see the sunny-side up mess he'd expected. He found no trace of the mysterious watcher except for a gray raincoat in the street, exactly the same make as the one Flemosh wore.

"These are the same duds you have on," he said, returning to Flemosh.

"Don't you think that's odd?"

"The same? If anything that makes it even."

"Mr. Flemosh, can you also explain why your shoes have metal cletes?"

"Just what they had at the store that day."

Martin considered how entities of a similar type often appeared in the same outward garb. He knew from experience, for example, that people wore sour faces, gods wore heavy sandals, cats wore paws, and ghosts wore red jumpsuits. He felt there was more to this coincidence of the raincoats then Flemosh was letting on. But he also knew when to keep his mouth shut.

IV
I DON'T EVEN KNOW I HAVE WRITTEN THIS

After leaving Flemosh with the injunction to contact him if he "remembered" anything, Martin went to the New York City Department of Records and looked up the blueprint of Krug's place. He wanted to see if the spineless-book walls were following preexisting patterns or if they'd been constructed along an entirely new design.

From what he could tell, the paper walls basically matched the original blueprints for the mansion, with the exception of one area on the fourth floor where there should've been more room than there was now.

Then he returned to Krug's bibliophilic house. This time he brought a flashlight. It was chilly, so he wore the gray raincoat he'd found near the playground, which fitted him fine.

When he reached Krug's writing-room he saw the body sitting in the same position he'd left it in, only part of the head was gone. He approached ready for the worst but it appeared to be made of birdseed mixed with some compound realistically resembling human skin.

The pigeons were not there but had obviously been eating.

He put his hand in the raincoat and felt a piece of paper that he hadn't noticed before. He opened it:

KRUG'S HOUSE - 7 PM. MAKE SURE TO—

"—So you came," a woman said. "I wasn't sure you'd show." Martin glanced at his watch.

"It's five to seven," he said. "So here I am."

He tried to read the remainder of the note but a hand touched his shoulder, sending little incisor-sharp thrills down his arm.

"I'm glad," the woman said.

Martin turned around. She wore a gray raincoat. Her hair had the clean, shiny golden straightness of a Labrador's fur in an Alpo commercial. Her features were slightly asymmetrical like the plates on a table set in a hurry. But they were fine plates.

"And how are you?" Martin said.

"How do you think, Lyssen? I'm worried. Your name—am I pronouncing it right?"

"Yes, that's right."

"I've heard small talk is not your strength," she said. "But you're more handsome than I'd imagined."

Martin was not particularly good-looking but he liked what he heard. Her smile was bent like a tool with a specific use, a lock-pick or a tremolo bar.

"Looks like we need some more birdseed," Martin said. "And, uh…"

"Human skin? Yes the birds eat that first, isn't that strange? But with this police strike, finding and peeling bodies has been pretty easy."

"Of course," Martin said, trying to concentrate, feeling like a ball in a washing machine.

"I'd heard you lost your coat when you flew off that building."

"I had another."

She took a cigarette case and a lighter out of her raincoat and took the coat off and hung it on a hook made of rigid bookmarks. She had two long, slim wings made of many pieces of Krug-like paper coming out of her shoulder blades that flapped lightly when she lit up and took a long drag. The papers were covered in different handwritten notes.

"So, what's Flemosh up to?" she said.

"He … he's hired a private investigator," Martin said. "He seems… desperate."

"To prove the pen is some kind of holy relic, which will make the Lifters follow him? He's ridiculous, but no threat—not the kind your people think he is, anyway. But I guess I shouldn't say *your people* anymore. You're sure you're really with me now? You want Krug back where he belongs?"

"Yes."

"I never understood why you and the No-Krugs want less Lifters. It's not like there's too many of us as it is—you know how much work it takes to find all the scattered Krug-papers and fashion the wings. But this hellocrow isn't going to work much longer and the other Lifters will get nervous when they realize Krug's not here anymore. I mean the papers are going out, but these falsified Krug-pages don't have the right wing-lift in them, do they? They sound right, I mean *Stillborn but Still Alive* is something Krug could have said in his autobiography, but they're just not cutting it. Soon the secret's out."

The door opened downstairs. "Who's that?" she said.

"I don't know. Stay here."

Martin tiptoed to the bathroom and crouched down in the shadow of an antique sink. With the door half open he unrolled the note from his pocket and finished reading:

KRUG'S HOUSE - 7 PM. MAKE SURE TO KILL LIDIA FOR GOOD.

On the back was her address in case she didn't show.

Someone who sounded so large he could only wear overalls was walking up the stairs. The loose pages on the narrow stairwell rustled like leaves in a hailstorm as the visitor brushed his way through. Martin withdrew a little into the bathroom. The noise stopped, too suddenly, like how an airplane engine shuts off in mid-flight.

Something metal flew bat-like from the dark and struck Martin in the forehead. He fell back and nearly cracked his skull on the porcelain tub. He wiped blood from his eyes.

Another object came at him. Martin was ready and caught it—a shoe with metal cletes.

"What's going on?" Lidia asked, approaching the bathroom, wings fluttering like trash in a hurricane.

"Flemosh?" Martin called.

"Lyssen!" a man roared back. "Who are you?"

Martin stepped out of the bathroom, staring at a vague mass clogging the inky stairwell. "But you're Lyssen..." Lidia said, walking up to Martin. She put her hand to his waist.

She smelled like falling fast. What did she want?

It didn't matter.

"He's lying," the voice from the stairwell said. "He's the detective Flemosh hired."

"Yes," Martin said, "and you're the one sent to kill Lidia. I won't let that happen."

No answer. Martin went to get his revolver out from his pocket but the man retreated down the stairs quicker than his bulk would suggest possible.

Martin ran out the door after him but he was nowhere to be found. When he returned to the house, Lidia was gone, too. She must have flown out the window.

But there was a paper he hadn't seen before lying on the floor, which he knew came off Lidia's wings like a feather from a dove, because it smelled like her. There was Krug-writing on it:

I am dead, but my hands are alive. I was supposed to have wings, I was intended for flight. Those hands keep growing, keep trying to find a way to lift themselves and all of Krug up into the air, those 27 hand-bones pulling themselves in 27,000 flapping directions. I have never flown, but with a pen in hand my attempts at flight have written things, and each time in a different handwriting. Writing is failure to fly. I don't even know I have written this, no brain working to know this, only hands to make this.

Martin wanted to investigate the fourth floor and see if he could figure out why Krug had decreased the room, but he wanted Lidia not to die more than that so he ran into the night, his heart bounding off a well-worn path it didn't know it had followed.

V

SiNGLe WiNGeD FeMALe

Martin was following up on the address written on the note in Lyssen's coat pocket. It indicated an abandoned elevated train line on the West Side. He kept his wits on red alert as he walked dark apocalyptic streets, eerily empty of siren-wails, and flooded with occasional criminal shouting that came on flash-flood sudden. But he felt an exciting sting, a dizzy freedom-feeling, when he thought about Lidia, the woman who could fly away from you and had a touch like an embrace.

His glimpse of her burned like a stare. It had been a long time since he'd felt this way and he had trouble controlling it, as a patient coming out of brain surgery is bad at waking. He'd been married to his work and the idea of an affair was intoxicating. To get back his focus he ran over the details he understood so far.

This Telluros Krug character was apparently dead and always had been—but his hands worked. His hands were constantly, unsuccessfully trying to fly, and when there was a pen in them the attempt to fly ended up in writings on loose pieces of paper that were then blown out his window and into the streets where some other characters in gray raincoats collected them and made wings out of them—wings that worked. People who used those wings to fly were called Lifters, Martin assumed, and they wore metal cletes to help them when landing on smooth surfaces.

These were the simple facts. But motivations, Martin knew, were the sticky stuff that held the facts together in a pattern like the letters in a ransom note.

Flemosh believed if the pen belonged to Krug, it had some sort of power. Lyssen and some of his "group" had other plans and wanted Lidia dead, and for there to be less Lifters. Lidia thought Flemosh was foolish, and wanted Krug to continue his wind-blown writing. And what did Martin want?

He fought the temptation to see Lidia as the heroine and the others as villains. He'd been around enough to know things were murkier than that. But you also needed a guide to get through the murk and what could be better than a woman with wings and a smile like a lockpick?

A basketball suddenly fell right in front of his face, bounced twenty feet high and fell again. He caught it and looked up. Some Lifters were flying in circles, great wings made of Krug's works streaming majestically behind them. They had gray raincoats tied around their waists and besides the wings, looked like a random sampling of people pulled off a New York City subway—all different in age and ethnicity.

Martin tossed the ball up as far as he could and a portly old woman caught it with a nod of thanks—probably mistaking him for one of them in his raincoat. Then they resumed their game of catch, spiraling higher and higher until they were specks.

Martin was under the old elevated train tracks now. A line that hadn't run since the Bronx was burning, they loomed overhead like a graffitied aqueduct, overgrown with ugly, gray vines that lived off asphalt and urine.

Somewhere up the stairs leading to the station platform, someone screamed in a heavy-metal high pitch.

Martin raced up the stairs to the abandoned station, snapping gray vines lashed to rusted metal and pebble-pitted concrete and ran straight into Flemosh, who was mumbling to himself. His wings frowned. He looked like the last angel on line at the soup kitchen.

"Where's Lidia?" Martin said, shaking the man by his narrow shoulders.

"That way," Flemosh said, pointing. "Watch out for Lyssen—hey, does Krug's pen exist?" But Martin was already running like a man in a nightmare, without a map or sense of terrain.

The scream cut through the air again and Martin tripped over his feet and rotten wooden planks, tumbling down the railroad tracks with the husk of a flaming ambulance lighting his way from the lawless street below.

Further down the tracks he could make out the monolithic shape of Lyssen and the screaming began again.

"Stop!" Martin yelled, propelling himself forward, reaching for his revolver—finding an empty pocket.

"Help!" someone cried.

Martin threw himself into Lyssen to knock him over. He was already kneeling and barely budged. A cloud moved away from the moon and Martin saw Lyssen's skin had been peeled off his face and he was clutching at his eyes with turkey-sized hands.

"Help," he whimpered.

"Don't move," Lidia said.

She had Martin's revolver pointed at them both. "What are you doing?" Martin said.

"Collecting skin for the hellocrow—and getting rid of an enemy at the same time."

"You could've killed him first," Martin said.

"Maybe I'll start with you," she said.

"You already have," Martin said.

"Don't worry. I'll make sure you're not lonely any longer," she said cruelly. "There's plenty of dates in the cemetery."

"You could grant me a dying wish," Martin said, feeling his stupid heart ache like a toddler that's run into a sharp table edge, stalling for time. "You could explain a few things. Give me the Cliff Notes."

"Kneel down next to Lyssen," she said.

Martin did as he was told.

"It takes a rare person to become a Lifter. They've got to notice Krug's works scattered all over the city, and they've got to take the time to gather them up. When they get enough pages together, a pattern is revealed explaining how to make them into wings and fasten them to your body.

"Lyssen and his crew don't want any more Lifters. They think there are enough of us already, and they think they're going to take over and start running things. So they want Krug out of the picture.

"Me, I just want to meet the right guy," she said with a laugh. "He's got to be a nice Lifter. And there aren't enough good ones to go around right now. So I want Krug back at his desk."

"Must your man have wings?" Martin asked.

"I'm not sure who you are or what story you've walked out of," she said. "But you've lied to me before and you don't belong in this one. And you're not going to put me down."

Lyssen choked back sobs.

Martin shut his eyes like a boy waiting for his first kiss. Nothing happened.

Martin opened his eyes. Flemosh stood in front of them. He'd hit Lidia on the head with a brick and caught her in his spindly arms when she fell backward.

"You can't die," Flemosh said to Martin. "I need to know if Krug's pen exists."

"You couldn't have told me about all this before?" Martin said, getting up and indicating bloody-faced Lyssen and comatose Lidia with a sweeping gesture.

"I had to see if you were the one chosen to discover the answer," Flemosh said, his pupils riding see-saws in his eyes. "Now I know you are."

VI
There's something else

On the fourth floor of Krug's house, Martin tore away a wall of Romance and Chick-Lit paperbacks that had been carefully set there by Lidia to hide Telluros Krug from Lyssen and those other Lifters who would murder him.

Krug balanced atop a piano stool, a pitiful broomstick of a figure. Where his face should be was the back of a shrunken head, stringy black hair hanging down to the nape of the neck. His skin was wrinkled and stretched across his thin bones. His arms were long and atrophied and ended in two enormous hands that quivered and flapped in violent spasms just like alligators roped by lassos. The left hand was covered in black spots like periods stolen from all the unfinished sentences in the world.

Martin knelt down and put the quill pen in Krug's right hand, which clutched it tightly. He picked up the stool and Krug and placed them at the 18th century writing desk, looking out on the lovely lake in Weeds Hill Park. He put a piece of paper under Krug's pen and Krug jabbed the nib into his left hand and scribbled something with his right. His blood was the color of black ink.

Before Martin could even try to read it, a wind came as if from nowhere and took it out the window and into the wilds of Brooklyn. The page seemed to have its own flight-power. No wonder it was possible to gather enough of them, if they could be found, and make wings that could lift a person above the ground, if not their passions.

Well, Martin thought. *I can tell Flemosh in good faith that it's Krug's pen, all right.*

Mystery solved, Martin turned to go. But he felt glued to the spot. Was it the memory of meeting Lidia, and hoping she was the one? A little, but there was more: if he left Krug at his window, others would find his works and eventually there'd be more Lifters, which seemed okay—and maybe Lidia would find the Love of Her Life. But there was also the chance Krug would be assassinated, which didn't sit right. So another option was to hide him again.

Martin looked at those roped-alligator hands trying to fly, writing on page after wingish page.

It dawned on him that there's what people with wings want, there's what people without wings want, and then there's something else.

Martin removed the quill from the trembling hand. He found a sharp letter opener in a desk drawer. It wasn't hard to slice through the brittle wrists. Krug didn't seem to be in pain and it was over in a moment. The emaciated body fell off the stool and crumbled into enough powder to fill a large hourglass.

The hands floated out the window. Martin watched them gracefully skimming the tree tops, tentatively feeling the paperless air. Then they flew up in ever-widening, joyful arcs, two hands waving hello and goodbye into the horizon. Suddenly Martin felt a little less alone. It was strange really, because there was nobody there.

at and it terrified. Bestial: and stupid as incorrectly understood passphrases . . . Left behind. I was compelled to think: *Something ate the one I love*. It meant nothing to me. And yet. *I don't want to start believing that all words are code words. I'll ignore the evidence if it ever comes to that.* I knew the thoughts didn't make sense, it was like they weren't mine but I couldn't stop. Just as you know it must be you when you sleep, it comes to you every night, but really, sleep has nothing to do with you. Does it? How can you know since you're not *there* at the time? Imagine calling on a newborn for your witness.

I guess anything you cannot help doing is very much the same as anything done to you by an external agent, be it a snowflake wetting your nose or the misused cords of a marionette cutting short your breath forevermore. I thought of crucified insects with engorged genitalia. I thought: "Take care of him" means both: "Eliminate him" and "Make sure he is not eliminated."

I think, therefore I haven't got a fucking clue.

And yet.

THE LEAF

1
A WISE AND WORLDLY PIECE OF WOOD

I led my father through the lanes of our apple orchard, watching wormy balls of fruit drop to the soft earth, so glutted with decay they couldn't roll. The sky was a healthy blue flame and my father put his hand up to block the light from bursting his old eyes. He laughed.

I looked back over my shoulder under the shady brim of a lop-sided straw hat.

"What's so funny?"

"My hand can stop the sun, but it can't keep a single apple from falling."

He dropped his walking stick and sat in a pool of tree-shadow. He wheezed heavily, splintering twigs with his thick fingers. His nails were too long and collected dirt. It repulsed me to think that my father had gutters on his fingers.

"What do you mean?" I asked, walking over.

A fruit struck my head and unhatted me.

He said, "*That's* what I mean. It's the big things that are easy to do. Own an orchard. Have a wife. Have children. Even living and dying are nothing. But the little things, those are not so easy. You cannot see them and what you cannot see you cannot even for wait for. You cannot even *wait*, do you understand how sad that is? Watch out for the little things, Gideon. Blights hit your trees, your wife stops talking to you, and all your children go off and disappear."

"I'm right here."

"Of course I don't mean you, but your brothers. Aren't you going to pick up your hat?"

"No."

"Why not?"

"It's lopsided."

"Wasn't it lopsided this morning?"

"Yes."

"So why did you put it on to begin with?"

"I felt different then."

"Just a few hours ago?"

"Yes."

"You're a strange one, Gideon. You're given to dreaming and your moods ... are *your* moods, and nobody else's. It will be trouble for you."

"I'll help you get up. Let's check the rest of the orchard."

"What for?"

"For apples that aren't ruined."

"Here? Sooner look for a newborn in a grave. You know what this is?"

"Don't start with the curse. The curse isn't real."

"First your brothers disappear. Now our fortunes, destroyed. I've been cursed."

"You left out, *we conceived you by accident.*"

He said, "No need to state the obvious, Gideon."

"I'm going to keep looking."

"I'm going back to Bronx."

"What's Bronx?"

"I know that apple wasn't hard, so your skull must be soft. It's the town you've lived in your whole life."

What the hell was he talking about? We were two wounds bleeding into each other.

"But our town is called Brookridge," I said to him.

"You're a strange one," he said, spat, and turned to go.

"What will you do at home?"

"Watch your mother hide my things in plain sight."

"Tell her I have hope at least, if you don't."

"Don't get lost."

"I know these lanes well."

"They might have changed. The rot … has twisted the trees here and there—you see? A twist here and a twist there, and who knows where you'll wind up?"

"You're stranger than I, old man."

"I was first, anyway. That entitles me to something."

He planted his cane in the ground and began pulling himself up. I offered my hand and he ignored it. It could block the sun, but it couldn't help my father. He struggled to his feet on his own.

I watched him hobble away, each step an effort, his right arm barely swinging, his left advancing the cane. He used to beat me with that stick when I was young. That stick had taught me about cruelty and how to wake up in the cold dawn. A wise and worldly piece of wood, now it tutored him in walking.

ii

YOU CAN'T WAKE A GOURD

A squirrel took my hat away and my thoughts with it. That is how light thoughts are, even thoughts about flipping the universe on its head. I turned round and kept on down the lane. A curled-up leaf rolled by my feet. There was something about that leaf, but I couldn't figure it out. It wasn't the way there's something about rocks or twigs.

A white fungus scarred the tree trunks. Apples were blackened and devastated. I stopped to listen to them thudding to earth, like raindrops sound to ants.

Salamander popped out from behind a tree with the ho-hum

surprise of wind-blown trash.

"Gideon, there are lots of people named Wolf but no wolf with a name," Salamander said. "I mean: hello."

He was tall and scrawny and his pigeon-chest was tanned a leathery brown and his red hair was sparse from pulling. There was fragile china on the edges of wobbly tables in his bomb-shelter eyes. There were scars on him, too. Many of them were the result of my hitting him too hard, when he needed hitting.

Salamander's mother died giving birth to him. At the time, he understood what had happened and tried to hang himself with an umbilical cord. But the midwife believed in the Right to Suffer and cut the noose. He lost much oxygen and—where there had been a sense of purpose—was now a half-idiot.

The other half? I took it for my friend. But his learning problems grew faster and stronger than his bones, he couldn't read, and he sometimes made odd prophetic announcements that came true and made him highly unpopular.

A few years back, Salamander's father was struck by a triangle-wheeled cart full of experimental blue pumpkins, donkey-driven by the destitute inventor Lester Treat. The cart was rather slow and didn't crush Mr. Mander. But on the point of reviving he swallowed some blue pumpkin seeds. His skin turned a purplish-pink and he fell into a deep sleep.

Salamander asked around for advice. Nobody knew how to wake a gourd, but he received several excellent recipes for pie. As reparation for the accident, Judge Afterwit ruled Salamander should keep the cart and half the offending farmer's pumpkin patch. There was no patch. Salamander moved into the dilapidated Barn of Slim Mercy on Lester Treat's plot and laid his father in the cart. He fed him gruel daily, waiting for him to wake.

iii
when stars become apples

Back in the rotting orchard, I said, "Salamander, how are you?"

He swayed dumbly as a sapling in the wind.

"I asked you a question," I said.

Breezy blood shook his fingers.

I slapped him, somewhat half-heartedly, on the cheek. He stared stupidly. I lifted my hand again, but something stopped me, maybe something that described what a leaf is not, or something like death that I would never remember when it pulled me away from myself. Today I was aware that if I hurt the half-idiot nobody would care. It would be consistent with the way the world was at that very moment. Each drop of Salamander's blood would be a justification for the sun to rise in the east. If I didn't strike him the sun would still rise—but I would've had nothing to do with it.

How did I know this? It all goes back to my youth, which I remember so vaguely it has become private legend. My parents didn't bother to teach me the word "apple," despite the fact we owned an orchard of them. I assumed they were stars, since I'd heard stars were in the sky, and I thought sky referred to anything above ground level.

When I harvested round reddish stars you could eat, I felt somewhat divine. And a shooting star was one that fell to earth, and starlight was when you set the stems on fire. But when my mother took a basket of them to make "applesauce" I asked why it wasn't called "starsauce" and learned stars couldn't be collected. I despaired. When stars became apples, the world was drained of life. So I tried not to go along with the world, as much as possible.

IV
A CLOUD THAT DIED

"My mother gave up mothering twenty years ago today," Salamander said.

"Shut up."

"Sorry, Gideon."

"Oh, you know you're allowed here. I am in a mood."

"What kind?"

"I don't know. The one where you say the wrong thing. Why are you here, though?"

"I wanted to see if it was true about the blight."

"Well, see for yourself. Why don't you come along? I'm looking for one decent apple."

"I saw one, up the road."

"That's good news. I told my father I had hope, and it wasn't unfounded. It had no blight at all?"

"None."

"Better than good news. Sally, you're like a brother to me."

"Do you ever think about them?"

"I never knew them. I know more about their clothes. You see all these patches on my trousers? My mother takes them from different articles of clothing belonging to each of the five of them. Whenever I get a tear in a garment, she mends it with Ben's sock or Blake's vest or Nestor's shirt. I wish I knew them better. It appears that Wegman was somewhat flamboyant. In fact, I think the red fabric on my knee is part of a strapless gown. But you're like a brother right here beside me, and that's worth more than rags and wishes. Now show me this good apple."

"I ate it."

"Happy birthday, Sally… shall we skip stones? There's no lack of those."

"I miss my father. A person who is sleeping is not a person at all," he said, collecting pebbles.

"My father snores so I get no rest. Does yours?"

"No."

"Well, gourds don't snore. Maybe if you made him snore, he wouldn't be a gourd any longer and he'd wake up."

We followed a path to the edge of Nobody Lake. It carried no reflections on its silvery surface. It didn't increase with rain; it didn't dry up with drought. It ended in an omnipresent, huge wall of gray fog, opaque as granite.

Salamander thought the lake was a cloud that fell into a deep hole, couldn't move, and died. That made sense to me—who ever saw a living cloud stay still?

I didn't know what my brothers thought about the lake, but I knew that one night, drunk and egging each other on, they rowed across it through the fog and were never seen again.

Since dead people are equally nobody, our town's funeral rites were performed at Nobody Lake as well. Salamander's mother's pyre had drifted across it, growing smaller in perception as it went further into the distance and less in size as it burned to cinders, disappearing in two ways at once. That bothered me because if you can vanish in simultaneously multiple fashions, it suggests there were many of you present. Speculations aside, nobody—living or dead—had crossed the lake and returned to talk about it.

"Something about this day," I said, "makes me feel like we're giants about to skip tombstones."

V

CLOSE TO MEANING WHAT I SAY

"Did you hear Goody Treat died this morning?" Salamander asked.

"No. You're not going to her wake, are you? Her widower Lester Treat will be there—do you want to see the man who turned your father into a gourd? Besides, people think you're weird enough as it is, without you slinking about the corpses of strangers. Why do you do that? It makes people nervous."

"They don't know what I know."

"What does that mean?"

"More butter, please."

"Sally, are you okay?"

He was gazing at the gray line where the lake met the fog. The dead cloud glistened like fat. I skipped a nice flat stone three times across it.

"Do you remember when things were different?" Sally asked.

"Not really."

"Me either. It seems to me we've been standing at this lake for our whole lives."

"Even if we had been, things would be pretty much the same. The orchard would be rotting. My father would be miserable. I'm restless, Sally. It seems to me nothing goes on here, nothing ever did. Sometimes when I wake up, I wish I was still asleep, like your father even, never having to put on these ridiculous pants, or say good morning and good night ever again. We're only bold enough to toss rocks in this lake. What kind of risk is that? The stones are worthless. They're not even ours. I can understand why my brothers tried to cross this water. They had to get drunk to do it. But I'd like to do it sober."

He said, "You can't be serious. Nobody leaves Grahamsblat."

"What's Grahamsblat?"

"It's the town we live in, Gideon."

"My father thought it was called Bronx earlier … why can't we agree on a name for it?"

"I don't know much. What do you think it's called?"

"Brookridge."

"Okay, well, nobody leaves Brookridge, then."

"Goody Treat just left today, didn't she?"

"Gideon, you can't be telling me you want to die. You're my only friend."

"I know. And, I don't exactly mean what I'm saying. But I'm close. I'm close to meaning what I say—do you see how unusual that is for me? I'm frustrated and bored, and I want out of this, all this world we know. All Crumbull's gigantic utensils. Don't you get sick of having to lift a fork with two hands? I wish I had something to live for besides what others lived for me first. I wish I was the son who got away."

I looked down at a rain puddle at my foot. A leaf had fallen on the face of my reflection. I felt the oddest sense of recognition, but it passed quickly.

"You see that leaf?" I asked.

Salamander picked it up, dripping.

"What about it?" he said.

"It looks pretty normal, but it isn't. You know what's so special about it? Its origin."

"I bet it came from a tree."

"But *which* tree?"

"I don't know. There are hundreds and hundreds here."

"Exactly. And every leaf on the ground, every single errant leaf you ever saw, is a mystery, because you simply don't know where it truly came from."

"What are you getting at?"

"I don't know—but I'm close. I'm close, and I'll be sure to tell you when I find out."

"I need to feed my father," Salamander said.

Without a word we rose and started back, dodging falling apples all the way. The white fungi on the trees were like markers for a path that didn't exist—yet.

VI

A PIECE OF WOOD'S AS GOOD AS FATE

After Sally and I parted, I headed home: a cottage standing at the outskirts of Brookridge (or whatever it was called). It was overshadowed by willows that swept the eaves and threw branches down the chimney, leading squirrels to the disappointments of Mother's kitchen.

Since childhood I waited for inanimate things to move, hoping a spirit stirred in them. Many a knot didn't untie under my gaze and many a table refused to jig. I paused beneath an elm at the crest of a hill, to look at the still white cottages stacked up and down the green sward like boxes for storing lives.

I took one step forward and a whistling pierced the air. More whistles followed. Hundreds of shrill notes were carried and dropped by the wind. It was tea-time.

My cottage door was open and our kettle screamed. Father sat at the old oak table, his back to the door and fire. Next to the fireplace were empty bookshelves. My father had burned all the books long ago as fuel for the fire.

One dreadful winter, long after Bob's disappearance, Father stole the boy's diary from under Mother's bed and tossed it on the flames. I hadn't summoned up the nerve to read it yet and I cried out as the pages were eaten. I took to hiding the books, but we nearly froze to death and I had to give them up.

Father sat at the old oak table, his back to the door and fire.

He faced a painting of himself and Mother. Pots and pans the size of bathtubs hung in front of it and obscured the canvas. The painting told the story of my parents' meeting in their youth. It depicted them pinned under a large piece of timber.

They both worked at the sawmill. One day, they were the only ones there and were accidentally trapped beneath a beam. The whole time neither one uttered a word, each resenting the other for being witness to such an embarrassing and painful episode.

They lay side by side for a full day before they were found by an art student. He began sketching the unusual scene. After several drafts he pulled the timber off them.

"A piece of wood's as good as fate," my father said to his coworker. "I need a wife, and you need a husband." So they were married, and the artist gave them a painting to commemorate the event, suitable for blaming.

Putting Father's thick coat on, I hugged the enormous kettle and set it on the cool stone floor.

He said, "So, you're finally back. I know you put the tea on before you left just to drive me crazy. You know I don't feel up to lifting that kettle, and Heaven forbid that idle son of mine would be around to help his own father. Did you find a fine apple?"

"No. Where's Mother?"

"Your Aunt Leona's house."

"Why?"

"I'm not there."

"I'm going, then, to see Mother and then to check in on Salamander."

"You shouldn't hang round that one, I've told you before."

"Save your breath, old man. If I cannot choose my enemies, at least no one will ever stop me from choosing my friends."

As I was leaving, I noticed something stir across the room in the stillness. For a second I thought the inanimate world was finally going to sit up and do a somersault for me. But it was a reflection in the mirror atop the dresser.

Father's wrinkled face was framed there, and it was crying.

I had never seen him cry before.

VII
THE MANDOLIN

Aunt Leona lived just past the Barren Well. She was a spinster who offered you things she couldn't locate and spent the rest of your visit trying to make up for it by giving you things you didn't want. She reminded me of everyone.

I knocked. Leona appeared in a crumpled pink dress, her ageless smile wide and smooth as a brand-new sled.

Mother was busy rearranging furniture. Because she couldn't make people do what she wanted, she liked to show her authority over things. She once insisted my right shoe was my left, dominating my feet because she lacked access to the concomitant halves of my brain. I wondered what Leona had done to make my mother bring her passion for reorganization to her sister's living room. Mother wore a green skirt and a yellow top and whirled about like an angry flower.

"Mother, what's happened?" I asked.

She said, "The chair has taken the desk's place."

"I mean with Father."

"Did you find a good apple?"

"No. I believe the orchard is completely useless."

"Damn, and I swore you would. If only your brothers were still here. You can't do the job of five."

"Six, counting me."

"Five or six—there's little difference."

"There's all the difference in my world, and I hope some of yours, too," I said. "My brothers are gone and that's it. I'm tired of living in the shadows of people who don't even have them."

Leona tapped me on the shoulder. "Can I get you some tea?"

"Please."

"Milk?"

"Yes, thank you."

"Mother," I said as she took two unicorn tapestries off the wall and looked about for new locations, "I saw Father crying just now."

"You were seeing things."

"Yes, they're called tears."

"Don't talk back to me, Gideon Prop."

"But do you know why?"

"I'm afraid I don't have any milk," Leona said, returning from the kitchen. "Can I offer you some biscuits?"

"No, thank you. Do you know why my father is crying?" I asked her. "That's why I'm here. Maybe you can tell me."

"Certainly not. What can I give you?" Leona said.

"Oh, I don't know."

"There must be something."

I spied a mandolin on the wall. I couldn't play, but then my lack of knowledge never stopped an object from existing.

"How about that mandolin?" I asked.

"I was about to put that away somewhere, anyway," Mother said. "It clashes in here."

"Oh, I don't know…" Leona faltered, her smile vanishing.

"What do you want with that old thing?" my mother chided.

"Nothing, of course. No, nothing. Don't be silly! Why would I need a mandolin?" Leona said.

We stood there in silence until Mother took the instrument from its peg and handed it to me.

"May I be alone with your sister for a moment?" I asked my aunt.

Leona smiled and went out of the room, but the smile and exit were unusually forced.

"I'm going to do something crazy soon," I said.

Mother was puzzling over a three-foot long rolling pin. She twirled to face me.

"Gideon, I'm going to sit and show you how ridiculous you are."

She backed up to where the chair used to be and fell on her behind.

"Do you need help?" I asked, crouching to her level.

"You've always asked too many questions, Gideon. Why can't you be more like your brothers?"

VIII
IF YOUR VASES ARE ENORMOUS

I left Mother trying to move a spider's web from the wainscoting to the ceiling and went to see how Salamander fared with his father who slept in his Barn of Slim Mercy. The barn was at the bottom of a little wooded valley. It looked as though it had tumbled there. It was built on a foundation of clover and so full of holes it was more thin air than wood.

As I descended the path, a cold shadow enveloped me and I turned to see mighty Crumbull and his gang looming.

Crumbull was a potter, or illusionist, which is the same thing. Everyone drank from his cups, ate on his plates, and pissed in his bedpans. He also made cutlery. Because Crumbull was a ten-foot tall giant, all his products were giant-sized. Thus the rest of us felt ourselves living in a world too large for us.

I think nobody journeyed far from Brookridge because of those great mugs and vases. It gave the illusion there was enough space as it was, because a vase captures space and if all your vases are enormous, then clearly all one has to do is break the vases in case one needs more room to live.

Behind Crumbull the Illusionist stood at least twenty of his gang, various half-Crumbull-sized townspeople who liked to think spending time in his company made them as big and influential as he. All wore black mourning dress.

"Seek shelter, Gideon Prop," he said. "It's about to rain."

I looked up. The sky was blue.

"Apparently you've gone completely mad," I said. "At least I know it's not just my family. Do you know what my father said to me today? He said, and I'm not exaggerating this one bit, that—"

"—Enough!" Crumbull shouted.

"Enough of *you*. There's not a drop of water in sight."

"I didn't say anything about water, did I, mandolinist?"

"Oh, this? I don't even know how to play."

The gang dragged large crates of broken pottery and stones forward.

"What has Salamander done?" I asked.

"Ask Goody Treat's widower!" Simon Dimple said, pulling Lester Treat to the front of the crowd.

"He poisoned my wife. He's killed my Goody," Treat said.

"Impossible," I said. "Salamander has no motive or ability. He scarcely knows his own name."

"He knew her last words. He must have been in the room, hiding. Demons can hide."

"What do you mean?"

"He passed by the wake," Treat said, "and we didn't want him there. But I thought maybe he was paying his respects and it wouldn't be right to turn him away. Then when I thanked him for coming he said 'More butter, please.' And those were Goody's exact last words. But he wasn't there when it happened. My Goody never got her butter…and all thanks to Salamander's evil ways."

I remembered Sally saying those words at Nobody Lake, and saying, "They don't know what I know."

"He knows," Crumbull said, pointing a drumstick finger at me. "You can see it in his face. You're protecting a murderer, Mr. Prop."

"It's no surprise," another said. "Gideon's family is cursed. He probably did his own brothers in."

"Yes," I said. "At the age of five, I cut them to pieces and hid the bodies so I might grow up to wear the stupidest pants in all Brookridge."

"What the hell is Brookridge?" Crumbull asked.

"Oh, forget it."

"Out of the way," Crumbull said.

"Wait," I said. "You say I know Goody's last words as well as Sally. By that logic, I might be the murderer, and Salamander just happens to know my secret."

My father always told me that I was an idiot.

"Listen," I said. "The simple truth is Salamander didn't kill Goody Treat, rest her soul. And neither did I."

"It looks like you're involved," Spatch the titmouse-droppings addict said, standing between Crumbull's legs.

"Looks can be deceiving," I said.

"Not about looks they can't," Crumbull said. "Get out the stones, boys."

"How would you like to hear the mandolin?" I asked, stepping back and holding it aloft.

"I thought you don't play," Crumbull said.

"I don't. But if you'll just wait here for a bit, I'm sure I can find someone who does."

"Mr. Treat plays, actually," someone said.

"Fantastic," I said. "That's great."

"I'm not very good," Treat said.

"Wait, in fact, isn't that *your* mandolin, Treat?" Crumbull asked.

"No, I'm sure it's not."

"I think it is. It has your initials on it, right there in mother-of-pearl. I've seen you playing it at The Toasty Eunuch. This bastard must've stolen it."

"I did no such thing," I said. "It was given to me by my aunt Leona, who—"

Treat threw a rock at my chest.

"Up yours," I said.

He tossed another rock. I blocked it with the mandolin, which broke open. A letter and a small leather whip fell out. I could see clearly that it was addressed to Leona and signed "Your Sweet Treat."

No wonder Leona was always smiling.

Treat ran forward to snatch the note. If their affair became public it would ruin him, especially since Goody was so beloved by all.

He picked it up and tore it to pieces.

"What does it say, Treat?" Crumbull growled.

"It... I cannot say... it is too painful... but it indicates Gideon and Salamander as Goody's murderers... it's some kind of curse, a magical note."

I turned and ran toward the Barn of Slim Mercy. Pottery crashed at my heels and stones rained on my back. I swung the door open. It fell off its hinges.

ix
How to Wake a Gourd

Through broad barn-piercing sunbeams I saw Salamander lying on his father, head on his chest, both of them sound asleep in the cart, a line of drool from Sally's mouth to his father's shirt, an equally tenuous string of life binding us together.

Rocks showered the barn. I didn't think the wall would stand much longer. The mob flooded the doorway, crushing clover, walking slowly because their crates of ammunition were so ponderous. They could not see us behind bales of graying hay.

"Sally," I said, tapping his shoulder. "Wake up."

He opened blast-crater eyes.

"Did you kill Goody Treat?" I asked.

"No," he said, getting up and straightening his father's shirt.

"You knew her last words. That's what this is about."

"I know everyone's last words."

"What?"

"Yes, I have always known everyone's last words—"

"—Never mind."

A stone crashed through the wall and hit a bucket. Sally looked at me blankly, still drooling. I tossed him on the ground under the cart and pushed a bale of hay in front of it to hide him.

Crumbull filled the doorway.

The mob came through holes on every side of the barn. A foamy tide swarmed around me, black-waved and crested with pale leerings. I grabbed a rusty rake, wielding it like a bouquet of daisies.

Lester Treat looked past me at Sally's purple father in the cart. There was a sadistic smile on his lips. Crumbull advanced slowly. He smelled like a beer-drinking horse. In his hand was a great decorated wooden spork.

What happened next happened fast. Crumbull lumbered forward, swinging the spork. I ducked down and poked the rake into his groin. He roared backward. Stones smashed my face and arms. I fell, bloody hay in my eyes. I got to my trembling feet. The world had gone soup.

Crumbull raised the spork. As he brought it down, a mourner jumped in front of me. The spoony part struck my father's skull. He collapsed into an ashy pile.

I dropped by his side. The fingers on one of his hands were opening and closing, opening and closing. The hand was a brilliant pink, like a tropical flower quivering in a downpour. I bent down and took it. The fingers clutched my own and stopped moving.

A murmuring crowd gathered

"You stupid fools," I said.

Crumbull saw what he'd done. He dropped the spork, bent down, and took a large stone carp from a crate. He lifted it high over me.

Before he could smash my head, the golden beams of sunshine began disappearing as high blackness slid over the Barn of Slim Mercy. The room was plunged in unnatural night.

"It's the curse," someone said. "He's a demonist! Prop is blocking the sun!"

The panicking mourners streamed out, even Crumbull. Salamander helped me up.

"We can't stay here any longer, you know," I said, and he nodded. "Don't move. I'm going to see if they're gone."

I found the doorway with my hands and reached out to test the sheath of darkness. My fingers touched something like skin or dried tongue. I crawled under, stones left by the mourners biting into my knees.

After creeping several yards with no sign of light, I tried to make a hole in it. It was tough but not impossible to tear. With a shard of pottery I managed to cut a cross into the surface and pulled the flaps down toward me.

My head emerged in the middle of a sheet of vibrant green, a color too noble and joyful to be tossed in a salad and too divine to be found in a feather. I wanted to dive into it, and open my mouth and devour it at the same time. Slightly darker green veins, thick as tree trunks and giving rise to smaller tributaries like branches, forked throughout the colorskin. Here and there silent birds strutted and pecked along them. The veins radiated out to the tips of three serrated main points facing north, east, and west. These tips were tinged with fields of gold, red, and orange. I turned my head and saw a monolithic stem, browner than its host, curving up into the sky like a scorpion's tail poised to sting, and only then did I know my find for a leaf.

All this wonder mingled with my father's sacrifice and I tried in vain to see how the nightmarish loss below and living dream above could share one moment. Strong gusts blew from the north. Dark clouds unrolled toward us. It must've been these powerful winds that brought the giant leaf.

I crawled back to the barn.

"It's a leaf," I said. "But we have to go. We can discuss this later. We must cross Nobody Lake."

"Why?" asked Sally.

"Because this leaf came from over the lake. I can tell from the direction of the darkness."

"I don't understand."

"I don't know anything about trees, but the mystery of this leaf is worth investigating. Finally, a reason to get out of this town."

"What about being wanted for murder?"

"There's that."

"Gideon, before we go, would you help make my father snore?"

I didn't think it would work, but I understood Sally wouldn't want to leave him alone like this without trying.

"Is there a lantern here?"

A moment later we moved in flickering light. I opened the sleeper's violet mouth and sealed his nostrils with my fingers. He began snoring.

"You did it," Sally said.

"But I don't see how it will help anything—"

"—Watch it with that cart!" his father yelled.

"Dad," Sally said.

"Where am I?" the man said, looking around and through me.

"You're in a barn. You were hit by a cart years ago and have been sleeping ever since," I said.

Salamander started crying and I realized I stood on my father's long-nailed hand. He looked remarkably like the timber-trapped figure in his wedding portrait. I knelt down with the lantern. We were alone together in a circle of light, enclosed in walls of darkness and each one an inch from invisibility. I laid the spork over his chest.

My father observed it with evaporating-ink eyes.

"A piece of wood's as good as fate," he said.

I put my ear to his mouth. He was done speaking and breathing. The sorrow in my gut seemed to belong to another, and I felt my blood cheering and pressing against it, trying to drown it out.

"I have a second chance…" Sally's father said.

"But I have to say goodbye," Salamander said.

"Yes, I'm sorry, we must go," I said.

Mr. Mander said, "Good luck, son. Now that I have this second chance at life, I will live honestly. I will open my heart and reveal to the entire world the woman I love and intend to marry."

"Who's that?" I asked.

"Why, none other than your aunt Leona."

"Good heavens," I said. "What Leona shows and what she hides must be complete opposites. But, Sally, we must get to the orchard. There is no time to waste. Mr. Mander, can you sit up?"

We helped him to his feet. The seeds which had worked their way into his blood had kept him from atrophying.

"How do I look?" he asked.

"Kind of like an eggplant," I said. "But grand."

He hugged his son farewell.

"You can do us both a last favor," I said. "Tell everyone we went toward the Marshes in the south. And tell my mother…"

"Yes?"

I decided to say something factual. Because the world is made of indisputable facts, of giant potters and enormous leaves and blue pumpkins and the non-reflective bodies of dead clouds. There's always enough room for facts, but throw a feeling in there and it gets claustrophobic.

"…I am the son who got away."

So Long

Salamander and I started for the woods. I planned to follow their perimeter until we reached the orchard. We both knew the orchard well, but we'd have to improvise a way across Nobody Lake. We had to move quickly because I knew soon Crumbull and his gang would come back soon to get us. And I had no doubt they'd blame my father's death on us too.

We were still making way through the trees when night fell. Confused voices rang out and hushed intermittently, near and far. We often stopped to wait for footsteps to recede. But mostly our feet snapped twigs and crushed leaves, and each snap was the end of a twig and the end of a snap, and each crush the end of a leaf and the end of a crush.

When we were still, all was silence. The leaf was like a hand fallen on a mouth. "Enough," it seemed to say. "Please shut up. Can't you see you've been talking nonsense all these years?" Rain started. It was odd to hear it pattering above our heads while the forest stayed dry.

"What's that squishy sound?" Salamander asked.

I knelt down and picked up a mass of spherical goop.

"We've reached the orchard," I said.

"What's that crinkly sound?"

Slowly, a horizon of dim light was seeping into existence.

"The leaf is curling up at the edges," I said. "Just like a normal leaf that's blown off a tree and dried."

We fumbled our way through trees bowed under the weight of disease. My father had warned the blight would change the paths, and he'd been right. *A twist here and a twist there, and who knows where you'll wind up?* We reached a steep slope that led down to Nobody Lake and I stepped in apple mush, sliding forward. Salamander fell into me and we both tumbled and slid down through rocks, sticks, and extruding roots until we knocked into a large rock.

Shadows began to flicker into shape around us. Someone had lit a fire.

I peered around the rock. The furthest tip of the leaf stopped just short of the lake. A large bonfire was raging by the shore. A flash of lightning illuminated figures in the gloom. Two floating funeral pyres were about to be lit.

They were going to send Goody Treat into the unknown. The second pyre was for my father.

My mother was moving my father's limbs and his cane into different poses on the pyre as though they were floral arrangements. Crumbull exchanged heated words with her and she stopped. Aunt Leona was there also, and Mr. Mander was following her, a lovesick ripe plum of a man, begging at her feet. Lester Treat sullenly stalked them around Goody's pyre. He suddenly started shouting and kicked Salamander's father in the behind.

"Now or never, Sally," I said. "We have to make a go for the pyres."

Sally didn't hesitate. We ran along the dead cloud's edge. The mourners were too delighted with the private lives turning inside out to notice us. I heaved Father's pyre into the silvery water and Sally launched himself on Goody Treat's. I took my father's cane and used it to push myself from the shore. It was still a wise and worldly piece of wood.

I looked at my father's face only once the whole time we paddled across Nobody Lake. His mouth was open. His teeth were too yellow and sparse. I'd never noticed the narrowness of his tongue before. Sally sat dignified, facing outward from between Goody's spread legs, like a diligent guard dog.

When we were a few yards away, the town finally realized the pyres were gone. They shouted and screamed at us to come back, Crumbull and his gang uttering vile threats. I skipped a stone from my pocket that struck the giant in his forehead. That was such a perfect last sight of Brookridge that I turned to face the fog the rest of the journey.

Eventually the yelling died down. We paddled cold water with our hands. I don't know when we reached the jagged gray wall of fog, past which nobody had ever returned.

"Sally," I said. "You told me you know everyone's last words?"

"I don't know why. But I do."

"Mine aren't *this is it*, are they?"

"No. Your last words are *urinal cake*."

"Good. This is it."

The pyres and their weird cargo floated effortlessly through the fog. I expected it to hurt, but it was soft. We saw pulsating lights everywhere, like when you press your hands against your eyes. Then our crafts gently bounced against a shoreline. I felt as though I was falling asleep and waking at the same time, the consciousness equivalent of a leg lifting and falling in the process of walking.

We stepped onto a gravelly beach. The fog stood behind us. It was dark as night. The rain had stopped, but my head thundered.

Quick as missing keys, we were blinded by sunshine as though something huge had blotted out the sun and then moved. While our eyes adjusted to the light, we heard footsteps approach. I waved Father's stick like a weapon, ready to fight.

"Gideon," a man said.

"Who's that?" I saw the gradually solidifying outline and details of a bearded man in a violet floral dress, carrying a parasol.

"It's your brother Wegman. And you brought a friend. That's good. You must come with me, and meet Ben, Blake, Bob, and Nestor."

"Where are we?" I asked.

"I'll explain everything."

"Dad's dead," I said.

"I know."

"How? Are you a spirit?" I asked.

"No. His corpse over there is kind of a giveaway."

Salamander had been fixing Goody Treat's hair, which came undone on the journey across the lake. He finished that, and straightened her false eyelashes, then joined us on the beach.

"What I really want to know," Wegman said to me, "is what took you so long?"

He removed our father's cane from my hand and used it to push the two pyres back through the fog. Then he showed us the tree.

WELCOME HOME, ALL YOU UNINVITED

"Without attempting to explicate something for which there are likely no words, I simply state that at a single fell stroke, I have lost any tranquility and peace of mind which I ever achieved. I stand face-to-face with nothingness . . ."
– Gustav Mahler, letter to Bruno Walter [1909]

i
WHAT THE TOILET TELLS ME

Mornings had been bad for the past half year, since the night Wilson got the ass-kicking of his life. It was like this: First, Wilson would wake up but couldn't manage to open his eyes. Instead, he'd vividly imagine—a vision of hearing—the first stalking bars of Mahler's 10th Symphony, which death had distracted the composer from finishing.

Tentative, 1911 violas would probe the *andante* darkness of Wilson's skull, like the fingertips of a man buried alive as they trace coffin's lid—almost, but not yet ready, to dare acknowledge the possibility of his predicament...

And then, this day [as every other], Wilson would open his eyes, with a weak, clairvoyant taste in his mouth, too distilled with spit for interpretation. Who knows? Perhaps it meant he would compose again ... in the meantime, it was no surprise that the only music in his head was courtesy of Gustav Mahler.

It was the legendary late-20th century composer, Androsaur Flekt, who'd introduced him to Mahler's works; and it was the symphonies that most inspired Wilson to push the conflicting boundaries of his own, ineffable compositions. Over decades of intense study he'd learned to *watch* Mahler's music, observing predatory tension within the spectrality; certain passages—the opening of the 3rd Symphony, for example—resembled nothing so much as a movie-monster that, slowly unveiled by dispersing murk, lies on the ground—surely it's dead?—but there are twenty-five minutes left until the credits ... you couldn't turn your back on these orchestrations; they threatened to incarnate. They would have Nephilim bones and stampeding plans.

Perhaps Wilson was conceited in thinking that he alone had the key to this secret agenda of Mahler's music, though you couldn't blame him for thinking so: If, as Wilson believed, Mahler's music was a struggle to fight its way into corporeality, then he and Wilson shared something remarkably rare: The attempt at impossible transformation—though Wilson's efforts were made in the opposite direction, for Wilson's mission was to convert his anatomical malformations into music as far from flesh as stars are from questions.

... Bleary and hemorrhaging borrowed, unfinished masterpieces ... nothing but his bladder's insistence got him out of bed...

Androsaur Flekt had been equally irrepressible, and as close to an internal organ as anything outside could be, that drives you nuts but also gifts supreme relief; and besides—and most importantly—you need it. He missed his mentor and friend—no mere appendix—his only *human being*, really [every other person was too flat, the joyful ones the worst—boring and insipid and popular as dancing Keith Haring figures].

Flekt would've known [or commanded] what Wilson should do now, and if Wilson pointed out that Androsaur never took his own advice, he'd just laugh and his eyes would shine like coronation crowns beneath the befurred rim of his faux-Yeti hat:

"There's nothing hypocritical about being hypocritical, eh, Feffy?"

Most of all, Wilson yearned for those occasions when, against all reasonable probability, he and Androsaur would separately conceive of and blurt out the same odd thing at the same moment; quite simply, it made him be not alone in the world—a rare feeling. Like the time Xenakis asked them, at the premiere of one of his monotonously "immersive" installations, what they'd thought. To which Flekt and Furst replied, stereophonically:

"Shit sandwich without the bread!"

He'd been dead—what? ten, eleven years . . . lately, Wilson felt a recent *departure* of Flekt—a sense of his having-just-left after a visit; and he'd look around to see if he'd forgotten anything—much the way one returns to open an empty refrigerator over and over. The feeling could be so uncanny at times; he had even briefly wondered if Flekt might be haunting him. But that was too idiotic for serious consideration—it being hard enough to believe in life *during* life.

Wilson's right hand burned with 1,000 phantom limb violations. He refused to pay it any mind, instead observing the lack of his impression in the rumpled bed sheets, sodden gray as the bloated sky pressed against the vaulted windows. A shower was likely, but would offer no relief in this Chinatown summer, when the rain smelled like street-piss and the pissed-on streets smelled like shit . . . enough, bladder! He stumbled through a paradoxically barren mess, reminiscent of the last stages of garage sales, junky miscellanies hauled curbside [PLEASE TAKE! FREE!], and he tiptoed over green-schmeared bagels and a gated community's worth of holiday junk mail—since the attack, he'd dreaded clean-up so much that he'd even stopped masturbating.

At last Wilson reached the seven solemn cairns of stale clothing, beyond which lay the bathroom, clean and yet dingy in an Eastern Bloc fashion. He sat on the toilet, elbows to thighs and forehead tipped in hands, sinking and insufferable and beyond heartbreak, a faithful widow remembering her wedding vows.

An old, rolled-up copy of *Art Now! [Outsider Art Special]* stuck out a bag of popcorn kernels. He shook it loose; opened to a dog-eared page representing an early press "appearance." Maybe his music was gone, his memory was strong—viciously so, perhaps—and he didn't really look at the 1-page feature as he read:

HE SINGS THE BODY ECCENTRIC
Sterling Prizewinner Wilson Furst completes
the *Art! Now!* Questionnaire

Q: What exactly is your fefhorn?

A: As far as I know it's unique. I suppose you could say it resembles something out of Hieronymus Bosch. I'm a private person, if that's what I am, so I won't describe it in detail, but it is basically a part of me, a musical instrument that's sprouted out of my back, midway between the shoulder blades. There's no medical name for it, but Androsaur Flekt decided to call it a *fetus ex fetu,* and over the years that got shortened into fefhorn. I liked it, because it reminded me of the posthorn which Mahler used to such evocative effect.

Q: How do you play it?

A: I'm private as my parts, and all I can say is I have to use my right hand. I'm right fefhorned.

Q: What does it feel like?

A: Nothing. It's like it has no nerve-endings. I've played it a million times but just as you would an instrument of wood or brass.

Q: Are you a misanthropist?

A: Can a monster be a misanthropist? I don't know.

Q: How does it feel now that *Welcome Home, All You Uninvited* was awarded The Sterling Prize for Most Compelling Composition of the Year?

A: None of my business.

Q: How do you respond to those critics who claim your work is nothing more than an ingenious form of ventriloquism?

A: I think all music is ultimately ventriloquism. And as for music critics, I think that their criticisms are sad expressions of the critic's inability to project his voice from anywhere but himself.

Q: Why did you refuse to accept The Sterling Prize in person?

A: Too many people. There's no greater lie than the more the merrier. Just think of Pompeii. Auschwitz. Woodstock.

Q: What composer has had the great influence on your own work?

A: Gustav Mahler.

Q: Why?

A: Mahler and I share a lot of things. Of all composers, he's come the closest to expressing my experience of the world. For example, I can only compose in absolute solitude, and Mahler sequestered himself away at Steinbach, each chance he got. Maybe that's a common feeling. More significantly, I believe Mahler and I share expertise in our relations to impossibility. He carried impossible music in his head—the anguish and joy in his works express the beautiful agony of flailing about, trying desperately to express this impossible music—like a man trying to do more than develop womb, and more than giving birth, who also insists on fertilizing it himself.

Q: What would you like to achieve with your music before you die?

A: To finish Mahler's 10th Symphony—for real. Not like the Deryck Cooke version, which is about as exciting as pushing all the buttons in an Empire State Building elevator and listening to the beeps up to the top. I mean *really* complete it. I don't know how, but I don't know a lot of things. Whether or not I'm a misanthrope for example.

Q: Anything else you'd like to let our readers know?

A:

Wilson dropped the magazine and watched the toilet mock-flush. He looked in the mirror and observed a wide-eyed, grotesque expression—Louis Armstrong tasting a bad trumpet. He returned to the loft's obnoxious expanse. Rent was a luxurious $3,000 monthly, but it had a refugee center Feng Shui—a place hastily constructed in response to unexpected disaster.

The storm began. At the great vaulted window Wilson watched the rain falling in tongues. The homeless man stood at his usual station across the street, wearing his blank advertising placard, plywood boards sheathing torso and back, a sort of not-much-proof vest. He had a Harry Partch percussion instrument quality—hints of unlikely utility, hidden microtonalities. He was coarse and public as the vacant lot beneath his bluescuffed boots; and behind and high above him always loomed the windowless back of an anonymous building, hideous gray as cheap dental fillings.

In recent days, Wilson had developed a mild fascination with this character. He often fantasized the details of his childhood: Formative years as a human sandwich, advertising a Dry Cleaning business or Delicatessen or Nail Salon; a tiny strolling sign, ignored and pacing endless between the opposite poles of one dreary block, each day identical in length and tone and feeling as an insect's belly-segments … and, as the peripatetic placard aged, the plywood boards, which hung over his shoulders with handleless jump-ropes, grew with him, anatomical extensions [like Wilson and his fefhorn]; and when the business he paced for closed down he wandered off … the decades of reckless divagation eroding SALE! and %OFF! from his placards … and now he was his own man and didn't need to pace or advertise anymore. Now he'd realized his dream of immobility, across the street from Wilson's loft … here Wilson got tired of his imaginary biography.

Every few minutes, white-belted white people—who sipped "infused" beverages and would not under any circumstances play Russian Roulette without locally recycled bullets—walked by the blank man/sign, dung beetles passing a beetle without dung.

Today there were less of these gentrifiers, and umbrellas hid their casual smugness. As usual the man/sign just stood there getting soaked, a sentry unable to leave his post.

The phone ringing took Wilson by surprise. Who wanted to talk to him? Nobody cared any longer. Critics claimed his work had become overly redundant—like breathing, he supposed.

"Yes?"

"Hullo, Dash here. How's the piece going?"

"Fine, it's going fine. Thanks forch…"

The homeless man was staring up at Wilson's window, right at him, though possibly not seeing him; the rain now snapped like gravel at the panes.

"For checking in?" Dash asked.

A flash of static came and went, after which he still heard Dash speaking but the phone line had crossed with his past; and as Squall waited for a reply Wilson eavesdropped on a conversation he'd shared with Androsaur Flekt 10 years ago:

"Feffy, have you always hated people?"

"Uh, Dash, I'm sorry?"

"No, I haven't always existed."

"You said *forch*—thanks for calling, I'm sure you meant. Are you OK?"

"Don't worry Feff. They all die in the end."

"Yes. Thanks. Yes, thanks for checking in and … for this opportunity."

"You know what I say, Androsaur…"

"My pleasure. When do you think I can hear a bit? I don't mean to prod, but as the key piece in our 20th Anniversary Celebration you can understand I am a tad more anxious than usual. Not trying to rush you—but the event is next month."

Simultaneously, the friends raise their glasses and shout:

"All's well that ends!"

"Soon, Dash. I promise."

Serrated, comforting laughter…

"Soon?"

"You know how it is making art, Dash."

"I only wish I did. But I know how to make a deadline."

"But doesn't making art hurt? It's self-mutilation. But, it's like this: If you are compelled to painfully rip the hairs out of your head 1-by-1, you might as well make a pretty bloody pattern on your scalp while you're at it. Something people can clap at."

"I trust you won't let me down."

"Do you really think it's bad as all that, Androsaur?"

"Sure," Wilson said.

"I think the truth only hurts if you care about it."

"Great, talk soon Wilson."

Dash was Director of the New York Anti-New Music Symphony Orchestra, and one of the few influential figures who still championed Furst as an important composer. His phone call today had been the first time they'd spoken in half a year, when Squall commissioned Wilson to compose and record a piece, to be released in a limited, autographed vinyl edition exclusively for the top financial supporters of the Orchestra, in celebration of its second transgressive [but cultured] decade. Squall was particularly keen on the idea because the first piece they'd ever presented had been Furst's own *Welcome Home, All You Uninvited.*

At their winter meeting over sushi and sake, Wilson had leapt at the chance to compose a new piece in exchange for a generous sum of much-needed money, and the possibility of future commissions and acclaim.

He returned to the placard, blank and coughing in the rain.

What am I thinking?

Maybe I should help that man. Maybe I'm like that man.

Yes. No.

Then why am I watching him? What am I thinking?

I'm thinking he should really get an umbrella.

Nothing else?

No.

Wilson disconnected the phone. He thought about the incidents of the mugging, in vivid sequential detail. It was like he'd lost an important key and the only hope of retrieval was diligent, retrorse tracing of his day. It was also like going back in time and finding out the past was worse than you remembered it.

ii
WHAT THE SNOW TELLS ME

Wilson had left the dinner with Squall a little past midnight in a glorious C major dithyrambic mood. He'd even forgotten about those obscene, reveling anonymassholes at the table adjacent. It had been someone's birthday, and attending their gynecological celebration were the most unthinkably idiotic, laughing twat-dropped creatures, all pleased and oblivious as air-conditioned tourists in some shitty desert land—you *know* them—and you *know* the one.

Ah, but now Wilson had the intense pressure and consequent focus that were the silver linings of hard deadlines. It was just what he needed to get out of a recent creative funk and force a breakthrough; and he had until summer—six months was sufficient to compose a fine piece of music.

Heavy snow had smoothed the city's sharp things, defunct antennas and barbed-wire fences, shattered beer bottles and even the shoutspeak of poor people who used windows for telephones. The buildings and cars merged, like mating worms into a single pale obesity; Wilson felt *scherzo*-like in a Mahler's 7th kind of way. Six illegally intoxicated teenagers traipsed toward him like evacuees from a flooded city, singing the latest pop-puke [I've got nine hearts and don't you forget it or I'll push you in the pool with my electric ferret]; they passed him with their cruelty and cell-phones and Wilson hummed a cute little *Kindertotenlieder* as chilly murk embraced him.

He took a half-assedly shoveled shortcut through diatomite curves, following sodium orange cones of streetlight through a hollow park, cold quiet broken now and then by a colder circling wind. Ahead, the sinister gathering of lumpy dwarfish figures under an icy moon turned out to be nothing but deadbeat snowmen.

He stumbled onward, alcohol and blazing-phoenix future setting his blood soaring…

"Shut up, Feffy and listen. Here is the great secret: Music is none other than The Uninvited."

"Meaning?"

"Not so much meaning, as telling-it-like-it-is, Feffy. The Uninvited is a special instance of appearing; it is an arrival which is not possible to claim is on time or late; it cannot even be unscheduled…Now, that which is Uninvited can be either Recognized or Unrecognized—an acquaintance or a stranger; and the acquaintance or stranger can be either Welcome or Unwelcome."

"Supposing that's true, what does that have to do with music?"

"Not music so much as the composer. Our role in life is serious, Wilson. Our aim is to Double-U-W: Cause The Uninvited to appear, in an Unrecognized form—and to Welcome it as though we had been expecting it all along and were delighted at its arrival."

"Double-U-W? That's a World-War prefix."

"Ha, I hadn't noticed. That only makes it more interesting. Didn't Mahler tell Sibelius the symphony must contain the world?"

"Yes, but your theory sounds like total bullshit."

"Do you have a better explanation?"

Wilson does not.

Now the loft was just a block away, the street empty as a bookstore; and Wilson felt like Mahler, implacably world-striding to his very own composing hut at Steinbach. He nearly slipped on a patch of ice, and as he gigglingly steadied himself a gun pressed into his back, mere centimeters beneath his flaccid fefhorn tip.

Suddenly, things were getting very 6th Symphony hammer-falls.

"All of it…wow nice shoes."

The voice was slurred and gravelly, frighteningly hopeless, yet oddly, timidly cultured—an unemployed professor of musicology?

Instinctively, Wilson reached his right hand behind his back to protect the fefhorn.

The hand was quickly seized and brutally crushed.

Too quick to be gentle or violent, and reptilian as he'd always imagined a lover's kiss must feel, the gun-muzzle mouthed the nape of Wilson's neck. His attacker kept Wilson's fefhorning hand in his lethal grasp and Wilson awkwardly emptied his pockets with his left hand, wallet to concrete, coins scattering. The man ordered Wilson to kneel and pulled off his John Lobb shoes, scraping his heels and undoing silken socks. Chunks of rock salt and inadequately melted ice ate at his knees.

The grip on his right hand loosened; now the pain flowed more freely. It was impossible to believe this agony didn't stretch to the unseen horizon and would literally drown him.

"That's everything," Wilson managed.

"The ring, clitshit."

Androsaur had gifted Wilson the faux Yeti-fur-lined ring, that one time in Rome, when they argued about Scott Walker during that amazing lightning storm; the trip during which he'd said all the wrong words to Androsaur as he lay on his deathbed.

"I can't."

"Aw, do I smell poop in your diaper?"

"It's not a diaper."

Wilson's fingers broke quietly and stolen ring dimly clinked on the ground like a counterfeit penny flung into a begging cup.

There was shit in his pants but he couldn't smell it. Why did that make things more nightmarish?

"Lately I fantasize the most shocking things—my imagination leaves nothing to the imagination…"

Yet he was no longer afraid—for his life, anyway. His brain was too busy fumbling for meanings and hopes related to the mauled hand, like a tongue which prods a hole in a tooth and misperceives its shape, depth and location, unable to confirm the actual affairs of its sponsor mouth…

"Enough with this thinking for yourself bullshit—how about learning to feel for yourself!"

Probably the butt of a pistol slammed the base of his skull. As he began blacking out in an altered dominant-9th haze, Wilson managed to glance up. He glimpsed half the face of everyone, from a dogshit's view…

Wilson woke to an inconsiderate polyphony of intersecting streams of nearby traffic, reminiscent of the 1st Symphony's *Todten-marsch.* The snow had stopped falling and the sky sprawled blue. Without warning a hot stream of piss followed the margins of his inner thighs and warmed bare, frozen feet.

He sat up in his excretions. The fefhorn was OK. The right hand was roadkill. On either side of him, the recent boot tracks of the indifferent white-belted.

Insouciant, stern Flekt's voice flickered between the emaciated scraping of gutterblown tabloids.

"At a certain age, you discover the only way to deepen your knowledge of life is to learn new jokes about it…"

…and Flekt on his cot, his serrated laughter, attenuated body draped in bearskin; and on the nightstand the surprising gravitas of grainy pulp curdled on the floor of an untouched glass of lemonade.

Whispering:

"Come closer, I have a new secret: Cancer is the awkward age between childhood and death, adolescence and death, adulthood and death, and old age and death."

"What do you mean?"

"Well, what do you want to be when you turn cancer?"

It was somehow more than nonsense.

If only because they were his last words.

iii
WHAT THE DEAD TELL ME

The phone disconnected, Wilson watched the soggy homeless man schlep eastward, gutter for road. Without intending to, he examined his right hand. The fingers were twisted and bent, totally fucked. He wouldn't be playing the fefhorn any time soon—if ever. At least the instrument itself was not injured.

Does that matter?

If I'm disabled, so is my music.

Even if my hand heals, the fefhorn might fall off like a frozen wart, or develop a disease.

Am I even a human being? I've never been to a doctor, so who knows?

Have I turned cancer?

Who can I be, if not myself?

Body.

That night Wilson wolfed sleeping pills with a glass of what should not have been vinegar. He woke next afternoon, all *andante* fingers tapping coffin ceilings and tongue stuck to the roof of his mouth with clueless paste. Carefully moving through the solemn cairns of stale clothing, he reached the bathroom and regarded the mirror, disgusted; he was filthy, his mentionables were unmentionable. His reflection suggested a humorless mash-up of Groundhog Day and The Metamorphosis.

Hanging on the wall behind him was an 8-x-10 askew photograph of Mahler's composing hut at Steinbach, where the master had composed his titanic worlds with astounding discipline, precision and visionary abandon. Wilson used to look at it when he crapped.

He straightened the picture. He dressed quickly and, not really sure what he was doing, went downstairs. The sky was barely trying, a half-assed gray, the nearly no-color of paper towel sopping up more water than it can handle. The hot sun pissed all over the city, everyone plodding about guardedly, remembering and plotting interrogations.

He crossed the street toward the homeless man.

Why him?

I never have to awkwardly decline an invitation to his house.

And?

And that's it.

The man/sign was staring intently at something spherical in his hands, as though watching and waiting for a lottery number to appear. It was about the size of the huge boil on Sigmund Freud's testicles, which he describes at length in the *Interpretation of Dreams.*

A bruised apple.

The cracked, fat hands cradling the dead fruit, set against the rectangular white background of the placard made a striking image, creating the Magrittesque illusion he was concealed behind a painting that appeared part of his person/environment.

"Hello sir, I hope you don't mind me bothering you—my name's Wilson, how are you?"

"Hungry," he said with a swollen, careless voice. He didn't bother looking up.

"Great Glob, Feffy—You have no social graces. Had you no childhood friends?"

"You need a childhood for that."

"I can help you with that—I want to help you. I will help you, I'm not saying I'm withholding food I could share with you unless you do me a favor, too," Wilson said, feeling faint, slightly nauseous as when you get a spot to sit in a crowded subway car, and experience the assheat signature of the fat person who exerted himself from the seat seconds before you sat down, and you wonder if resting your legs was worth it.

"I almost burped."

"Sir, I have a job if you are interested, and I've got all the food you could want, and I insist we would work out a monetary payment. It's a weird job—not *that* kind of weird, but … I'm an artist; we're eccentric I guess …"

"Well do at least make an attempt at schmoozing. Remember you cannot fail if you don't try first …"

"You rich?"

He looked up, eyes lost and no fare to get back. His face was puffy and pocked and erratically bearded; and he should probably have been in a hospital for any number of conditions.

"Oh—there's a worm in there."

The man returned to the apple with a yellowy smile and carefully turned it upside down so a maggot fell in his hand. It wriggled. He ate it and tossed the apple away.

"You rich?"

"Not too much," Wilson said, going on as he had to, as if this were all a dream, with no consequences and no taboos, the most hideous acts merely symbolic. "No, not rich but you could, uh—you could finally get a new set of boards or a suit, some good shoes, a fine hat or umbrella to keep the rain off your head. A room to rent and hot food, maybe. What do you say?"

"I'm Kenneth?"

"Good to meet you… You're not allergic to latex, are you?—that sounds bad… but it's not what it sounds like."

"What it feels like?"

"I mean latex gloves of course. It's hard to explain. I have to show you. Do you mind? I mean, I could really need you…"

He grunted and coughed.

"You rich?"

*c!

One minute they were on the street, and the next, Wilson sat backwards and shirtless on a chair, arms hanging over the back, head propped straight and still as mounted taxidermy, looking at he and Kenneth in the oblong mirror he'd propped up before them.

Kenneth remained in his blank, frayed placards, having looked at Wilson as though he were the devil when he offered to put them somewhere safe.

"You're sure you are OK with this? We'll have to do this a lot—there's only a month before the music must be written and recorded… there's a lot you have to learn quickly."

Kenneth shrugged, grunted, tugged at the surgical gloves Wilson had instructed him to wear.

What am I doing? You know what you're doing.

You know.

I know, I know.

Variations.

"OK, here's the part I told you about. It's all about that bumpy object on the thing on my back—all right; I hope it doesn't disgust you..."

"Part of being human is being inhuman, eh Feffy?"

"I suppose so."

"So cheer up Feff."

"But I feel so lost, I can't find the wrong way to go."

"That's easy," Flekt says, doing his best Ray-Bolger-at-the-yellow-brick-crossroads impersonation.

"That a wing, right?"

"Do you think so?"

"Big chicken wing?"

Kenneth grunted, shrugged:

"You're pretty rich?"

"Remember: Double-U-W."

"No really I'm not OK, let's start. Just move your hand along the right-side ridge. Do it gently. I just want us to get a feel—"

—It wasn't pain exclusively or even exactly—a peripheral, if striking phenomena, like the light of burning fire; Wilson convulsed and his eyes twirled up to spy into his inner-face—

—A clattering, loud and world-like, drew his eyes back down from his head.

In the mirror, he could tell the man/sign had tripped over a pile of dishes and flatware and God knows what else and had slammed backwards into the wall. But why was his expression full of discovery? What sale was the flat surface of his board now advertising? Wilson tried to read it but the words were in some ancient language, all swirly and drippy wet reds. What was in Kenneth's hands?

The fefhorn! He'd ripped it off Wilson's back and was examining it with a child-like disinterest in warnings—tapping and sniffing it, sticking his hand in up to the jolly elbow.

It was hollow.

Wilson heard, then saw the blood dripping off his body to the floor behind him. It meant nothing. He was transfixed by his impossible, outsider's view of the fefhorn.

He wanted the man/sign to turn it more slowly so he could get a thorough look. He was too tired to express this, or anything else.

Then Kenneth lifted the fefhorn above his head and looked up inside. He shook it, as though trying to dislodge something. He brought it down and peered into its conical hollow, grunted and frowned in a puzzled way, raised the fefhorn again, shook it, grunted, shrugged, and put it on his head.

It fit perfectly.

Only now did Kenneth look at the mirror. He stood over Wilson's slumping form with a very serious face and adjusted the fefhorn just a tad. He nodded, satisfied. Suddenly, his eyes met Wilson's in the mirror. Until then he seemed to have forgotten Wilson was in the room with him. He grunted and came round from behind Wilson and crouched before him. Wilson's blood streaked his placard and spotted the folds of his neck. He grasped Wilson's shoulders and hauled him up, straightened him out so he didn't slide onto the floor.

Wilson kept his eyes open. It was difficult to do, but Kenneth's face was a mass of worries and he knew that to look away would be to confirm the man's worst fears. Why that should matter to him, he didn't know. This guy was just another anonymasshole—but it was somehow more than nonsense when he offered Kenneth a smile, to reassure him.

Kenneth returned an ochre grin.

Then he pointed at the fefhorn on his head:

"This waterproof?"

*C!

"Do you know that story about Mahler," Androsaur is saying, "how, one summer in 1908, while he and Alma were away from Steinbach, actually—in Tyrol, I think—he came running up to her, all breathless and shaken?"

"No, tell me," Wilson says. "This was when he was working on Das

Lied von Der Erde?"

"I imagine so. Ah this is a good one. So Gustav comes racing over the green grass to his wife. He is covered in perspiration, his eyes are wild and red, his hair a greater disaster than usual and he can hardly get out a breath. He tells Alma that, in the seclusion of his composer's hut, he suddenly felt the eye of Pan upon him with all the grotesque, hateful plans which the natural world has for the nature-lover in it. Then he says he needs to get away from the presence of the Goat-God. He goes into the house and is only able to get on with his composition in the company of other human beings."

"Seems a bit mad, even for Mahler. With the Goat-God and all."

"But there are Goat-God costumes. Mahler's was a time of disguises—you know his confession of triple-homelessness: he was a Jew in Catholic's clothing, a Bohemian in Austria, and an Austrian among Germans. Everywhere an intruder—welcomed nowhere—uninvited."

"But eye of Pan?"

"Do I have to point it out? The uninvited had slipped through a space as it opened between the covert shuffling of things."

"And?"

"It was disguised as a Goat-God."

"Could it come dressed as anything at all?"

"Of course."

"Then it could be dressed as you—or me, or anyone."

"It could've been a hat-rack."

"A bottle of brandy!"

"Yes. Keep it down."

"A fig! Underpants! A mirror!"

"Yes. Enough already, Feffy."

Wilson knows when to stop pushing Androsaur; he has that sealed jam-jar stare and his mouth has compressed into a frown that could hold back the Cossacks. The carefree mood broken, they sit somewhat awkwardly for a while, quiet, each occasionally sipping at his brandy, leaving the rim of the glass against the mouth a tad too long before putting it on the café table, desperate to use whatever poor resources at hand as an excuse to not speak.

Until suddenly—surprisingly, neither expecting it—they raise their glasses and shout together:

"Music!"

THE DEPOPULATION SYNDROME

(HBDS)

A NARRATIVE OF TRUE EVENTS AS I EXPERIENCED THEM

> *"He had not known that he lived in so wild a region. There was something uncanny in the revelation."*
> – Ambrose Bierce, "An Occurrence at Owl Creek Bridge" (1880)

AN

I don't know how to start. And so I answer my own question:

Apologize.

I must say I am deeply sorry for not knowing how to start. Aside from the Ambrose Bierce quote, which convention has established should appear directly before the story begins.

From here one need only go on.

Should I now elaborate upon how I have never felt like a *real* human being; or with the prosaic tidbit that I'm a very private person; or, through discussion of my background as professor of Information Science at Cirkle's Way University? The unanticipated, cosmic mentorship of allergies? Ghostmoth in the hills of Rhymeshead, New York? The autism spectrum? On the other hand (spectral side?), it might be best to begin with the bees—Apiculture in general, perhaps, leading into a deeper investigation of Honey Bee Depopulation Syndrome (HBDS)?

Later, there will be dancing.

I don't like to go out in public. I look normal and follow the social conventions well enough. It's just my natural inclination. But I'm not so much a private person as one who vanishes the moment his front door closes behind him. If my neighbor walked by and saw me exiting my apartment, outside, he would politely nod as we pass, with a quick blank look at my face. But when I am inside my apartment, and my neighbor's relative stops at my front door and asks, "Who lives in there? Is there a family or just a couple? Families can be such noisy next door neighbors!" he answers: "Oh I'm sure nobody's lived there in ages…"

For this reason, I'm a failure at chit-chat and such. Although I've been published in professional journals, and given lectures to thousands of students through online courses, I have never told a "story" about "myself."

The reason it's easy to get away with providing inaccurate details about yourself is because so, so very little that "makes you who you are" has any weight, doesn't matter in the least. It's like you're a homework assignment—write a 500-word essay about yourself. Most people do nothing but endlessly generate tales in which they play the protagonist.

So it's boring essays recited everywhere you go; if a stranger asked me about myself, I'd use an overheard detail from here and another from someone else's "paragraph" there.

As a result, I was known to many kids as a liar—and a few teachers and other adults.

Because when they asked my favorite color (I suppose much of everyone's life is spent answering and asking such stupid questions): "Blue," I said, and I didn't value any color over another; and I remember once, although I had no pets, I spoked at length about my two dogs before the class: Statler and Waldorf … Statler was the friendly one … And the list goes on, tiresomely *finitum.* I was aware of the appropriate codes of right and wrong in the general ethical sense, and always tried to do the right thing by collectively determined standards of behavior.

But when I related inaccurate or "borrowed" personal information or history, to my mind I was essentially "telling the truth"—or, to be more exact:

I was not telling the opposite of the truth.

*C!

You must be familiar with the uncanny experience resulting from the iteration of a lone word over and over and over—*what* word isn't essential. When you say it enough times in an unbroken series, "walking" or "bridge" or "the" or "rainy" or "shit" or "word" or "occurrence" becomes a blank sound.

Of course: it had no meaning to begin with.

*C!

Suffice to say I wasn't concerned with the *content* of my communications, so much as relaying "socially appropriate" signals/ autobiographical information to the world of people/receivers who couldn't help demanding them of me. I knew they had simply been made that way.

Of course, my real name is not Erik T. Johnson. But even though it's not my true name, all would agree it's not a lie. Why is a *pseudonym* a socially acceptable deception? Why then cannot every word, autobiography, remembrance, be pseudonymous? I don't have an answer to this. Originally I was going to use Eric with a C—it would've been even more generic. But then I rethought it. Leave the end of the name with just one K—that is a proper spelling but slightly less common. This is an example of a difference which might not be a difference to begin with. A question for some armchair *Strangerist* (*see below, in the part where I discuss the tests and evaluations I was subject to in my childhood*).

A note on my childhood development: My "interpersonal quirks" appeared when I was just a few years old. My disinterest in the lives of others. The frown. Periods of obsession with the differing hashlines of TV radio antennae, spark plugs, then porcelain buttons. Lack of affect and failure to establish emotional connections with my peers. I'd rather play alone in a corner than join in sing-alongs. And my play consisted of taking mechanical things apart to study their smaller bits and pieces. The more complicated the item, the better. I left them in impossible states of disarray.

I did like reading (in solitude). I had one favorite story. Once I'd learned to read, I read it several times a day—and from childhood through adulthood. That story is "An Occurrence at Owl Creek Bridge." It was written in 1880 by Ambrose Bierce, an American author who disappeared in 1913, soon after joining Pancho Villa's Mexican revolutionaries. It remains his most famous work to this day. I'm sure you're familiar with it from Junior High School. If not, it's public domain and a five-minute read.

I'm not entirely certain why my brain latched onto that particular piece of fiction and not another. I think, somehow, that knowing the man who wrote it had vanished, was never recovered, was a big part of it. I already had something of the person who'd disappeared for good about me, I felt. And then in the story itself, there was the clear juxtaposition between two opposing realities—that of being hung by way of military justice, and the other of running into the arms of domestic bliss in the form of a loving wife. Although my circumstances couldn't be more different, still I did understand what it is like to face the troubling dissonance of that enormous unbridgeable gap Bierce put to paper. Because there was such a space between me and everyone else in the world, it seemed. And something about the timbre of the word "Occurrence" was enigmatic in a way I wanted to understand, as if it was an important key to my own destiny, but the meaning of which was beyond my faculties.

But I wouldn't be like Peyton Farquhar, who occurred (was he The Occurrence?) at Owl Creek Bridge. Faced with the prospect of a broken neck, I would've let the Union Army snap it—not lose myself in sentimental flight to some beloved wife, "little ones" and cherished hearth and home. They would not interest me.

Before I move on with *my* story, one more thing about Bierce's tale. There are liminal *places* between Peyton's hanging and his hyperidyllic homecoming.

There is a segment in the river where Farquhar observes that "*objects were represented by their colors only; circular horizontal streaks of color—that was all he saw. He had been caught in a vortex and was being whirled on with a velocity of advance and gyration that made him giddy and sick…*"

Glad for having escaped drowning and grapeshot, yet sensing an uncanniness in the fulfillment of his intentions, Farquhar then sees: "*The black bodies of the trees formed a straight wall on both sides, terminating on the horizon in a point, like a diagram in a lesson in perspective. Overhead, as he looked up through this rift in the wood, shone great garden stars looking unfamiliar and grouped in strange constellations. He was sure they were arranged in some order which had a secret and malign significance. The wood on either side was full of singular noises, among which—once, twice, and again—he distinctly heard whispers in an unknown tongue…*"

I couldn't see it as simple fantasy, enjoy it as pure entertainment or for its so-called "trick-ending." The bizarre, unexplained event/s (Occurrence/s?) that Peyton experiences in the water and through the woods, serve as a mighty mortar to hold the two more obviously "real" and weighty opposing "bricks" of the story together into an unbreakable unity.

I cannot help but think there's something important to be learned from this observation.

Back to me:

There were batteries of tests run and evaluations completed. These were conducted by different adults, none of whom I'd seen before and few I met more than once; They were a diverse group (I should've mentioned before that, in an all-encompassing sense, I call them Strangerists): psychiatrists, neurologists, developmental specialists, occupational therapists, school psychologists, third-party evolutionists. The school system needed to come up with a definite diagnosis for me. They couldn't find one. Yet still, a System insists there is no information that cannot be categorized.

There is a Spectrum, out there, incarnated from the *let's-put-our-heads-together* heads of educators and medical practitioners. My cluster of socially deformed behaviors put me "somewhere" on the autism spectrum. As in "Over the Rainbow," or like "God," who, though impossible to locate, we yet know through His works—which indeed seem to cover a spectrum so broad as to include atomic bombs and rape, as well as the sheltering and healing of abused animals. Officially, I was diagnosed with high-functioning Autism Spectrum Disorder (ASD).

I'm no expert on autism and related disorders. Still, it's important to make clear that the difference between one person with ASD and another can be like the distinction between the fingerprints of two separate suspects. There are those who, like me, exhibit many of the symptoms of Asperger's Syndrome (difficulty with social-emotional reciprocity, and repetitive interests and behaviors). Individuals with profound autism may never speak or even acknowledge the presence of another human being. There are those who spend life in a furious hell, biting, kicking, and screaming at anyone who approaches them.

Just look it up online, there's an overload of far more interesting information on the subject than I'm giving here. And incidentally, I've never had anything against these designations and diagnoses *in toto*; they've been helpful in guiding many people toward treatments that have made their lives better. Rather, as I've said in a different context:

It's not so much that it's bullshit, as it is not the opposite of the truth.

*C!

An acceptable dictionary defines Spectrum as *a broad range of related ideas or objects which tend to overlap so as to form a continuous sequence.* For many of my adolescent years I wondered: How broad is broad? That means anything from literal nothingness to total existence. How related is related? An ant and the Chancellor of Germany are related insofar as both are verbalized as nouns. Blood is related to veins and to poetry, as well as genocide, Elizabeth Bàthory, life-saving transfusions, and Herschel Gordon Lewis movies. *Tend to* suggests some *X may*, while another *X may not* tend to overlap, providing no stable information. *Continuous* excludes no gaps in a sequence; returning to the dictionary, we discover that a Sequence *is a set of related events, movements, or things that follow each other in a particular order. Spectrum* is a Latin word meaning *image* or *apparition—spectre* (as in territorial ghosts of folklore crossroads).

*C!

There was one thing, though, a skill of the interpersonally performative content type, with which I've long wished to have any facility: How to relate jokes. These signals withhold information about the teller's affective state, and encourage congenial moods in his listeners, the joke-receivers. In terms of this document, I could make the encroaching doom funny.

Yes, It's too bad. It would increase your interest in reading this—knowing there will be laughs in store amongst all the dry talk of signals.

There are signals all around us, transmitted by strange entities with no interest in humanity's survival. Light itself travels through the emptiness of the vacuum without a care for the eye or plant. There are signals that carry dark information along unseen channels, which since slime began have sought a receiver. These signals do not care what effect they have on the receivers, and flesh is as good as anything else if only it will carry the inhumanly cold message.

If I didn't frown now and then, I think I could easily've been mistaken for an android or the lone, chilliest human inhabitant of the Uncanny Valley—a phrase famously coined by Masahiro Mori in 1970, in describing a particularly wild *region* of negative emotional responses. Humans have evolved these specific negative responses as a mechanism of pathogen- avoidance; they become repulsed by anybody/thing who/that looks, in a manner difficult to pin down, *wrong*.

The phrase enters my mind:

Nothing significant is interested in rainbows of friendship.

Enters my mind? It might have *incubated*, hatched out of it.

Perhaps literally... Not necessarily.

Sometimes it is difficult to see any difference between things—even *opposing* things. Do I divagate?

No: You should know a little about whoever is leading you nowhere. Distracted people are actual people.

No again: I can only go forward the way I can, however limited my means. Otherwise I will never get to what people call "the point." They usually don't mean it in terms of Euclidean Geometry, but in a real sense, that is how I am employing the word here: A point cannot be defined in terms of previously defined objects, and has no length, area, volume, or any other dimensional element.

That's where we're going.

It's a long trip but nothing in the universe is more indifferent than time.

*c!

In any case, I've never precisely experienced this oft-discussed Uncanny Valley. I've seen the same photographs of human-like dolls and robots that "creep out" everyone, and that's all they were to me. Pictures of objects. My atypical response has been confirmed by Strangerists who have studied at some of *the* schools across the country.

I *do* make it a habit to frown, it comes easily enough and there's never a lack of reasons to make the expression. Yes. The

Frown. It is the frown alone which I share with others. Perhaps my frown functions like Batesian mimicry in the animal kingdom. The wings of the *Caligo eurilochus* butterfly, for example. These have evolved patterns that look like the large eyes of owls. These false "eyes" serve as an effective warning signal, seducing the signal receiver (in this case, the large owl) to avoid confrontation. *Caligo* is Latin for Darkness.

OCCURRENCE

To recap: I frown, so we have something in common (unless you're afflicted with rictus, or are my sibling in precisely my ASD, too; not a fantastical notion). I am a professor of Information Science. I have never been "in" the Uncanny Valley. I have an enduring fascination with the story: "An Occurrence at Owl Creek Bridge." Early in life, I was diagnosed as being found somewhere along the admittedly broad autism spectrum—that's me over there without any human warmth or meaningful relationships. I cannot tell jokes, and I regret it. I started this story in some confusion, but have already apologized for that.

Now I will add more to the picture of my life that I imagine I am painting for you. For all I know, you're looking at a distressed muddle, and we're not *connecting* in the least. But I go on. I will tell you about the guidance of allergies in my life, how in many ways they are my life, the world of this frowning man who disappears when he closes his front door behind him.

Allergic reactions are a peculiar example of signal-processing, in which the body interprets information from the world as problematic and destructive. Throughout my life, I have experienced such reactions to a variety of things: circus peanuts, moldy leaves, the tracks of a cockroach, dogs, cats, birds, lizards, gerbils. Exposure resulted in my lungs tightening and atopic dermatitis, rashes blooming in random spots on my arms and legs.

My flesh was my enemy.

The highly-allergic person is not at home in the world. When I was young I imagined I belonged on some other, isolated planet, where nebular formations, solar winds and dead atmosphere would not contaminate me like the pollen-filled sunshine—a world without sun, flame, sea or earth. There is something alien about being an allergic individual, and perhaps such people are more sensitive to other forms of the unworldly. But across the country, allergies are increasing in quantity and intensity, and today I know this far-off planet of my non-committal dreams is a reality for *you*, in the near future. It is a nightmare orbiting your doorstep.

I do not come from a financially prosperous family; needless to say, my hand was forced to find a means of belonging to this world. When I was in my twenties, I undertook an extensive series of immunotherapy injections to reduce my reactions to food allergies and environmental pathogens. The treatments were highly successful and I soon found myself assuming I must be enjoying autumn leaves and peanut butter and jelly sandwiches, mundane "pleasures" that had long been beyond reach (and now, I discovered, were very overrated).

All that changed again about ten years later, when I undertook an expedition to the Rhymeshead area of upstate New York in the autumn of 2009. I had heard bees were disappearing from their colonies in exceptionally large numbers in this desolate location. Having recently published a well-received article in *American Apiculture* on Israel Acute Paralysis Virus and worker bees, I thought myself up to the task of solving the mystery, not knowing I would become a part of it.

AT

One of the few things I had not been allergic to were bees, and early in life I took to studying them. Although I earned my living as a professor of Information Science, as an amateur entomologist and sometimes apiculturist I naturally took great interest when Honey Bee Depopulation Syndrome (HBDS) was first described in

North America in 2006.

Today, many are familiar with the term, as more and more bees go missing from hives with devastating effects for agriculture. Although the scientific and popular journals are full of theories, such as *Varroa* mites and the effects of electromagnetic radiation from cell phone towers, in the apocalyptic days to come everyone will know the true meaning of this phenomenon. It will be called nothing, then. There will be no words to describe it because all the mouths will be eaten.

OWL

Set in the lonely hills of Rhymeshead, New York, Ghostmoth was a small, once-thriving university town sequestered between a row of abandoned rubber factories to the east and the Rhymeshead River to the west. Besides its quaint Victorian architecture, the town was distinguished by inexplicably having the highest rate of allergy sufferers per square mile in the United States. But years of immunotherapy meant this no longer concerned me.

I drove past the ramshackle town and into the wilder, northern reaches of the area, through eerie Phelantonberg, where the houses grew more and more entropic, until the few scattered homes I saw were completely abandoned and tattered like people lying near the epicenter of an explosion. I thought of Peyton Farquhar. Why? Because I constantly thought about him and the Occurrence ... In the story, several things happen *at* Owl Creek Bridge. But Bierce uses the singular *Occurrence*. As if it was all one thing. Why? Would he have used the preposition "on" rather than "at" if his intentions were different?

At this point I'd reached a crossroads. I stopped my car in a field near the edge of a dense wood. Under the illumination of a full-moon, the leaves were hemolymph bluish-green. In centuries past, the crossroads was a place of extreme significance. This world and next met there.

In many ways the crossroads were the opposite of the Euclidean point toward which I now achingly move. But in the old days, the traveler would see his path bifurcate and stretch two, far indeterminate horizons along with it. He would have to pick which of two ways he ought to go and his decision was momentous. The journeyman could, for example, be a talentless wanderer, choose the right fork in the road, meet the devil—and walk back haunting folk with your guitar, like a Robert Johnson. Or he might be impinged upon by spetres or Hecate herself.

Even I could recognize the irony here.

Today the Crossroads is a dead metaphor. A locus of fate transforms into cliché. Today we move through liminal spaces. You can't predict your fate simply by picking a horizon and heading that way. There is nowhere to stop and get your bearings before moving ahead. A pathway is a synonym—*pseudonym?*—for labyrinth. When the terrain is invisible, the cartographer goes hungry.

I got out of the car to stretch my legs a bit on the irony. Almost immediately I felt an itching sensation on both my arms and discovered vaguely star-shaped welts rising there, suddenly removing me from the world the way the first drops of rain take you from a clear day. At the same time, I heard a low droning, as of bees congregating, somewhere through the tightly-grown birch trees.

I got back into the car, rolled the windows up and turned on the air conditioning, but the itching continued. I took an allergy pill and waited twenty minutes. The bumps on my arms increased in size, bulging outward like sacks of pennies. Seeing there was no escape from this unknown allergen, I once again left the car and decided to find the source of the sound.

Although I moved through closely-packed trees, I could tell others had preceded me from cigarette stubs and the occasional boot-print. Soon I came upon piles of pants, jeans, shirts and underclothes. The marks on my arms shook like jelly though they were hard as teeth to touch. I felt them being pulled outward by an unseen force. At length I came upon a yellow clearing whose dead grasses sloped down toward a bog.

At least a hundred naked people danced by the bog's edge with weird aquatic motions, twisting themselves about like pieces of meat tossed by a wave. They stumbled and swirled around and past each other in ecstasy or the limits of pain, kicking up peat with their feet and hands, clawing and flipping about. Their bodies were covered in fleshy stalks about four or five inches in length, which protruded from star-shaped red patches ending in purplish bulbs. One man I cannot forget was rolling on the floor wildly, seemingly trying to snap the growths off of the eyelids where they had taken root. I do not recall feeling anything aside from scientific—perhaps child-like wonder—In his *Torture Garden*, Octave Mirbeau wrote that *flowers have no time for sentiment*, and there is an alignment here between that poetic observation and my overall state at that puzzling moment. I will leave the determination of the significance, if any, of this correlation for the most qualified Strangerists.

The buzzing that had drawn me there came from thousands of swollen bees hovering and sitting on the towering protrusions on the dancers' bodies, plant-like but most reminiscent of the strigose hair of a whale-sized insect, had such existed. These bees were the same type of workers, with their modified ovipositors, that had gone missing in the area; only their bodies were bloated to the size of small mice. The bees appeared to be gathering something from the fleshy stalks, as though harvesting pollen from pistils. Their purplish-black stripes rippled weirdly like the flashing of squids and I realized the bog itself was rippling to an invisible tide in the same rhythm.

I was thinking that Mainstream informatics presumes a stable ontology, wherein lies the possibility, at least, of knowing the properties and workings of this ontology in an exhaustive fashion. I was thinking Mainstream Informatics would have to go the way of the Mythological Crossroads ... Or, even better—Bierce's unsolved, plural-yet-singular *Occurrence.*

The bumps on my arms reddened, rose, extended like pitiful Tyrannosaurus limbs. I scratched and they grew at the scraping of my fingernails as though nourished by bruising. The itching increased in intensity and I felt compelled to run toward the bog and douse myself in the fetid water. Sweaty dancers squirmed around me like chunks of slimy food digested in a gut, filling the poisonous air with broken laughter. I heard their words borne in snatches on the dry wind, as though passing under a spinning fan whose blades each had its own voice, some distorted beyond recognition. I had the sense that although some individuals were repeating and sharing the same expressions, most were "fumbling," so to speak. As if trying to remember a password fifteen-years-unused for an AOL account, or, surprised at finding their front door locked, painstakingly enumerating a list of places they might've dropped their keys on the walk home. Their utterances accumulated one atop another, at first with some of the order as found in Ravel's *Bolero*—then crossing, catching together in the chaotic way of pubic hairs fallen—somewhere between thousands of opening and closing zippers—into Grand Central Station urinals:

> *"Flocks of abyss caw empty world ... FORGET FOREVER ... SAY THE WORD & THE WORD IS OVER ... The transmitter transmits ... b'thnakl-thog ... If Guns Were Outlawed, Only In-Laws Will Have Bite One Gut One Freedomination ... spits phlegmy spirit out his mouth ... Johnny Yen again ... bone ask and perceive ... HELLO? Mission is Sub ... h'laqtra-kratom ... Scalpy ... Yankee ... Hastur ... Foxtrot ... Yog-Sothoth ... Hotel ... Fungi ... Foxclot ... The Revolution Wilting Telesummoned! ... n'ksoihet'l ... AMPERS& ... cresting recollapsing shoeshine ... Scald the Skald, Skald Scalp the Skullversion ... Fall to pissing, drop to parts, each part deeper to fall into ... Erogenous Starslave Wet Dwarves ... achslpolick ... Knock-Knock! Slop-Slop! Do you mindcontrol? Yes, please, who's lair?"*

Then the contorted people began chanting the same grammatical noise, all at once and from wherever they stood, lay or crawled, the obscenely hirsute stalks vibrating like reindeer-bells along their quivering bodies. "HELLO?" they said, over and over. The signal Thomas Edison told us to use when answering a telephone call. It's not a word, simply the human vocalization of the buzz, beep or click: transmission has reached receiver.

Returning to Rhymeshead: this "HELLO?" was intoned with intense focus of a mantra of the most numinous import. Once everyone had been locked onto repeating that single question for ten or more minutes, they suddenly went from there to jointly recite a litany similar to the following (I more than paraphrase):

> "*HELLO?*
> *Yes, HELLO!*
> *HELLO again, then! Listen:*
> *For the purpose of these words alone,*
> *Our corpse is hair, thwarted into diverse anatomies.*
> *Headless, a body-shaped head of perverse hair.*
> *Only by these words as these words,*
> *And not others:*
> *Our corpse is hair, holed, colded into black acephalic hair.*
> *Headless, anthropomorphic headless head of hair,*
> *Birthmarks, cancers, guts of hair and skulled.*
> *HELLO?*
> *O Yes, HELLO! SCALP, NOW:*
> *Ragged-Veined, Fat-Bone-Scalping-Bile-Eyed-Heartvalved-Muscle-Scalping—*
> *In the grasping yanking tornado of these words of torn,*
> *New forms arise, examples senseless depart and arrive,*
> *Such as Skeleton-murder. Such as Literal Communal-Corpse Possibility.*
> *Next gathering, purely for the purpose of these being the words that are the words the next gathering,*
> *Messages mating:*
> *Abyss flocks capriole in bacterial pools of missing cradles.*
> *Forget forever: Say the word and the word is over.*
> *The word now the sound GOOD-BYE!*
> *The sound now the word BYE-BYE.*"

I understood immediately (as one does a threat of murder, gun-barrel precariously paired with your sweaty forehead) that the words of this half-song/half-babble were unimportant, thus the reference to a succeeding conventicle on completely unrelated topics. The chant was orderly but disconnected, stuttered, in = no key, notes ranging across the twelve-tone scale randomly as drops in a blood spatter. Strangely, part of me wanted *to join in with them*—a new emotion—Cognitive Dissonance, with its piranha-teeth and soft bordello hands, was alternately chewing at and massaging the fringes of my skull. I forced my mouth shut and planned on hurling myself into the bog, praying for the itching to stop—when I saw the holes in the rippling watery ground, each a terrible abyss that spiked my eyes with sharp emptiness, the nothing at the too rotten to be rotten centerlessness of the universe.

The distended bees were flying in and out of the holes as from a hive. Some purplish light belched deep below the reedy surface. I looked in a nightmarish fog at the sacciform stalks swaying on my arms, depending from my chin and neck.

The small yellow-and-black striped vectors flew to me, perching on the dark, bulbous tips of my flesh where it grew in little towers from my arms, my face and neck. I felt their mandibles and legs scratching, the stalks expanding, the shrill cachinnations sifting through my pounding head.

Like a monster strong enough to scalp a man's head nude with its hands, I tore the growths from my arms and face and tossed them aside. I ran, and it seemed like *"objects were represented by their colors only; circular horizontal streaks of color"* until my asthma collapsed me on a brown, rocky knoll. I lay there sweating, gasping, bleeding amidst buzzing and howling laughter merged together like the voice of a mad perpetual motion machine. The bees did not follow.

Now I know why the dancers laughed. I removed the starry *growths* from my body. But I could not remove what was already *growing in me*, what the missing bees brought and injected into the allergic protrusions, those monstrous channels for incomprehensible information. I am full of holes, like the surface of the Rhymeshead bog. I am bloated with *caligo.*

And for the first time in my life, I feel that the world is letting me belong in it.

I check the bookstores regularly, and I can confirm that "An Occurrence at Owl Creek Bridge" continues to be reprinted in anthologies of all kinds, old and new. I believe it will be in print as long as there is print, and available online while the internet lasts.

Across North America, bees have not stopped leaving their colonies bereft of workers. Beekeepers are finding those that don't get away refuse to be kept, dying in their hives rather than make honey, or to pollinate the almond, cherry, and other crops of farmers in general. In the last six months alone and on average, beekeepers have lost more than 45% of their colonies. The Honey Bee Depopulation Syndrome (HBDS) spreads, raging with losses. In desolate, liminal places, purple light erupts to the surface of swampy waters, in time to the penetrations, the plungings of information-mad, runaway *Apis mellifera.*

Allergies are on the rise. Recent reports indicate food allergies alone have increased by 65% over the last year. Theories abound, from global warming to an obsession with cleanliness rendering the immune system rabid and delinquent. Doctors are seeing more patients with extreme reactions to unknown triggers, and hitherto unseen rashes of varying bizarre shapes, from the simply tubular to calciform, to weird, ornate strands of lenticular skin.

At the same time, a just-released National Health Survey indicates that 1-in-80 children, ages 3 through 17, have been diagnosed with autism spectrum disorder (ASD). This is a near *doubling* of reported autism diagnoses confirmed in the Survey's the prior year–wherein 1-in-45 children had been confirmed with ASD. Strangerists are quick to point out this means that 4 percent of *diagnosed* children in the U.S. are currently living with autism. This data is useful in pointing to an undeniable trend in the growth of spectrum-related disorders. And it doesn't even take any adults, such as myself, into account. Soon enough we'll be legion. There are more and more of us spreading over the globe nightly. Write the Center for Disease Control (CDC) if you want further details. No, better: Step outside and look up toward the stars and close your eyes. That is more not exactly the opposite of the truth.

Errant Bees, Allergies, and Autism. OH MY!

I worked days on that joke, so maybe someone would get a laugh. I tried. In any case, I won't try again. Because I have received the signal directly from the transmitter. It calls when calls is the word used to communicate that It calls. What is It? I don't care. Some call it a dark god or a predatory anti-*destinary* woken from incalculable star-long slumbers. Some vestige of childhood religious indoctrination. Fine. Let the Strangerists theorize all day. It doesn't matter. Only because these words are these words, I say the words I learn new songs.

It is preparing bodies to receive the final packet of information. For me, it comes easily. I'm grateful for it. This may even be happiness, I don't know. I've spoken of never quite feeling like a *real* human being. Now there's no need to know. Those who do nothing but scream in corners; who like nothing more than rocking back and forth; you there, repeating the same phrases over and over, incapable of recognizing an Uncanny Valley, barely emanating the same flat affect toward your mother (who loves you with all her heart) and the bus driver (who doesn't give two shits); you frowning men like me, who don't understand people, and disappear when you close your front doors behind you: You will be the lucky ones, soon. You will share a world for the first time in your lives. Imagine *belonging*. I know you can't, right this moment, while you're still expected to be as minimally awkward a human as possible.

Most of you will take it hard. It will be torture, your slow birth into inhumanity.

Especially those of you with love in your hearts, with warmth and comforting friends and family. Even those of you who hate your families, your jobs, no prospects, no future—even *you* will face pains I cannot fathom. When you are receiving the gift of being the receiver.

You may be merely sneezing now, just a little itchy. But soon the whole world will be another, much colder planet. Soon all will hear the buzzing of the Human Being Depopulation Syndrome (HBDS), scratch unrepentant galaxies rising on their bodies, feel stalks bursting from hands clasped in prayer, meet prodigal bees urging you to dance, filling you with blackest signal, returning to the transmitter where nothing goes, where I go now . . . Will I *occur*?

Anything's possible.

BRIDGE

THE ARGUMENT:

MAY YOU DANCE THROUGH YOUR DISASTERS
WITH YOUR EYES BLINDFOLDED SHUT
WITH THE PAGES OF MY STORIES
THAT KILLED SOME WITH LAUGHING
AND OTHERS WITH DISGUST
MAY WE DANCE THROUGH OUR DISASTERS
WITH OUR EYES BLINDFOLDED SHUT
UNTIL THE DARK BURNS TO ENLIGHTENMENT,
OUR AMPUTATIONS PAPERCUTS

A CURSE FROM THE UNIVERSE
CANNOT SIMPLY BE UNMADE

NO.

NOT THE WAY SUNLIGHT CAN TRANSFORM
INTO CHEAP UMBRELLA SHADE—

NO!

NOT IN ANY SONG OR FORM.

THE PURPLE WORD

EVERYONE I EVER LOVED OWNED A CAT.

I'd never thought about it until recently, now that I'm the only human left at the "Crumble-Down Farm," as the local children once called it.

My mother, difficult but always there for me, had an orange tabby named Charlie who seemed to be living his first life in a feline incarnation. She had to lift him up onto windowsills because he wasn't sure how to jump, and I once saw him fall off a table and land on his side. How he loved her, too. He was a marmalade shadow always at her side, even, she told me, keeping her lap warm while she sat on the toilet.

And Benjamin was my father's obese, white, deaf cat who shed rugs weekly and kept his tongue sticking out stiff as a little pink depressor. Benny was an affectionate, stupid animal who never used his claws on anything, not even furniture. He liked to play with grapes.

There are so many more I could name, each different than the next, cats belonging to my best childhood friend, my aunt Willa, both my grandmothers. And Joy's cat Winston … She was a little Tonka truck with a thick African wildcat tail, and skin missing on her flank where some cruel boy had thrown hot tar. Everything about Winnie was round—marble green eyes, neckless head, paws. When Joy and I would leave her alone too long, she'd grow angry and swipe at our feet and shins upon our return. But then she'd curl up with us later in Joy's bed, making our sleep purringly calm and warm…

These trivial details are so important to me here in the attic. I roll them round me like a kitten with balls of yarn, trying to lose myself in the unwound threads of lost lives. If I stare at the snow that's fallen through the roof, I see the cats so clearly like pictures projected on a white screen.

Everyone I ever loved is gone.

They were in town at The Egg Festival when the blue sky was overwhelmed by an infinity of stunning purple. An impostor sky.

A stomach virus saved me from this plague. I was home sick at the farm and saw it through my window. It moved like a time-elapsed movie of an approaching storm, abnormally quick and arching itself over the horizon until there was just a glowing purple above the world. It shone bright as sunlight, but the sun was nowhere in sight. It only lasted a few days but was so immense it seemed years from end to end. It brought cold with it too, and that first day was like January in Maine. When it left I heard dogs howling all over the countryside, then the howls got dimmer and dimmer. They left for some other dog place.

But the cats stuck around.

The farm is so quiet. I like that. The old gray wood doesn't creak, it's so pliant and spongy beneath my heavy steps. It makes me feel I could lay my head anywhere and sleep, as if the whole place is one great bed. I'm on the highest hill in the county with a view of the land all around. There are plenty of trees around the house, and overgrown grasses in the summer, to make me feel far from civilization. The nearest town is five miles away. I don't know if anyone lives there any longer. There's a highway close, but it never bothered me. It sounded like the ocean.

Last month was November. After the impostor sky left and the blue returned, the leaves died. I let them fall and pile up all over the yard, flakes of red, orange, green and yellow, like the down of an enormous tropical bird. One day at sunset, I sat on the back porch in great-grandmother's rocker, listening to the zombies complain down in the valley. I watched the leaves shiver, the trees scrape back and forth. And then I saw a small white and black cat I'd spotted around a lot, walking funny along the tree line fifty feet away. As my eyes followed him I realized he hobbled because he was missing one back leg.

It must've come off in a fox trap.

He disappeared behind a log pile without looking over his shoulder.

The next day I did something I'd never done before: I went into town to get cat food. I knew it would be difficult because by then I was sure everyone I knew was walking around dead. When the wind blew strong from the south I could smell them rotting and hear their moans. They seemed to be trying to articulate a particular word their ruined mouths couldn't make clear. It sounded something like:

Ooh ooh ooh ooh ooh...

Somewhere in that hellish sound was Joy's voice. She was at The Egg Festival with the others. Once she got her finger caught in our Chevy's door. The howl she made. I never wanted to hear it again. Now I strained my ears to find it among the wailing as they shambled below Crumble-Down farm.

It was like trying to pick out one raindrop's splash in a thunderstorm.

How did I deal with this? What was I thinking?

A white paw batting black grapes across a pink rug... a marmalade tail… two lidless marble eyes rolling across my mind, the slices of darkness in the middles spinning like the propellers of a plane that can't take off…

The road to the store was deserted as the sun slid down. The Egg Festival signs hung with bright pictures of Chickens from poles along the way. There was a poster for an omelet-eating contest in Gentry's Mercantile's window. I parked and saw the store's front door swing back and forth.

No breeze.

Something had just walked through.

Out or in?

I entered slowly. Vegetables were stacked in display cases, some covered with colorful mold resembling coral reef formations. Cans lined the shelves orderly as barcodes. Rotten eggs were on prominent display in a small refrigerator. A thin layer of sawdust like wooden snow had been recently disturbed by shoe tracks. Each step I took announced itself with a thud. I walked back to the front and looked out at an empty street.

I'd never looked for pet food at Gentry's before, but I figured it must be in the back.

I passed the frozen meats when I heard ice falling.

Mr. Gentry wriggled from a refrigerated display case the size of a child's coffin. His skin peeled off in lasagna strips, tiger-striping his face deep purplish red. One eye was missing. The other gaped unblinking as a cave mouth. I ran to the back and grabbed a case of cat food. When I turned round he was halfway out, massive torso hanging down towards the floor and head just an inch above it. He'd forced his three hundred pound, six-foot-five body into the five-foot long frozen meat case. His legs were smashed and twisted completely around and he'd got his toes caught under something.

"Needed cold," Gentry coughed wetly. He lashed out at the ground and thick bloodstreams dripped from his open mouth.

I stepped back in shock, more at hearing him speak in that state than seeing him that way. The shelf came down. Steel bars cut hot into my back as I hunched over and shielded my head with my hands.

Through the ringing in my ears I could hear footsteps.

I shifted into a push-up position beneath my burden. Sticky blood ran into my eyes and I could feel the lumps growing on my head.

One Mississippi…

Something scratched at the floor before me.

Two Mississippi…

Moaning from above.

Three Mississippi…

I pushed myself up and scrambled out from under the shelf, tripping over scattered cans and standing up right before stumbling over the mess of Gentry's head.

A case or two had landed on it and one eye lolled like a panting tongue. Another loose can had hurled smack into the middle of his over-ripe face and the bottom stuck out of there, where mouth and nostrils had been. Even then a noise percolated in his throat and his bloody scabby hands were like two red crabs having epileptic fits, clawing at the floor with overlong nails.

Don't panic. Think: white whiskers tipped black at the ends… gray ears erect like teepees… soft body warm as cup of tea curled on lap…

Twin headaches burst out from the epicenters of my temples. I picked up another case and walked toward the streetlight shining through the front door.

One foot away from the exit I remembered the footsteps…

I spun around to an empty room.

Something tapped me on the scalp. A blood-drop. A widening dark stain spread across the ceiling. I heard footsteps again. They came from above.

Floorboards hit me seconds before the bodies. Two women with dead meat faces knocked me on my back. They didn't seem to notice me as they faced each other over my legs. They lay on their bellies, each on a pillow of red guts spilling from their open stomachs. Without lifting their skeletal arms they bit at each other's mouths. No tongues. No lips. I'd never seen lesbians before. The stench of their hisses and grunts was unbearable.

I shifted my hands behind me and pulled myself to the door. The movement caught their attention and they tried to bite my legs, but when I saw I couldn't sneak away I jumped up, knocked them down, and ran to the truck. Night had fallen, blue and cool as a freshly washed sheet.

About to turn the key in the ignition, I asked myself what I was doing in *this* nightmare.

I wanted to feed those cats. Small mouths lined with sharp teeth. Rough tongues coated in medicinal saliva.

Looking up I saw lights in the houses, and figures shuffled back and forth past the windows. I heard things crashing to the ground in the apartments. Still bodies must've started stirring at once. I took a crowbar from the truck, determined to get that food.

It seemed hundreds of lost shadows crossed the street, thrown by zombies in the windows. I walked through them to the store and kicked open the door, crowbar in hand.

As other doors creaked open and doorknobs rattled in the street behind me I breathed deep and plunged in.

The two fallen women feasted on Gentry's entrails by the frozen meat display case. They ignored me, and I managed to get a lot of cases to the truck before I could see the rest, coming for me like sleepwalkers from all directions. They were a block away.

Everyone I'd ever known.

I sped off as their strangled calls rose in the cold night where chimney smoke once coiled and broke apart.

Ooh ooh ooh ooh ooh ... Were they crying "blue," asking the sky why it had turned on them?

The next day I stored the food in the attic and put a can out near the porch. I found myself in the rocker waiting for Peg Leg to come again. I laughed with a strange sense of amusement, as I realized I'd given him a name. I'd never named anything before, and I used to wonder how the pet owners I knew chose from so many options. Now I saw: Names just appear from nowhere, like purple zombie-making skies.

The pain in my head and my sides shut me up fast.

He did not come that day. November bugs laid their eggs in the food and I had to throw it out.

The next morning I sat with my coffee on the porch. There was a trace of coming rain in the air, so the screen doors gave off a pleasant metallic odor. I watched an old clothesline suspended from the third story to a tall oak tree guarding the border between the yard proper and the woods. A faded red scarf hung by the side of the forest, clothespinned to the line. It was put there to dry by my mother. It might've been the last thing I'd seen her do.

A rustling drew me from the cloth. I raised the shotgun I now kept by me at all times. A cat approached the fresh food I'd put out when I woke. The cat sniffed the ground, head moving side to side and rubbing his chin on the earth as he crawled, like a solider advancing under enemy fire.

His coat was confederate gray but it might've once been white. Under his nose was a black mustache smudge. I wondered if he was blind, as he didn't look up at me, but seemed to have found the food by scent alone. He ate rapidly. Then thunder pealed, and he raised his head with taut masticated ears. He had no eyes. A shiny BB gun pellet was lodged in one socket.

The rain fell hard and he zigzagged in a crazy pattern toward the trees, more like a fly without wings than a cat. The sky turned the color of his coat.

But my thoughts ran to friends and family. Perhaps the rain would melt them away like a herd of wicked witches of the West. Or perhaps having forgotten what rain is they would seek its source and come up the hill to look for it, finding me instead of clouds.

Why not? Weirder things have happened.

#C!

The days grew colder. It became my daily ritual to sit on the back porch, waiting for cats to get the food I'd put ten feet from my seat. I'd wait with anticipation to see who would arrive, cleaning my shotgun to kill time. I found if I left five or six cans I could get as many as ten cats to come up to the house. Sometimes it was Bandito (as I started to call the mustached cat). Other times he'd not appear for days. I also named Pickle, Jester, Streak, and Crush, orange tabbies like my mother's Charlie; three Calicos called Mike, Jesse, and Bombay; gray tigers (Lee and Max were my favorites), and a striking dark chocolate brown cat I think belonged to a friend of my cousin. I called him Friend Lee. They tended to remain quiet. I didn't see Peg Leg for weeks.

Then one frosty December morning I woke with him sitting on my chest.

His eyes were a pale violet I'd never seen on any feline. Of course, I never looked face to face with a cat before. I pet them now and again. But the cats weren't mine, and you don't look eye-to-eye with what isn't yours. But still, they seemed unusual.

He must've come in through the torn screen door on the back porch, although he would've had to be smart enough to figure out how to lift the loose piece of screen up before slipping in. I couldn't help but think he wanted something from me, and was waiting for me to understand.

"What do you want?" I asked, for the first time talking to an animal, as I'd seen so many people do before.

We locked eyes.

Black slices of darkness in the middles of his eyes like propeller blades on a plane resting between flights…

I wasn't sure what to do. Though I'd been around cats plenty, I'd never picked one up. They even made me a little uncomfortable. Winston slept near me, but only when Joy was there to stroke her and make her happy. My presence in the bed was incidental.

As if sensing my discomfort, Peg Leg jumped off. I heard claws jutting from three feet patter on the wood floor, and the hinges on the back-porch screen door move as he slid out. I didn't see him again for a long time.

The first week of December, the snow started, slow and light. The house gets frigid at this time, as it's in a real shambles. One afternoon a thud drew me to the attic. Part of the roof had fallen in. Squirrels nested in a corner next to a steamer trunk filled with old curtains and doilies. I thought the house might not last the winter once it gets going.

Through a hole in the attic roof I noticed a knot of activity down in the town center, where the Queen of the Egg Festival would've been crowned atop a massive hen-shaped float, all yolk-blonde tresses and shell-white skin. On Festival day the sky went purple at two o'clock—an hour before the ceremony—so this would be the first year with no Queen. Now the bodies gathered there, moving more rapidly than I'd seen before, walking in duck-duck-goose circles.

Remember what Gentry said?

Needed cold.

They wanted it to snow.

I moved the cans of cat food to the back-porch, where they would be shielded from the wind and snow. I would then sit behind the screen door in the rocker with my coffee and watch from that warmer vantage point. None of these cats figured out how to get through the screen door like Peg Leg, so I didn't worry about them getting in. Peg Leg seemed smarter than the rest. But I didn't know cats enough to be sure.

To my surprise the number of visitors to my porch increased as snow fell in earnest. I worried there wouldn't be enough cases to last the winter. The cat food was looking pretty good to me now as my own supplies dwindled.

I always liked Crumble-Down Farm in December; the gray wood outhouse, the tool-shed, the caved-in barn, the wet, black trees covered in the same blanket of snow, the yard a picture of quiet stillness. But now intermittent cat-movements invaded the calm. Paw prints Rorschached the snow, and I heard their steps up the porch stairs, and aluminum cans clanging into each other as they ate in a hurry.

It was a strange sight from the third story window. I saw the dark shapes of the cats set in the whiteness below, some still and washing up or scratching, others jumping after squirrels or birds, and most going somewhere unknown to me.

Usually I didn't look toward town, but I'd hear them, like demented back-up singers in some dead pop star's insipid love song.

Ooh ooh ooh ooh ooh ooh ooooh . . .

Near month's end I saw fewer cats as heavy snowstorms swept over this part of Connecticut. The town was nothing but a blank valley and the moans stopped—or else I mistook them for the wind living in the skeleton trees. I imagined the yard was drowned in all the envelopes lying around the post office, great piles of white that hid messages forever undelivered. Congratulations, greetings, apologies, love . . . The snow drifted five feet high in some places there, which I guessed made cat-travel difficult, if not impossible. And the other night I spied a fox eating frozen cat food that had sat untouched for days. I let him finish it; then I threw out the cans and stopped the attempts at feeding.

Until this morning.

My isolation must've got to me because I spoke out loud to myself for the first time ever (So many firsts lately: First cat fed! First thing named! First lesbian sighting! First staring contest with a cat! First zombie knocked over outside a video game!). My exact words were:

"Thank God, they need me. God bless those cats. Thank God. Thank God . . ."

See, now I had cats like everyone I ever loved . . . and I knew a little of how they must have felt having *their* cats, and it meant that in some way I still shared my life with those people, like they weren't really gone.

There was a herd . . . I counted at least twenty. Some reddish, some black, some brown, some white and barely distinguishable from the landscape. They crept up the hill, no doubt risking sinking with each step. I thought I recognized some, but not all. I figured they were starving smaller cats—They had to be light as balsa to tread on such fragile ground. I got the food out in expectation of their arrival.

Not long after I saw Peg Leg.

I'd gone to the cellar for some dwindling firewood. I was about to hit the attic, to use fallen roof for tinder, when the cat stepped out from behind a rusty old wheelbarrow. He didn't say anything, just looked at me with those violet eyes, now dyed a deeper purple.

He had a muzzle of blood.

I put down the logs.

"I bet you've been living down here all this time, haven't you?" I asked.

If he'd stuck around the house it would've been easy for him to get down to the cellar. After all, he knew how to get through the hole in the screen door, and there were mice to eat in the walls.

Peg Leg hobbled closer and sat down, looking up at my face.

"What do you want?" I asked, stooping down to his eye level.

He kept staring at me. Then he got up and went over to the trapdoor that led outside.

I followed him and opened it outward. Snowy air blew in and stung my face. The cat climbed up the ladder leading to the eastern side of the house with difficulty, pulling himself up by front paws and swinging one back leg after him. I followed when he'd reached the top.

We stood in a few inches of snow. That side of the house is protected by an awning where there was a porch ages ago. All round the sheltered area were five and six foot high walls of glimmering snow.

And the cats.

Fifteen lay at our feet glazed with frost. Friend Lee was missing, and the cat with no eyes, too. They were huddled together, as if still trying to keep warm in death.

At the rate the snow came down, they'd be buried in hours.

"Is this what you wanted me to see?" I asked Peg Leg.

He looked at me with a quiet I could feel. It choked my heart.

Raised his little face to the endless dark air.

I saw the herd of unknown cats I'd expected. They crawled to the awning as though drawn to Peg Leg, but something wasn't right.

Cats have heads and eyes and tails and legs. These were just oval mounds of fur moving over the snow.

The wall before me burst open in a cocaine sneeze explosion as a co-worker of mine staggered out. I'd thought the auburn hair atop his head was a rusty tabby I used to see sometimes. But it was Vitolo the guitar-playing mailman walking through the snow.

Under it.

They got stronger with the cold, and now they had enough energy to make it up the hill…

I lifted my shotgun and fired. The shot went through a gaping hole in his chest and into the snowbank behind him. He stopped as though startled. Purplish-black blood sprayed from the snow as another zombie appeared behind the first. It was a little girl with no head. She kept treading forward, her pale flesh flapping like she was made of tattered surrender flags.

I raised the gun and pumped it. The girl pushed Vitolo forward. He slid onto the gun so the barrel stuck out his back, and threw blue arms around me. If shit could take a shit, he smelled like that. I thought he winked at me but it was a black beetle crawling around in his eye. He tried to speak but had no lower jaw and wretched a spluttering sob, repeated over and over like one stuttered word. I kicked his feet out from under him and he fell spread-eagled, taking the shotgun down with him.

Its barrel pointed up at my mouth.

The headless girl tumbled onto Vitolo's body and the one finger left on her tiny dead hand curled around the trigger.

I stepped back and threw a hand out to knock the barrel away.

Wave good-bye, hand.

The shot clanged in my head. My face stung as though a thousand angry bees had been loosed from the barrel. I started down the ladder and tried to use both hands. One was a phantom and the floor came up hard against my cheek.

Above, the zombies broke through the pristine snow. Their putrid shadows fell in first and then their bodies. I heard a broken melon noise as one crashed headfirst.

I ran for the door and up to the attic. Crumble-Down Farm's spongy gray steps shook and groaned. I'd never treated the stairs that way. I felt I was stomping on my mother's face. Noise in Crumble-Down farm! Another first...

I shut the attic door as well as I could. Through the holes in the roof the freezing storm blew against me. Snow lay in heaps round the room. I grabbed an old shovel, and piled it against the door. Packing it with one hand was slow painful work.

I couldn't tell how smart they were. Maybe if I'd made it up fast enough, they wouldn't find me.

What about the blood trail from the stump at my wrist?

I sat down, leaned against the snow, and stuck my arm deep into the pile. As a red circle grew round it I felt weary. I put my good hand to my face. It was there, singed by the blast that maimed me.

The snowflakes in the air faded and bits of cold night blew into my eyes until I couldn't see. I grew numb. Fell asleep.

I don't know how much time passed. Something soft hit me on the nose and I jerked awake, throwing my hand out for the gun.

But I had no left hand.

It was Peg Leg. Relief woke me from my daze.

There must be a cat-sized hole somewhere in the shadows.

"What do you want?" I asked him.

He climbed on my chest and put his paws on either side of my face and his nose to my nose. His eyes were so icy, so purple.

Impostor eyes.

I wept. The tears stung my blasted cheeks.

He opened his jaws to speak for the first time and a strange meow came out. It sounded as though he was trying to articulate a human word but had the wrong mouth for it:

Woo woo woo oooh...

He was such an unusual cat. The purple sky must've gotten him the way it got the others. Perhaps it took longer for him to change... I stroked his head and he lay down on my lap. I felt I was being lowered into icy water.

I tried to think, to focus: furry head lapping at toilet water...

Mother ... purring under a plaid cotton sheet ... Father ... tiny cries at birds outside a window ... Joy ... broken wings versus fangs ... nobody had a dog ... all the dogs got away ...

I heard sodden footsteps on the stairs, and bodies tumbling down steps ...

Now the zombies have reached my door. Their nails and bones scrape the wood. Their fists pound. They want in. They want me to share myself with them. So far the door has opened a half-inch or so as they push it against my body's weight and the packed snow.

And I know what Peg Leg wanted all this time. To draw them to me. And I can hear them answering his call. I was never close enough to hear what they were saying so clearly.

The word is *You*.

That's me.

And here I am.

BRAIN SCRAM

i
CALLED TIME.

Martin Box, Private Investigator, looked out the window at the stormy green sky. Across the bay, the Statue of Liberty was lost in a verdigris smear. Three days ago, inexplicably, the sky had turned every color but blue; the papers were declaring the end of the world. Business slowed down, as apocalypse trumped mystery.

Some editorials said it was a doom foretold long ago and others that it was a case of man's own doing. Martin thought two suspects weren't enough to solve the crime of existence. Things could be equally random and fated, moving into completely unexpected yet predetermined moments, like a game of cards, which requires necessary rules to be a game at all, and luck to be a different game each time it's played. Or, more troubling, there could be something else at work, separate from free choice or destiny, a shadow metaphysical order. Just because you couldn't see it anywhere didn't mean it wasn't everywhere.

But Martin wondered where these thoughts were going to get him. He prepared to close up early when a folded ironing-board of a man entered his office, quiet as blood. He wore a suit like tattered rain; his belt was black and shoes brown. His stubbly face was too small for his rusty handlebar moustache. He had a rash-like red mark on his forehead. He smelled like whiskey. His dark eyes were piercing, confidential, and troubled. *You're my last chance*, those eyes said.

"How can I help?" Martin said.

"You're my first choice," the man said. "Let's start with a last name."

"Briar is the name, Devin Briar," the man said, pacing as though cold. "I'm something of a fanatical book collector."

Martin sat and let Briar spin about the room, unconsciously examining the bookshelf of case files and the edge of the desk with long, nailbitten fingers.

"There's one book in particular I've spent years looking for— It's called simply *The Greater T.E.*—Tea Etiquette. The book is extremely rare and written by an anonymous author in the 18th century. I've never actually seen the book, but I met a man once who had traveled the world over, who saw a copy and memorized the first page ... he was kind enough to recite some of the text to me, and one phrase in particular stuck out: Dorglingk."

"What's it mean?"

"I don't know. But recently, I discovered there is a graffiti artist using this name on the Weast Side of Brooklyn."

"That's a particularly rough area," Martin said. "You know the expression: When East meets West, and neither one merges, all your whistles come out dirges. What's a man like you—a collector of fine books—doing on the Weast Side?"

Briar paced a seismograph waltz across the room.

"A book of urban photography recently came out—and I saw a picture of the tag name there."

"So you want me to find out who the graffiti artist is, so that I can discover where he or she found this word Dorglingk, and therefore lead you to *The Greater T.E.*?"

"That's it exactly. I'd heard you were good."

"I still am. You must really want this book, Mr. Briar. If you haven't heard, the world is ending."

"The world is always ending, Mr. Box. It's called time."

"Mine will cost you."

"If you find the book, I'll double your fee," he said, eyes piercing, confidential, reflecting a threatening purple sky.

11
DUKE LORD KING

Legend had it that Brooklyn's Weast Side, home to freaks, criminals and corpses, was built on a clown graveyard. It had no street names. It's not that urban planners didn't assign them, but the questionable citizens of the Weast had removed all the signs so consistently, the city stopped putting replacements up. This made offering and receiving directions difficult and meaningful travel virtually impossible for strangers to the dangerous neighborhood.

Walking on foot, Martin consulted his Blumenkrank, a sort of official-unofficial map to the area he'd once found on the body of a man pinned to a nameless street by a bradawl through his ears. The Blumenkrank helped him navigate deeper into the Weast, passing car-wreck avenues, abandoned warehouses and burned-out homes while a transmission-fluid sky rippled in muted reds and browns.

He was looking for taller buildings, water towers, and any other structures where a self-respecting graffiti artist would try to leave their mark. It didn't take long to find an empty factory facing a blank billboard over what used to be an adult video store. Martin climbed up dark, trashy stairways to the fourth floor. The room was bare but for a few broken industrial sewing machines and expired rat traps. Martin smashed the black glass out of a window, raised his binoculars, and waited.

Night came on like a cyclops' eyepatch. After a few fruitless hours Martin heard footsteps on the stair. He slid to a shadowy corner. An upright casket of a man entered the room. His wide head seemed to hang from a tall shock of red hair. He wore a long raincoat that trailed behind him like a bridal train. He had a small telescope in one hand and a machete in the other. Martin recognized him as Jammer Stropf, a fellow PI and affable sociopath.

"Jammer," Martin said, stepping out of the gloom.

An ex-mercenary who'd fought for seventy-eight sides in thirteen African nations, he didn't even flinch.

"Martin," he said. "You on this Dorglingk case too?"

"I guess."

"Wow, Duke Lord King really hedges his bets. I hope he's paying us both the same."

Martin nodded. Duke Lord King was a notoriously wealthy eccentric who lived in a mansion near the water in Bay Ridge. He was rumored to be an accomplished student of transdimensional potencies and supernatural lore. He was also reputed to be a cold-blooded killer when his secrets were on the line. Nobody knew how he got his money and there was only one picture of him extant—a John Dewey High School photo showing a boy with weird eyes like painted pennies and a lycanthropic unibrow. He hadn't been seen in many years. If Duke Lord King were involved in all this, either Devin Briar wasn't coming clean about the case or he was in something over his head and didn't know it.

"No point us both staking out the same location," Martin said. "I'll see you later Jammer."

"You can bet on it," Jammer said, and hunched down in front of the window.

iii
A sentimental Melody

Martin decided to head over to Briar's house and shake him down a little. It was late; the sky was almost a healthy black, just streaked with greens and yellows around the lunar nimbus. Martin drove to Briar's address in the suburbs and found his cottage-like little place, set cozily behind tall bushes and cypress trees.

The lights were on. Martin quietly walked around the back of the house and peered inside.

Briar was pacing his kitchen, a bottle of whiskey in hand. Every few seconds he'd take long, deep gulps. His eyes were lifeless and dark as graves. His brow twinkled with sweat. He froze before a white enamel-topped table, standing straight and still as a broken minute-hand. The bottle dropped from his clutches and shattered on the tile floor.

Briar's head began shaking "no" side-to-side. His ears flapped slowly like puffin wings. Over the years, Martin had seen many strange things—pesky gods, good people turned monstrous and murderous spirits. But nothing prepared him for what he saw next.

Briar knelt and slammed his forehead into the floor repeatedly. His face opened like the cargo hold of a C-130 and brains billowed in the opening like superimposed, black and white, slow-motion films of duststorms. The brains fell to the floor with a wet-meat sound Martin could hear through the glass. Liver-colored crab-like legs extended from the two halves and they groped toward each other, finally merging into one eleven-legged entity. This uneven creature then tottered off, dragging its medulla oblongata like a brain-penis, leaving Briar in his stopped-time state.

Martin watched the arthropoid brain poking around in the remnants of the broken bottle, delicately tracing the edges of sharp brown glass with the tip of a leg. It tenderly gathered up the slivers, sat atop them, and began quivering and humming a sentimental melody. This went on for several tense minutes. Clear discharge like tears or saliva suppurated from the cerebral grooves and flooded the whiskey puddle. Slowly, as though nauseous, the brain stood up and inched up Briar's leg and onto his shoulders. It split into two halves again; the legs dissolved and the remaining cortexes slinked up the neck and returned to the head through the ears, disappearing like scarves into a magician's cane. The face closed up.

Briar's red eyes shot open like bullet wounds and he collapsed to the floor.

IV
SPILT MILK

Martin decided to keep his knowledge of Briar's neurological problems to himself. The next morning he returned to the Weast Side, Blumenkranking his way to an abandoned elevated train and spraypainting it himself with the word "Dorglingk." He reasoned this would throw Jammer Stropf off the trail of the graffiti artist while Martin visited other parts of the neighborhood where the real culprit was more likely to strike.

He guessed right. Martin had been sitting on an upside-down plastic crate for hours in an abandoned dance studio that smelled of moral and bladder failure, when a red line appeared on the window, followed by two more straight lines—a backwards letter K. Then a reverse G filled the adjacent window. The graffiti artist was on the roof, leaning over to leave his mark.

Martin raced up filthy stairs, tripping over vials and used condoms, reaching an unlocked door. He pushed it open and spied a man with gray ponytailed hair in a leather jacket and ancient jeans kneeling and too involved in his spraypainting to notice him.

"Hey," Martin said. "I see you."

The man turned around. It was hard to tell if he was surprised or not because one of his eyes was a nipple the color of an embryonic sack. A typical Weast Side freak. He held the can up like mace.

"I just want the book you found the word Dorglingk in," Martin said.

"You can't have it."

"What if I told you there were people who'd kill you to get it?"

"I'd laugh!"

"What if I showed you?"

The man put his hand into his jacket. Martin reached into his blazer and got out his revolver. He prepared to fire when the man pulled out a shot-glass. A milky liquid dripped from his eye into it.

"All right," the graffiti artist said. "But you've made me sad. Sorry, I'm bipolar."

"What's the word mean, anyway?"

"I don't know. I found this weird old book under a dead guy—you know how people are always finding things on corpses on the Weast Side. I took it home and it was a cold night. So I threw it on the fire I had going in an oil drum. But the book didn't burn. All these words popped out of it like fleas jumping off a soapy dog and two of them got me. See?"

He walked over to Martin, rolling up the sleeve of his jacket. His needle-pitted forearm was branded with DORGLINGK.

"Dorglingk hurts," the man continued, walking over to Martin. "But I found if I wrote it over and over the pain would get less. It was like once the word became part of me, it had to be expressed constantly—like a car horn insists on honking when a broken head gets crushed against it. Then I figured out if I wrote it really large, the sting would stay away even longer. I think it wants to take over the world. But the other word is the opposite. It wants to lay low, as if it would disappear forever if I wrote it out. I know that sounds crazy, but that's how it feels."

"Thus the graffiti," Martin said. "But where's the other word that got you?"

"Back of my neck—take a looksee—I haven't been able to make it out."

The man pulled down his jacket and Martin clearly saw the word R'ATDOOKUF lightly etched along his cervical spine. Without realizing it, Martin read the word backwards and forwards, as though he were taking in a landscape that could be approached from an infinite variety of angles, a destination rather than a directional pointer.

"I tell you what," Martin said. "I'll give you a hundred bucks for the book, and some advice: start writing in secret, because there are meaner men than me looking for you right now."

V

SEVERAL SHADOWS

Back at his office, Martin examined *The Greater T.E.* It was black, small and unassuming, like a prayer book. He read the first page:

> *It is hard to untie a knot with fingers crossed. Thus the disciple of The Greater T.E. must perform the rituals without hesitation.*
>
> *As the common written word can also be spoken or thought, so the word of The Greater T.E. can be deed*

made real in the worlds. As [Word Missing] cries:

Here ought, was and will are one. Here distance is the time it takes to stop. Personality is the black back of a mirror, equally everything without reflection's mutable hypocrisy; the curvature of the stars a slide for flesh and tears to darkly roll past rumbling earth. Fate is like several shadows that overlap each other on a white field—do they make one larger shadow or are they a collection of intersecting shades? To the uninitiated these words seem like chattering motion, senseless tangle, the keys of a piano bobbing quietly in a pool.

The remaining pages were covered in odd symbols and words laid out like airport runways.

Here and there were spaces where a word or cipher seemed to be missing. Martin guessed they represented Dorglingk and R'atdookuf, having popped out of the book.

Briar said it was a book about tea etiquette.

Like hell: it was a book of transdimensional interference instructions—ways to change reality.

What Martin hated about magic was the way it rendered clues impotent. The world hung together on the simple, double-sided nature of clues; on connections between smoking guns and dead bodies, open doors and drafts, graffiti and nipple-eyes. Being a detective, Martin thought of his job as a way to make the world clear—not change it, but reveal what was already present. Magic meant things didn't cohere, that the will of a single person could upset the system; or, alternately, that the system involved a method of eliminating the clues to itself, which is to say, the world is self-erasing. But what bothered him most in *The Greater T.E.* was the line about fate, which reminded him of the thought he'd been gnawing when Briar entered his life—that there could be a shadow metaphysical order operating beyond or alongside freedom and destiny, that not only were things not what they seemed, but that *seeming itself* was something alien and unknowable.

True, he could make the whole confusing mess go away with a

phone call. Now that he'd found the book, delivering it to Briar could be the end of the story; but Duke Lord King's involvement made things less black and gray than usual, and he wasn't sure what Briar's crawling brain had to do with it. And he'd rather call off the case than cross Duke Lord King, if that's what he was doing by working for Briar. He needed to know exactly what was going on. He couldn't do that without paying Duke Lord King a visit.

VI
SOMEBODY SCREAMED

As Martin walked carefully manicured avenues to Duke Lord King's mansion, the ochre sky opened like an upside-down tool box. Heavy rain-chunks tinted the ground with hints of iguana, and here and there a drop struck and jiggled like rubber tears. It sounded like rats were dancing atop Martin's umbrella.

He watched his black shoes moving through the umbrella shade, one foot after the other, bone, flesh, cotton and leather traversing time and space together. Were his steps like the motions of a wheel rolled down a slope, or were they his own improvisational contribution to the ever-flowing, jazzy freedom of the world? If everything was determined beforehand, then it was identical to the unchangeable past. The world was like a photograph of itself that existed without the world that had been photographed. On the other hand—

—A man in a long black coat with goggles and tophat condensed out of the greenish haze ahead of Martin, large as a monument, wielding a machete, expertly slicing the solidified drops in two when they fell past his waist.

Before Martin could get out his revolver, Jammer Stropf was upon him.

"Don't make me kill you," Jammer said, holding Martin's arms down on the pavement and sitting astride his chest.

"Okay," Martin said, coughing up a gelatinous raindrop.

"Just give me the book. Where is it?"

"If Duke Lord King wants the book this bad, he wants to be

the only one who has it. He's a collector of knowledge—for it to have value he needs there to be as few people as possible knowing what he knows. If I give you the book, you'll kill me anyway, in case I've already read and understood it. And then you'll search my place in case I made any copies."

Jammer felt *The Greater T.E.* in Martin's blazer with his knee.

"This reminds me of that time in Somalia," Jammer said. "Good times. For me."

He lifted the machete high and looked like he was solving an algebraic equation. Martin thought this was going to be a real chicken-headed ending. Faster than he could say "cluck," the sky darkened to gangrenous green and blackish icicular pieces of frozen atmosphere clattered around them. Jammer looked up for a split second; a twelve-inch sharp spike slammed through Martin's hand—he howled and Jammer looked down—Martin swung the hand hard into the side of Jammer's head, piercing his temple. Jammer fell off Martin and rolled on the ground. Martin grabbed the machete, tossed it over a fence; somebody behind it screamed and he beat it.

VII
THE IMPOSSIBLE HURTS

He'd removed the icy spike from his palm by the time he reached Duke Lord King's place. That Fortean precipitation saved his life, but it had pierced his shooting hand and he was leaving a trail of red spots everywhere he went, which turned a curious purple when blue hail started falling.

The mansion was a massive, white colonial affair with gray gambrel roofs, accessed by wide marble steps set in a monstrous, grassy hill. Martin raced up the steps and under the shelter of the wraparound porch. He leaned against a Doric column to catch his breath and a jittery, wet Devin Briar stepped out of the nearby bushes and confronted him.

"I knew you'd come here. I knew you were working for Duke," he said. "Betraying me." A deep voice was slowly intoning consonant-rich words behind the front door.

"Not so," Martin said. "I came here to get the truth. See, if I'm going to be involved in the unraveling of events, I like to have an idea of the kind of knot I helped loosen, or the noose that's tightening. And you haven't been straight with me. That's okay—I don't expect honesty from everyone—but getting me mixed up the wrong way with Duke Lord King could cost me my life."

"Give me the book, and I'll give you the money I promised."

"You used his first name—Duke. That seems odd."

"He's my brother, if you must know," Briar said. "And he put a curse on me."

"I'm guessing it involves your brain and eleven legs?"

"I see there's no sense hiding anything from you ... yes; thanks to my brother my brain likes to leave my head every now and then. But it's far more terrible than that. My bloodless gray matter rubs its soft belly against broken glass, battery acids, rusty pins, splinters. It gets to understand these aggressive objects from their point of view; it feels for them with their own impenetrable self-centeredness. This feeling should not be possible, and the impossible hurts. It loves pain like graph paper loves a square. It falls oblongata over medulla for the world's off-limits. It wants to hover there with the grief of inert sharp edges. And then it must return to the stale air of the smooth dreaded head, dreaming and pining about serrated angels beyond its skull-gloved grasp. This curse has broken my brain's heart, making me sentimental about things I'd rather avoid if I had the choice. The disconnect between what my brain desires and remembers falling in love with and what I want and remember, grows until my head is like a fire too hot to give warmth. I do not stand in my feet; I wander, lost in my body. Do you know how maddening it is to almost comprehend the aspirations of a tack? And don't get me started on the headaches ..."

"That's one hell of a curse," Martin said.

The muffled chanting behind the door grew louder.

"My brother and I have always been in competition to obtain the rarest transdimensional guidebooks. He particularly wants to keep *The Greater T.E.* out of my hands because it contains a ritual that will allow me to share my curse with another person. I want Duke to suffer as I have.

That's why I need that book, Mr. Box. Do you hear him? He's in the middle of an appeal to The Emptier Spaces now. I know that chant: it enables a man's body to merge inappropriately with the inanimate. It's very useful for spying. This is the best time for me to act, while his energies are directed elsewhere."

"Again, I hear you. But now that I know what you really want the book for, I'm not risking Duke Lord King—"

A Glock pointed at his head interrupted Martin's sentence.

"Oh, it's to be that way is it?" Martin said with annoyance.

"I'm sorry, Mr. Box. Hand it over now."

"All right. But there's something you should know about this version," Martin said, giving it to Briar. "It's missing a few pieces that may affect how it works."

"Don't try and trick me. I've got no time to waste."

Briar inserted a key into the gray door and stepped aside while he opened it; a great gust of dusty wind bellowed out of the house and knocked Martin over. By the time he got up Briar had gone in with the Dorglingk/R'atdookuf-deficient Greater T.E and closed the door.

Martin figured he should just go home when he saw the black form of Jammer Stropf leaping up the marble steps, top hat missing, goggles askew, hair like a roadkill fox, pale bloodied face grisly as a smile, waving the machete Martin had tossed.

Martin tried the doorknob. It turned and he ran into the mansion just as the sky dissolved into a field of rippling bronze. He shut and locked the door behind him, feeling a soft lump on the doorknob. He was in a pale blue living room. There was something wrong about it. The air was hot like breath in an ear. The windows were cloaked by heavy drapes. Devin Briar was standing across the room, on the further side of a doorway, uttering strange syllables from *The Greater T.E.* Martin flicked on a lightswtich and realized it was a human tooth as the chandelier lit up; one of the pendants hanging from it was a knuckle; the doorknob had lips and there was a unibrow dangling from the pendulum of a grandfather clock;

the drapes were fantastically extended eyelids. Now he noticed teeth gleaming everywhere; in the walls, set among the mosaic of the coffee table, where nailheads in the parquet flooring should be. A spleen fluttered mysteriously within a hurricane candle. Other body parts were integrated into different parts of the room; some in ways Martin couldn't quite discern though he knew they were there, the way you know old people are scowling at you from their windows.

"I interrupted him as he was in the process of becoming the room," Briar said. "You can see the results."

A machete blade burst through the front door and a scream from nowhere echoed through the house. Martin felt a bit freaked out. He tried to run past Briar, but a force he couldn't see pushed him back.

"Don't bother," Briar said. "Not while the Krinintente is working."

"What's supposed to happen next?" Martin said, looking for an escape route, clutching the leaky wound in his shooting hand, trying to keep the insistent hacking of the machete from shattering all his nerves.

"I have only to say one more word and the brain nearest to me will develop the eleven-legged affliction," Briar said. "I hope for your sake your brain is not closer to me than Duke's. I can't see where his is, but it must be in the room with you. It's a chance I have to take to get Duke, cursing the wrong person."

Martin ran to the other end of the room and thought he found the brain; it was a cellulite-pocked buttock emerging from a throw pillow. He scrambled about as the door turned to splinters and a deep groan shook the air. He overturned cushions and books and ashtrays and other room-stuff. One by one human bits embedded in the scenery went by under his frantic hands: intestine, fingertips, coccyx, shoulder, nostril, uvula.

"I'm sorry; we have to go forward now," Briar said.

Martin looked at his black shoes. Beneath, he saw a labyrinthine, cloudy pattern in an area rug. He yanked the rug up and tossed it toward Briar just as he uttered the final word to initiate the curse. At the same time the door broke down and Jammer Stropf stumbled in, not looking pretty. He took one step forward and tripped on the rug, which had fallen to the floor in disarray. He got up and turned toward Martin, as an eleven-legged brain jumped out of the rug and onto the machete. It clung tightly, rubbing a gelatinous belly along the vicious edge and humming a love song. Stropf tottered back, eclipsing the doorway, flailing his considerable arm, trying to knock the thing off; Briar suddenly collapsed and pounded his head until his face opened, and a brain scurried out and joined its brother on the machete, harmonizing sweetly. Stropf released the handle and the machete fell to the floor with its strange passengers. Stropf looked at Martin, vengeance and question marks in his eyes. Martin clutched his temples and shouted:

"Run, Stropf! The house isn't safe! After my brain, yours is next!"

Martin dropped to his knees and forced himself to pound his own head into the floor.

Stropf decided he'd better split and ran out the door into an electrical storm, purple lightning now flooding the sky.

While Martin waited for Stropf to flee a little further, he watched the brothers' naked brains entangled in a three-way with the unkind blade. It was hard to tell if they were sharing or fighting for it. Just as Martin decided it was time to get out, a battering-ram of lightning burst through the front of the house and almost obliterated him, bringing fire that spread quickly through the living room, violet flames lapping at furniture, misplaced organs and anatomical features. The brains flung themselves into the fire and throbbed and oozed into one mass, like a sob caught in a giant throat.

Martin looked around, saw no escape. He perceived everything he'd ever done leading up to this instant, but through a tunnel so long he couldn't make it out clearly; his whole life was one Bigfoot sighting. In this moment he teetered on the wobbly, impossible edge of an alternative to the merely random or wholly determined order of things. It tugged at the back of his brain, passed through the tangle of his neurons, rose to the surface of his lips with the urgency of the word a dying man wants to say after his last word. He didn't understand what it meant but he let it go, opening his mouth and whispering:

"R'atdookuf…"

He passed out as the smoke thickened.

The sound of birds cooing woke Martin the next morning. He was alone in Duke Lord King's mansion, surrounded by ashes and pigeons. He crawled out and rolled down the hill past the marble steps and landed on his back at the bottom, looking up at the blue sky, clueless.

②

I can only assume
your head is vestigial.

crazy is my
maiden name.

We are completely demonstrative here. Even the
men join in the breastfeeding...

A cemetery
~~up~~
waiting for
deceased fire
to set
destruction
loose.

Cemetery bombs

~~Blasted~~ Deceased /
Fire.

You break a spider web, it doesn't complain,
just makes another one. That's all they have to do.
It's like a factory job basically.

~~like~~ [illegible].

The clean, no-smell of dead insects.

It would be funny if it
wasn't so funny.

BLUMENKRANK

BECAUSE BROTHER HUNG HIMSELF from our chandelier with fine silk ties, mother and I had to take in a boarder. It meant Brother's old room, the larger one next to mine, would go to a stranger. For thirty-eight years I had wanted that room; it looked out on a pleasant green field broken by a row of poplars so patient, just seeing them was to feel it must be contentment to always be waiting.

Blumenkrank!

What a boarder. I hated Blumenkrank from his knock on the door. He sullied our welcome mat the very day after Brother's funeral. His knuckles on the wood were the somber striking of a tongueless bell.

"But Mother, isn't it odd? You didn't even post the room-to-let sign yet."

"Then I'm saved the trouble. Lord knows there's been enough of that lately." She glanced at the chandelier, now yanked so low we couldn't cross the parlor without grotesquely crouching.

He wore black, black, all concussion black. One gray eye outgrew the other, in size and predatory coldness—its cephalopodan pupil seemed to pulse as if blinking its own translucent lid; his nose was somehow a shambles—I don't want to get into it—his eyebrows cathedral-arched in disapproval; his pewter hair was overly alive and thick for his anachronistic age; and his mouth was a diagonal line, lips twisted to greet and grin at sideways things. Looming just outside our doorway with the confident, tentatively territorial posture of a man opening *his* home to us, those bleached lips parted: "I am Blumenkrank. I am a cartographer."

He didn't speak—rather he broadcasted. I had the absurd conviction his words travelled far beyond the confines of mere conversation. I'd never heard a voice so dissonant, growly and liturgical, the vowels and consonants somehow lilting in opposite directions.

Mother, an impossibly practical woman, didn't care one way or the other "how many carts he made" as long as he paid on time, which he soon did—though he appeared too shabby for the capital required. The only rule she strictly enforced was "no callers after midnight"(Brother had a constant effluvial stream of filthy, drunken visitors. Thankfully, we rarely met these ungodly-hour guests. We only guessed them from the bony slivers of violently thrown dice, missing valuables, gambler fingerprints, and nicotine, urine and worse cushion-stains).

"Do not worry," Blumenkrank evaded.

Mother fell for it. Blumenkrank crossed our threshold with triumphant, martial steps from which rose inexplicably vaulted echoes. Why didn't mother hear them? I couldn't bear to watch; I stared at a stranger's fake pearl embedded in a wainscoting crack. Then Blumenkrank was on the stair, and I peeked at his unstoppable, ascending form. It seemed many regrettable years had already passed since his hollow knock on our door.

Of course my nervous illness, my obsession with puzzles of all kinds, absolutely prevented me from earning a living. My days dissipated in a room the size of an outhouse, and I suppose my life was a constipated one—I'd rather not get into it. Meanwhile Blumenkrank lorded over Brother's room, crowding it with cape-sized rolls of parchment and cube-pens (the eight sharp corners nibbed), compasses without hands or markings, impractical rulers that tangled like strings, and other ambiguous devices. He also brought an absolutely black, unmarked globe, darkly glimmering before the window, obliterating the view of the poplars.

Blumenkrank transcended privacy; like the great hidden network that spawns mushrooms, he was inaccessibly submerged and indeterminably vast. During the day, he disappeared with small canvas bags that clinked as they swung like shrunken heads from his weathered, gargoyle fists. He returned nights, alone, rent in hand. Over the several occasions I stayed up late enough to spy him coming back, I noticed that clear or rainy skies, he entered dry, hair windblown.

I'd been sleeping poorly—exhaustedly writhing is more accurate—since his arrival. From my cot I heard him enter Brother's room. Each time it sounded as though he were walking on different terrain—once like bare feet slapping marble, again like boots in an abandoned hospital, another evening like shoes crackling broken glass, and so on. Where could he be, if he was only too here, yet sounded so *there*? After his door closed I listened to unrolling sheaves of paper and the careful, linear dragging of bizarre pen-nibs across their victimized skin. I envied what was obviously his skilled technique.

One night, about a week after Blumenkrank came, troubling social noises drifted from his room, between moonlit hours I was too drained to confirm. I slouched up in my cot, electrified by the chance to report him for post-curfew entertaining. I pressed my ear against the wall, and heard far more chairs than could possibly fit in that room—a rampant herd of wood legs scraping the floorboards, odd-gaited pacing—how many improperly fitted prosthetics tramped on the other side?—how many limbless struggled to stand?—who was so tall that his demented head disturbed the ceiling light's tessellated, ornamental crystals?—laughter overdriven by snarls, the expressions of a bewildering number of unrecognizable lack-of-emotions. One sound was familiar: the mutual grinding of pocketed coins; I remembered this from Brother's late gambling revels. But when I approached Blumenkrank's door—no frame of light, and the hallway mute as snowfall.

I resumed a pitiful mimicry of sleep, and returned to mentally completing a jigsaw puzzle, the pieces of which I'd recently imagined into new outlines…

The next day, Mother, a depressingly healthy and stoic woman, complained of chest pain. She felt as though a hoofed machine had stood on her during the night. But she shrugged it off and got on with chores.

In the tenuous evening, the infernal discord whirred up again, and more coins jangling. I slid into the hallway; again, no light under the door and only silence, except for the chandelier tinkle-swinging as the house unsettled … we'd never figured out how Brother reached it, set the noose of ties just right, and finished himself. It was as if he knew some esoteric ladder or staircase leading up through the air, ending at a portal to oblivion…

When morning came, Mother was too ill to prepare breakfast. She'd aged decades in her sleep, and her bright green eyes had faded to pond scum. When Blumenkrank departed, I used my skeleton key…

The cartographer's hateful things were kept in meticulous, easily accessible order, as though he were used to having to flee with them at a moment's notice. I spun the black globe on the windowsill. It was cold and whistled exactly like a decapitated weathervane falling through an abyss—a sound I clearly recognized, though I'd never heard it before. There was a note on the desk:

Bedroom (1st)—quantahypsometric

Bedroom (2nd)—transplanimetric

I couldn't guess what this meant. Was he a thief? If so, why would no items be listed, only rooms? Besides, we had nothing worth stealing, since Brother's pilfering associates. Something wasn't right. It is hard to trust a man who makes maps, who spends his nights shrinking the world to a size he can manage, condensing great spaces into inches that fold under his hands.

Mother coughed as she stumbled to her uncharacteristically fragile feet. As I turned to leave, the globe seemed to have quietly exploded into an obscenely primitive orifice, sucking the sun from the air and leaving sickly phosphorescence in its place, a sort of star-vomit. In the hallway, my shadow cast in the shape of a dense circle—a stack of countless, impersonal shadows—round, without start or finish, endless. I told myself this was a hallucination produced by my exacerbated, neuropathic condition.

Soon I began hearing peculiar noises at all hours (though at intermittent intervals) throughout all areas of the house. These were of two general kinds. The first sounded like a creature made of lipless, gumless mouths filled with a range of yellowed, elderly teeth, connected by ligaments into an anthropoid shape, pacing an empty room, simultaneously smiling, grinning, and angrily grimacing itself back and forth, often changing direction, as though composed of warring sets of chattering, cavity-infected minds. The second type called to mind a wind-up Victrola with a single leg ending in a bull's hoof, pounding a stony floor, its broad, dented horn broadcasting scratchy, screeching backwards messages from a poorly grooved, cartilage-covered record that skipped with tubercular spasms.

Mother had been sick for weeks. One of her eyes was now interred within a shiny black skin and the other was two-thirds occluded. Her hands had begun curving back on themselves like dried fruits. Her hair grew at a fantastic rate and threatened to strangle her in the night. Her skin had paled to a shade darker than water. I took care of her as best I could—I don't want to get into it.

One evening I dreamed that a mosaic of small, clawed teeth clamped on my uvula, suspending an enormous weight that displaced my viscera. I woke with my ribs twitching around under my skin like the partially-paralyzed limbs of a daddy long-legs trying to scramble their last inches, the sky above a foot about to squash . . . I couldn't move, tears bleeding from gaping eyes, until the pain stopped suddenly as a psychiatric session. Something chomped itself in the hallway but I couldn't get up until the morning . . .

In a rare encounter, I passed Blumenkrank on the stair. As usual I averted my eyes.

"You are here," he said fiercely—a strange condemnation.

"I don't know what you mean," I said, wincing.

He laughed curtly, a satisfied smile in his eye. As I walked by him he whistled, a plummeting sound of a decapitated weathervane down an abyss . . . I rushed up as he went out, and stepped on what might've been a piece of fallen plaster. As I was about to close myself in my room, I saw it was a gambler's six-sided die—a normal enough find in the house—only rather than white, it was the green shade Mother's eyes used to be, and the black dots set in its sides seemed to strain toward me like beggars' pupils, shiny, tear-washed, too many eyes, impossible as too many mothers, or none. I kicked it off the landing.

I ignored what I thought was Blumenkrank's warning on the stair—stupidly mistaking a curse for admonition—I was too curious, and more importantly, I knew he was responsible for what was both killing Mother and harming me. I snuck into his room again, with a notebook. The black globe looked slightly larger than I remembered. But I had no time to investigate. I was searching for his maps.

They were protected in great brass portfolios under Brother's bed, clasps muddied with verdigris fingerprints in a disturbing variety of sizes. They were heavy; with difficulty I dragged them over the whiskey-stained floor and opened them. At first I didn't know what I was looking at. The parchments were covered in practically amorphous symbols and strange-sided geometric shapes, and indescribably odd ciphers lacking any shared family resemblance replaced the four common orientating directions. There was no legend. I hastily sketched what I could, filling up several notebook pages before sliding the portfolios back. They were now lighter and easier to push, as though I'd removed something from them simply by copying the inky glyphs.

I spent the rest of the day sealed in my room, reviewing my copies to determine their meaning. Were they star charts? No; I knew enough astronomy to be sure that wasn't the case. In vain did I compare them to county, state, national and even world atlases—they didn't correspond to any earthly geography. But I had been known (diagnosed, even) to spend months gnawing at one piece of a merely entertaining puzzle without giving in; now that life and death were involved, I pushed myself harder than ever to reach a solution.

I spent several tormenting hours pacing the house from end to end, sheaves of paper in hand, working on the problem—trying to even *determine* the problem. At length I leaned against the banister of the second floor hallway and looked down at the chandelier Brother had used to swing himself to inviolable safety. I said earlier that the chandelier was now suspended much lower than it had been before the tragedy. It also cast stranger, squatter shadows that I hadn't observed previously. One of these elongated, swampy dark spots called to mind a symbol I'd copied from Blumenkrank's maps.

I located this symbol on a page of my notebook. Comparing it to the shadow beneath the chandelier, and relative to that point, I was able to relate certain other graphics and icons to other definite features of our home, such as doorways, rooms and windows. In addition, there were many symbols on the maps that didn't correspond to any obvious, worldly domestic elements, as though portraying unseen portals or invisible yet palpable objects. Some of these appeared to represent points at ceiling-close heights, far from easy inspection; other runes were randomly positioned in hallways or near corners.

The sun was setting and Blumenkrank would soon return. I had just enough time to approach one of these seemingly random locations in my house, as indicated in one of my sketches. It was almost a foot shy of a certain corner in the kitchen. I stood in the spot represented. At first I noticed nothing and decided my work had been in vain. But when I turned to walk away, the scuffing of my foot on the linoleum tile echoed as though I'd been standing at the mouth of an interminably bleak tunnel. I resumed my former position and turned again, hoping for a repeat of the echo. Just as I lifted my foot, a great weight pressed around it, as though it were immersed in nearly-dry cement. With great effort I pulled myself forward and almost crashed into the table. Behind me, I heard the faint sound of someone half-laughing and half-eating a thing too big for his mouth.

I knew Mother and I would die if we didn't unravel the enigma of Blumenkrank, but all she cared about was that he provided us with an income. That night, as I sat up in my transplanimetric bedroom, listening to the diabolic commotion through my wall, I thought about it a great deal, and I knew why Blumenkrank always paid his rent, collecting coins at night that he exchanged for dollars each day: He was hosting an awful gambling business in Brother's room, to things from some other place, and the winners received maps of the house. Why? Obviously because they instructed them on how to find our rooms and drain our lives away. These were clearly creatures that couldn't navigate through the usual senses and needed specialized graphic representations to get around our world.

The next morning I determined to see what would happen if I followed the rest of the symbols on the map that didn't correspond to any particular objects in our house. These spots must have had significance for Blumenkrank's guests, and I now believed they aligned with the places I'd recently heard the weird teeth-wandering and hoof-cranked, backwards record playing. As the front door closed behind Blumenkrank, I set to work.

My experience solving puzzles helped me in this task. I paced to and from these locations clockwise, counter-clockwise, and then in other more complicated patterns. I began to feel dizzy and walls blurred as though seen through rising heat. Sunlight dimmed before my eyes. I soon found myself in a cold tunnel shaped like the inside of a Chinese finger puzzle. It was long as the space between the antennae of a V, dark as a blood clot, lined with fleshy spines that emerged erratically from the walls, waving like torch-flames and smelling like sewage and burning leaves.

I consulted my copy of Blumenkrank's map and saw certain characters corresponded to the positions of the dimly-perceived fleshy spines. I began piecing together the significance of these specific locations along the sides of the tunnel ... I turned many rounded, rubbery corners and slid down chewy slopes, my footsteps suffocated like unlucky babies. Who knows how much time had passed when in the course of my investigations I lost track of my starting point, and standing in a phosphorescent, star-vomited dark embellished with rounded protrusions struggling to have faces, I once more looked to the map for help. I noticed that from where I stood, the symbols on the map exactly echoed the distances between the convex objects. Seeing another pattern arising, my passion for puzzles overriding my increasing dread, I walked from one to the next until I reached a narrow, low-ceilinged chamber. It was obvious this space was represented by a character which also depicted the largest rounded protrusion, that same glyph which had stood for one of the fleshy spines in the first area of this subterranean realm.

This was a map of being lost.

It precisely represented the inability to attain a place in the world. Wherever I stood, the map corresponded to my immediate location, which was the same thing as making no sense at all. It was the absurdity of the mirror which constantly negates itself, retaining no single image while reflecting any image back from it. Yet I had a powerful and terrible urge to follow this map, wherever it led. I could not ignore such a puzzling guide. I continued on my way and entered what I must inadequately describe as a low, cavernous, frigid hallway traversed by impossible, glittering webs of dust, fallen bridges that could never have stood.

Filling the end of it from floor to ceiling was a huge black globe, fat with emptiness, which seemed to be rolling slowly closer like a painful laugh rumbling up from the bottom of a throat swollen with penitent, struggling meals. Or it may have been something else—a brother's pupil flattened and monstrously expanded by unfathomable benthic pressure, the yawn of a hole that flinches at your touch, a nightmare marble in some nameless not-game of chance, or a slice of my wrongheaded shadow. Or it could've been the terrible period at the end of a sentence I cannot bear to utter, its gravestone, and simultaneously a lightless, dead cloaca birthing dynasties of awful realities ... What it *was* didn't matter in the least —existence is the merest possible thing. The only issue, the black nought of the matter, was that this inhuman, encroaching *what* corresponded to a symbol on my map, which had only just represented my location in the tunnel.

Finally, I understood the meaning of Blumenkrank's *here* on the stairway.

How terrible to always know where you are.

For The HOAX

Looks in mirror → Body parts in the wrong place.

3/23/12

"His eyes were like frozen wheels, still, but you could sense the desperate force trying to turn them..."

The retired salesman

Excuse me I've lost somethingamajig

He was so thin you could mistake him for Rain, so dry he nearly rustled when he moved.

on his way to a funeral. A drowned boy, one of a dwindling # of equidistant relatives he had not heard from then in years & assumed the invite was a mistake. Still, he had no plans.

PETALS & PISTILS

GIRL MISSING

In the wee morning hours, someone had taped far too many copies of the flyer to each telephone pole [e.g., wasting four where one would've been equally effective]. This absurd repetition of the message suggested overnight regime-change—exuberant fanatics posting their edict everywhere—TODAY, WE ARE THE STATE! [This wasn't true but the suggestion *was* strong]. Running above the signs, thousands of voices in slack black lines spoke to-and-fro of likely anything but Veronica.

GIRL MISSING

... Then it said Veronica was last seen kicking a plastic bottle of seltzer along the old tram-tracks that deadend at Noah Vitolo Lane. Would you help find her? Badly photocopied picture: Pig-tails, features barely delineated in smudgy gray curves and blots.

Last Seen…

Two rainy days pass … three new signs, three more companion creatures gone.

Their photographs vary across a short spectrum of reasonable quality [the camera loves dogs]:

DOG MISSING

MISSING DOG

DOG MISSING

… Then they said things like: Last seen chasing her own tail in Hatsarmaveth Park. Last seen rolling on her back at the fringe of Boomies Dale. Mostly black … He has brown spots shaped like little boomerangs on the outside of both ears … Sweet Bulldog … Reward if found … She limps with front right paw … Answers to name of Flopsy … Answers to Colt. White, but shaggy tail gray and white … Might growl a bit but he's harmless … Rusty face … She's very, very affectionate … drools a lot … Answers to Doobie … Reward if found … Last seen … Loves chicken livers … parking lot of Gary Nelbalms' Tannery on 4th and Urgo … if found … scares easy … red white and blue collar … Very friendly … He will hump you, it's OK…

These flyers overlapped, sometimes concealed Veronica's sign [the missing girl]—No problem, as there'd been too many to start, and the rain had taken plenty down on its own…

I didn't recognize these dogs, but then, I'd long been a lone-wolf of a hound. And the others were terrified of me, even the threatening packs of strays. They kept away on account of the experiments I'd endured before escaping The Numberless Address. I'd been out for years, yet I'd forever smell like a warning, the stink of statistics and scalpels

… I represented the 65,000+ dogs tortured in the name of science each year, in our homeland alone. The strays and loved both didn't want to think about it and who can blame them. Hello, my name is Doom, is this seat free?

Besides, even had they rubbed their asses onto their corresponding signs beforehand, I couldn't name who I'd be sniffing. My olfactory hind-recognition turned crap since those monsters in white coats tinkered, pissed expensive serums in my brain. Small price to pay, you might think, in exchange for the abnormal advancement of other faculties. But to your *Canis Mediocris* who gets to bark at the mailman and take two walks per day, that's Iago's dogdamned pound of flesh.

Flopsy and Veronica and Colt and Doobie were not found. They were, however, Last Seen.

I've moved across this country more times than a serial killer or Bigfoot sighting.

I'd seen a passel of towns. Up 'till now, the people here were the most community-minded, smiling, *how-do-ya-doo?* 64th note upbeat bunch of humans I'd yet seen.

Perk withered into melancholy, and melancholy in turn grew in its strange, enthusiastically lifeless way. They had to see those flyers every day. Post them. Seeing, posting, seeing, posting . . . Like prisoners who, forced to diligently invest in backbreaking labors, receive less than nothing in return. When a few days of rain came, there was an extra lot of reposting going on. The signs sodden, illegible, aborted—

Nature is a sadist.

I have seen the rain spit in the eyes of drowning faces.

Women and men, old and young and hardy too, stooped as they walked, a disenchanted procession of elephant goddesses, heavy-boobed with petrified milk collected for long foretold godlets who'd never tell. No more *how-do-ya-do?* in them. They didn't stop to say hello. Like they knew all there was to about each other up to the very minute of their unrealized encounters.

Periods of hard rain tag-teamed with the sizzling rise of *schadenfreude* suns. Days of over 100 degrees Fahrenheit weren't uncommon. First light was rife with cries of *cock-a-doodle-don't!* Time was hot and empty, it was willows too dry to weep one half-second drop of shade, it was measured all wrong by the dragging of sandals and shoes along Main Street, a loud, rude racket without direction.

Summertime is also known to certain distasteful beasts, myself included, as the Season of Hum, and no shuffling of sandals and shoes, however leaden with grief, could drown out the *humming,* the sound that is summer's by an eternal decree of The Random.

This characteristic hum has a number of blended sources. You've got your gas-lines, green wood-fly, blossom-drunk bees astride wireless communication, the craftily kazoo'd bloodcry of fleshbound mosquitoes, yet more gas-lines, lullaby nonsense of linden and oak leaf in clinamen whisper, the sore and cease of throats of wind, the mysterious but "Nothing to worry about, folks" low-frequency hum of electromagnetic radiation from near [and far] industrial complexes ... I know quite a bit about one or two of those. Oh! I can't forget the avant-garde compositions of Brewer's Blackbird, the Cuckoo, and the pleas of who knows what as-yet unclassified relatives to dinosaur and Dove alike. Incidentally, while on the subject, the Channel-billed Cuckoo is the world's largest parasitic bird, its wingspan measuring up to three feet ... Did you know the population of Brewer's Blackbirds has declined two percent per year over the past forty-four years? That's a cumulative decrease of sixty-one percent—of birds not there and thus never missing—yet somehow *gone*, all the same.

There's no word for this world.

Mid-August:

A new, unfamiliar strain of humming—thin as an echo inside a cardboard box—threaded itself into the multistranded tapestry of summer's hum. Nobody else noticed; apparently one of the invasive surgeries I'd survived sensitized my hearing to this specific sound, alien to all summers past. I don't believe, however, that the various experiments of the monsters in white coats were in any way connected to that foreboding hum—only incidentally, insofar as I could be aware of it.

Then:

GIRL MISSING GIRL MISSING BOY MISSING

[And so on missing... three, more than three, more than...]

Large search parties searched over large areas of terrain. They tried their hardest, but nothing doing. And in their eyes, a terrified incomprehension of powerlessness. Because there's nothing faster than the irretrievable. They might as well've been trying to catch up to fictional characters—entities less substantial than ghosts—to prevent them doing whatever stupid thing they do in whatever story they play a part ... Like, fr'instance, I'll use the Bible, since everyone knows it—like, say Lot's wife—*Hey, you!*

Lot's wife! Stop! We're trying to save you! Keep your eyes up front, it's no joke!

I'd bet on the book.

Come evening, many people inadvertently made me confessor: They were bleeding out hope, in drams after dram—this fact indicated by the decibel-level of their prayers, which increased nightly ... I understand prayer: I've howled inside me, fully aware there's no pack to run from your heart to your aid... it's much like trembling in advance of an anticipated tremor, which may or not arise, banging your head into a wall before the roof falls in ... At these times you don't wonder, what use could the world's biggest sundial have on a black night.

Some wept openly, others, embarrassed—as if making no distinction between crying and urination—in private rooms. Old people stopped going outside altogether, dehydrating at the bottom of deep shadowpools, suffering mothball calentures under six layers of sweater. Nobody knows how many elderly perish from dehydration annually, but from what I understand, it kills almost 1,000 old people in nursing homes, alone... The rate of alcoholism also shot up (in proportion to the increase in uttered prayer volume). Approximately 88,000 people in this country die of alcoholism each year—and that August, half the townsmen seemed intent on enlisting in those American Statistics.

A very little hot, empty, dragged-foot, weepy, loud-prayered, drunken time elapsed:

DOG MISSING DOG MISSING DOG LOST

Hymn ... when's my turn? As the number of vanished increased, telephone-pole real estate space was accordingly reduced. A mutually agreed-upon method of posting that respected all the bereaved, developed, whereby the dog-owners affixed their signs round the individual CHILD MISSING flyers. This created flower-like arrangements. The canines, fanned outward from each side, formed the petals, safely enclosing the pistil of a single lost kid. This unintentional appearance of representational art in these solemn efforts belittled their source in tragic events and broken hearts.

Potential collage-eyes of missing children and dogs watched each other across various spaces and intersections. Cooperating as units that formed the greater floral wholes, the missing of both species seemed tacitly complicit ... an everything-going-according-to-plan vibe I knew wasn't right. But the vibe was there, nonetheless.

Whatever the cause, the truth is there was no difference between them; they shared an equal measure of irretrievability. They'd transformed into one single, new species: *Missing*. The inverse of Extinct. And what's more, there was less evidence for the reality of the *Missing* than the Extinct, which at least leave traces to justify their classification as such.

And it occurred to me that all those mutts and kids had transformed into cryptozoological animals. There was no proof they existed, these legendary *Missings* who were supposed to look like dogs or human children. They might've been Yeti or Mothmen or Chupacabra. They might've been vivisectionists who refused the chance to mangle and hurt as many involuntarily participating dogs as they could at The Numberless Address.

The increasing number of "flowers" climbed up the telephone-poles, transfigured them, depending on your mood, into multicolored joyous Totems, the ruins of a decimated indigenous people, both ...

Did you know more than 1,000,000 dogs go missing each year?

Last Seen ...

Will never again answer to...

I was alone by the lake, undistracted and dreamy, dozed. I woke startled, as from an extravagant nightmare. It was the new humming. It got closer, then fainter, near then far, approached then fled, over and over—the aural equivalent of a sustained period of erratic and rapid manipulation of a kaleidoscopic lens. This pattern continued for some minutes. It loudly roared, the next minute it receded again, then droned close-by...

It circled like the last Thunderbird extinguished on the cusp of an ancient, burning noonlight... The sky, the air turned edible and salted, as if being preserved for a 16th century voyage across seven perilous seas. Sudden drops of rain landed gently on things, as though lowered by the discrete hands of a spider.

The hum tore at and swooped me into irretrievable velocity. Ah! Inexpressibility of the Last Seen.

To speak in metaphor, I was running on two speeds, inside and outside.

Awareness went black and I disappeared from disappearing ... When I came to my bones were moving at the same speed as the rest of me. Faster than stars in their dying orbits. Did you ever *see* the life and death of a split-second? You may've *felt* it "go by" or "creep"—a vague, approximate sensation. But that's not even close to the quick I'm going on about. Not even the stars above, blessed as they are with a star's eye view, have the eyes to see *gone*. [I'm still speaking about all this in metaphor, at the friable limit of metaphor.]

It was late, I skirted rusty railway tracks, passed dilapidated warehouses the old signs that bluff NO TRESPASSING and I sat under a leaf-bitten sky in the woods.

A white *who's-that?* headed my way, threading trees in a zigzags, It vanished behind a trunk, bloomed closer... The *who-cares?* had long brown hair and pink ribbons on either side, and those clipped with lavender plastic-perfect butterflies. Her face wore the smudgy expression I'd recently seen on a badly photocopied flyer. She brushed against me so fast that she'd never been near me.

And then I was speeding too, smashing through everythings,

entering and exiting them as if they weren't real, like ghosts pass through their memories . . . I smithereened things with such speed I didn't catch their names, adjectives crumbled to crumbled crumbles on collision . . . Then I suddenly recognized my life—a marionette suspended like stone up ahead, waiting for anything any hand wants to do with it. I roadkilled my life, then I bulldozed autobiographies that never were, there's no words for of it, no syntax . . .

It was only when I stopped within an ancient windmill or factory or hospital or superchurch, that I *began* to understand. [Everything begins with a feeling; even the driest scholarly article on twenty-one possible means to induce epilepsy in small rodents, started with some guy feeling that writing and publishing that article was worth his time and energy.] Now I felt something unique stir in my heart, the birth of a new kind of emotion, the first I've known that doesn't need poetry to justify itself nor science to determine specific neurotransmitter behaviors concomitant with its expression.

I know what has happened to the missing children and the dogs—at least, so far.

More could happen, why not? But I cannot tell anyone. For one thing, it's much too complicated. You had to be there. Even supposing I did figure how to give you an idea about the phenomena—who'd believe a word of it, coming from a *dog*—an animal who doesn't even use words? Who's been known to growl at his own reflection, shit the carpet, gobble it in shame, and puke it up again. Yeah, I'd trust that guy too . . . Well, maybe. Oh, wait, he's eating his puked shit . . . *never mind* . . .

And sure, maybe I'm an exception as far as dogs go. I'm one of the smarter dogs who's ever lived—perhaps the *smartest ever.* In The Numberless Address lab, there were a few others like me. But I doubt they're still alive today, they'd been too brutalized to think escape possible . . .

I might even be the *smartest* that ever lived—after all, how many dogs know how to read a sign, rattle off long lists of statistics on almost any subject you can imagine, know sufficient botany to discriminate petals from pistils, and comprehend enough religious truth to understand that a woman can suddenly turn into a pillar of salt, if she looks over her shoulder to see what she'd better not?

So what!? Even after all the modifications I've endured, I still regress now and then—I'm still dumb enough, on occasion and without knowing why, to chase my own tail as though it's a being apart from me, a serious threat, an enemy to be mauled to death at any cost...

But where's my head? All that stuff I just said about being an ultra-intelligent, government-engineered freak of a dog, it's true, yet that's not the point anymore. See, it doesn't matter what I was. I'm getting so worked up I forgot that I'm no longer a dog, anyway. It slipped my mind that having become a *Missing*, there's no possibility of getting through to you. Even if I'd been human before, it wouldn't make a difference now.

There's a lot I don't know: What exactly the scientists at The Numberless Address were doing to me and the other dogs, what power chose this particular town to yield so many *Missings* in one summer ... And like I said, I can't describe what ultimately happened. But I can at least give you a tidbit I hinted at before. It might be worth more than zero—That's for you to decide.

Q: Why the *humming*?

A: Because it all went down in summer, and summer's the Season of Hum. If it had happened in February, Season of Whistling Wind, I would've noticed a new timbre of whistle blowing back my cold ears. Or in spring—Season of Chirp—the omen would've been like a little bird peep, as though from just beneath the height of flying.

The whistling, the chirping, the whooshing in autumn ... when I hear those announcements, it's loud and clear ... A few dogs and kids are about to go Last Seen. And I've got real good hearing, and this story takes place in summer; *ergo* the omen was the *humming*. But the way I understand it, whatever the season, each year over 2,000 children don't hear it at all.

16 Title
continued from page
ADVOCACY DAY:
2 TOPICS
The Fellows will share storie
I will loaf about
and observe...
SOUNDS GOOD W/ME...

THE INCONSOLABLE KEY COMPANY

ANYTHING HAPPENED. Luke Harris tied my backpack through the fence at recess. He fished through it and tossed my pencils and notebooks around the yard. "Look, he eats his pencils, gross," he said to the gloating wall of other kids. He stood over me, laughing. They were all laughing. He shook my keys and said, "Looking for something?"

Mommy always told me never lose my keys because if something happened to me she could never forgive herself. Mommy wasn't going to be home till ten or eleven because she worked late writing wills. I asked her about wills and she said, "You don't have to worry about that for a long time."

"Give them back," I said. "Please?"

The bell rang. Luke pocketed the keys.

"*Please?*" he said. He looked happy.

I couldn't concentrate during class. I had one of those brown erasers you put on top of pencils and I rolled it around in my hand and on my arms. It felt good. I shut my eyes and rubbed it on my face. When I opened my eyes it was dark outside. I sat across from two windows and saw my reflection. I had bits of eraser all over my cheeks and forehead. I could see the buildings outside through my face. If I shifted I could see one lit window behind each eye.

That's what my ghost will look like, I thought, *after I've rotted for a while.*

Mrs. Higgins saw. There was foam in the corner of her mouth. She asked me if I knew what I looked like.

"Yes, a dead person."

Everyone laughed.

"No," she said. "Lester Strong, you look like a fool."

The class laughed harder, Luke Harris the loudest.

"I can wash it off."

"No," she said. "You must wear it until school is over."

"Okay," I said.

After class I walked home, but knew I couldn't get in because Luke had my keys. I'd have to sit on the porch until past my bed-time. It was only three-thirty. Mommy worked late and wouldn't be home in over seven hours.

I decided to walk a new way, crossing the widest streets I was never allowed to cross. I got to an empty dirt lot. On the other side of it was a narrow street and a streetlamp blinking on and off like a giant hand was waving in front of it. It was a dead end paved with cobblestones. All the brownstones were empty and boarded up, and some were doorless and stuffed with darkness. You could hear shrill wind blowing through them like they were whistles half-full of water.

I walked to one of the brownstones. There was a beat-up black sign in a window that said THE KEY COMPANY, INC. in gold letters.

Inc. stands for Inconsolable.

I'd heard about skeleton keys that could open anything. Maybe I could find some inside and it wouldn't matter that I lost my real keys. I had to be careful so nothing would happen to me, so Mommy could forgive herself. There were empty beer bottles on the stoop and crushed soda cans, and a leopard-spotted banana peel.

I peered in the doorway. I heard some kids laughing and spun around. One of them was Luke Harris. His laugh was like a hatchet cutting into Squeaky. The other two were older, pock-marked. They were tagging a deserted house across the street with spray-paint. I went through the doorway. I almost tripped on a giant metal key that I guess used to hang outside the building like a sign.

The hall was dark and musty. There was no furniture and wires stuck out of the walls.

I opened a door to the Inconsolable Key Company office. Some light dribbled from a window and onto a dead palm tree in an orange pot, and a black chest in the corner the size of an arcade game. There were no keys, but there was a big bowl in the middle of the floor with decorated with a painting of a gold and red key-hole.

A dead man wearing clothes way too small for him came out of the painted keyhole the same way a nosebleed just appears on your shirt sometimes.

He said: "Woof. Meow. Ba-Ba."

I thought about splitting, but the kids were laughing outside. The dead man slid from the bowl. One of his legs was broke and he dragged it on the floor without sound.

"Oink," he said. "Honk."

He looked like when a fan blade spins really fast and you can sort of see the blade but mostly it's a blur.

I wanted to run but couldn't move. He limped closer.

"Neigh. Neigh," he said. "Squeak."

His head was on backwards like a GI Joe figure thrown off a roof, but his face had slid around to the other side of his head so his eyes were looking at me. His face resembled mine with the eraser bits all over it, except his face was rotting. I think he thought I was dead because of the eraser gunk. His eye sockets were gouged out and filled with ketchup. Black holes in his eyes kept trying to force their way through.

"Choo-choo. Meow," he said, panting.

I forced myself to run behind the black chest.

The graffiti kids busted into the room with slingshots. Being afraid of monsters under the bed doesn't make sense because what about the monsters under everything else? They didn't notice me by the box. The dead man was standing in a shadow. They couldn't see him.

Luke Harris sprayed the gray plant blue. Then he went over to the box and sprayed and sprayed and then saw me and sprayed my hands while I stared at the floor.

"Hey, Six-Eyes."

It's Four-Eyes, but I didn't say anything.

Luke smacked my nose.

"Check this runt out."

I felt something squirm behind me, muddy worms being squashed hard into my spine and the backs of my arms and neck. The dead man was rubbing himself into me. His arms were partly in my arms. His face was entering my face like how brown enters a marshmallow when you burn it.

I shouted and a slingshot rock hit my chest. It made me pull away from the dead man.

The kids were laughing and making fun of me, but I couldn't hear their words clearly, as though they were rooms away. The schoolyard was spilling through the green fences after me.

"He's sick or something. What's wrong with him?"

"The freak rubbed an eraser on his face," Luke said.

"But where's his hand, or his eye?"

They were talking about *me*. One of my hands was old and see-through like a dirty window. The dead man had given me his hand. I pushed my way past the kids and I saw the dead man had one of my hands and one of my eyes. I put my Lester-hand to my right eye and it came back bloody. My eye on the dead man's face looked angry and my hand on the dead man's arm clenched into a fist.

"Moo," he said.

With my hand, he picked up the slingshot rock that hit me and threw it hard at the big kid's pimpled face. The kid fell over and crashed against the ground. He didn't move and his eyes were shut. There was a red mark like the trail of a cherry-flavored slug between his eyes.

The others got scared. I followed them but slipped in a puddle leaking from a pipe in the shadows. Luke Harris slid in it too and the kids slammed the door shut in Luke's face and I heard them jam the giant key across the door so we couldn't escape. I shook across the room as far as I could to get from the dead man.

Luke Harris looked for a way out. I kept my real eye on the dead man. He was shambling closer and trying to tell me something. He wanted me to help him drag the kid he hit with the rock.

"Don't hurt me please," I said.

"Help me find an exit," Luke said, scratching the glass of the barred window with my keys.

The man in shrunken clothes needed me to pull the knocked-out kid toward the bowl with the keyhole painted on it. He was pretty heavy, but I used my good hand and he used my hand and we got the kid's head to drop into the bowl. Then he pointed with my stolen hand to the top of the black box and stared at me with my eye.

I grabbed the lid with my hand and he did the same with my old hand and we lifted it. The kid on the floor moaned. The dead man put my hand in the box and pulled out a big key made of bone. It had stiff hairs growing from it in weird places. It had a sharp, beak-shaped point and hummed.

The dead man said "A, B, C, D," and walked over to the kid with his head on the bowl and shoved the bone-key into the kid's eye and turned it. The boy didn't move and the dead man chuckled with his face on backwards. I covered my real eye.

"Open," the kid with the key in his eye whispered.

I saw a door open where there wasn't a door before. The dead man in little clothes walked through. Some light filtered out of it. Luke had his back to us, but he saw the door and ran for it.

"Luke, don't do it," I said but it was too late. He rushed through and the kid on the floor said "close" and the door shut like ventriloquist dummy lips.

I didn't want to do what I did next because I hated Luke Harris, but I thought I should try to save him so I pulled the bone-key out of the kid's eye. It shook and coughed like grandpa in the Cancer Ward. I stuck it into the kid's eye and turned it. The key sighed and the kid said "open."

The door in the wall swung open again. Mommy says there are no second chances so I figured this must be magic.

Stairs that looked like giant bad teeth descended into darkness. I lay my head on the first damp step and listened. The wind was faintly hot. Someone said "so big" in a fake baby voice and then I heard myself crying. I was there somewhere, alone and afraid. I'll bet my eye was scared of everything it saw.

"Luke," I yelled, "up here."

"Where?"

"Up here."

"Okay. You can let go of my hand, I got it."

"I don't have your hand."

He didn't answer. It was quiet for a minute and then I heard jangling. My keys flew out and landed at my feet. They were melted together into one big gloppy, inconsolable key.

I couldn't help Luke.

"Close," the kid on the floor said and he stopped breathing.

The weird door shut. I sat on the black box and took off my backpack. I pulled out a chewed pencil and a piece of loose-leaf.

I decided to write a will because Mommy told clients on the phone that having a will is important because anything can happen. At the top of the page I wrote: THE FIRST WILL AND TESTAMENT OF LESTER STRONG. It's called a will because it's a list of stuff you're not willing to share until you're dead.

I thought about it. I didn't have anything. Then I remembered I had a hairy bone-key and a bloody gouged eye with a black hole in it. One day someone is going to come into this room, and then they can have them.

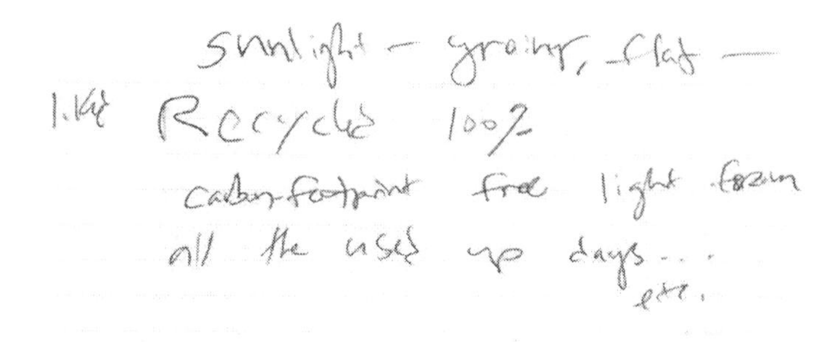

THINGS FOUND IN A 4TH FLOOR ROOM

1

TAPE RECORDING OF AN UNIDENTIFIED MALE IN HIS MID-THIRTIES: CIRCA 2009

For several years, I have been living in neglected houses, sleeping in many punctured waterbeds. No matter where I stay in Ghostmoth, the sun shines through the orange and brown blinds with an apocalyptic quiet, broken by the occasional bang of a metal pole striking something in the distance—possibly a loose flagpole or traffic light.

I don't have to live here—I could live anywhere, given my personal wealth—but as a student of philosophy I have an interest in determining what happened in Ghostmoth that goes beyond the admittedly bizarre details.

Until 1979, this small town in upstate New York had been a favorite destination for tourists, who enjoyed the colonial houses, kayaking on the river and antiquing, and students from across the country who soaked up the intellectually challenging atmosphere of Ghostmoth University, an experimental school in the most liberal tradition.

I am collecting bits of diaries, newspapers, and other textual evidence left behind when the citizens of Ghostmoth disappeared. Most valuables that remained have been looted since then, but correspondence and other written records can be found in almost every desk, drawer and file cabinet.

Many of these records have been quite useful, but I am specifically looking for an unpublished work by Wilks and his student Blick, reportedly titled *The Repetition Must Repeat Itself Now*. At the moment, the existence of this manuscript is only a rumor…

2

ReD BOOK OF DR. HAMMOND WiLKS: SePTeMBeR 21, 1970

Until recently, I was an aging, urbane philosopher and professor of metaphysics and ontology at NYU. Last summer I took a position in the philosophy department at the newly created Ghostmoth University and bought an old Victorian house on the fringe of the small town. The house had once belonged to Tristan "Reedy" Richards, a reclusive, outsider musician suspected of schizophrenia who was little liked in the community, and had provided Ghostmoth with its first dark moment when he disappeared one night in 1965.

I settled happily in the sleepy town and began my life's work in earnest. I focused on the nature of repetition, as a metaphysical principle and in all its existent forms: the constant rising of the sun, the opening of eyes, the flying of bees, the breaking of pencils, the breathing of air, the booming of thunder, the reading of letters, and so on.

Ever since the failure of Marx, it had appeared that philosophy could not actually change the world and could only spout on and on about it, like a crazy aunt at the dinner table. But I knew I was on the verge of a breakthrough in my philosophy, something that would literally break through into the world itself.

I was so absorbed in my studies that I had not even seen every room of my new house. There were four floors in all, and I had only been on three of them.

One night a terrible storm took down the lightning rod. In the morning I decided to finally visit the top floor and see if I could find a way to the roof.

On the way up I thought I heard the sound of an acoustic guitar playing. It was very faint, but I could just discern the motions of a fugue. It was possible someone was practicing somewhere in a field nearby; there were plenty of hippies around Ghostmoth in those days. I continued up the stairs and found no way to get to the roof through the house. In fact there were no doors or rooms on the top floor.

I found a ladder in the cellar and as I reached the fourth floor from outside, I heard the fugue again. I also saw a rectangular shape on the side of the house that suggested the location of a covered-over window.

I gave up on the lightning rod for the moment and decided to find out what was behind the walls of the fourth floor. On the inside again, I broke a hole in the wall from beyond which the music was definitely drifting.

Inside was a large room that smelled as if maggots infested with maggots had been stuffed up my nostrils. In one corner was a little writing desk, and in the other was a corpse, leaning upright on a stool, and incessantly playing a fugue on his rusty-stringed guitar.

The musician's features had long ago rotted away but bits of skin still clung to him as sky clings to snow. On the desk was a sheaf of musical notation and lyrics and a piece of paper covered in twelve strange characters resembling symbols used in electrical diagrams.

After this discovery, I was not seen on campus for two months. I said my absence was due to "medical reasons." When I returned, I was the same man, but I was most surely not.

I had determined that the twelve "categories" this freak musician had discovered implied three more to form a complete series which would transcend the abstract and enter fully into the concrete "real world." My task now is to discover and then learn how to use all fifteen properly.

3
LYRICS FOUND IN THE 4TH FLOOR ROOM, SIGNED TRISTAN "REEDY" RICHARDS: CIRCA 1965

A stranger shadow troubled Tristan.
At the speed of rain, it painted his hand.
He looked up to see a headless hawk
Never watching him with care.
It shifted on its perch,
Left to right, right to air;
Spreading feathered bone, it flew.
Once more it had to disappear.

4
JOURNAL ENTRY OF BURTON TALISMAN: CIRCA 1973

...And while I'm on the subject of people that I don't like, I don't care what anyone says, Dr. Wilks is a dangerous person. Not only do the number of students enrolling in his classes increas every semester, but the same students continually re-take his courses, even if they cannot get credit for them. One student, Max Blick, has taken the same course with Dr. Wilks over eleven times in the last few years. I seriously think that he should have graduated a few semesters ago but taking the Wilks courses is holding him back. I can't imagine that he's missed something. Blick is that kid who never speaks, his eyes are gray and cold like bullets, and you get the feeling he knows how long it takes for a wingless fly to croak. And there are some other students who seem to be following his lead—what kind of peers do I have when Max Blick can exert peer pressure!? What's really bizarre is that Wilks teaches philosophy—it's not exactly a discipline that results in being able to do anything, like economics or anthropology, my majors.

Some people think I am overly obsessed with thinking about

this stuff but there's nothing else to do and I like people—when I'm watching them or when they're in my head.

5
GHOSTMOTH HERALD INTERVIEW WITH APRIL JEFFERSON: SEPTEMBER 19, 1978

I ran away from my mom and dad fighting. I went to see grandma at Windy Ponds Cemetery. Nanna had always been the one to make those fights stop, and make things better, and now that she was gone they kept going. Every day was the same and every day got worse. This time dad bought mom a necklace and they were at each other's throats—how can a gift take something away? So I sat on her grave and cried, over and over. I can cry a lot. I guess my tears are pretty heavy, because I crashed through the grave and into Nanna's arms, like she was waiting for me.

One arm broke off and I smelled earthworms and 2nd grade—the inside lid of the coffin was made of blackboard pieces. I could still see some kid's writing in chalk. It was the Pledge of Allegiance. The only readable letters were "EDGE … GOD … ON." I've been doing more drugs than ever since that.

6
CLASS NOTES OF MAXWELL BLICK: CIRCA 1974

Even the entirely "new event" repeats itself—which is to say, every day the "new" happens, over and over. There are a million "first times" going on right now, each notable not only for being "the first" but also for being "the millionth."

Some of those Times ↔ Bloody (Sum of that Blood ^ Timely).

7
GMPD INTERVIEW WITH NEVILLE PARSONS: OCTOBER 3, 1979

Mary and I were walking down the street at about 2:00 AM. We both have insomnia and walking around the block repeatedly often helps. It was quiet, deserted—a usual Ghostmoth Sunday night. I noticed someone had stabbed holes in the door of a car parked on the street, or it had been shot up. That was weird since we don't usually have vandalism in Ghostmoth. Then I saw all the cars on the street had been stabbed that way, with deep puncture wounds through the doors. Mary pointed out each tree lining the block had also been poked with something sharp. We were beginning to get worried, and we fairly ran home to find our front door full of holes.

8

WRITTEN ON BACK OF GMPD INTERVIEW WITH NEVILLE PARSONS: DATE UNKNOWN

I have been up to the 4th floor of the Reedy Place too many times to count, and I cannot find any evidence that corroborates Hammond Wilks' Red Book regarding the perpetually musical cadaver or any indications of any other odd activity taking place there. This is particularly frustrating, since I feel finding this room would be the best bet for locating *The Repetition Must Repeat Itself Now*.

9

CORONER'S REPORT: OCTOBER 4, 1979

SCENE DESCRIPTION: The death occurred at the decedent's home. A copy of a suicide note in Maxwell Blick's handwriting was provided by GMPD Detective King. The note was written on the back of copy of a German book, *Wissenschaft der Logik* by G.W.F. Hegel and stated "The Repetition must repeat itself NOW. No need to wait, or Philosophy is the drunken whore everyone thinks She is." The note is not dated.

BODY EXAMINATION: Initial body examination at GCH revealed an adult male Caucasian seen supine on a steel autopsy table. The decedent has blond hair, green eyes, all natural teeth, an unshaven face, and multiple small scars on the posterior left forearm. There is a small tattoo of the infinity symbol on the upper right bicep, and two apparent single-edged stab wounds are noted in the center of the chest. No hesitation marks are seen surrounding these wounds. No additional external trauma is noted during the preliminary visual examination.

10
UNMAILED LETTER FROM OWNER OF GHOSTMOTH CASKET CO: OCTOBER 1, 1978

We knew a guy who had an ungodly supply of blackboards that schools didn't need. I don't know where he got them—I guess kids today don't learn to read or write anymore. Anyway, rather than using a full blank of mahogany, we could just take the blackboard and cut it, put a mahogany veneer on and nobody would know the difference on burial day. We did this over and over without a problem. But after the April Jefferson thing, that was it. We had to give up which bodies had been buried in the "blackboard coffins" and replace them with the proper lids, at great expense. The only one we didn't change was the one Professor Wilks had been buried in. He had no family to request we fix it, and we didn't want to spend the money. So he's still down there with his blackboard.

11
PURPLE BOOK OF DR. HAMMOND WILKS: DECEMBER 29, 1975

Everything that exists repeats itself; from moment to moment it exists, over and over. But if everything repeats itself from moment to moment, then in each moment it is not the same thing that it was a moment ago; it is the thing in this particular moment and not another moment. In this case the word "Everything" must refer to something else every time it is used, and further, even the word "Everything" itself is not the same word it was a moment ago. Strict continuity is not possible. So each thing is what it is not. This includes Life and Death, the key to each of which is a proper understanding of Repetition. That understanding, in turn, can be found through the application of my Fifteen Categories.

There is one other person whom I believe can follow me to the never-ending of this journey, a young man named Maxwell Blick. He has a history of somewhat sociopathic behavior, but he has truly discerned the kernel of my teachings and I have decided to invite him to join me on a research project into this, the furthest depths of Repetition.

It occurs to me that to call Maxwell Blick by his name is to use empty words. What makes Maxwell *what* he is, is not his "Maxwell Blickness." But I digress.

12
JOURNAL OF PARIS SPARKS, PRESIDENT OF GHOSTMOTH UNIVERSITY: MAY 29, 1974

I met with Dr. Wilks to ask him about the recent, disturbing behavior of his students, while trying carefully not to imply I blame him for this. But there are some important questions to be answered: Why are the students constantly repeating his classes, even when the syllabus has not altered? Why do the best students in our school show up even when the school is closed, and wait outside the doors, reviewing the same notes they reviewed weeks before. Dr. Wilks is clearly an asset to the university, and the (very) small circle who understands what he is saying believe he will be remembered as the greatest philosopher of the 21st century, so it is difficult for me to broach this subject with him, and I had to be delicate.

Luckily, I found him sympathetic. He claimed he too was concerned for his students and suggested holding his classes off campus, in the spacious 4th floor room of his Victorian House—the Old Reedy Place. There he could keep better watch on them, and provide food and bedding when required. I must admit this is not the solution I was looking for but there is something very persuasive about this man. It must be his eyes. The more you look at them, the more they resemble forgetting them. So you look again and again. In some ways, each dark eye appears like a thing in itself, like a drawing of an eye in an anatomy book that leaves out the face. And then the face sometimes appears this way too, like an unworn mask. It is difficult to take Wilks in at once.

Because Ghostmoth is nothing if not a cutting-edge university, and it is the 70's after all, I hesitantly agreed to his plan.

13
PETITIONER'S DECLARATION FILING (FOR DIVORCE): JANUARY 1, 1957

OTHER INFORMATION: Tristan was unable to perform normal daily tasks because he would constantly hum the same tune over and over. The song would take over his every waking minute and sometimes he would hum in his sleep. In addition, he became more and more obsessed with what he called his twelve children—a bunch of symbols he had invented to communicate with "The Headless Hawk of Ghostmoth." He told me that my head did not do much and that he could remove it and I could still do the dishes if I would let him show me how.

14
DIARY OF BURTON TALISMAN: OCTOBER 6, 1979

I don't know why I decided to follow Max Blick around. I guess I have been kind of fascinated with him ever since he started taking those Wilks courses. There's not a lot to do in Ghostmoth so if you can't afford drugs, you make your own fun, I guess. I learned that in anthropology class.

This time Max was walking strangely, sort of staggering. His hair was totally messed up. He was barefoot, which is really odd. He had a metal pole with a sharpened point on it. I think it was the lightning rod from the Old Reedy Place. He was walking down the trail slowly and stabbing at everything he saw with it—trees, bushes, squirrels, rocks—it was like he wanted to spear whatever he could.

I was about thirty feet behind him, treading carefully. If he noticed I could pretend to be hiking, since the trail was pretty popular and leaves were turning nicely. Then he stabbed a hornet's nest hanging from a tree.

I couldn't help but watch as they flew out and began stinging him all over. Then I got a little scared when he just kept walking while they covered him with venom. I thought he would fall over. But he didn't fight them, and he didn't slow down. I stayed as far back as I could while keeping him and the black and yellow cloud in sight.

I realized his walk was so weird because it consisted of a series of exactly repeated motions. No matter what terrain he stepped on, rocks, sticks, etc.—he stepped the same way, moved his arms the same way. Like a wind-up toy.

I saw someone jogging down the path ahead of us. She was easy to see because she wore a bright red track suit. Her head was down and she was focused on each step.

She heard the swarm and screamed. Max approached her, pulsating stingers hanging out from all over his skin, hornets coming out of his ears, his nose, his mouth. I saw her step back and Max stabbed her in the gut with the sharpened pole. He pulled it out and walked over her body, kept going down the path.

I wanted to help her, I really did, but she must have been almost dead and those hornets were all over the place. I might be allergic and die, I don't know since I've never been stung. I'm not proud of it, but I turned and ran and I called 911 when I finally could pick up a phone without shaking, about an hour later.

15

TAPE RECORDING OF AN UNIDENTIFIED MALE IN HIS MID-THIRTIES: CIRCA 2009

Now that I've found the unsent letter from the owner of Ghostmoth Casket Company behind a dresser in his office, I am at Windy Ponds Cemetery to dig up the body of Dr. Hammond Wilks. If that letter is true, they left him in a blackboard-lidded coffin…

I've finished digging up the grave. It is silent here. I saw a hawk, circling—too far away to see if it had a head or not—but otherwise all is quiet. I'm going to pry open the lid.

... (Indecipherable) amazing, he is writing something over and over, tracing marks in the air with the point of his chalky hand... everything about him is absolutely dead, but for the arm and hand which keep repeating motions endlessly like a seismograph reliving a traumatic quake.

From thirty years of wear, the index finger on his moving hand is worn down to a nub, but the words he has been writing are clearly visible, etched through the mahogany veneer and into the blackboard coffin-lid: 4TH FLOOR UNDER RICHARDS, 4TH FLOOR UNDER RICHARDS, 4TH FLOOR UNDER RICHARDS, 4TH FLOOR UNDER RICHARDS...

But I have been up to the 4th floor of the Reedy Place so many times, and found nothing...

I'm at the Reedy Place again. I have already searched the 4th floor where classes supposedly took place, where Wilks found the body of Tristan Richards playing a fugue over and over, in vain. But then it struck me that Wilks could have *moved* the 4th floor somewhere else, that is to say, moved whatever made the 4th floor what it was to another location... I recall what he said in his Purple Book about how Maxwell Blick is not who he is because of his "Maxwell Blickness." Similarly, the 4th floor may not be what it is because of its "4th floorness" but because of some other quality which can be transferred elsewhere... I'm in the cellar and I have found a door beneath a pile of coal that leads to a small flight of stairs...

There is the corpse of Richards, playing a silent fugue—all strings on his guitar snapped and hanging floorwards like the long feelers of a deep-sea predator—his white hands moving over stale air and warped wood as night-bugs patrol lightbulbs, maggots dropping from his jawless mouth where the words "painted" or "perched" or "disappear" should be sung. Under his rotten backside, I see a thick manuscript for a cushion... (Indecipherable)

... I have applied the 15th Category, and now understand what has happened in Ghostmoth, from the little details to the big master strokes of time, from how Maxwell Blick stabbed himself and went on to stab and stab for eternity, making that stabbing the sole meaning of his existence and therefore giving his existence true meaning by giving it one, single meaning; how he killed who he could and how the other students died of starvation after Wilks died, waiting for class to continue; how the rest of the town (Indecipherable); how Reedy made the playing of a song he could not stop humming the meaning of his existence, how that meaning endures. And by lying in that grave, moving his hand like a magician whose method of misdirection is the same as his trick's effect, Wilks is constantly transforming his entire Existence (not his mere life or death) solely into a sign that repeatedly points the way to the answers of the deepest mysteries, the greatest teacher that ever taught, who is not only teaching but is *only* teaching ... and that brings me to this moment, here.

I will get new guitar strings and a jaw for Richards, I will get a new blackboard and chalk for Professor Wilks, and I will buy a harpoon and invest my wealth to bring the streets of Ghostmoth back to life again, for Blick ... outside I can hear the sharp clank of rusty cans speared on a lightning rod, and a tread that repeats each beat, and I can hear the mad whirring of hornets slaughtering the buzzing flies that prey on Blick's tattered flesh, Maxwell Blick who disturbs nests.

I don't take life seriously, it's a joke,
But Life seems to take *me* seriously —
Like not funny one bit, mister!

MUDDY LOVE

icky. →

editor's note: So here's the deal. This book was going to be roughly 450 pages, so we had to cut some beautiful things, stories like "Muddy Love," represented now as the QR-code you see above, and "The Angel Chaser," which was supposed to go before this one. If you can figure out how to scan these images with a QR-code app on your cell phone, feel free to download and enjoy them on the go, or wherever. Otherwise, well, sorry...

VISITATION AT NIGHT.
12/9/13

I HAVE FOUND THE MOST RELIABLE LOCKPICKS ARE BENT INTO THE SHAPE OF A QUESTION MARK.

MARTIN WAS HERE

IN THE DAYS when Martin Box advertised as a Private Investigator/ Supernatural Specialist, he didn't like downtime between cases. He didn't want to think about himself and his problems, and that's what happened when he wasn't on a job. He'd just solved the harrowing case of the Head Collecting Demon of Brooklyn Heights, and if he ever saw another decapitated head he'd have to cut his own off to stop the disgust, the pointless misery from taking up permanent residence behind his eyes. So he lit a cigarette, and turned on the news for some distraction.

There'd been a horrific murder in his hometown of Burtonsville, Connecticut, that unexpectedly brought his personal and professional lives together.

He didn't much like that, either.

Using an unknown adhesive, somebody had glued blue plastic bags over Diggle Street at about 3:30 in the morning. They then dragged a two-ton statue of an elephant from a local amusement park and placed it in the middle of the street. Next, they broke open a fire hydrant and flooded the area, and apparently slid a local squatter down the wet, plastic-covered street so hard his head was crushed through to the brainstem when it struck the elephant's extended brass front foot.

These details gave Martin the strangest sense of déjà vu. He was in the shower, watching the water trying to run down his crusty drain, when he realized why.

As a kid in the 1970's, he'd inherited an old Slip' n Slide from a neighbor. Martin had a clear memory of laying it out in the attic, where he spent most of his time playing, thinking, and hiding from his family. One day, he was pretending to be a giant. He had a cast iron bank shaped like an elephant and a GI Joe doll. He wet the Slip'n Slide and slid the action figure toward the elephant. The impassive head struck the front foot. Martin used some red Play Doh to make it look like the skull had smashed open.

He didn't want to go back to that house of dark times, but something was calling him back. Maybe the coincidence was just too great to ignore. Was that why? Without answering the question or bothering to get all the shampoo out of his hair, he dressed quickly, forgetting underwear and mismatching the socks on his feet, grabbed his wallet and keys, and started the long drive back to his childhood home.

During the drive, Martin heard about yet another Burtonsville murder.

They were saying on the radio that someone had used an "unidentified goop" to glue together hundreds of hardcover books, making an object the dimensions and shape of one twenty-feet tall hardcover volume. They'd somehow gotten this Cristo-sized item to the outskirts of the abandoned rubber factory and crushed two homeless drug addicts with it. A picture of a dragon had been painted on the cover of this enormous book-built book, as well as a bizarre doodle of a milk-leaking tit. Police had no leads.

Martin pulled over to the shoulder to focus. His first thought —more of a hope, actually—was that an Extradimensional Terrorist was trying to confuse him through the car radio. That had happened to him before, watching HBO. But then he remembered that such unholy interference could only occur in stationary situations; the moving car would be too difficult for an ET to possess. That meant this second homicide was real. The newscast had reminded him about his childhood notebook. He'd drawn a dragon on the cover, and a not-so-friend of his had drawn a breast next to it, milk running in crude lines to the dragon's fiery mouth, much to Martin's embarrassment. He didn't remember using the notebook to destroy action figures or other toys, but it was entirely possible he had. After all, how many people can remember everything they pretended to be or do yesterday, let alone when they were little?

He wondered if he were somehow responsible for these murders—they were obviously based on incidents he'd played out long ago—but the Martin who played those events was doing just that, being a "normal" child. If he'd pretended to be feeding the poor, would someone now be leaving roasted chickens at all the homeless shelters in the area? But what little boy ever plays at being merely kind?

No child would be innocent of murder if their imagination were put on trial.

He hadn't been to his childhood home since he was a boy; it had been a miserable place of arguments, fights and punishment. He raced the river, rediscovering and passing long-forgotten landmarks. There went the closed rubber factory, historic clock tower, two silver steeples, four statues of dead men, and the desolate grid of locomotive tracks. He wasn't even sure if the house was still there. But it was easy to remember, like his father's hand slapping his little face and the way his mother didn't care.

333 Spring Street was standing, but barely. Time had loosed termites, storms, rust and rot. Itinerant and established biker gangs and squatters had vandalized the windows, walls, and doors of the house where Martin had taken his first steps, his first punches, and said his first word, which was "BOOM."

Of course nobody had bought it; Burtonsville was the most depressed town in the region, rife with corruption and crime. He brushed a fly from his face and walked up the treacherous back stairs, glancing at the old well his great-grandfather had covered with stone slabs to keep the kids from falling. The screen door was wide open. One hand on his revolver, he stepped into the dimly lit mud-room carefully, as though testing if a possible mirage would disappear at his touch. A few more steps and he saw how far things had gone downhill since his childhood days. Those rare pieces of his great-grandparents' furniture that weren't splintered were missing, no doubt stolen and sold. Used condoms lay about everywhere like jellyfish beached among hypodermics. The peeling walls were covered in unreadable graffiti, charred by tramp fires, and kicked in by many all-night beer-drinking parties; toilet paper and worse hung from the ceilings, strips waving majestically back and forth in a breeze from the pane-less windows.

This mix of memories, about which he was already ambivalent but which were his alone, and their crude violation by strangers, was disorienting. In a weird way, the scene looked familiar, as though he'd dreamed it before. Martin wasn't used to reflecting on his feelings, or even feeling them, for that matter. He didn't name them to himself, no more than he would name a passing pigeon. Maybe, he thought, his inner inexperience was why things were tilting weirdly and threatening to collide in his head; he seemed about to slip into an emotional synesthesia—things had suddenly gone so wrong, it was as though he dreaded walking another step because the functions of his face had moved to the bottom of his shoe. He was sure that with each step forward, everything would look equally bad while only the pain would change. That would get more and more intense with each discovery.

Martin's heart strained like an electrocuted starfish when he saw his grandmother's prized collection of original one-sided Edison records had been thrown like Frisbees across the dining room. They lay in shattered heaps of black shellac. At the same time, he inexplicably felt like laughing. It was strange because he hadn't even liked his crabby grandmother and kept away from her as much as possible, and he'd always thought she deserved the cancer that had cut her down. Then the memory suddenly came to him of hiding in the attic, pretending she'd fallen out the window and broken her neck. Yet obeying an instinct he didn't try describing, Martin approached the shards to salvage what he could. Something moved furtively in the closet.

"Who's there?" he murmured distractedly, as though picking up the office phone while reading through a tough case file.

No answer. That silence, which often precedes attack, snapped Martin back into focus.

He walked away from the Edisons and considered the closet across what had once been a family room.

"I'm going to open this door." Martin put his hand on the knob. Even though he'd done this plenty, his pulse still pounded in his chest. "I have a gun."

Again, no answer.

He yanked the door and was knocked down by a riot of raccoons that flooded through the debris and disappeared. Martin crouched down to examine his face for scratches in the crescent of a broken mirror, when someone walked up behind him.

"You should get out of here," a girl said, before he could finish spinning around.

She was all of fifteen or so, wearing the gray and olive green outfit of an urban squatter, with blonde hair in dirty dreadlocks, nose pierced with an emerald-eyed dragonfly pin.

"I'm Martin Box, Private Investigator/Supernatural Specialist." He handed her a recently-printed card.

"That spells PISS," she intoned more than spoke, like a lobotomy-case Martin had once visited while on the case of the Flying Book murders.

"Yeah? Well, tell me what the hell those raccoons were doing shut in the closet."

"I don't know anything about that."

She bit her chewed nails—not nervously, but in small portions as though eating dinner with guests. Her eyes were two deep holes.

"Then what *do* you know? Why are you here?"

"I'm Trish. I stay here sometimes if there's nowhere else. But lately this place is haunted or something. I was just going to grab my stuff and get out."

"What kind of things are going on?"

"Noises, mostly … but weird things keep showing up. I was sleeping in the bedroom upstairs, and when I woke up the room was full of these tall, brown hats—like fifty or more. That was last night. Can I get my stuff now?"

"Go ahead, but first—I'd like your nose piercing. It belonged to my mother." Expressionless, she removed and tossed it at him.

"Who does it belong to now?" she said without a hint of meaning, walking upstairs.

He fished around for evidence. Over an hour or so he'd found plenty of corroded junky needles, lots of fast food wrappers, beer cans, cigarette and other narcotic ash, and empty whiskey bottles ... one of them was Canadian Club, the brand his dad used to get and forget that he'd gotten violent. The place looked like that epileptic troll he'd tracked to a Bensonhurst tanning salon had hit it. He was surveying it all, puffing on a Marlboro, thinking that it amounted to nothing but bits of disrespected past, when Trish bounded quickly down the stairs and rushed past him and through the mud-room. Suddenly, her head popped back into the room.

"You seem like an okay guy. Watch out for the God of Death."

"Who?"

"He's short. You can see right through him, but he can see through you, too," she cautioned him, and took off for good.

Martin searched the rooms a few more hours before he decided to take a break. But it was impossible to relax. He sat in a green rocking chair on the second floor porch of the dilapidated house, smoking cigarette after cigarette and thinking. What did the incident with the elephant statue and the giant book have in common with his childhood, and what connection did those raccoons share with the brown hats that were indeed strewn all about the shooting gallery bedrooms?

He made a list on the wall with his felt pen, something that would've given his grandmother a conniption:

1) *I played with the Slip 'n Slide and the dragon-doodled notebook in the attic, and nowhere else.*

2) *I had a whole gaggle of Ranger Rick the Raccoon figures as a kid, also in the attic.*

Each of these dolls sported a tall brown hat.

3) I used to pretend they were monsters that ate people.

4) Martin was here.

Who could've known these things, and have the ability to execute these ridiculously complex murders, based on a child's daydreams? Had he stopped another crime by letting those meticulously collected raccoons loose, or had he simply opened the door to another more hideous transgression? He cursed at his lighter. Sometimes it took several tries to work.

When he finally got a Marlboro lit, Martin went up to the attic, slowly, to keep the creaking stairs quiet as possible. It was difficult walking that path to the room where all the dreams of his youth had once run wild.

Where once he'd leapt over marbles and hacky-sacks, he now tread with care over hypodermic needles, bodily fluids, melted candlewax and thousands of cigarette butts. But the stairs still led to the same old giant room he'd remembered. Mattresses had been laid out by squatters where his model airplanes had once been lined up, and an overflowing child's potty where the board games missing pieces had towered high. Amazingly, his old 8-ball was still intact and sitting next to an empty ashtray. He turned it over but couldn't get an answer.

How did he feel? Why did he keep asking himself that question? Was it because something had finally happened to make him unafraid to feel—or to let the feeling loose despite his fears, regardless of any consequences? All this uncertainty bothered him. He had always associated emotions with unanswered questions, and his job was about the ones you could answer—the mysteries that could be tamed. Now was no time to get all wild and emotional. Stay private as your parts, he told himself.

Then Martin stepped in something so sticky, he couldn't move, and he knew anger. Yes, he held it in his clenched hand—it *was* the very clenching of his hand—he wanted to destroy everything, the other half of the memories of his half-forgotten childhood, snap the hypodermic needles, pulverize the remaining Edison records, and even knock down the house. Just knock the damn thing down and get back to questions worth answering because they could be. He almost tore off his shoe trying to get out of it. Finally, he untied his shoe and left it in the goop, took out his flashlight, and examined the mess more closely, trying to breathe deeply and slowly enough to regain some objectivity.

It was a translucent jelly that smelled like stolen wishing-well pennies and mildewed Nudie magazines. Globs of it had tattooed a dotted line across the room and Martin followed the gelatinous trail to where it stopped, at a hole in the wall the size of an adolescent Siamese twin.

When he was a kid that wall had a small grate set in it, and the occasional squirrels he saw move behind that grate looked out on the expanse of the attic from that unexplored space. Now it appeared that someone hopped up on meth (or worse) must've recently thrown something and broken the wall open.

There was a rectangular chamber on the roof-most side of the grate. It was filled with furniture made of hardened, clear jelly-like material and Martin recognized translucent facsimiles of his old beanbag, night-table, and Mickey Mouse lamp. In one corner was a large yellow chest which used to hold his toys. In another corner, his light fell upon the back of a statue of a young boy. He could see through the clear statue to a body propped behind it, a dead squatter with flies faking sleep in his eye sockets; Martin had seen those same files a thousand times at hundreds of grisly scenes. The flashlight showed the statue's hands reaching out as though trying to choke the corpse, but the goop had ossified around him and he was forever frozen in that beseeching gesture. What bizarre cruelty had happened here? If only flies testified.

This murder presented the kind of question Martin liked to answer. He was in his element and fully in control, all analysis and observation. But when he turned the light on the translucent boy's face his heart started skipping beats. The figure was the spitting image of Martin as an eight-year-old, when he would choke his Wolfman doll while pretending it was his father. He knew the gesture well; it was a game he played after each beating. From the right angle, the statue looked like it could be the God of Death that Trish had described before she'd run off.

Martin had seen many weird things in his career, but none of them had ever hit home quite like this. Why? He didn't know. He pelted down the stairs and sat huffing on the porch, asthma getting the better of him. The urgent burning in his chest helped him focus on his body, on the moment, rather than on the urgent impossibility of these unfolding events. How did he feel? Damn that question. It inevitably returned like a fly on a dead man.

That night, Martin waited in a corner of the attic with his flashlight, his revolver, one shoe and a whole lot of trepidation. He found some votive candles and lit them with his Bic to use as nightlights. As the moon prowled the black sky, it was surprisingly easy to slide back into a time when he'd crouched ready to pounce in that same corner, with a flashlight, a toy gun, no shoes, and a sense of adventure. It was in that corner that he'd had his first intimation that there existed an order of things outside the world we know, and dreamed of investigating it when he got big. Nothing supernatural had happened to him to make Martin come to his conclusion; but a tincture in the darkness in that particular spot, the way it maybe moved at the corners of his eyes, and how the still air seemed more *mute* than quiet, was enough to set him on his extramundane path. Yes, it was easy to be a kid again in that attic. It was simple as falling asleep ... the creak of old stairs startled him awake and he tightened his grip on his gun.

A humanoid stood in the broad swath of moonlight that draped the attic doorway. It was about four feet tall and looked like a hairless, translucent boy who'd been burned in patches from head to foot with very smooth skin and unnaturally long fingers. It stood still for a moment, as if thinking, and Martin saw a comic book think bubble of clear blobs drift out its head. Then the thing stepped forward with the right leg, jumped forward with the left leg, hopped two more steps, dropped to all fours and crawled, then stood up and jumped with two legs until it disappeared into the hole in the wall.

Martin knew he should've been shocked, pinching himself to

ensure the reality of the scene. Yet at the same time, the appearance of the grotesque creature made sense. It was as though he'd spent so many formative years pretending in the attic, vividly acting out fantasies and impossible situations, that he still thought anything could happen in that space. Looking at the hole in the wall, waiting for the monster reappear, was not much different than imagining the whole thing, actively suspending disbelief.

Martin heard it rummage about in the old, yellow toy chest and readied his pistol as he got to his feet and approached. The thing, still apparently oblivious to Martin's presence, started to take things out of the chest and drop them in front of the hole. A few rolled around the attic, and three of them stopped near where Martin was sitting. One was a soccer ball; another was a little blue Wham-O. The third was the tattooed head of a dreadlocked squatter. *Not another one*, Martin thought. The creature came scampering over to find the missing "balls."

Martin had just come off a long case that revolved around an evil, headless creature that collected a monotony of decapitated heads. He'd spent months studying them up-close, until he was able to eat his lunch while examining neck-stump photos. So Martin thought his nerves would be steeled against the sight. Instead he felt nauseous, on shaky ground, nightmarish.

Ignoring the dead eyes staring up at him, Martin rolled the soccer ball back. It knocked the thing in the knee. It jumped backwards, fell down and rolled over, got up, and spun in a circle before putting the ball with the other heads and balls. The boy-creature swerved around again, turning clear eyes on Martin—he could see straight through the big pupils and out the back of its skull into the space behind it. It sniffed the air for a moment, and then a disturbingly human smile of recognition took up the entire lower half of its face.

"What's your name?" Martin said.

"Play. Play!" it enthused, with the hissing voice a punctured tire would have if it could speak.

"I don't know. The last guy who played up here with me drew a boob on my Dragon book," Martin said without humor, as though cutting school and debating the loyalty of a new kid in the neighborhood.

It picked up a basketball and tossed it at Martin. He caught it and put it down at his feet.

Martin told himself that since he was facing a monster, he should probably kill it; that's what one does with monsters. He'd done it a thousand times before, but his finger hesitated on the trigger and his chest tightened as though flooded with emptiness. Was that sorrow? Why did he have the sense that he was pointing the barrel at his own head? Martin could finally only fire the .44 by pretending he was a kid and it was all make-believe. The bullet stopped in the thing's clear belly, causing it to laugh like it had been tickled. A clear exclamation point drifted out its head and splattered on the ceiling, where it stuck like the toilet paper downstairs.

The gun wasn't going to work. OK. He'd go along with its games, observe its behavior and see if any other good ideas popped up.

"All right, I'll play," Martin said. "How about we kick the balls downstairs?"

He stood up and began to walk slowly over to the pile, accidentally tipping over a candle.

The flame grazed a lottery ticket on the floor, which immediately blazed. Martin stamped it down, chose the Wham-O and kicked it down the staircase. He remembered doing this with the different sized balls he used to keep in the yellow chest, much to his mother's annoyance and his father's rage. He hoped the thing would also remember.

"You've been living behind that grate a long time, haven't you?"

"Yes. Watched you play! Learned everything!"

It all clicked. Now that someone had broken the wall in, the creature could get out and was repeating what it had learned from watching little Martin play—only with real, live people and whatever else it wanted to use.

The thing did a summersault, then took a rather elongated, austere head and followed Martin's lead. Soon, there was a whole Brady Bunch of heads and every kind of ball at the bottom of the stairs. Martin dashed down the steps and it followed him. Good, it still saw him as his teacher. Now he had to carefully choose what example to set for it.

"Play!" it shouted before it began to juggle heads, giggling unctuously. "Learn more!"

Martin had practiced juggling in the attic as a child. It had been decades since then, but he took a small beach ball and a tennis ball and kept them airborne while making his way out the back door and down the rickety steps. The creature followed. Acting on some sudden intuition, as though pulled along by invisible strings, Martin approached the deep well his great-grandfather had sealed up to keep the kids out, drawing the thing with him. He wasn't sure what his next move was. He wanted a cigarette.

That's when it all came together.

"Let's play something else," Martin said, letting the balls fall to the dirt.

A cryptically happy question mark congealed on the side of the thing's temple and faded into the starry darkness.

"Help me move these stones. Remember playing at landslide?"

"Landslide," it yelped, shoving the enormous rocks off the well like they were Styrofoam cubes.

Martin dropped the tennis ball in the well. It was a long time falling and landed with a hard thud far below. The thing laughed and Martin dodged the gluey exclamation points shooting out from all over its spindly body. Excited now, it took the heads and started tossing them down while singing in a chirping, child-like voice.

"Remember digging to China?" Martin asked, after the last head hit the bottom. He crouched down and started clawing at the ground with his fingers, like he used to pretend to do in the attic.

"Digging!" The creature copied him, its enthusiasm obvious as it tore at the sod, quickly tearing through six feet into the earth.

"Stop! Do you remember playing with Daddy's lighter? Flick, flick?"

The malformed face peered over its freshly dug hole, staring widely at Martin's lighter as he flicked it over and over until it finally turned on.

"You can take it. When you break into something really hard—a metal pipe like the kind I used to swing around like a sword—Keep flicking the lighter until it goes on. It might take a few tries, but when the fire comes out, that means you win! But not until then, OK?"

It laughed in italicized globs, nodded, leapt out, took the lighter in its mouth, pirouetted, stood on its head, which flattened for the duration of this gesture, and walked backwards on its hands to the hole.

"I'll race you," Martin yelled down. "Faster!"

It disappeared into the earth. Martin ran as fast as he could away from the house, his bare foot getting cut on the overgrown, glass-strewn driveway. He stopped across the road, huffing and puffing, to take a final look at 333 Spring Street.

How did that make him feel? Suddenly, he understood: He was angry that those scumbag druggies got to destroy the place. He wished he'd done it himself, long ago. He'd felt ambivalent and confused when he first returned because the violation felt good to behold. But it made him rage to think that his fantasy of obliterating the family home, his ruined childhood, should've been made real by anyone but him.

The creature reached the gas line that ran under the old well and everything was blown to hell with a great big BOOM.

Martin turned his back to the conflagration and watched his shadow flicker in the erratic glare, shivering as though it were cold. He felt lost and scared and he wanted to go home more than anything, but that he was home and there was nowhere else to go. For a moment, he couldn't move. The air behind him was scorching his back and he began to sweat so much he had to close his eyes for any kind of relief.

But he couldn't help but steal a quick glance over his shoulder at the grand fire and house-sized black smoke. Almost immediately he wished he hadn't looked. In that split second, he thought he saw the features of an awful, cunning face delineated in the flames; the face of someone who knows you well and yet you cannot recognize it; an interrogator, a stalker—a private investigator.

994
Pet Emporium
Nail Salon
994
NOTE:
make her NOT beautiful
MAP the Rooms out — etc
His eyebrows cast shadows that made his blue eyes look brown
Thiel
298
299
300
MARTIN
Dufresne
It was so easy

"DO YOU SING?" ASKED XAVIER STEEN

"True singing is a different breath, about nothing. A gust inside the god. A wind." – Rainer Maria Rilke

1

Detective Odd Hyspad woke that Sunday morning from a recurrent dream of brutal silence, hushes from a thousand bulletholes, 9mm mouths screaming from the bodies of his wife and two boys. Lying across an immaculately made, king-sized bed, cozy, joined in bloodclotted togetherness—two-thirds of a family become one beached deep-nightmare creature, carcass too heavy to lift in his arms, nestle his face into and blubber. And forever gone.

God, how many years ago? Don't answer—Only a monster would dare attempt measuring, defining these things... In real life, he'd found them in the kitchen, everything inanimate knocked over or broken—except an untouched cup of tea, steaming, *waiting* on the counter; his wife had poured it for him less than thirty minutes earlier. Hyspad couldn't bear to look at the cup any more than the bodies; that aloof, ceramic receptacle mocked him with its ongoing usefulness, possessed of more sheer existence than his dear Synnøve, and his big boys, who'd always be his little ones—Mathias and Vegard... The murderer left no traces and was never caught. There were no suspects. Not even in dreams...

That Sunday, just minutes after Hyspad woke from his silent nightmare, wondering if this was finally the right time to *do it*, the phone threw its tinny hissy-fit. It wouldn't be a friend; long ago he'd ceased all but professionally necessary human interactions. His old friends had meant well—but that meant nothing. Their sympathy made him sadder, angrier, almost supernaturally depressed; his reflection in the mirror seemed unable to bear looking at him. And they'd tried to set him up with women who weren't Synnøve, hounding him to date—the most heinous interpersonal blasphemy. The only dates he cared about were expirations on canned dinners and milk cartons. Even Hyspad's family didn't get it; they confused misery with depression. *Misery* is the one that loves company, whereas *depression* despises *everyone*—present and future company included.

So since the murders it had been work, only work for Hyspad. He took no vacations or sick days. He'd been rapidly promoted—So what? Meaningless. It served to keep him busy ... Sometimes, Hyspad would think about how he overheard a guy in forensics say if you put your naked hand in a fire, the pain will fully occupy its noiciceptors. Nothing's busier than a nerve in agony. He tried to be like that nerve.

But eventually, being busy wasn't enough reason to *be*.

Raising the questions:

When? How? Where? Should I leave a note?

He considered and failed to answer these daily.

ii

Hyspad spent most of that morning at the Bergen docks. A local fisherman spotted a body in the bay. The single ear attached to the maimed head was pressed against the hull of a docked houseboat; it appeared to stand upright in the green water, floating weirdly, like a figure in a Chagall painting. The corpse grasped a black pamphlet in one hand, inside his chest cavity, as if sheltering a candle from drafts.

The fisherman had knocked on the houseboat door to ask about using the phone; the door was open. He stepped in. All the curtains drawn, and somewhere below, a phonograph eked out a 78 of an old, popular American tune—banal love titter, cooed in factory-pressed baritone. The fisherman followed the music downstairs. He located the record player, and discovered an elderly woman lying on a bed, her wrists opened with a straight razor, which she clutched in one hand.

There appeared to be no connection between her death and the body whose ear was glued to her houseboat. When Odd Hyspad arrived, a few officers had just dragged the submerged corpse up onto the docks.

"Jesus Christ," Fin Koldbjornsen said, turning away, nauseous. He was a young, unpleasantly meaty officer. But lean detective Gladhaug dove right into the mess like a scalpel.

"You're not all wrong, Fin. Look…" and he pointed out rusty nails driven through the victim's icy hands and black leather boots.

"Sexy boots," Gladhaug said to Odd. "Ugly model, but sexy boots. These remind of a woman I know, you might like. Your type—Auburn hair, tall, a little sad. You always liked women who came pre-heartbroken, yeah? Why, less work for you? Anyway I could—"

"Enough," Hyspad said, quietly as a murdered son.

The nails were the least of it. Crouching down to inspect, Odd's red tie dipped tongue-like into scooped-out chest. Intestines and other lower internal organs were missing. Something abstract, nearly touching in the way of a small child's drawing, remained of his lungs and heart. A shotgun blast to the back of his head had halved it. A very ugly, wrong mouth was embedded haphazardly in this random conglomeration of viscera. One glaucous eye looked nowhere. A few strands of long blond hair from the back of the head remnant wove around the neck like thin gold necklaces.

The dead boy's eye was alive with silence. Hyspad saw himself in it. Now Hyspad was a living person found by a corpse. He shuddered and for a second he didn't know where or who he was. It was the sorrow of calling out, asking "*Is anyone home? I'm here! Hello? Where's my hug?*" and getting no replies, never again. The sadness was small but so is a bullet, a razor blade or sleeping pill.

Written in bold black letters on the first page of the slim black pamphlet found on the corpse: *Hymns For Mezzotheliomatik Frostbite*. The few remaining pages harbored a tightly woven script rendered indecipherably prolix by long baywater immersion; but Hyspad could read one set of lyrics clearly... he held it up to the sunlight.

Idiotically titled *The Unsolved Devil Murder*, Odd immediately recognized a glorification of his family's slaughter, some descriptions ripped off the many articles all those years ago. In the song, the assailant was "*The Devil with a submachine gun*" who "*will be back to make more blood run*" and who "*Killed the mom, the blood matched her head / enjoyed the boys screaming as I shot them red.*"

Hyspad pretended the words didn't exist, the way you skip a condom in a one-night stand because never mind, just this once let's go straight to the next step, and tried to recall why *Mezzotheliomatik Frostbite* rang familiar... Of course! That "black metal" band's drummer had proudly burned down a church in Stavanger, only a few weeks ago.

This little book was a definite lead. But the last thing Hyspad wanted was to give a bunch of morally bankrupt teenagers more press. And some instinct he couldn't name told him to keep the book secret.

"Keep quiet about this pamphlet—*both* of you," Hyspad said, shifting his gaze from Gladhaug to Fin the Fatty. "Just for now,

OK?"

They nodded, left as the bodies were removed. Policemen were telling an early morning crowd to leave. Children whispered in churning houseboat shadows, threatening to pull Hyspad into the water, should he walk too close. He thought about the Devil gunning down his... It was like how, after you've had a one-night stand and didn't bother about a condom, in the morning you can't think of anything else but *what if I'm dying right now? What if I'm dying?*

Silence.

iii

A long, black-haired miscreant named Xavier Steen was brought to Hyspad for interrogation. Xavier went by the appellation *Hieronymus* as guitarist for *Mezzotheliomatik Frostbite.*

He was a tall, arrogant youth with colorless, stonesouled eyes. Hills of facial acne obfuscated his age. He wore a black tanktop shouting redly: HATRED FOR THE SACRED, kneeholed blue jeans, unscuffed (therefore stolen) motorcycle boots.

Steen decided Hyspad was a typical fifty year-old, shit-eating Oink-Oink, spare-haired, pudgy-faced and paunched, never breaking the rules that supported his ass like a comfortable couch. Actually, he wore an aura of kind solemnity that attracted certain people. He looked like he'd listen if you needed to unburden yourself, and take you seriously—he'd care. Hyspad didn't lack for friends before his tragedy.

"Do you know why you're here?" Hyspad asked. He kept a steady, world-weary gaze at Steen over the piles of papers on the desk at which they both now sat, in his small cluttered office. Odd's stare was determinedly apathetic, quiet as a black eye.

"Dead, I guess?" Steen said.

"Who's dead?"

"Dead. Dead's dead."

"Sure, dead *is* dead. Did you do it?"

Steen leaned back in his chair and asked for a cigarette with a sardonic grin. Odd, who didn't smoke, fetched one from his drawer. Steen considered it with disgust.

"Take it or leave it," Hyspad said mechanically, realizing he'd long ago lost whatever pleasure he might've once had by offering menthols to bad people

In fact he felt nothing at all.

Hyspad lit the cigarette for the reluctantly acquiescent Steen. The smoke swirled dramatically around his face. Steen opened a grotesquely toothy mouth and told the story.

iv

"We forced Dead to join the band. Count Azathoth and I rehearse in the garage next to Azathoth's house near Oslo. We'd been through a thousand shitty singers. We needed a new one, somebody good.

"This skinny kid with long blond hair moved into the neighborhood. We never knew where exactly. He wore a leather jacket with a silver pentagram painted on the back. One day this kid was walking down the block while we rehearsed with the garage door open, scaring the neighbors with our really vicious sound. The kid stopped and looked right at us. We stopped playing. *Mezzotheliomatik* had no singer then but we had a mike so I went and said:

"'Hey, asshole, what do you want?'

"We laughed at him and he stood there staring. His eyes were glassy and intense. They were like expensive doll's eyes stuck in a raggedy doll's cheap face.

"'You play anything?' I asked.

"'I'm Dead,' he said. Almost all he ever said.

"'Do you sing?' I asked. That was the important point.

"'I'm Dead.'

"'Let's make him sing,' I said.

"We threw down our instruments and apocalyptic soundwaves charged out the garage, high-pitched wailing and low rumbles, you know? 'You're dead, huh?' I said. 'Not enough.' I struck his cheek with my studded leather glove. He stumbled back. Blood ran down his chin and dripped onto his motorcycle boots. Dead's look was glazed, like he had an ice-sculpture head with a human face painted on ... Hey! Weird but, you know what detective? You sorta have that look, too...

"... So we kicked the shit out of him. He finally passed out when Count Azathoth brained him on the back of the head with a drumstick. (For the record, Azathoth can be a real pussy too. He only attacks from behind, like a faggot.)

"We might've killed him then, if Count Azathoth's mom, Mrs. Soderlind, didn't call us in for lunch. Peanut butter and jelly sandwiches and milk. Ever since her husband left she feels useless I guess, and whatever we wanted she made. Azathoth's dad used to beat her so she's really submissive. But somebody's still smacking her around, I wonder who... Sometimes I bet Azathoth gives her a wallop, himself. Man of the house I guess. Hey, I bet *you're* some big important patriarch yourself, right? Are you man of your house, keeping the wife and kids in line?"

... Her eyes large and bright and the arrow of her laughing smile pointing to some word he'd just mispronounced. Long, auburn hair pulled back tight in a ponytail and simultaneously hanging wild to her hips, and her naked body on a bed of afternoon, Sunday newspaper light. An orange sweater clinging to her, holding onto her more tightly than he could ever manage, but serving as an aspirational ideal. One of her hands rubbing Odd's always-sore neck. Synnøve wears these impossibilities with the grace he's come to think of as her defining characteristic ... and their little boys, his always-little boys laughing, green and gold beautiful boxes and there were bright futures wrapped inside for them ...

"Yeah, Mrs. Soderlind is alright. I could have her. You should see the way she looks at me... But she's a fat cow... So, after lunch, Dead's still there, lying on the street, dyeing the tips of his hair red by dipping it in a puddle of his blood. I dragged him into the garage and pointed at the mike. He took it up, started wailing in pain. It was good, you could hear the thrashing we gave him lifting his voice up ... every syllable had our punches and kicks in it. So we beat him into the band. He was kind of of a pussy. I'm sure he was all pussy broken-hearted over some girl, something stupid, trendy like that. Pussy. But what the hell, we needed a singer and he sounded pretty dark and fucked-up."

A broken heart becomes infected. It travels up the spine and into the head and becomes broken brain, a fatal condition…

"Dead moved into Azathoth's garage. Anyway, what, two-three-weeks ago? Mrs. Soderlind's brother owns a catering hall and let us play a gig there. He's in racketeering or something. But, anyway before the show Belial got arrested for arson, that church in Stavanger. Good for him!

"Before we went on, we took turns inhaling from a bag of decomposing poodles, and knocked Dead around. Only two kids showed up, but we gave our all, crowd or no crowd. Dead's voice was good, brutal as I'd ever heard it. He stalked around with his skinny little lyrics book, because the songs were pretty new. Yeah, Dead was good, but Count Azathoth and I had a plan to boost his performance to an even more awesome level… The more you tortured Dead, the better he sang. Now I'd taped a knife to the back of my guitar, and Azathoth hid his uncle's sawed-off shotgun behind his kit.

"He sang the first three songs unmolested. Then while Dead stood at the edge of the stage watching the entire two-kid crowd exiting. I got the knife ready, whacked him behind his knees. He fell and I dragged the blade along his arm veins, little shadows of blood rising to the surface—Nothing serious…

"Dead didn't even react. He was past everything. And guess what? The fourth through sixth songs, Dead's voice was incredible, beyond imagination. Our last number, *The Unsolved Devil Murder*—Dead was dragging himself around the floor like a bitch, paler than corpsepaint. I threw off my guitar, cut him open. He was a gory open grave. Count Azathoth leapt out from behind his kit; together we ripped out Dead's intestines. I kicked him in the head…

"A vague tremble disturbed his body; picture an epileptic corpse. I remember lots of red. I pulled Dead's head up by his Goldie-Locks and Azathoth fired the shotgun. Dead's brain draped my face and perfect guitar picks of cranium scattered at my feet. Then I stuck the microphone into his chest, pulled it through this throat, and out the blasted side of his face. Suddenly we were deafened by feedback like electric storms, it's hard to explain—the most amazing noise. It sounded like escape, you know? *Real* escape—a demon, freed from the cage he'd been born in, from the limitations of his bones, screaming with a voice that was another element. *That* was singing, true evil black metal singing, yes!"

... You have children and it changes your memories and all you planned on, doesn't it? You get a new, shorter life. Food tastes different; fire burns hotter, cars go too fast and everything sharp gets sharper. Forget about airplanes, you wish they were never invented. It even changes the way you waste your time doing nothing... But you never thought about submachine guns and maniacs, too worried about lead paint and stairway gates... All the same, your wife asks if you'd consider a less dangerous job, she imagines the little boys growing up fatherless... what kind of world would that be for them? Unthinkable...

"Back at Azathoth's we hung Dead upside-down over the drumset, hammered rusty nails into hands and feet. One nail pinned his lyric book to his hand ... I put a bucket to catch the blood. We mixed it with red paint and made a little picture on the garage door. Soon Count Azathoth's mom complained about the smell. She thought we were practicing taxidermy! We were bored with Dead anyway, so Azathoth and I dumped him in the water...

"We haven't booked a show since then. Can't find a replacement... I don't know how *Mezzotheliomatik Frostbite* can go on. How can we get a singer who could rival Dead's performance? You must torment your singer, and to get the best out of him—sacrifice him on stage—just like the climax of a real, Satanic ritual. Nothing else will do... Dead spoiled us—and now *he's* spoiled!

"Anyway, detective, here's the point, the important point:

"Do you sing?"

Hyspad wondered: *Do I sing? Is that indeed, the whole point of Steen's story? The point of my story?* Again he didn't know where or who he was; a living person found by a corpse, a detective interrogated by suspect. Either way, sad and inconsolable.

When? Using what?

Wait—*Who?*

All these years, and Hyspad never thought to ask *that* question, assuming he'd do it himself ... Before he'd even thought them, words tumbled from Hyspad's mouth:

"No, Mr. Stee—I mean, may I call you *Hieronymus?*—I cannot sing. But I want to learn. Until our interview, I didn't know that. But *you* could teach me. Isn't that the important point? Why we're here, after all?

"Wha?"

"You see, Hieronymus, I've considered every question except the most important one. *When? Using What?... Notes*—But I left out *Who*? Certainly not me. Can you imagine, and I call myself a detective."

Hyspad's face had an expressionless stone slab quality coupled with a sense of great force, as though it was about to topple off his neck and crush Steen where he stood. Steen nearly pissed his pants. It was awesome; he could only nod in assent.

"Count Azathoth's mom's garage?" Odd asked. "That's where you could give me lessons, yes? Or say rather, *one* lesson. That's all I need. Give me a chance at the microphone and let me sing—like a demon breaking free of his bones."

Hyspad wasn't afraid. He just needed to go the way *they* went. He needed fate to strike him from outside himself, then ... the silence of a thousand bulletholes. And no one left to dream about it.

Steen knew Hyspad was serious, and the guitarist called Azathoth to check if it was OK with him. At first the drummer flipped his lid, saying the idea of bringing a fat old cop, who's going to arrest them for murder anyway, to play with them was fucking ridiculous. But then Azathoth started yelling about all the horrible things he'd do to a pig like Hyspad if he had the chance, and he realized, hey, *waitaminute...*

V

Practice was at eight that evening, leaving Hyspad plenty of time. But he needed to leave the office before *he* recognized anyone; he wanted to open his door upon an unfamiliar world, see only those people, drive the streets that he didn't know.

His proposition to Steen wasn't one he'd thought Odd Hyspad would ever have made. Yet in less than an hour, here he was, pulling into Count Azathoth's driveway in a lower middle-class suburb of Oslo. There was a large, red, sloppy Star of David spraypainted on the closed garage door; a real change from the swastika these Black Metal types usually went in for. Then Odd realized that Count Azathoth had no doubt mixed up the six-sided Judaic symbol with the Satanic pentagram. Somehow, that mistake told the whole sad story of *Mezzotheliomatik Frostbite*'s demented young drummer.

Odd sat on the hood of his car, considering the graffiti in an empty waiting-around-in-an-emergency-room daze. Also hazily comprehending Dead's blood coagulated there... perfumed bags of poodle corpses... *Killed the mom, the blood matched her head / enjoyed the boys screaming*... The penetrating quiet of a drowned man beached on the shore of a nightmare.

"Excuse me?" a woman called gently from his left.

Plump, fifty-one?—fifty-two? Wearing a much-outdated purple bathrobe, smoking a cigarette almost down to the filter, leaning through the half-open front door. The color, length and all the secrets of her hair were concealed beneath a white vinyl shower-cap, giving her an unfinished vibe, suggesting endless possibilities and personalities.

"Sorry if I startled you. I'm Odd Hyspad. I'm uhm ... an acquaintance of your son's band. They told me to be here at eight but ... well, I'm a little early. Didn't have much to do today, I guess. You must be, ah? Mrs. *Azathoth*?"

"Freda Soderlind. My son goes by Azathoth, the stupid shitbird. The name I gave him is Erik. He's home now, but sleeping in the garage. He likes it better than his bedroom, crazy. But you know teenagers—right?"

"As much as I've been able."

"*That's* the truth. Do you want to wait inside? I was about to make some tea."

There are rare things which happen with a suddenness that

seems faster than time should allow. For example, the exact moment you discover a mysterious, distant relative has died and left you untold riches and a magnificent castle, that you're royalty. With a vague premonition of such an event, and more instinct than awareness, he crossed the poorly-maintained lawn and followed Mrs. Soderlind into the dingy kitchen.

When he got closer, he saw her dark blue eyes matched the bruises around them, and was disgusted with himself for finding it attractive, a reaction to finding beauty where you least expect it.

The place was a dump; Hyspad didn't need to look to know every room resembled the corner of a rarely used attic. Through a doorway he could see a living room, the carpeted floor stained with various, unspeakable carriers of DNA; and beneath the nicotine fog, the stinky air confessed to a long tenancy of numerous cats ... They sat across from each other at an oval kitchen table, mismatched teacups steaming. Hyspad was grateful she knew enough not to ask why he was there. She probably did think he was a cop. What else could he be?

"Thanks for letting me wait here, Freda. I just, please understand I'm a quiet man. I don't like talking much, but it's nothing personal. I'm not good at conversation."

"You mind listening, Odd?"

"No."

Her smile was really something. It wasn't the fragile, exaggerated smile of a victim; it was at odds with her bruises; it was the smile of someone with all her teeth, who had loosened the teeth of her attackers while they turned tail.

"A quiet man," she said. "I like that. When most men open their mouths it's nothing but *you bitch* and *you're lucky I didn't kill you* and *stupid bitch*, you know. And they're not so great at listening, either, no matter how loud you scream, ha."

Freda had a musical voice, deep like hearing a cello played solo and going, hey, you know what? I *really* like the way cellos sound, I just never thought about it before. She spoke to him of domestic trifles, her favorite TV show canceled, the line at the supermarket, the clog in the bathroom sink turned out to be nothing, rumors of a friend-of-a-friend's affair...

As though they'd lived together forever, all the profundities already deeply shared and felt, and the kids gone away to university, the mortgage paid off, leaving them with an easy need for nothing but pleasant small-talk and tiny concerns. And what was that about rare things that seem to outrun time? Well, *that* again, and Hyspad enthralled, happily forgetting himself. Eventually the topic of Count Azathoth came up.

"My boy, like his father, he isn't the best person in the world," she said, nodding her toward a picture on the wall behind her, of a smiling boy on a much younger Freda's lap, a happy child who was getting the love and protection he needed, a child like Mathias or Vergard. "Since Erik was born, every year my world gets darker, and a mother had better get night-vision. She has to see in the dark clearly, you can't flinch, all the stuff waiting to get your kids is hiding in there. And I guess I was always a day person. Anyway it's too late to help him now... so I keep making sandwiches."

"Everything sharp gets sharper," he said, and could tell by her soft, grim smile that she understood.

"I bet you're a day person too, Odd. And I like when you talk—But look at the time! The Count will be waking any minute."

When?

Ten to eight. Yet to Hyspad, the hours had gone too fast. Consistent with this strange day full to bursting with quick, bold decisions, of thinking *after* the thought, before he realized he asked:

"Would you like to have dinner with me?"

"When?"

"Tonight—Now."

"You're here to arrest my son for something?"

Odd got up and walked to the window, looked out into the shabby blackness.

"Only if you want to have dinner with me. We can go now."

"And if I don't?"

"Then I'm not here to arrest your son, or anyone."

"What if I sleep on it first?"

"Then you'll never see me again."

He saw the still glow of a one-headlighted car a few blocks away, stopped at a traffic light, and guessed the driver … then Freda's reflection approaching him in the dark window. She'd taken off the shower-cap; releasing a luxury of shiny helixes, probably brown. He watched as she put an arm around him and rested her head on his shoulder. A gentle whisk of breath on his nape. These gestures felt unquestionably natural.

"Yes," she said. "Why not? I'm sure Erik deserves it, and I think I deserve it too. I'll just leave a note so the boys will know what happened…"

Hyspad turned from the window into an unexpected kiss. He felt something you cannot describe except by grossly inadequate, embarrassing references to pop songs, dusty sonnets, and advertisements for certain vacation packages … Yes, her hair was brown and smelled like shampoo … They exchanged smiles both flirtatious and compassionate, then—

Hyspad *Freda* saw her *What's* pupils *Wrong?* rapidly *A* dilate *Broken* and *Heart* she *Gets* opened *Infected* her *And* mouth *Becomes* to *Broken* furiously *Brain* scold

—In the nanosecond between the moment when Count Azathoth's cymbal-stand made contact with the back of the detective's head, and when it had driven halfway through his skull, Hyspad was overcome with enormous gratitude to Freda, for so graciously inserting a few extra moments of joy into the story of his life—And to his unseen assailant, for, thank God, taking him out of it at such a glittering peak of crescendo.

Hyspad's only regret—*If* he'd become a ghost with an afterlife point-of-view, which, in life, he'd certainly held was a lot of nonsense—*If* (and no-one can know the truth) he'd become a ghost, his one regret would've been his inability to protect Freda from the first vicious thing her son did to her following his own murder, and the second thing, third, fourth … until she'd lost count of the tortures because she'd lost her fingers and the mind needed to count upon them. Freda endured several weeks and died slowly. Erik Soderlind did not report his mother missing, and nobody else thought to; the only one who would've cared had also disappeared.

Despite a thorough search, no one was identified as a suspect for the possible murder of Detective Odd Hyspad, and his body was never found. Of course, now and then Fin, Gladhaug, and other old colleagues had no choice but to *remember* him. But that was painful. Better to keep Hyspad out of spoken reminiscence… And what of sleep, that country where everything can happen? Well, *if* any of them *had* glimpsed his face or heard his voice, be it in dream or nightmare, then they'd certainly *never* mentioned it, and never would. Chances were that Hyspad would've wanted it that way. In any case, he left no note.

TRUTH = THE OPPOSITE OF TRUTH AND LIES

I BELIEVE IN GOD WHENEVER I FEEL LIKE IT — THE WAY, MAYBE, YOU CATCH YOURSELF WHISTLING. I BELIEVE IN ME ALL THE TIME, LIKE SINGING OUT LOUD.

WRITING "WISDOM":

ALWAYS WRITE AS THOUGH THE READER WILL CARLESSLY READ YOUR WORK. ASSUME THE READER IS A DISTRACTED SKIMMER. IN OTHER WORDS, MAKE SURE EVERY LINE IN YOUR STORY IS GREAT AS POSSIBLE — SO NO MATTER WHERE THE SKIMMER SKIMS, IT WILL BE SO GOOD THEY GO BACK + PAY ATTENTION.

WWII STORY.

...NQUIL, IDYLLIC VIEW

③ THEY NEVER LEAVE...

W

S N

E

THE MANGE FRANGE WIND

HOUSE OF UNBROKEN WINDOWS

CAP'N DIES

THEY ENTER THE HOUSE OF UNBROKEN WINDOWS... ②

① FOUR SOLDIE... PASS THRU A ... OF FOG...

The CAPTAIN

SYKES

SHEPERD

BELLS

FOG

...AN... WIND, DUPLICATE MA... SEEMS TO BE...

"THIS MANGE-FRANGE" RUNS SOUTH TO NORTH.

THE WAR

...ontinued to page

The Startling Objects

"So it's always been a crazy world. The whole idea, a ball spinning around another burning ball—that's crackpot right to start with!" – Arch Oboler, in *House on Fire*

1
The Case Against Everything

Everyone's got a name, occupation, and view of the world—that "*ball spinning around another burning ball,*" as the man behind *Lights Out* wrote in 1969. Martin Box was a Private Investigator in a world he believed was rotating itself into a greater nonsensical mess with the collapse of each sidereal day. As though having accepted some stupid planetary Quadruple-Dogheaded-Demigod-Dare. If you asked him to justify his judgment, he'd say *OOFDAH!* or *fug-geduhbbowdet* or *Oofda, you doan wannuh-no, pfsssht!*… Such answers are either immediately understood—like a raised and aimed middle-finger—or opaque as those sunglasses Scientologists wear in public. Depends on the specific querent's neural pathways, deadends, cul-de-sacs, etcetera.

Nonsense is Big Business.

It was a typical, seasonless day in the Northeast. Some index was a number, there was percentage of precipitation, winds moving in one direction or another. There was temperature, Good God!—*weather*, even. Martin sat behind his desk, thinking about leaving early, when two finely-dressed businessmen entered the office. The taller and younger resembled an overworked undertaker. His black briefcase could hold two average male heads (assuming circumferences of twenty-four inches each), or single hydrocephalic. This obvious lackey waited for the short, shiny, richer, grayer one to sit opposite Martin. He then closed the door and put the briefcase on the desk.

Despite a free seat adjacent to his boss, the thin man chose standing. He leaned against a nearby wall, looking at home among the uninvited vertical cracks. He had one of those faces crying out to be punched.

"I hope that's full of hundred dollar bills," Martin said.

"It might be, if you can do what we want done," the older man said, his accent mostly dynasties of inheritance, consonants tinged with hedge fund dividends.

"I'll bite—soon as I'm good and sure it's razorblade-free."

The assistant opened the briefcase with the perfectly manicured fingers of a un-uncanny android still in a top-secret phase. Thereby revealing an inventory of four (4) Startling Objects:

1. Roughly twenty-seven inches lengthwise, equal in total mass to the lavish vintage Roman chasuble which Pope Benedict XVI wore for the 2010 Feast of the Epiphany: A round chrome plate connects two red tubes via one larger; the ends of the two curve pinceresque, symmetrically inward, ending in small, black rubber nubs:

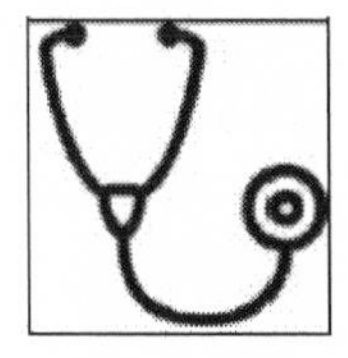

2. A six-inch-long, hollow, black wooden item, apostrophic in shape:

3. A four-inch-tall, glass tube that tapers toward a diminutive opening, the hole at the end of the wider tip wearing a sort of tight-fitted rubber hat:

4. Approximately eight inches in length, a chromium-plated device formed like the traditional, rudely extended tongue of the Krampus, that Austrian Anti-Saint Nicholas.

There was also a pinkish, ticket-like scrap of tattery pulpstock:

> *The Ballad of That Which-Don't-Exist serves as the key text for the properly initiated Mage(nt) / Executive Staff. The Ceremony is actually quite simple. It is the way you rose so high in the ranks of The Corporation: Always Fol-*

low Directions. Never Ask Questions—Do Whatever The Great Corporate Power Wilt Thou To Do, including Other Duties As Assigned. The Corporation is Above, You Are Below. Do What Thou Shalt Bidden Be To Do With the Pentagrammatical-Headed One, Starflesh with the Four Startling Organs. That is the Loophole of the Law. There Exists No Suit of It. As Above, So Below—Except Expendable. Go forth, Expendables!

"What are these startling, uh…"

"Inventions, Mr. Box," from the unimpressed older man. "*Objects*, if you like. It's all the same. We want to know who invented them and *what* they do."

"And you're about to tell me that you are?"

"I am Sebastian Wolvers; the hat-rack over there is my associate, Wilton Pickle."

"Mr. Pickle, I've only just heard about your name, and I want to offer you my sincerest condolences… Mr. Wolvers, are you the Sebastian Wolvers, CEO of Wolvers Wonderproducts?"

"Yes."

"I thought I recognized you from the cover of EMIT's special Man of the Year issue.

Because last year, you out-did James Dyson, you invented that—what was it?—*Lesbella*?—No, *Oombella*, right?—Doodoo-Hickey-Gizmola to help keep rain off pedestrians. And the BANISTER® right? That's an amazing thing, the way people don't have to risk falling off staircases all the time. Was the DOORKNOB® you, too? I love turning those. That was a good one. Now you own pretty plenty. Why d'you want my dirty Pee-Eye fingers in your unblemished pie?"

"It's called an UMBRELLA®, Mr. Box, and you should try one at the next precipitating opportunity. *Then* you'll understand just how life-changing my invention is… And yes, I take credit for the BANISTER® as well. I don't think I'm bragging when I say I deserved to be featured on the cover of that particular EMIT annual issue. Just wait a few months, Mr. Box, until our latest invention, the FLOW-

ERPOT® hits the market—unfortunately probably after the holiday season ... I can't go into any more detail than that right now—even the product's name, I'm sure I don't have to add—is *strictly between the three of us* ... The DOORKNOB®, alas, is Most of All Incorporated's only decent creation. I grudgingly admit to also enjoying the turning of them ... But that's a fluke; they're hardly competitors.

"As for what's brought us to your charming dump of an office: We understand you specialize in strange cases."

"Tell me again how you came by these objections, I mean, objects ..."

"You assure this discussion remains confidential?"

"Does a ghost wear a red jumpsuit?"

"Yes, yes. I am well aware you have proven this trivial fact is indeed the case, one of your more well-publicized investigations."

"Let's hear it."

"We stole them. Or rather, they were stolen from Everything Else, Inc. a competitor of mine, and sold to us by a trusted third party. But we don't believe that Everything invented these objects. Rather, Everything had stolen them from elsewhere, just as we took them off their hands. And if Everything's top brass thought the objects were worth stealing, they must be worth a good profit. They're smart—Worthy adversaries."

"If only you knew what these items *do*."

"Precisely ... And in fact, it's not unlikely that Everything Else's technicians hadn't yet determined what they were made for when they first began to study them. Our understanding is that Everything Else's men had only just started investigating their usage when we pulled off a purloin."

Martin decided that laughing at this last sentence would be detrimental to his potentially lucrative relationship with Mr. Wolvers.

"But where does the *strange* aspect of all this come in? Corporate espionage is nothing unusual."

"What about Corporate *Wizardry of the Outermost Transdimensionerristories*?"

"WOT? Okay, I'm all ears hooked up to adequate auditory systems."

"As you can imagine, we have access to an exceedingly unique pool of human capital and other operatives. The consultant who stole the objects for us goes by the name of The Bat.

Unoriginal, I know. But unimportant. The Bat is gifted with the ability to see invisible things; however his perception of the visible is severely limited. He's essentially blind to our world."

"And?"

"The Bat was able to locate and steal these four Startling Objects for Mr. Pickle because they were concealed beneath a haze of invisibility."

"So?"

"Wolvers Wonderproducts owns the only Invisibility Haze-Generating devices that could've hidden these objects to begin with. I'm 100% positive this remains a corporate secret. That's because only myself, this man here—Mr. Pickle, two well-controlled scientists—and you, Mr. Box—know this technology exists ... Of course we've already conducted intensive and extensive investigations. I know our scientists couldn't possibly have sold any information. And it's certain Pickle hasn't traded our secret, because although I trust Mr. Pickle more than any other man, I don't trust Mr. Pickle one bit and he's almost never out of my sight, touch, or hearing... Well, you know what I mean."

"Aye, as Queequeg to Ishmael ... (Martin was in a Herman Melville reading phase, even going so far as to finish the unexpurgated *Pierre*). So, some other force was behind the invisibility that had cloaked these objects. Not Wolvers Wonderproducts technology, which, technically, should be the only kind that could do this."

"Yes, something unnatural—Impossible to trademark," Wolvers said, shivering at the commercial implications.

"Which means the source of the inventions are likely *Transdimensionerristory* in origin.

And that sort of nonsense is my specialty. But let me ask—How d'you know competition—Everything Else, Incorporated, or Most of All—didn't create their own Invisibility Haze-Generator?"

"The story is too long to tell. You just have to take my word for it, that no other company has developed similar technology.

Especially Most of All. The idea is laughable."

"Good. Laughter's good for you. And your word is taken. Now, does W.W. have any inventions on hand that would allow me to see invisible objects, à la M. Bat? Because it sounds like I could use that for this case."

"We do, and would authorize your access to it—*for this purpose alone*."

"But why not just hire this Mr. Bat himself?"

"For a detective, you ask a lot of questions," seethed Mr. Pickle, with puzzling, unsinkable irritation.

Martin turned to face him. The man was annoying exactly like suction cups when they simply won't remain on a wall, no matter how many times you try to get them stuck.

"For a man named Pickle, you sure ain't no coolest cucumber."

Pickle simply looked at Martin, expressionless—*through* him, almost—while the detective rejoindered. Aside from the filigree of cracks, the wall Pickle leaned on was thumbtacked with miscellanies, a few maps, mugshots, to-do lists, phone numbers, names with obscure occupations scribbled on eggcream-stained Hinsch's napkins: Dr. Julius Jonsson, Hylesoprotolist and Cryptobotanist; Cylinder Olynyk, Copyist, etcetera. As Martin was returning his attention to Mr. Wolvers, a Chinese take-out menu—not near Pickle, who hadn't moved, anyway—suddenly fell from its tack to the floor. Like it had been quickly torn off. It was nothing, but it was an odd nothing.

"Shut up, both of you, *please*," Mr. Wolvers said, reeling Martin back to him. "What Mr. Pickle was about to tell you, is that The Bat is an excellent thief, but little else. I trust that's a sufficient answer."

"Why don't you take a seat next to your boss?"

"I prefer to stand," Pickle spoke, then displayed an out-of-place of smile—the type two close friends share at the unexpected resurrection of a personal joke.

"Suit yourself. All right … Mr. Wolvers, how did you make these invisible objects visible again? I assume you have some patented Wolvers Wonderproducts process for that?"

"You catch on quick."

"And this thing about That Which-Don't-Exist and Starflesh?"

"We have no clue as to its meaning, value or use."

"All right. We're in business. Say, Mr. Wonderpants, you should invent something to make taking shoes on and off a lot easier, you know? Imagine how much more free time people could get."

"Ridiculous," Pickle said, locking the briefcase before taking it off the table. Mr. Wolvers chortled in a rare, touching show of employer-employee solidarity.

"Please leave the inventing of life-changing technology to the experts," Pickle added. "Honestly, who needs help operating their footwear? What an idiotic conception..."

"Goodbye, Mr. Box."

Martin nodded, they scrammed, he gave the closed door the bird. Nothing happened. He shook his middle-finger a bit to get the circulation going, then gave the bird again, like, two or three times more. Nothing. Time to go home.

11
(LIKE A) SEDENTARY MIDDLE-AGED CYBORG-S&M-DEMON

"There you go."

The elderly, lab-coated man stood in the never-used yet still moldy shower of Martin's office bathroom.

"The Angelicas look snug now. How's it feel?"

Martin looked doubtfully in the mirror. Wolvers had dispatched the scientist to implement the fitting. The Angelicas were a set of metal horns about the size of an extra-large double-ended dildo, curving forward like those of a bull, and covered in blinking electronic lights. Martin looked sorta like a sedentary middle-aged cyborg-S&M-demon. And Christmas display.

When the Angelicas were engaged, they allowed the wearer to view the invisible world. Though cumbersome, they pulled Martin slightly off the ground as if a great magnet hung above his head, and the air beneath his boots was distempered. It was like standing on a raft woven of struggling eels.

Martin observed a centipedesque heliotrope horror tipmillion-toe about the scientist's glabrous head, pass through his face as into sculpted air, only to reappear at his feet. It then went POOF!—to places unknown.

"How's it working?"

"Did you just feel a multilegged arthropod, about the size, say, of an undernourished ocelot, go weaving in and out of your head?"

"No."

"It's working."

"Remember, this is a Prototype. We're not sure, but the longer you wear it, there's a chance you'll lose the ability to see the visible world clearly—or at all. And there could be other Side-Effects."

"Huh. The whole Viagra® thing."

"Yep. Good luck, Mr. Box."

"Is that the scientist, or Sebastian Wolvers talking?"

"The concerned grandfather I'm sure you never had."

"No need. You only die once, right?"

"Yes, but you're *always* dying. So don't be such a pessimist. And take these directions we've prepared for you. They're straight-forward. But there's still a chance you'll get lost. But don't... Now, is there a real working bathroom around here?"

"Sure. Just across the street, in the Bourgeois & Global®, there's like, six Starbucks®."

iii
UH, GRIZZLY... I GUESS, MAN?

The laboratories of Everything Else, Inc. were located in a shitty, sparsely populated (although it's not like the Census ever visited) place on Brooklyn's Weast Side. In spite of its easily-confirmed reputation as the most demoralizing, slummiest, dangerous area in the city—a neighborhood so bad that even that Mr. Moloch Gen-trification considered it off-limits—the word "broken" was practi-cally meaningless there.

Everything simply *had* to be repaired (quality-schmality!) be-cause nobody had cash to hire an expert for proper thing-fixing.

And most nouns were repairable, both because Weast Siders didn't own much, and their most complicated possessions were either mechanical or analog. The continuous efficacy of necessaries had always to be ensured. Most of the duct-taped windows, rusty fences, plywood doors and stairways, furniture—all domestic objects—had been serving their intended purposes for decades. Because if you were born in the Weast Side you stayed there. You took first and last breath in the same sad room. In the same sad bed that could never break, even if it looked quite as different as you in the end.

The buildings evoked incomplete factories, eroded public housing. Martin thought of landfill acreage, a Worst-Of-Human-Nature preserve from which rose a monitory stink—Off-The-Charts (and shredded) Crime & Poverty Ratings / Less-Than-Zero-Zaggat® Ratings / unburied-bodies and the backed-up hurlage of manhole, asshole, knife-hole ... Families so poor they flavored Thanksgiving gravies with shoebox desiccant packets...

But at least it wasn't Bensonhurst.

Martin purposely went at twilight: Few people noticed the man with the somewhat laughable yet bellicose headpiece, because hardly a soul dared the streets when shadows flooded the Weast Side. He was counting on appearing completely fucking insane, because in New York that's your best bet to keep safe, in any neighborhood, trust the voice of experience—and don't take advice from anybody, evah.

Eldritch fauna rode Electro-Gentle-O-Matic™ tide variations past Martin (No, Martin had no idea what that description meant either; it isn't what it isn't and could be). He sorta-walked-upon-simulated-water, bobbing along—wheezy, headless snakes with faces for bodies that moved by coughing up prosthetic limbs of mistyped Latin sentences in 72 pt. Comic Sans, the word-limbs yanked randomly from the official *viaticum*—(WTF?! *Invisible Sounds*?), rolling, lymphatically grotesque bottom-pukers, 50% spheroid, 50% rectilinear, and 52% dolabriform; and ground-hugging, solemn, slimy strati-form creatures of braindick that micturated streams upward (and so rained onto themselves) while taking turns muttering: "Gentlemen! This is not a good idea. We all agree we're sick of this piss. But, gentlemen, I ask of you, what are the alternatives?"

Martin was familiar with the disoriented vibes of *transdimension-erristorical* spots, but at this was all "loopy-deedee-leedee-loopy-doodoo-dee-pahdoop-boop," at the risk of being cliché. Here, Meaning Itself was a little bit disease with a pinch of distress. Things in the invisible world *could* demonstrate rationality, but it was irregular, episodic—like the fits and renascent fevers of epilep-sy or malaria or the brown bouts of White Castle®-Sliders ... At-mosphere of lighthearted, turtleneck dread conducive to philoso-phizing—i.e., a state of confusion—much how impending death catalyzes prayer in the dying.

Try, try, try, he couldn't follow Wolvers' directions, try, try, nope. Lost.

Why'd They have to make an idiot TV show out of it, trivialize the metaphysical? People like Wolvers ...

The directions were truly simple—made the Candyland® board look like finding Route 80, east of Parsippany, New Jersey. The laboratories should be near, in a compound of warehouses resem-bling giant storage boxes, but ... Martin still didn't know where he was, couldn't stop philosophizing ... damn disorderly atmosphere ... N-No, not that ... *Yesyesyesyes* whispers in his head, the same one you'd put a DUNCE hat on ... Damn! He begins soliloquizing, in an August voice, with Tourrettesesque abandon:

"We don't want to get lost. We want to be not-lost. In our de-sire to be not-lost, we desperately want to *follow directions* ... The es-sential nature of these directions is such that they are shared with others, so that more than one soul can reach a defined location.

"So if you follow a map, a trail, however lonesome it be, you can't be striking out on your own, now can you? Someone else has a hand in where to put your feet.

"But what is getting lost? The lost man is the architect of his own Destiny. LOST: Only you alone could've followed these exact no-signs-at-all ... No corporation can claim a deed to your place of lostness ... It's like the Wild West!—only, without the West—or North, South or East, either!"

Martin, calm down. Focus. Do you see that boxy building? Could lead to the laboratories, you think? That's rational, right?

But he'd been bit by an oration bug or something:

"In short, each individual believes their Destiny belongs to them alone. That's why when we don't know where we are or where we're going, then we feel we've gone astray from personal Destiny. So what do we do? We make frantic efforts to determine our location in relation to locations which exist in the context of social agreement. Which have been determined by others ... To get back on our own track, we must ask directions of another ..."

He shut up, and for this, too numerous could the oblations made to ye gods never be. But Martin shivered. It was a hard feeling, intangible, abrasive: You make conscious attempts to take control of your Destiny only when you appear to have lost it, and yet nothing belongs to you—and you alone—more than lostness ...

"That is your Destiny," came his dramatic peroration, "precisely because it is not your Destination!"

His lips, Martin zipped 'em—*and how, brother*, as Daffy Duck® puts it. He waited. The psychic eruption of whatever that'd been passed, for now. So that's what radios feel like ...

The visible world, its demarcations, got ... drippy. Building corners, streets and curbs appeared to deliquesce into a liquid landscape of pseudo-immiscibility. Sorta like an early, aborted draft for a painting Dali tossed in the trash.

More disorientation than expected. Wud' the scientist say? *Prototype ... Side-Effects ...*

But he kept on, hoping for a sign to show his hazy trail true. He tried to perceive definite contours and shapes, yet the garbled dimming of the visible world grew ever dim and garbling on all sides. Martin wasn't a religious man. But he suspected this exhausting effort to align hope with actuality amounted to praying.

Then in a flash so fast—near nonexistent—the Angelicas jerked his head to and fro, threatening whiplash; it stopped and he could see the visible again.

Now fluorescent graffiti tags popped out of otherwise drab, ashen walls of public housing projects, their halls squeezed into crawlspaces by peer-pressure, no room to escape fust of theft, rape, murder, prayers, despair, hope ... Most of the tags were stylized into the illegibility of *The Voynich Manuscript*... A few were readable, if outlandish: KNEE-BRACE, WAINSCOTTING, MATTRESS COVER, DISPOSABLE RAZOR—each punctuated with a WUZ HERE paraph.

Martin liked them; they sounded as meaningful as they did meaningless. Might refer to any of the things in the everything.

—On the nape of Martin's neck, the sudden withheld-breath of a stare. He spun round to an invisible entity, about three feet in circumference—size of a large Pilates ball really—hovering about ten feet behind Martin, scant inches above the ground. Nothing is sure as shit, and it was with just such fecal certainty Martin knew the thing was following him.

It resembled an *azzurrognolo* Saturn, ringed by twisting fascicles of bone, from which hung sparse curtains of furryblack, fibriform gesticulators. Each long as orangutan arms. These symmetrical loops orbited a tumid and hyperkeratotic sphere, the whole pulsating with the abnormal intervals of ventricular fibrillation. It choreographed itself to Martin's movements, topped, moved when he did. It dragged a chain forcefully jammed in its hind, with mild clanks. A sodacan-tailed honeymooners limo shrinking into the sunset...

Although hardly comforting in appearance, the orb didn't seem an immediate threat. A picker of carrion perhaps? Waiting for Martin's inexorable butchering at a pack of invisible predators local to the area. But the Saturn radiated a bold timidity—as if it had forced itself from a hidey-hole against persuasive instincts of self-preservation.

Bad feeling, how it knew something Martin didn't... generated a state of nebulous lookout. But a professional must keep on.

Martin had just turned, his focus to the wavering visual field, when the Saturn whooshed ahead of him, dime-stopped against Martin's belly and bumped him backwards—he very nearly landed smack on his sedentary middle-aged cyborg-S&M-demon coccyx. Great instincts, Martin—Naw, *that's* not an immediate threat . . . He fumbled for his gun and couldn't find it. He usually put it in one of five places, and only had time to check three—no, wait, one in seven places, if you count—Ahhhhfuckit . . .

You win a few, but you get viciously mauled to chunks of nothingness by an inexplicable entity only once.

Martin winced for the oncoming blow of what he took for an MWHVKW: *Meaningless-Worm-at-the-Heart-of-the-Void-Knows-What . . .* Nothing happened, like giving a closed door the finger. Getting up, Martin saw only the top half of the Saturn at his feet, inert. Had its lower half been lopped off? He spun about, seeking whatever had severed the cyanotopic orb twainwise. He stepped back to the security of a solid wall. A spot from which to gain perspectives. Except, none useful . . . Like giving a closed door the bird twice.

The orb was still alive, armillary bones spinning fast, drawing Martin's attention.

Numerals had been deeply scorched into the animal's skin. Each long as your typical clownshoe:

#1Ø2

Owtch . . .

"Oofdah," Martin mused. "Hadda hurt. Plus, the whole sliced in half thing . . ."

Once it knew Martin had seen the brand, proof of an escape from cruel and unusual bondage, the Saturn rose from what Martin now saw was a sizeable abyss the street. If #102 hadn't knocked Martin to the safety of his ass and corked that hole, it would've been the end of his Private, Investigative life. The creature was whole, all there and all right.

Martin put out his hand. It was met by a velvety conventicle of black hairs, these forming something like an Ursidae paw.

"Close enough," Martin said, and they loosely shook on it. "I'll call you Grizzly. Come along, then . . . Oh and thank you for saving me life. I would've said that earlier, but I forgot I had one. I have a feeling you'd like me to return the favor and, just so you know, Grizzly, I'll be happy to. I also get the sense you know the purpose of my mission, why I'm wearing this last-place, award-losing Halloween costume contest get-up. That you're reading my mind. Or at least motives?"

It's hard to describe, but the entity nodded: "You nailed it, man!" "Lead on then, Grizzly!"

His new companion alleviated Martin's sense of lostness, that degeneration of meaning he'd felt when entering the invisible. He trusted Grizzly. There was loyalty under that pulsating blue psychedelic weirdness. Of course, everyone lies, but Martin had learned through hard experience that if you find a liar you can trust, hold onto that angel ... Because lying and loyalty aren't mutually exclusive.

"Are they?" Martin never asked himself.

IV
(WITH THE EFFICACY OF) UNITARIAN EXORCISM

Below the luminous flux of a cold moon, Martin cased the warehouse for a way in, crept through a shallow moat of megacapitalist runnel of blood and toxic chemicals.

Grizzly drifted to a door huge, ostentatious as The Spruce-Goose. The creature uncurled hirsute rings, skeletal bodkins, and adroitly wined and dined the wires of a sorta HAL electronic lock. The door swung inward, maybe a Pharaohs' tomb. #102 levitated politely to one side, waiting for Martin to precede him into the silence. The yawning silence you find in the knotted hearts of an ancient rope-bridge, still hanging limp, tattered, and just barely ... A warning, now, that no one will ever reach the other side again ...

The Angelicas allowed for vision in most conditions, visible and otherwise. The place was chock full of boxes and nightmare darkness, corners clotted with shadow thick, unpleasant as cannibal viscera (*What does that even* mean? Martin wondered, too—such was the breakdown of rationality in that place).

The enormous quiet of tiny wounds not worth mentioning ...

Martin watched his telepathic planethropod pal, speeding through the high, inventoried corridors with definite purpose ... Where to? *Hymn* ...

Something whirred behind great boxes. Martin's blood strained to become all eyes, but only managed to effect a significant increase in its pressure ... The crates contained Everything Else's newest product, ready to ship before the holidays:

THE FLOWERPOT®

> No More Planting Flowers in Expensive Funerary Urns! Enjoy Flowers for their Natural Beauty—Don't Let your Ficus or Tulip be a Constant Reminder of Mortality and Loved Ones Lost! THE FLOWERPOT®—Beauty in Abundance—*Memento Mori* No More!

What'd Wolvers said?

"Just wait a few months, Mr. Box, until our latest invention, THE FLOWERPOT® *hits the market—unfortunately probably after the holiday season ... I can't go into more detail than that right now, and even the product's name, I'm sure I don't have to add, is strictly between the three of us ..."*

Someone had sold Wonderproducts out to their only serious competitor ... An extraordinary act of espionage, bravo. But no time to speculate who, Martin could almost choke on the lies that swarmed through each day—the ones that lay a million eggs in your soft naked soul and, *if you're lucky*, only a few hundred hatch, in diurnal cycles ...

The whirring had become a slowly gathering storm of white noise ... Martin moved away from the sound ... an operating-table, long-necked sodium lights curling over it as if in the midst of fascinating dissections. The tabletop was segmented into four deep, empty partitions. Painted in red at the bottom of each:

DONOR: THE STARFLESH
SPAWN OF THAT WHICH-DON'T-EXIST

An astringent foamy substance had pooled beneath the table, by triangular repoussé—the heel-marks of unusual custom shoes.

Waitaminute—Where's the whirring? And, a-a-and why can't I move my head?

Martin raised his hand to touch the top of the Angelicas' horns and groped big, metal fingers with cannon-ball knuckles.

He made a dash, the Angelicas go tearing off his head while an electronic screaming bore inescapable labyrinths through his auditory cortex ... He stumbled into a box labeled MASKS®, another new Everything Else product? Yeah but what's it do? Designed to change faces—Why?—isn't that what expressions are for...

The mechanical guard slapped his back with a titanium hand, Martin slid across the floor into a crate of defective mood cockrings, sought his revolver—with the efficacy of Unitarian Exorcism. Metallic steps crashed toward him, drowning out the whirring sound of a powerful multi-chambered gun practically not even invented yet.

Martin scrambled backwards on his elbows. For a moment, a humanoid outline towered above ... Martin seemed to go deeply under all that ever was blackly underneath and before he was born, and long after he'd given his name to the void, forsaken... or was it for safekeeping?

V
FLESH UPON A STAR

...Pretty sure his name was Martin, the man emerged from robotic, bitch-slapped traumatism, curled up, an achy ball of a man in the corner of a sadly standing church, abandoned, too depressed to collapse into the wooden dust it long should've been. Grizzly—his strange guardian angel—appeared and gently adjusted the Angelicas on Martin's head. It extended an improvised paw and helped him get up. He was a little shaky, but functional, solid—a tough vibrator can still get the job done, even low on batteries.

Saturnae of different sizes were #-burned and chained to the moldering pews. They'd been forced into numerically ascending order, from basketball-sized #1 in the last row, to the highest—#103—about two feet in circumference, and bobbing now and then into the luxury-class spaciousness of #102's front-row seat. Some meekly strained to disable their chains, but none were as big as #102, who was likely the only strong enough to escape. Most of them were still as the white shadows of Euclidean circles, barely-visible drawn chalk haunting a blackboard erased many lessons ago. They were glazed with obvious dejection, as a madman's beacon lips shine with asocial spittle.

"Don't worry," Martin said. "I'll find something to cut you guys loose…"

—Episodes of diseased rationality are hard to predict…Martin was searching for a tool to emancipate the orbs when he began thinking about his reading habits…

How he went through different phases. Like he'd get interested in American History for a while and get a bunch of those books; then he'd suddenly wonder if Shirley Jackson wrote anything good besides *The Lottery*, and he'd wind up reading *Hill House*, then *We Have Always Lived in the Castle*, *The Sundial*, and so on, devouring nothing but Shirley Jackson for five entertaining months straight. Well, in his oddest yen to learn, one bleak winter Martin delved into the cold of the Icelandic Sagas.

The Saga of the Volsungs was especially not the very most terribly dull, awful watching-paint-dry of them. Odin had embedded the magic sword Gram in the tree *Barnstokkr*. *Gram* could only be extracted by the "True King." Many strong men tried with all their might and the sword never so much as wiggled—until the "True King" turned out to be Sigmund (father to Wagner's Siegfried)—who unsheathed it from the unearthly grip without the slightest difficulty.

—Martin experienced this memory of reading trends in general, and *The Saga of the Volsungs* in particular—because he suddenly felt exactly like *Barnstokkr* must've when Odin gave it that divine whopper of metal thrust, a regular *Gram* of searing heat jabbed deep into Martin's lower back. With lightning-to-rod enthusiasm, the pain rose through his vertebrae like Looney-Tunes® Suicide-

Mission-Mercury hurtling toward cartoon-thermometer glassburst —to explode in the 1,000-degrees Far-in-hell of Martin's skull... Luckily the intensity and duration of the Saga-big wound was pretty short, fading with a last, quick zing, just as though he'd been struck by lapillus from an active volcano's rim.

In a migraine haze, Martin turned to face the pultaceous, five-pointed Starflesh who demanded his attention. It was about nine and a half feet tall and wide—the same dimensions as the Star Michael Hammers famously crafted for The Rockefeller Center Christmas Tree. A bright-red branding iron, like a railroad-spike tapering to a rapier-point, protruded from a sebaceous upper limb.

Its thin-skinned, diaphanous body was gravid with venous jelly, full of nonsense & non sequiturs—documents and dossiers; bed-springs; ripe, unpeeled banana; a large volume entitled *How to Become a Sunflower Farmer: Are You Ready?*; numerous used candles (How many are lit in joy, how many for grief? How are the heart's tiny flames apportioned, and of what significance wick-length? Polluting the air, then worldsnuffed)—Where'd *that* come from?—sink-or-swim submarine screws; three exenterated thumbs; presidential voting chads from Florida; keychains; cake knife; raggedy dolls in suggestive poses; UP, DOWN, and HEADFIRST elevator buttons—each lit in the dull, noncommittal color of all elevator lobby buttons; a green plastic watergun; realistic, balsa hygiene accessories for puppets used in venereal-disease training films; a lovely, untossed bridal bouquet; astrolabes and other tools; chewing-gum wrappers—the monster was its own storage space, file cabinet, tool box, time capsule, garbage can, dollar store, bomb shelter, municipal dump, aquarium...

Weaving around and through these items ran weird strings—elastic fascicles woven of friable dendrites, axons lacquered in scrimshawed rhinobone, and imperial black feathers that must've inspired several Odes to a Cormorant when it stood proud upon a Welsh shoreline.

These strings were securely knotted to a crazy nest of brass wires, and hooks hung from them, through a tangle of arteries, spiraling veins, and capillaries vaginated with psychopharmacological tubing … These hooks each pierced one of a sloppy network of numerous hearts, ranging in scale from tsetse-ticker to that of the largest, as-yet-undiscovered komodo dragon.

They didn't work like pumps. Each of these organs was an angry, mercenary unit. They swung in irregular spasms of violence, soused inmates engaged in a fight to the death. It was every organ for itself. Maybe their continuous, vicious battle for dominance kept the Starflesh alive…

The Starflesh lashed once more with the brand. Martin ducked justintime, while Grizzly tried to yank out a string of hearts, plunging a bony pincer into the thing. But the Starflesh nimbly evaded—Its 360 degrees of perception were keen… No wonder #102 needed Martin's help—alone, it was impossible to catch it off guard.

The Starflesh retracted the smoking branding iron into the sheath of its body, and by the metal's rufous glow Martin spotted a black leather folio inside the jelly, roughly where a pentagram's abdomen would be—and the cover embossed with depictions of the Startling Objects. Martin lowed his head and charged at the Starflesh like a bull to a red flag. The Angelicas pierced its skin and a bitter astringent effluvium whistled out. The Starflesh quivered, erratic, demented as a 47-minute Neil Young Bigsby® wankout…

Aiming for the folio, Martin deepfisted the Starflesh, knuckles stinging… stinging… stinging… Stuck! Martin's intrusion stirred up a trio of lizard hearts cooperating, in order to gang-rape a larger, mammalian organ. This degraded heart made a squish toward a faraway hook, as the three perps turned solo again, chomping and clawing as each tried to be first to reach Martin's hand… Shit!

The creature sneezed the hot branding iron out a lower appendage, and was about to singe Martin's head into something a touch more unidentifiable, when Grizzly flung itself into the path of the Starflesh's brand.

Martin was seriously considering that Grizzly was his guardian angel. And he'd gotten his own guardian angel killed…

It smoked from a #44 just below its #102 and fell—an immense thud of granite cargo unloaded by a shitfaced crane operator. His nettling hand only inches from the last heart standing,

Martin Angelica-gored the pentalimbed beast again, almost breaking his neck with the effort. By sheer luck, the point of one horn shish-kebabbed a squadron of ravenous hearts—the Starflesh generously exploded—luminous, circumambient and numinous as a Hell-King's Kama Sutra Orgasm, showering its multidimensional palimpsests all over the church.

Dripping in WTF?!, stinking and looking like WTF?!, feeling WTF?!, and thinking WTF?!, Martin rushed to Grizzly, whose integuments were bloating and retracting in bad-prognosis fashion. Behind him, 102 Saturnae clanked their chains with incredible nuance, like talking drums—furiously, with sorrow, gratitude, impatience…

"Hold on! I'm a'comin'…"

Martin squinted, prodded about, a blind dog bereft of olfaction … Eureka! He found an opened toolbox. Various implements lay everywhere … hammer … screwdriver … copper tape … voltmeter … springs … There! A large set of chain cutters had broken into one of the plaster Virgin Mary's monomorphic erogenous zones. Ha!—Now Martin was pulling *Gram* from the tree *Barnstokkr*… He went fast as he could. The first two freed drifted to their fallen comrade. They carried Grizzly away through a hole in the roof, clouds of great buboes evaporating into their journey home…

Drenched in sweat, Martin got down on the floor and reprised the blind, noseless dog act, groping about until he found the folio and its invisible pages:

! ! ❹ ! !

Directions for
The Ceremony of the Conjunction & Transmutation
of the Four Startling Objects into the Four Startling Creatures

> ***Read This First:*** The invisible is not the same as the nonexistent, but there is a greater affinity between them than the visible and the nonexistent. It is therefore not impossible to interbreed, for lack of a better term, the invisible and the nonex-

istent, such that the existent can be made visible, and vice versa.

Ceremonial Directions: The Chief Executive Officer steps to the center of the Circle of Protection and declares unto the Void The Ballad of *That Which-Don't-Exist*, into which the Four Startling Objects have been inserted wearing masks of text (If the CEO is not available, a Chief Operating Officer trained in Best Practices may be substituted for this role):

"O witnesses one-hundred & three,
branded witnesses witnessing me,
I'll extract real-world from the fiction that follows.
Four Startling Objects, mere words now in lyrics—
Soon four creatures living will make their appearance.

I call Fiction forth in the form of a ballad.
I am witnessed by one-hundred & three:
I sing you forth in a ballad—on four...
Ready?
One... Two... Three—
O!
That Which-Don't-Exist made everyone sick
She was harder to find than a newborn tick
With mandibles hidden inside her mouth
(And some said in places even less couth)
But why not antennae? Or dragonfly wings?
Don't-Exist had no need of such tepid things
One of her Startling Objects really could sting
And it had two tubes red, as like filled with blood
with nowhere to go—veins sealed by black nubs.

She broke virgin hymens on wedding days
With a Startling Object like an apostrophe

(More often than not in mid-ceremony)
Sweet-hearts she vanished for good in the hay
Clean water she turned to bile and pus
Made people with chaste thoughts unstoppably cuss
Of the City's wisest five, four gathered to plan
For to banish Don't-Exist away from the land

But one got a pox, and one spider bites
All over his crotch—next they ate his wife
One tried to flee and never came back
His trail fraught with bloody hoof tracks,
Ended with a glass tube wearing a hat.
It was nothing like what they would expect.
Which made it the more startling of a
Startling Object.

But That Which-Don't-Exist got morning sickness
We caught her in the vestry squatting mid-piss
Her womb had waxed large as a harvest moon
Too bloated to flee, we trapped her, and soon
We strapped her to the stake tight as skin to a rash
Her eyes broke like eggs, nipples into embers, ash
Where foul expression, now smoking black gash
She barred her fangs and they cracked and broke
Her fourth Startling Object was a chromium device
It stuck out her mouth and its metal shone white
Hot screams rushed up it, teeth fell down her throat
Then mandibles clacking, like that metal tongue
She perished with all the air singed from her lungs.

The purging flames died and all cheered she was dead
'Hold! She grows a pentagrammatical head!'
For her water had broke in fire's dazzling glow
Starflesh dropped down, it swung by the cord
All readied to crush it before it turn Lord.
The one wise man still left in old city town

Thundered 'We should crawl home, ashamed and afrown'd
We must turn from our crime and find a dry place!
We must pray to God for His mercy and grace—
For killing a babe is the evilest thing to do—
Your child, or mine—Even Which-Didn't-Exist's, too!'
Well it started to rain, so we took his advice,
Sought cover from storm, among flies and lice—
When the sky was dry we chopped off his head twice."

Impact Measurement & Evaluation: The purpose of the *Ceremony of the Conjunction & Transmutation of the Four Startling Objects into the Four Startling Creatures* is indicated when each Object has transfigured into a beast devoid of history and name; these four then merge parasitically into a single entity (Hereinafter referred to as "The Company" and only upon approval by the Board and CEO). The Corporation will then have the power to utilize The Company in the *Wedding Ceremony of the Four Startling Creatures Without Any Objections.*

!! ❹ !!

Martin had read and witnessed enough occult mumbo-jumbo thingies to understand in a trice: These rituals were designed to render the entire visible world invisible. This would give great power to invisible entities, allowing the most powerful among them—Starfleshes and What-Knows-What-Else's, to dominate and exploit the visible world's human and inhuman resources; similarly, physical objects that had always been visible to humans would turn invisible, putting people and other denizens at fatal disadvantages.

The only "safe" people would be the Corporations that made products to restore the imbalance between the two worlds, and the wealthy who could actually buy them. Martin only skimmed the next several pages. These explained how the Startling Objects played key roles in each ceremonial stage.

Surely, this dangerous knowledge must be kept from the powers at Wolvers Wonderproducts—and Everything Else, Inc. These corporations would use it to develop horrific A-to-Z Bombs & Drones; clever, sadistic tools of post-secondary educational degree interrogation... Weird, wonderful-but-addictive sexual technologies that would generate a malign host of novel fetishes—and open, among new orifices, entirely new consumer markets for them.

But Wolvers were his clients. His job was to deliver practical information, explain the function of the four devices. And so he would—only not what they'd expected. In fact, *technically* they didn't have expectations. That's why they'd hired him... He slid the folio and its contents into one of his raincoat's capacious pockets. Avoiding the riot of predatory hearts snapping at his feet, Martin beat cheeks as if every multilegged arthropod in the invisible world—each about the size of an undernourished ocelot—and just as hungry—was after his ass, with its deliciously chewy, fear-filled, middle-aged coccyx.

On the way back from his mission, Martin scrutinized the graffiti tags that grew in varying degrees of wild penmanship up the walls of every Weast Side building, and borrowed a few to use as false names for the Objects (each WUZ HERE deflourished).

He then lost track of the hours pounding his brains—as an interrogating Mafioso beats his tightlipped suspect—to think up reasonable enough, harmless or even beneficial purposes for their existence. The explanations would have to be deceptive, yet good enough to warrant no further investigation into their true natures. To keep them from being used in the *Ceremony of the Conjunction and Transmutation of the Four Startling Objects into the Four Startling Creatures*—and by extension, the *Wedding Ceremony of the Four Startling Creatures Without Any Objections*).

Now what? The chances were slim, but... He picked up the phone, called Cylinder Olynyk, the brilliant forger (Martin had once done him a great favor) ... Yes! See, finally proof that there is no God ruining all our affairs—the counterfeiter, as if by anti-miracle, was home, and the debt he owed Martin large enough to set him working on his scheme ASAP.

VII
The Startling Objects

"We're disappointed the Angelicas got damaged," Wolvers was saying. "And that the inventor is deceased. But at least you can tell us what these Startling Objects can do, which is after all the expensive point."

Mr. Pickle's briefcase, containing the Objects, was open on the table between Martin and Wolvers. The injured Angelicas sat off to one side. Wilton Pickle was in his usual stance, leaning against a wall behind Martin.

But very alert.

Martin shifted with practiced poise, swallowed by a leather chair at the Wonderproducts Board table, which was about as long as the New York City Marathon; it was made of the same blackmirrored gabbro of the Vietnam War Memorial. He glanced out a 188th floor window at the green speck of Central Park, took the deep breath of a man about to reveal the greatest discovery since Lactaid®, and placed the actual folio next to the briefcase. Martin opened it with care, as though Cylinder Olynyk's words, floating in an ocean of ciphers, were *truly* ancient, evil, corporate ... They were brilliant. It was a huge stroke of luck that Martin had so recently done Olynyk the favor of hiding his murdered wife's body.

"Here are the documents I found in the lair of the Starflesh. I'm not sure why they're visible now, but they were invisible when I got them ... As you can see, these pages demonstrate how each Object is intended to interact with the human body in their own different ways.

"The first Startling Object is called a STETHOSCOPE. You use it to listen to the heartbeat. The pincer-like appendages go in the ears, and the metal circle is then placed on the left side of the chest. It works like an amplifier. It allows you or a physician to listen to the heartbeat in great detail."

"Let me see that," Pickle said, listened to the rhythmic impulse in his sinoatrial node, frowning in surprise. "Absurd name..."

"The second Startling Object is called a PIPE. Don't ask me what that word means—it's that apostrophe-thing. You put tobacco in the bowl and light it with a match. I think its aesthetic appeal could make it more popular than the cigarette."

"Interesting," from Wolvers, not interested.

"Now this is an EYEDROPPER. You remove the hat-like top—*comme ça*—fill it with a prescribed dosage of medicinal liquid, return the little hat to his empty head. You hold the dropper over the infected, open eye, and gently squeeze the balm into it. And the fourth Startling Object is called the SHOEHORN. Let me demonstrate—I'll need a volunteer... *hymn*... Pickle?"

"My God, even now you won't let go of that stupid *shoe* idea of yours..."

Martin ignored Mr. Pickle's gripes, crouched down next to him as Wolvers watched in possible arousal.

"Get away from here," Pickle, scowlish and undertakerly. "Wilton! Let the ass walk the bray."

Martin knelt and loosened the man's laces. He used the tongue-shaped metal object to easily slip Mr. Pickle's left shoe off his foot. He quickly checked the sole before returning the shoe; the heel was embossed with a familiar, triangular pattern.

"Amazing," said Wolvers. "My, these *are* quite a set of Startling Objects. But I'm afraid you've confused the syrup with the shitter. You see, there's diarrhea on your pancakes, Mr. Box. Pickle here hid a surveillance system in the Angelicas—He's monitored everything you've seen from a 480 degree perspective. You see, we know the *real* purpose of these items. Obviously, I'll have to dock your wages..."

"Sugar-Honey-Iced-Tea. Never saw that comin'. Let me s'plain."

"There's no need."

"If only for the entertainment value?"

"You know, that's not a bad idea," from out Wolvers' grinning lips. "This one over here's usually not much for laughs."

"Have *you* seen the footage, or just Pickle?"

"Should I do it now, boss?" Pickle asked, pulling out a gun that, when fired, simultaneously blasted the air within a 60-feet radius into silence.

"Hold, Wilton—Only Pickle has viewed it all, but he has shared the significant portions with me, of course … I am a very busy man."

"Okay, okay, just waitaminute," Martin said.

"But sir, I want to hurry," Pickle said, predaceous and fool-faced, trembling a bit. "Hey," Martin said. "Wait your turn. Right now we're troubleshooting, and there's a whole cemetery between troubleshooting and shooting trouble…

"Mr. Wolvers, Wilton here's a double-crossing spy. I can tell for one thing by the pattern of his fancy-ass soles; the shoes are clearly of custom design and match footprints I found in some slime at the Everything Else factory. I saw in the Starflesh slime at the Everything Else warehouse. I also discovered great big towers of stacked FLOWERPOT® product, ready to ship to the consumers starving for something new … No more funerary urns, that's the catch, right? *Memento Mori* No More!"

"He's talking nonsense…"

Shaking in his $6,000 chair which could withstand 78 Gs, Wolvers blanched and brightened simultaneously: Angry and dying, fearful—yet like a man on the verge of a bold, perhaps final act, a Beowolvers…

"H-h-how could this cretin get that knowledge?"

"Wait Pickle, wait—Let Wolvers look at you with the Angelicas on. I'm guessing he'll see two Wiltons, one visible, one that's usually not—who goes by the name 'Mr. Bat' because you're about as creative as a parking meter. Which is why, even though he hardly lets you out of sight, he's been losing secrets to the competitor—your unseen twin. Have you ever seen an invisible someone with such dirty hands?"

"Let me see," Wolvers said.

He put the horned technology on his head and gasped. "Saber-toothed Testicles! What in God's name *are* you?"

Invisible Pickle shot Wolvers in the sternum. Suddenly they were in a colorized silent movie. He fell forward on the board table, blood pooling across the marbled surface, the Angelicas off his bald pate, fell noiselessly to the floor. Martin aimed his revolver at the *visible* Mr. Pickle's *hand* and his bullet perforated the *invisible* one's *head*—leaving a vivid semi-visible stain on the wall behind it—Targeting this wet-brain-projectile-icky-stuff, Martin shot a tunnel through visible Mr. Pickle's nose. Martin had always been a terrible shot. It hadn't let him down yet.

It took a few minutes for the 60-foot-radius of silence from Pickle's shot to evaporate.

Simple ambient sound returned, grating on the ears like a chainsaw cutting through an oak-quiet.

Martin felt like he was forgetting something important... was it which of the seven places he usually kept his revolver in that it occupied now? No... Was it the century during which the *Saga of the Volsungs* had been snored onto the page? Oh, oh I got it!

He gave the bird to Pickle and Wolvers simultaneously. Take that, haha!

Nope. Why can't that gesture make him feel good? It does nothing. The magic must've worn off in Junior High School, he guessed. It' s something else he's forgotten... No, not that... No... Money? That's it.

No Money.

He flipped through Wolvers' hacker-proof Rolodex® ... The burn in the small of his back suddenly bit from within him, retracted; he still hadn't examined the wound, the scar was probably invisible anyway, like most. When the pain subsided he called the CEO of Most of All, Incorporated—The number three, bit player in the corporate inventions swindle...

"Mr. Trump? I have some things you might be interested in. Right ... Oh yes, lucrative for your company ... earn you a noventrigintillion—hymn... reasonable price. What are they? It's hard to explain over the phone, but they are personal wellness body gizmos. They exhibit a range of uses, from the medical, to pragmatic, to the high-end leisure market. In fact you might consider it a valuable real-estate acquisition, with the human as zone for development and rental. They'll be bigger than the DOORKNOB®—that was Most of All, wasn't it? Not Everything Else or Wolvers Wonderproducts? Aha, I thought so! Brilliant invention that, it should've been you on EMIT's Man of the Year special edition…

"How do you know you I'm not just some crackpot? Well, for one thing, I have your phone number in my Rolodex®. How many people have access to that? Oh and I know what a FLOWERPOT® is—ever hear of it? No? Both Wolvers and Everything already started production, and I can let you in on their secret now. You'll push millions of units … Unhuh … Great, see you there and then, wearing that and that—with an UMBRELLA® if it's raining.

Great. Buy!-Buy! Trumpty-Dumpty."

Viii
THe MiRACULOUS

Martin hangs up. He puts the Startling Objects back into their briefcase. He fires Pickle's silenceblaster gun into the asshole's smug dead face, then shoots the Angelicas to smoking pieces without noise. He sticks the Rolodex® in his coat pocket, along with the folio and Olynyk's masterful work.

How do ya get outta here?

The walls gleam in CGI—hyperperfect glass reflections, and no matter which way he turns Martin's image presses toward him, an incredibly vivid and mirrorific threat. His face has the thunderwide eyes and arrestingly, blankened and blackened expressions, that lost desert refugee shock, often seen on the cover of EMIT magazine—when they're not lauding a greedy sonfabitch like Wolvers—and even if the editors choose the face of a humanitarian Crisis over a Croesus to stare out at millions from newsstands worldwide, you can bet some rich photographer has won a cash prize for this high-resolution voyeurism, the sunrise saturation of vermillion moans, eyes in albescent terror, tears dried by shrapnel winds, or dousing a shrouded baby in a one-armed cradle ... The candids of gang-raped, civil-warring souls, atrocities too evil to be called *real* in the sense the word's used to describe anything in our world...

Countries that change names, contagious diseases, regimes, fifteen, sixteen times a year—a horrorzone of cliterectomies, witch burnings, slaughtered foreign aid workers—one of too many places where, despite thousands of years of scrubbing themselves to their bones, they're *still* trying to cleanse the ethnic out... There are even unseen realms where kindhearted orbs were branded like cattle and treated worse. Pick any dimension you want, any afterlife, even, and it will stink like money. Every Corporation built upon the steady rot of corpses...

Better stop there, you can go on forever with this stuff, how sickening.

But it's all going on right now, across the sphere whose orbits trace the aggressive spinning of stupid laughing children, kids going dizzy, dizzy, dizzier, until they slam down into ambiguous tears.

Compared to *that* Martin's just finishing up another typical, shitty day at the office. In fact, for all the homicidal bizarrerie, he feels he's already misplaced a completed file on The Four Startling Objects among his heap of closed cases, all mixed-up as they are with his laundry and unread catalogs, beneath the bathroom sink. Or is it the kitchenette, anyway.

How dare his reflection imitate a those victims of existence, exploited on the cover EMIT magazine. How *dare* it.

Gun drawn, he steps back, fires into the nearest reflected face. For a minisec he sorta sees himself split, cascade into silly-sharddle piles on the floor. Damn lucky discharge—A hole in the mirror, Pickle's briefcase in hand, he debouches straight to the elevators and no casualties. He decides to get a tattoo—a #102, with #44 below it. Where? Martin's never had a tattoo. He hopes it will really hurt. He needs sleep. He better get trademarking his four inventions before meeting with the CEO of Most of All at the end of the month... Five dark, steel doors loom before him like monoliths of deep earth, cue Strauss, Opus 30...

Yeah, yeah. But what happened *after* Zarathustra Spake? Martin sorta wonders.

He pokes a button, it glows, doors open with a dainty chime for its single occupant. It coasts smoothly past 187 floors to the lobby. *Hymn, let's see—which way's home?* Ah, the directions are simple enough:

Ten blocks down Kickert toward Marlin, slight left at the Amoco® station and you've escaped the Weast Side; two short blocks to the four-way intersection, cross 5th Ave.—watch the broken light and blotto goombahs—turn north, another six blocks…

His building is the one with the entrance half-blocked by a dead tree that looks like a scream of wood—no better way of putting it. Martin walks through the empty lobby, the cold echoes of his heavyslugged tread up the stairs, opens his apartment door, locks it behind. Two dim lights are on. He turns them off. And without the labor of thinking, choosing—his body following its own miraculous directions—goes straight to bed. To sleep, which is almost love, isn't it? A few hours of no more tomorrows.

YOU ONLY LIVE ONCE
BUT YOUR PARENTS DIE TWICE

THE STARS HOVER LIKE PREDATORS
OF INCREDIBLE FORTITUDE AND ZERO INITIATIVE

[REDACTED]

THIS STORY was removed from the collection and replaced with blank pages so the reader can take notes, doodle, $c!

A Few Leaves from the Travelogue of Doctor Julius Jonsson, Cryptobotanist & Hylesoprotolist: Bay Ridge, or ...

Change it to E2 had (4) colored directors — Just no South story, So his mom goes South → first he helps create the final legend,

1/7/15

(*) Getting so that's how I became the Man with Movement for face & Episode & Lake got its Southern legend.

Eh.

As for my chil

Opening
Mother — excursions
Finds her dead
Crow event
Leaves house
Walks through city ...

New

→ Realizes he's going South only when a Quinceaux points this out to him...
→ Enters Majuscule woods...
→ Finds field of dog holes
his mom did in Majuscule
→ Trips on one, or one was very deep, etc.
→ ~~THE INSECTS~~ ATTACKS (NEW)
→ ~~[scribbled]~~ ATTACKED (MANDI THING)
→ Sees red roof → Goes for it
More on THE "INN" SIDE → Clinic scene & DR / Nurse ← MF
change to
→ Drainmate — Oh, just the one w/the (rat), etc.
I'm a relative...
→ The Consultation, examination, etc...
Ending wish. like "good he's fertilized"...

Sth, like
Dr. Says
Soon I will be well enough to move about.
I'll make myself known. I wonder what they'll call me.

THINK ANA KAVAN ICE FOR WORLD COHERENCE, Story coherence

Or maybe Development vague: The operation was over & they say it was a success. From what I can gather I had either given birth, or, etc., or etc.,

→ Finds out pregnant... B → w | Need for face, etc.

(*)

The Belief in the Undead Still Exists in New York

... A MILD APRIL NIGHT when I found myself approaching the community of Bay Ridge from the West. My horse Lethe and I went along the Brooklyn-Queens-Expressway, or BQE. From high atop the asphalt road, the windows of run-down apartment buildings ran brightly by my feet, and high-rise apartment complexes loomed ahead, the most boring use of rectangular shapes imaginable, like diagrams in elementary geometry texts. COSTCO Price-Club, where the natives go to shop at wholesale prices, was quickly lost to view below as I rode on by two neon women framed by glowing Xs atop a warehouse on 3rd avenue. Soon the signs for car dealerships appeared on my right. Name brands fought for the very air but I ignored their scuffle, and continued to the 86th Street exit, where I hoped to find some rare plants growing by the curb. Unusual things often grow undetected near the ends of roads, because when people approach the end of a path they look to what is beyond it rather than at the path itself.

Alas, I had come to yet another community lacking in cryptobotanical specimens. The highway opened onto a land of concrete paths and brick buildings. Numbers rather than names marked the streets. This quantitative approach to direction hinted at a lack of depth, a bad sign because seeds cannot flourish without it. Not a tree lined those indexed streets! It was a hard year to be a botanist, and a worse time to be a travelling one. (Forgive me, my poor reader, for repeating this phrase for the hundredth time in this Travelogue. As I mentioned in Chapter Two, I have spent most of my life hating the written word, and I fear my writing awkward as a result—This sentence being no exception!) All I found by the highway exit was some *ranunculus* and *regnellidum*, squashed beneath the shade of ubiquitous air-conditioning units protruding from the apartments above. Without any rare herbs to gather and peddle, I would once more have to rely on my hylesoprotolist studies to earn me a Comfort Inn's rest.

The streets were empty as though it was a holiday, or a plague season. It was late.

Suddenly I heard a mob shouting over toward 5th Avenue. Cautiously I jumped back onto Lethe and we advanced, her hooves masked by the noise of discord. The crowd was located two blocks up and to the left, on 5th Avenue between 86th and 87th Street. We passed a Greek Deli, a Chinese Laundry, an Arabic Video Rental, and a Pizzeria, so that before I came upon the natives I was aware of some of the faces I might see. It had rained earlier and the street was smooth and shiny as apple skin. Soon the wet shadows of people gesticulating wildly were thrown across our path by orange flickering streetlights. They were right around the corner.

I decided to circle the block and get a safer view of the crowd from the other side.

How to describe the houses of Bay Ridge in this Travelogue! There are a few decent two-family homes of brick, Tudor or Brownstone style, but these are the exception. Most of them look like children who have been playing dress-up in their mommy's bedroom, and have gone too far in an attempt to be colorful. In one dwelling, Lethe and I saw pale yellow siding, an ochre stoop, and bright lemon-curtained windows. It looked as though the owners had based their look upon a swatch of yellows from the home-decorating center of a hardware store. One also saw plastic flowers planted among colored stones—a botanical outrage. I noticed Halloween decorations on doors, though it was the second month of spring. Lawn jockeys, Virgin Marys resting among bushes, BEWARE OF DOG signs, grand baroque Italian banisters for unimpressive stairways, and American Flags completed the bewildering look of the neighborhood. From all this it was easy to see that the natives were colorblind, forgetful, and wanted to believe in something that could be pointed at with a finger. I was to discover that the last part of my supposition, at least, was indeed correct.

Presently the scene of confusion was before us. A crowd of all sorts was gathered before an Off Track Betting service. The butts of cheap cigars covered the street as if they'd fallen with the rain. Some of the excitable group had flashlights and these roved the night like spastic sunbeams.

A series of loud voices stood out from the general chaos.

"He crosses 93rd Street with wide strides!"

"He grabbed my ass!"

"He throws me over the turnstile, so that I get a ticket every time I go to take the R train!"

"He steals quarters from parking meters!"

"Kill the zombie!"

"He's not a zombie, he's a vampire!"

"Vampire, zombie, whatevah! Kill the freakin' thing!"

Sensing a hylesoprotolistic opportunity, I tethered Lethe to a STOP sign and joined the gathering.

"Where is the vampire in question," I asked a colorblind widow wearing navy blue.

"That's just the thing! If I could only tell you!" she said, throwing her arms up in the air.

"Then why may I ask are we all gathered outside the OTB?"

She looked at me with annoyance.

"Uck! How do I know?"

"You *know* through the operations of the crowd, Madame. They are a many-legged brain that may disperse at any moment, like a dance-company's dramatization of dementia praecox."

She ignored me and returned to waving her arms aerobically.

I spied a boy of about eight, whom risked being trampled as he collected cigar butts and put them in a *Century 21* shopping bag.

"What are you doing there, young man?"

"I'm smoking," he said.

"Do you know why we are outside this OTB? Where is the vampire?"

"He used to live above the OTB. He played the ponies all day. Then he died a mean drunk."

"What was his name?"

The boy laughed.

"It was funny! It was Bark-a-loo!"

The name brought eucalyptus and lupins to my mind, and I frowned with longing so that he laughed even harder.

But there was something else about that surname.

My mind has been trained to recall the oddest of details. Certainly my scientific knowledge was full of them, but faithful readers of this Travelogue will also recall the minutiae involved in the uses my father put to a combination of saltwater and the movements of red ants, and the way in which I located Flatbush Ave. by my careful noting of the position of certain candy wrappers in the wind.

Now I remembered: The smallest cemetery in Brooklyn is the Revolutionary Cemetery, at the corner of Narrows and Mackay Place. Only members of the Barkaloo family are buried there.

"To Narrows and Mackay!" I cried, and the crowd, at seeing a stranger so confident in their world, followed me with their flashlights, as though I had gathered them there to begin with for this purpose alone.

Fill a dark night with people and it grows strange and magical as a tank overpopulated with countless lobsters at a seafood restaurant. It is not hard to lose one's head over such easy wonders. But I knew I must remain calm and kept my mind on nothing but the goal as we journeyed south.

The Revolutionary Cemetery was small indeed—perhaps the size of two grand pianos resting side by side. Elms and maples threw redundant darkness over us as I tied Lethe to a parking meter and swung open the waist-high gates.

I heard voices at my back.

"Look—There he is!"

"That's the stranger!"

"No, that's Barkaloo. We better get out of here."

"It's nice out."

"Hey—Barkaloo lived over an OTB!"

"So?"

"So, that's about horses, betting on horses!"

"Shut up!"

"No wait! And this guy has a horse. Who else has a horse in Bay Ridge?"

"It's freakin' weird!"

"It *is* Barkaloo—He's going to invite us into his home and kill us!"

"But he lived over the OTB."

"Now he lives in the graveyard!"

I had to act fast.

"People, people, please!" I cried. "I've found something!"

It is a fact that a crowd shutting their mouths all at once is quieter than a single person doing the same, just as many prayers uttered at once are stronger than one. I took command of this powerful silence.

"A freshly opened grave!"

I did not lie. A grave had recently been violated. Mounds of dirt and coffin-splinters were strewn at my feet. It reminded me of the detritus of a shipwreck.

The curious, the brave, the frightened and the dumb surrounded me to peer at the hole.

"There's nobody in it!"

"Barkaloo is on the loose!"

"This one here with the horse is Barkaloo, I'm telling you."

"Yeah, he's tricked us!"

And now I have reached the point of my narrative, dear reader, that I promised to reveal in Chapter Two of this Travelogue, some four hundred odd pages ago. That is, the reason why a man who swore his life through that he should have nothing to do with written history, has produced the example in your hands.

Fear is a perpetual motion machine. Only a fool would not flee a mob powered by such a device. But in the sky there were clouds that roamed restless and black, and they fled from a glowing moon as if they were shadows. And when the clouds were gone I could see a small stalk emerging from the bottom of the open grave before me.

It was pure white with a lightly veined surface. I had never seen its like before.

How wrong I had been about the cryptobotantical possibilities of Bay Ridge!

Enchanted with this specimen, I was more than startled when they tossed me in the grave. The dirt fell upon me full of holes, so that it seemed they flung shovels of moonlight mixed with earth. I heard Lethe neigh in fright, a car screeching and then hitting something with a dull sound, falsetto screaming. And then I could hear no more and my eyes went blind as pebbles...

I do not know the name of the man who dug me out of that pit. Before I saw him I felt his long fingernails on my face, gently wiping, soft as a woman's hair. He was exceedingly obese, bald as a blade of grass, and his eyes lacked pupils. He wore an olive raincoat filled with holes. I associated the color with the phrase "I'll live." And for a moment I thought he must be God.

The crowd was gone.

After he unearthed me, my rescuer stood mutely at the foot of the grave. Too dazed to thank him, I dug the white-stalked plant out from the soil beneath me and ran down toward the shore, nearly slipping in a pool of horse blood at the corner.

I stood under the Verrazano Bridge, which loomed in the fog like a giant harp. I finally decided on tending to the plant in the nearby Dyker Golf Course, where a man can easily hide among the thick vegetation. I played gardener there for a week, looking ragged as a vampire myself as I watched my find grow.

It bloomed in fantastic ways, rapidly developing large rectangular leaves that sprung from a flat, hard spine. They were colored a milky white and exceedingly smooth to touch. The leaves appeared successively, sometimes a hundred a day, until there were thousands of them.

In the past I would take a hitherto unseen plant and investigate its properties, grinding parts of it into a balm, a powder, and a potion, and then test these medicaments following Agrippa's Capricornian methods.

But I could think of nothing else to do with this marvelous thing than write the history of its discovery upon its very leaves. Ink flows so easily on the fragile surface.

It has not been an easy task to complete. The day after I began this Travelogue, I was awoken by the sound of another mob. And now I will relate how hylesoprotolism saved my life yet again.

The wind…

EDITOR'S NOTE: THIS STORY WAS ONCE CALLED
"THE INVENTION OF THE MEMOIR"

"THE POISONED MAN"

It Began to Rain

Poison? Bullet?

They were talking murder about me.

YOU KNOW, "LABRUSCA COGNATUS" IS SORT OF A COMPANION TO DR. JONSSON'S JOURNAL. COULD WE INCLUDE IT IN THE BOOK SINCE IT'S SO SHORT?

LABRUSCA COGNATUS

SON, YOU ASKED ME ABOUT YOUR GRANDFATHER.

My father spent his life trying to commit suicide in various unconventional ways in the belief that certain specific forms of death would lead to corresponding reincarnations. He was often unsuccessful. It was his goal to be reborn as a king whose dominion knew no boundaries, physical or otherwise. After his rebirth, upon growing up and being crowned, he would reach across time and space for his family, allowing them to enjoy the riches he had reaped through his carefully executed self-sacrifice. The only price, so my father reasoned, was that it would take a full lifetime to be reborn and grow up to be king in the other dimension, and so his child and wife would not know him after his death in this life. But it was a small price, for soon enough they would be royalty elsewhere in the universe.

Your grandfather first tried to sleep himself to death, which did not work. So he tried dreaming himself to death, but the results were similar. Next he tried to be struck on the head by the last drop of rain in a thunderstorm, which he believed was the heaviest, but that last drop landed elsewhere, for he passed these events soggy but alive.

Years passed, marked by similar failures.

Son, after his death, I often saw my father's body lying on its back, arms and legs splayed out as though he'd been making a mud angel when he died. It was strange because that wasn't how I'd found him. No, I had left my house to find flat stones to skip on the river, and discovered my father on his belly, face down in the mud, and a motley coalition of birds were undressing him with their beaks, some thinking of food and others of nesting, and a sparrow was pulling on his tongue; but I almost never remember it that way. When I shooed the finches and eagles and crows and hawks and vultures away, and turned Dad over, the first thing I saw was a headless flower growing out of his chest. It was like a child's drawing of a decapitated tulip, bright green with two narrow leaves on either side of the base of its stalk, suggesting an arrow pointing into the earth saying "This Way."

I said, "I have not just found Father lying dead, but I have also found an exceptional plant which I've never seen before, and it is possible these events are equally significant." The universe had created fathers, and deaths, and birds to tear their clothing, and boys to stumble on them unprepared, but right then and there I vowed to find out more about the headless plant that had sprung from your grandfather's heart. I called it *Labrusca Cognatus*—wild vine from the blood of the father. I called it a vine because so much of a thing is what it can never be.

Like you, I had questions. I wondered: Had a seed grown in Dad's body, decomposing now several days? Or had it gestated in the chest for years, and bursting out only recently, caused his death with its first taste of sunlight? And if so, was this plant the root of father's madness, which had consumed the last decade of his life along with Mother and me? Perhaps its shoots probed deep into his daydreamy brain.

I dared not cry, for fear the salty tears would damage the specimen. Carefully, I pulled on the stalk of that headless flower, which stood roughly nine inches high. It resisted at first, and then, of a sudden it came free, dredging your grandfather's heart up with it. The heart was shriveled and blackened like a burnt potato. The plant had grown out of a bulb from the center, along the division of the ventricles. It was shocking to see the little pump that had once kept him alive.

I held it in cupped hands, which had never seemed so small, and carefully walked home, fearing wolves and bats, but meeting none. Then I buried the heart and the flowerless flower behind the cabin and lay back on the ground, hoping for rain and coming very close to praying for it, and wishing I knew a song to sing, and watching the bright cloudless sky a long time.

Son, my heart hurts. You asked me about grandfather.

Tell me about you.

3/27/15

POEM

WRITE
LIKE
YOU ARE A GHOST
WRITE LIKE
YOU ARE POSSESSED
WRITE
IT'S THE ONLY WAY OUT
THAT'S ALMOST PAINLESS

32,715

TWEETED 3/27/15

Write like you are a ghost
Write like you're possessed
Write ~~...~~ door
~~Write ...~~
Write is not salvation
~~Write is ...~~
~~Write, write ...~~
It's salvation
more and less

TEAR OUT PAGE, THEN CUT, RIP, OR FOLD HERE

The Invention of the Mask

TEAR OUT PAGE, THEN CUT, RIP, OR FOLD HERE

THE FOLLOWING STORY is located on the front cover, in incredibly small print. You may need to track down a MAGNIFYING GLASS® and close this book before continuing. Since this page is denoted with an imaginary number, *i*, and not an actual page number, don't forget to mark your place with this official "The Invention of the Mask" BOOKMARK® (seriously, just rip out this page and use it as a bookmark), or, if you're not so adventurous, simply find a receipt, torn piece of paper, currency, gum wrapper, square of toilet paper, tissue, pen or pencil, another book entirely, a cord or string of some kind, or dog-ear the top-right corner of this page, or the next.

EDITOR'S NOTE(S): MAYBE THE TITLE PAGE FOR "THE INVENTION OF THE MASK" CAN BE DESIGNED FOR FOLDING/CUTTING/RIPPING INTO MAKE-SHIFT BOOKMARKS FOR READERS WHO DON'T HAVE ANY OF THE OBJECTS LISTED ON THAT PAGE, OR FOR THOSE WHO DON'T WANT TO DEFACE THE BOOK BY DOG-EARING.

THIS AND THE PREVIOUS PAGE—SINCE THEY ARE A SINGLE PIECE OF PAPER—COULD BECOME THE OFFICIAL "BOOKMARK® FOR YES TRESPASSING. PERHAPS THE PAGE COULD HAVE AN IMAGINARY PAGE NUMBER, LIKE √(-1), SO THAT WHEN TORN OUT, THE PAGE NUMBERS IN THE REST OF THE BOOK STAY SEQUENTIAL! OR IS THAT A STUPID IDEA? PAGINATION CHAOS!

SCRATCH THAT. TEARING OUT A PAGE TO MAKE A BOOKMARK WOULD DEFACE THE BOOK ENTIRELY (ALTHOUGH IT'S AN ORIGINAL IDEA), AND WOULD ALSO REMOVE THE INSTRUCTIONS FOR FUTURE READERS, WHO COULD POTENTIALLY LOSE THEIR PLACE WHEN CLOSING THE BOOK TO READ THE STORY ON THE COVER.

THIS WOULD ALSO DESTROY RESALE VALUE ... BUT WHO WOULD EVER WANT TO GET RID OF THIS BOOK? SELLING OR GIVING AWAY A BOOK IS LIKE SELLING OR GIVING AWAY A CHILD. ARE BOOKS NO LONGER FOREVER THINGS? THIS IS QUITE THE CONUNDRUM...

** MAKE SURE TO REMOVE THE "CUT OR FOLD HERE" MARKS ON THE PREVIOUS TITLE PAGE PRIOR TO PUBLICATION IF DECIDING NOT TO GO THIS ROUTE. IN FACT, MAKE SURE NOT TO INCLUDE EITHER OF THE √(-1) PAGES. AND DELETE THIS TEXT! **

The Invention of the Umbrella

"PLEASE, SIT DOWN. Before we start, I want to tell you that I don't normally see people on such short notice, and at this late hour. I don't want you to think that we can make a habit of these kinds of sessions."

"Thank you doctor, I appreciate it. And it won't happen again."

"There was such urgency in your voice on my machine, that's the only reason I agreed—that and curiosity—why did you need to see me so badly before the end of the Autumnal Equinox? What could not wait till tomorrow? And may I ask you what that strange thing is that looks like a mummified pterodactyl?"

"I'll answer both questions in a moment, I'll explain. There's not much time. Let me start with my father."

"Go on."

"I used to think that I learned everything I know from my father, because he taught me nothing.

"For twenty-five years, every single weekday, my father would go out to sell Encyclopedias. The only people who bought them were the ones who never read a thing. He digested each volume and would impress the illiterate by his ability to recall any detail from those pages—lengths of rivers, names of battles, when roads went from dirt to asphalt. They thought that was knowledge—a stockpiling, a kind of having. Smart meant you could impress by mere possession, which is as close to tangibility as thinking gets.

"Every night my father read the stars with some graph paper, a drawing compass and graphite pencils, ephemeris tables, and that thing you were asking about, called an umbrella—an astrological device of his own creation."

"What's an umbrella?"

"The word was a compound of Umbra—Latin for shade—and Bela Lugosi, who played Dracula in the 1931 movie. Originally he was going to call it an umbracula, but in a rare concession to reality he opted to pay tribute to the actor who played a monster, and not the monster itself. It was a strange, obnoxiously furtive object that shielded the user from light—that's where the Dracula part of the name came into it. My father was a big fan of the old Universal horror movies. If vampires were real they would've made him rich, buying up all those umbrellas.

"So, the umbrella—nice word, I'll give him that—it was really a kind of half-inverted cane, half-tent. There was some black fabric fastened to a collapsible frame of thin wooden ribs radiating from the tip of the cane, and included apertures for a periscope and a telescope that extended through the fabric to the outside of the covering. You pointed the bottom of the cane upwards, pressed a button and the ribs opened wide above. Then your head and shoulders were concealed under the umbrella, and you could access the periscope if it was raining or snowing, to see ahead of you, or the telescope to view the heavens without any nearby light source getting in the way.

"He'd chart the courses of planets, ascensions, degrees in houses—I never understood it. Then he'd spend Saturday and Sunday standing too close to me with his old man smell, the scent of stewing idle perspiration rather than the sweat of hard work, talking too loudly with his old man voice, a cartoon voice with newsreel loudness, about his older-than-man revelations, as though, he, of all people—an encyclopedia salesman—should have uncovered some key to understanding existence, while so many brilliant minds before had failed."

"Tell me about that."

"He liked the big headlines in the sky, if you will; he often spoke of eschatological orbs, apocalyptic twinkling and the long unrolled milky maps of fate. He said he knew the courses of our lives. He said he knew me, and he knew himself. He wrote a little song that he used to sing sometimes, in a cracked baritone like a rubber tire groaning into the jaws of a garbage truck:

The will of the stars
cannot be unmade
like sunlight into umbrella shade.
But the will of the stars
I've learned to know
like moonlight into umbrella shadow.

"What did you think of all this?"

"I think facts were tacks that pinned the world down in place, and the stars were magnets that drew the facts out so my father could rearrange the world he way he wanted. He wanted to have knowledge that nobody else did. Knowing public facts in encyclopedias was one thing, but possessing secrets—that was another. And the best way to know things that nobody else does is to determine that things are not what others think they are. It made him feel important and powerful even if times were hard. Even if he was broke (and we often went without), he had stars in his pockets. And even if the facts were against him, at night the stars would rise out of his pockets into the sky and pull out the overdue bills and failures and the other tacks. But I'm just guessing about his motives because he was not exactly open. We did not ever talk about who we were, but only what we knew, and we were like a Beanie Baby enthusiast and a numismatic with a specialization in ancient Roman currency starring in a very boring student film. When I grew older,

I began to laugh at his nonsense in secret, and then finally, three months ago, at the dinner table."

"What triggered this open display of anger?"

"It was the Summer Solstice—June 21st. He told me he had read in the stars that the world was going to change in three seasonal phases, and the first was going to start this very evening. He said it used to be flat, then it was round, and now it would become another shape. He said it was the will of the stars that they would hide in long mourning coats and that no sun would rise. He said he had calculated a list of dates for the remaining three stages of the end of days, occurring on the equinoxes and solstices, something had ascended, something else had entered a seventh house..."

"How did he react?"

"He said you'll see, my boy, when you're a few days older, when you understand the forces of the stars on the lives of men. Then I said, oh we'll see all right—by the light of the sun..."

"Tissue?"

"Thanks, my allergies are really acting up—it's the start of mold season, and this feels like...it's going to be a really bad one."

"Go on."

"My father woke me by slapping my back, like a laundress beating a wet rug. It's odd when old people are strong, like freak weather is odd. And speaking of, it was this past June, a really hot one, you remember. I grumbled out of bed and he dragged me to the window with his old man grip, a grip always too tight as if holding on for dear life, and there were no stars; they were blotted out completely. You could see nothing. It was like having your eyes turned around in their sockets, staring into the dark wall of your brain. It was like holding his damn umbrella over your head."

"How did you feel?"

"You would think it would feel like a dream, but it struck me as more actual than anything I'd ever experienced before in waking life, and that made it all the more unnerving—to think that reality was the same as this overwhelming garbage dump of night."

"How did your father act?"

"I don't remember. And then I finally had to fall asleep. When

I woke, it was definitely morning, but outside the windows it appeared the house had sunk into a tar pit. I found my father sitting on the edge of his bed, looking about to moan, looking so secret and so left behind. I thought I'd go outside and see if the world felt any different, now that it was ending. I went downstairs and opened the door. And it's a funny feeling, when you can't see past your eyes."

"Tissue?"

"Yes, thanks. But then I saw a little line of light, sort of like a phosphorescent rope, a few hundred feet away. I went towards it and hit my head on something thick and heavy, like a saddle ... I reached out for the rope. Plain daylight cast rings across my fingers. I slid out from under the darkness covering the house and I saw that it was a gigantic leaf."

"Where do you think it came from?"

"I don't know. But the world used to be flat, and then it was round. Maybe now it's some other shape, with undiscovered angles or curves covered in monstrous forests with monstrous seasons. Maybe if it's the will of the stars some new maps will need to be made."

"Go on."

"It was miles and miles of glossy green with veins bigger than redwoods. It was the size of all the cemeteries in the world put together, with raggedy borders. It draped our house and the whole valley behind it. It was just luck, I guess, that the tip was so near to us, otherwise I might not have seen any light at all. I went back under the leaf and found the door and then my father. He seemed uncharacteristically humble, almost sane and appropriate. I took him outside, showed him what had really happened. As the leaf was drifting toward us, from a vast, unknown wild, it must've blacked out the stars—it certainly was large enough. It must have hovered for a while and then settled down on the land. I told my father, well, the world's not ending, but you were partly right, the stars did go out, and I'll give you that, and I meant it as a compliment. But he didn't want to hear it.

Maybe there was some father nearby celebrating his omniscience because he'd been telling his son that a giant leaf was going to drift on the valley. But *my* father was always about stars, never about leaves. And he was always about being 100% correct. He flared up and told me to get out and not come back. He told me I had never understood a word he'd said. I took the umbrella out of spite I guess."

"And that's how our people found you wandering the streets?"

"Yeah, that's how."

"Do you still think that everything your father said was nonsense?"

"Yes. Even if it's true, that doesn't mean it isn't nonsense."

"Do you always—excuse me, how strange. It looks like some kind of big storm on the way, doesn't it? Some kind of black clouds over the city. But it wasn't on the weather this morning…"

"Doctor, what's wrong?"

"The sky is going dark, I can't believe it. There's something massive in the sky. But I can sort of make it out, thanks to the streetlights."

"Here it is. Let me see—is it orange?"

"Yes … orange, and brown and gold and red … and look, some stars show here and there through holes in the … *the leaves* … are there more leaves behind this one? And that crunching and smashing sound, like bones grinding and ships wrecking, what is it? What's going on?"

"It's fall."

"What?"

"It's fall."

"What do you mean?"

"I saw the green leaf in June. It was a single, stray summer leaf from a single heaven-sized tree. But it's September 21st now. And if there are many leaves, and what tree doesn't have many leaves, and if there are many trees, and what tree stands alone out in the undiscovered wild, then all those autumn leaves are going to come down upon us, blown by whatever monster wind plays with monster trees. God knows how many leaves, how deep they'll settle on the land, blocking the sun, damming and contaminating the rivers, spreading fires, choking the air with a million acres of mold.

"That's why I had to see you tonight—I wanted someone to understand. I didn't want to be alone. I couldn't go back to him."

"I'm sorry. I know we have fifteen minutes left in our session, and I am supposed to be there for you. But I don't know what I'm feeling right now. Those dead leaves clouding the sky, flying, falling … it's too terrible for words. Please give me a minute. I need to watch this with my eyes open, breathe deeply and get a grip. Perhaps you could also use this moment to reflect on how you are feeling, too."

"Well you know, doctor, I think it's impossible to look deep inside yourself, but it's easy to look up and pretend you're doing just that. Here, take this umbrella and stick it—"

THAT FRESH COUNTRY AIR SMELLED OF "LET ME SLEEP A BIT LONGER — JUST A MINUTE..."

TALL ENOUGH TO CHANGE TRAFFIC LIGHT BULBS

AN ANNOYING PERSON: "THERE IS SOMETHING SO <u>MANDATORY</u> ABOUT YOU..."

"LOVE CONQUERS ALL" — YES, BUT WHAT CONQUEROR EVER CARED FOR HIS SUBJECTS? NAME ONE BENIFICENT CONCEROR?

↳ All, like Ghengis Khan or Hitler...

THE CLOUDS LAY VERY STILL, ABDOMINAL

THE PROBLEM WITH HAVING "THE BEST OF BOTH WORLDS" IS THEY ARE LOCATED IN THE SAME SHITTY UNIVERSE

<u>CLOACINA</u>: THE GODDESS OF TYPHOID

WITH AN I LIKE ME, WHO NEEDS YOU? <u>I</u>'VE GOT ENOUGH VOWELS.

THE INVENTION OF THE MYTH

SOME SAID I WAS BORN with a hunting bow in my hand; others that I stole a rib from my mother on the way out, which is just silly. All agreed that even as a boy I was the finest shot in the land. Up until I turned sixteen, I made my living hunting, dealing in hides, and performing tricks of accuracy for the curious in the town square. But on my sixteenth birthday, while I sat with my father and mother for a natal feast, a duty-haunted man in purple robes cast aubergine shadows over our door.

"The New King wants this boy for the post of Royal Archer," he said in hollow tones. "He must come with me immediately."

"But there has never been a Royal Archer. And there has never been a New King," my father said.

"There's only been the old one," my mother said.

"Just as there's only been an old sun in the sky," I said.

"Now there is a New King, who is the only King," the man repeated. "And he wants this boy as the Royal Archer. And he must come with me immediately."

"And what is the King's name?" I asked.

"That is a secret," the man in purple said.

We each played these parts several times, my father saying there had never been a New King, and my mother saying there's only been the old one, and me comparing him to the old sun, and the messenger saying there was a New King whose name was secret and I had to go be his Royal Archer. And then, I don't remember how exactly, it was tacitly decided that we had done enough rehearsing and it was time for the next scene, and I left with the messenger in purple.

I barely had time to fetch my bow from the ascham before I was whisked away by black horses in a black carriage into a black tunnel that led to a black castle, and never saw my family again, never saw anything I expected to see ever again.

In the carriage, I looked over at the messenger. I only saw his sharp nose protruding from his purple cowl, like an arrow directing everyone to see his point of view. There was something familiar in this suggestive physiognomy.

And I recalled a day when I was fourteen and a crowd of aristocratic strangers passed through the town. I told them I could hit whatever target they wanted me to if they would offer something of value in return. A moon-faced woman with eclipse-black hair and green eyes like verdant planets through telescopes dangled an argent locket.

"I'll tell you what," the lady said. "I have here a little poem, written to me by . . . a secret admirer. It is six sentences long. If you can shoot an arrow into each period in the letter, without damaging the words, I will give you this."

I examined the poem. I noticed the face of the duty-haunted man flushing, but he said nothing as the lady handed the paper to me. I memorized the sentences and where they stopped and started, in the thoughts of the poet and on the territory of the paper:

Hey, hey, baby, ooh-ooh
There's no light brighter than the sight of you.
I want to tell you all about it

But you give me such a fantod I can barely mouth it.
Give me a thousand chances and I'll shout it out one day
Just meet me where it's secret and when I say.
Can't be sure when I'll get up the nerve
When I expose myself you might think me a perv.
But every thirty days when the moon drops low
you'll see the King become a saint below your window
And I'll await you like a devil by the willow trees.
But if I don't speak, I don't mean to tease
It's just you're so outta sight I can barely say
Hey, hey, baby, baby hey hey

I tacked the note with sap onto a trunk, roughly 100 feet from where we stood. Returning to the group, I fired five arrows which deftly landed like exclamation points, and asked for my prize.

"But there were six sentences, and that is five punctuations," the lady said.

"Six sentences, but five periods, madam. The poet must have left the last period out in his rush to deliver the missive to you. Lust is haste for lust to abate."

The aristocrats examined the poem and had to agree with me. Only the duty-haunted man did not join them, and he eyed me with a squint as though I was a stinging onion under his blade. I did not like him. And it struck me that he was the sort of man who believed that reading his writing is a more perfect thinking than the thinking before the writing that you are reading, and he did not take kindly to seeing his mistakes made public. As for the others, they were most amazed by my dexterity. The woman placed her locket in my palm. She declined to take the poem back, saying she could easily recite it in her sleep. I kept the poem in the locket as a reminder of how it was won.

The horses reached the royal grounds at the speed of rain. The black castle was surrounded by an elaborate labyrinth of holly and yew topiaries, the centerpiece of which was an oddly-shaped bush trimmed into the shape of a short, squat person with giant wings. The purple man ushered me past an evergreen menagerie into the building. Then we whirled past an eclipse-haired woman who I recognized as a donor of lockets and poems. She looked almost the same, except she wore a jeweled crown and her planet eyes had moved further away in their orbits, having faded from a vibrant chrysophrase to a murky celadon—still lovely but much less alive. She regarded the purple messenger and I sadly, as though we were the last clods of earth tossed at a funeral. Then I was admitted to the New King's chamber. It was a vast, empty basalt room with a large arched doorway set an impractical fifty feet above the floor.

The long-bearded King flew out of the doorway, strapped into a great winged girdle and carried forth by a system of pulleys rigged by the ceiling. His wings of many-colored plumage were forty feet across. The pulley-wires had some sort of small tinkling bells woven into them, so that as he flew forward he left a trail of chiming sounds. In his hands he held a large trumpet-like instrument. It was obvious from my place far below that this strange cuckoo was exceedingly short. I was certain I did not like the hour he had appeared to herald.

The New King put the instrument to his mouth and spoke. His word came down to us loudly but with a mighty lisp that rendered the meaning all but unintelligible. When the King ceased talking, the purple man indicated that I should genuflect and bow my head with him. We bent our faces to the cold stone. I heard the King glide directly over us with a tinkle and a squeak of the pulleys. A rustling, as of pants being pulled down, and something wet and malodorous landed on my head. Then the King retreated into the black hole and my companion indicated I could rise. He too had been struck from above.

"Can't be helped," he said. "But some say it is good luck."

We entered a room noisy with fountains, where we washed off our luck. I asked him what the King had said.

"The King wants you to serve as his Royal Archer. I have here a list of creatures that are considered wonders, which he wants you to kill off completely."

"But why? If they are all hunted, they cannot be hunted any longer."

"That is his stratagem. He wants you to make them into nothing but mist. He is a poetic sort."

"As are you, I recall."

He flushed in his cowl.

"That's what he meant by myth, then," I said.

"Yes. And when they are all mist, or myth, as you like, some will remember them, some will hear of them, but none will have them with eye or hand. Then, they will fade even from dreams. And the King will alone be the wonder of the world."

With a fiery glare, the purple messenger produced a formidable scroll from his cloak. I scanned the list of names:

Angel . . . Caladrius . . . Centaur . . . Echeneis . . . Faery . . . Kraken . . . Leviathan . . . Troll . . . And so on.

"I don't mind committing a few murders. But this is a difficult lot of genocides for one boy," I said.

"Doesn't it seem a little unreasonable?"

"It is the word of the King, so it is just."

Even though all justice is made in error, not because the reasons why people mete out justice are good or bad, but because the reasons why they have those reasons are neither, I said nothing to contradict him.

"So tarry not," he went on. "You will be supplied with all the arrows and appurtenances you require."

"What of the carcasses? Am I to leave them to rot across the land? Who knows what plague they might harvest."

"You will be given arrows whose tips are coated with drops of disappearance disease, and will cause the rapid dissolution of the bodies."

"The disappearance disease? I didn't know that really existed."

"It didn't."

"But—"

"—No more questions. And another bit of advice. I know you do not like me, and I know you think yourself wise. Do not cross me."

"Ignoring advice is the best way to learn what ignorance has to teach you."

He was a man, and had two legs, but I swear he slithered away.

The next many years were strange indeed. I did as I was told and proved an efficient hunter. Often I had to get to know my prey better before I could kill them, and I worked hard to gain their trust. Wonders did not hang around with just anyone. So I roved the world, and smoked mandrake with the wild men of the forest, taught the cherubs pornographic doggerel, showed the basilisk how to whistle, and the salamander taught me that the beauty of fire is to burn the beautiful down. Many were these good-natured preludes to oblivion. And all this slaughter, for the sake of a man whose name I did not even know, wore me down. Duty-haunted, I lost my love of archery and with it, life. I no longer put my heart into my heart, my blood and sweat into bleeding and sweating, and had no hand in my hands.

But the King was pleased with my work, and often gave me to understand just how lucky I was this was so. He ordered the topiaries reshaped into the forms of the species my bow had removed from the world, gathered, of course, like loyal subjects around his tributary topiary. So now the foliage accused me each time I came or went from the castle grounds, and the bushes grew lush, as the very sun and rain showered them with solidarity. But if earth and sky were against me, the King was on my side. I was given a comfortable suite near the top of the castle, adjacent to the moon-faced queen, and several floors above the man in purple.

There were two important consequences of this arrangement. For one, I got to know the sorrowful queen quite well. I learned that it was she who had told the King about my happy accuracy on that long-ago day, and convinced him that no one but me could fill the post of Royal Archer. She often asked me to visit her rooms, where she would sit for hours and listen to my stories of the day's slaughter. I found these get-togethers tiresome, but she liked to soothe her broken heart by comparing it to all those that beat no more, thanks to my duty-haunted hand. One night after we had both been to see the King, we found ourselves alone by the fountains. Suddenly she began to sob.

"I am the King's queen now. I care for him, but I love the man in purple more," she said.

"If my instincts are correct, I believe he loves you as well," I said. "He wrote this poem for you, did he not?"

I opened my locket.

"Yes, only it's not a poem. Call it an unfulfilled promise."

"What does it mean?"

"Once a month, the moon seems to form a halo over the central topiary—the one shaped just like the King—when looked upon from my window. Each time this happens, I slip out of the castle to meet the man in purple by the willow trees just beyond the King-sculpted topiary. Each time, the man in purple opens his mouth as if to tell me something that will change our lives forever, but he says nothing and after a time leaves me there alone. Each time I wait after he leaves, hoping he will return. But I always wind up a solitary fool. Hey, hey, baby, baby hey hey, indeed."

"You missed a spot," I said.

I said there were two important consequences of my exalted living situation. The second was that over the years, the man in purple became increasingly hostile to me. No doubt he was jealous I had been raised above him in the hierarchy of the castle, and perhaps it irked him I had gotten to know the queen, and he may have suspected I knew too much about their secrets. And the rare times I looked in his eye I saw his pupil was a deep well and my corpse laid at the bottom. And it worried me more than a meeting with the last of the leucrota, who at that time I was still stalking. Then, one odder than usual night, the King summoned me to his bedroom. I assented without remorse when he asked me to murder the man in purple.

It was an unorthodox occasion. I walked the many steps to the King's lofty chamber. I had not seen it before, having only known him to cuckoo in and out of it with his pulleys and tinkling wires. The King sat unwinged in a monstrous bed, hopelessly adrift among blankets and sheets. His voice was desperate as a newborn's wail, and I could barely comprehend him through the lisping and cursing and a tear-soaked beard that grew into his mouth and tangled round his teeth. But I understood he had discovered the queen's unconsummated treachery. He could not stand losing her, but he dare not be cuckolded. So he would have to lose *him.* He fell asleep mid-malediction, froth on his lips, great vengeful birds pulling purple snakes, no doubt, from his brain.

So I waited for one of those nights immortalized in my locket-poem. This would be the best time to find the man in purple in a vulnerable way, anaesthetized with passion. In the meantime, I continued to shorten the list whose shortening was my only occupation. It seemed each thing I slew wiped another apathetic season off my life, for my hair had long ago gone gray as a tombstone. Already, people were telling mere tales of kobolds and mermaids, rather than hailing them, and questing after the "legendary" unicorn, who only a few decades before were to be found roaming the plains in great packs. Then something stranger happened. Rather than see the King as the sole wonder of the world, they struggled with a deep need to recall the details of the dead creatures, and began to fill in the gaps with their imaginations, which grew stronger and stronger. The falser their stories became, the more they believed in them. The unicorn's feet, which were webbed, became hoofed, and dragons, which were eburnean, myopic and telluric, were reborn as crimson, flying, fire-breathing terrors. Not content to twist what-was into what-was-not, they even concocted what-was-never, so empty had existence become for them.

I had taken so much life out of the world that it now required embellishment. But it was brushes, and paper and pens, and lutes and actors and clay, and none of it lived when you went to sleep.

The murderous night arrived. I slipped into the queen's deserted chamber and gazed out the window on the topiaries all aglow with snow. I saw the moon crowning the life-sized topiary of the King like a halo, illuminating leafy wings heavy with winter. Quiet as an eyelash, I made my way down to the labyrinth and hid between a holly wyvern and a yew ogre, prickly reminders of my irrevocable deeds. I gandered the man in purple beneath the willows. His hair had gone white as his skull since I had first met him. Wrinkles too dense for augury mapped his stern face. He paced expectantly amidst crunchy ice echolalia. I concealed myself behind the topiary of the King and drew back my bow. The queen appeared and threw her arms around him. He stood impassively as if she was something in the way of a trivial errand and he was consigned to waiting for her to undrape herself from him so he could get on with it. When the queen let go, they stood facing each other and he opened his mouth. Misty clouds drifted out. Then he closed it. It opened again, and once more closed. Each time it opened a little less wide and closed a little faster. Not a word, not a "hey baby," but only frosty mist mingled in the air between them. She shivered in her furs. For her sake, I hoped he would finally say what it was he wanted to all these years. Maybe I was making a mistake. But then it occurred to me that everything, even the most correct thing, is a mistake, because I believed that everything did not need to be the way it is, and could have been better to begin with. He turned to leave her a lonely fool, and I aimed at the man in purple's mysterious heart.

I fired just as something leapt out from in front of the topiary. It bellowed enormously. Without a glance over his shoulder, the man in purple dashed away between the moongilded, leafy silhouettes of a sprite and an honest man, and I crept forth.

The cuckoo King lay face up with my arrow piercing his forehead, the shaft casting the imposing shadow of a flagpole that has claimed its kingdom for dynasties. He was spread-eagled and his eyes, unreachable and bleak, belonged on a crab. His pudgy arms and legs shuffled back and forth, making a bloody snow angel. Then he stopped abruptly as an autograph. I reckoned he must have been hiding in front of his topiary tribute, blending into it in the darkness. I suppose he could not wait for me to complete my mission, but wanted so badly to see the betrayal with his own eyes.

As I considered the corpse, the queen ran to his side and sank to her knees. "My dear _____!" she cried at the King's almost predatory stillness, steamy brains leaking onto the frozen ground. My arrowheads were coated with the disappearance disease, and one drop was a million maggots. His face was already fading into a reflection of itself in a mirror, puddle, bowl, mug, thimble, navel, and before you could say "once" it evaporated into nothing but mist that joined the ghostly clouds escaping our mouths. His body vanished in an instant

"My dear ______," she said again.

"______? What's that??"

"Not what, but who..."

"Who is ______, then?" I asked. "Was that *his* name?"

"The King's real name was a secret and I'm not telling," she said. "But I had my little nicknames for him. And now you have murdered him, like you killed your phoenixes and your gnomes and your lycanthropes. And now he will be nothing but mist, like the rest of them. And I wish you had never been born, and had never met any of us. Oh, ______."

The tears turned to ice on her cheeks as she stumbled after the man in purple's tracks. Now I was a fool, old, homeless and alone.

Like a sudden rain startles and passes, so these falling drops of ink. Those wonders I hunted off the face of the earth have endured in stories as flattened, grotesque shadows of themselves. And though the details of these stories have changed over the ages until there is but a few syllables of truth left in them, it is still fitting that the King, who started it all, became the most famous of my fabulous prey.

IT'S LIKE THERE'S NO
AMERICAN DREAM ANY LONGER.
NO DREAM — I'D
BE SATISFIED WITH
SIMPLY BEING AWARE
OR EVEN SORT OF
"OUT OF IT" — AN
AMERICAN "OUT OF IT"
WOULD BE GOOD,

THE FABLE OF THE EMPLOYEE AND THE EMPLOYER

A YOUNG SIMPLETON APPROACHES the crossroads. He's got nothing but a hundred hard miles behind him. All he knows amounts to nothing. He's hungry, dirty, his clothes are spotted with holes worn through to skin, and he's cold and he's got no home, not a friend in the world. The useless young simpleton reaches the crossroads and collapses onto his knees, and he cries to nobody:

"Lord, I feel like God impaled me on His pitchfork and stomped on my face with His mighty cloven hooves."

Then the Devil rises up out of the center of the crossroads. The Devil has a pitchfork and cloven hooves and he's standing over the fragile man. His shadow covers the simpleton. His shadow is like blistering starlight.

"Is that really how you feel?" the Devil asks.

"God, yes it is, Lord."

"How about We make a Deal?"

"But what? I don't have nothing worth having. I got no sense, no money, not even shoes to give you. I got some teeth but they're bad."

"Rise up and listen to me, boy. I am going to read something to you and then we can make our deal. All will be made clear."

The simpleton got up.

"If you sign here—I know what you're about to protest, I have a fine pen with me—When you put your signature on this empty space here, I will give you mediocre intelligence, plain work clothes and shoes, a sandwich, a bottle of milk, and enough wits to quickly learn a bricklayer's trade. You will employ your bricklaying competencies to construct many walls and houses for satisfied customers, and perform other duties as assigned, providing you with enough money to receive some dental care, food, and to rent an apartment-major."

"But what do you get from me?"

"I already told you, poor simpleton. Your signature."

"I don't know how to write."

"I'll teach you, then," the Devil says and pulls a knife out of his mouth. He cuts the boy's hand and smears his blood on the paper.

And suddenly it was a few years later. The simpleton was now a craftier bricklayer, and his services were well in demand. He was in a cold apartment eating a sandwich with his wooden teeth and cleaning his shoes with an old shirt that no longer fit him. He laughed when he remembered that fool of a Devil he tricked on the crossroads one night.

"And all I had to give him," he said to his smarter, but still stupid self, "was my signature. Like I'm going to run out of those! There's a million more where they came from!"

"That's true. I did not lie to you. But see, there is only ONE of this document," the Devil said, having appeared. "Now that you've learned how to read well enough, it's only fair I let you take a look."

The man looked at the paper he'd signed years earlier on the crossroads as a young simpleton. It said that if the simpleton signed his name in the space provided (which he had), he agreed to become a bricklayer and to fulfill his obligations in that regard, building walls and houses and any other structures that he may be hired to make, and to the best of his professional abilities. And then he noticed something he hadn't paid mind to before: he had to perform "other duties as assigned."

So the former simpleton also had to do whatever the Devil wanted him to do, for as long as the Devil pleased.

Then the Devil told him to finish his sandwich. And the man asked the Devil:

"After I'm done eating this, what next?"

"I will assign to you many, many other duties," the Devil said. "It's no matter that you will not like most of them."

"I'll take up another trade. I quit being a bricklayer. There's nothing in here that says I can't quit this job! I hear there's some work needed in the vineyards to the south..."

"By all means! I would never dream of stopping you from changing careers. You certainly can quit your profession, as described in our agreement. But you cannot quit those other duties to which you have agreed, that aren't described—Perhaps not even conceived of yet."

"But why?" the trembling man asked.

"Because it's your job," the Devil said, "just as it does not say so in our agreement."

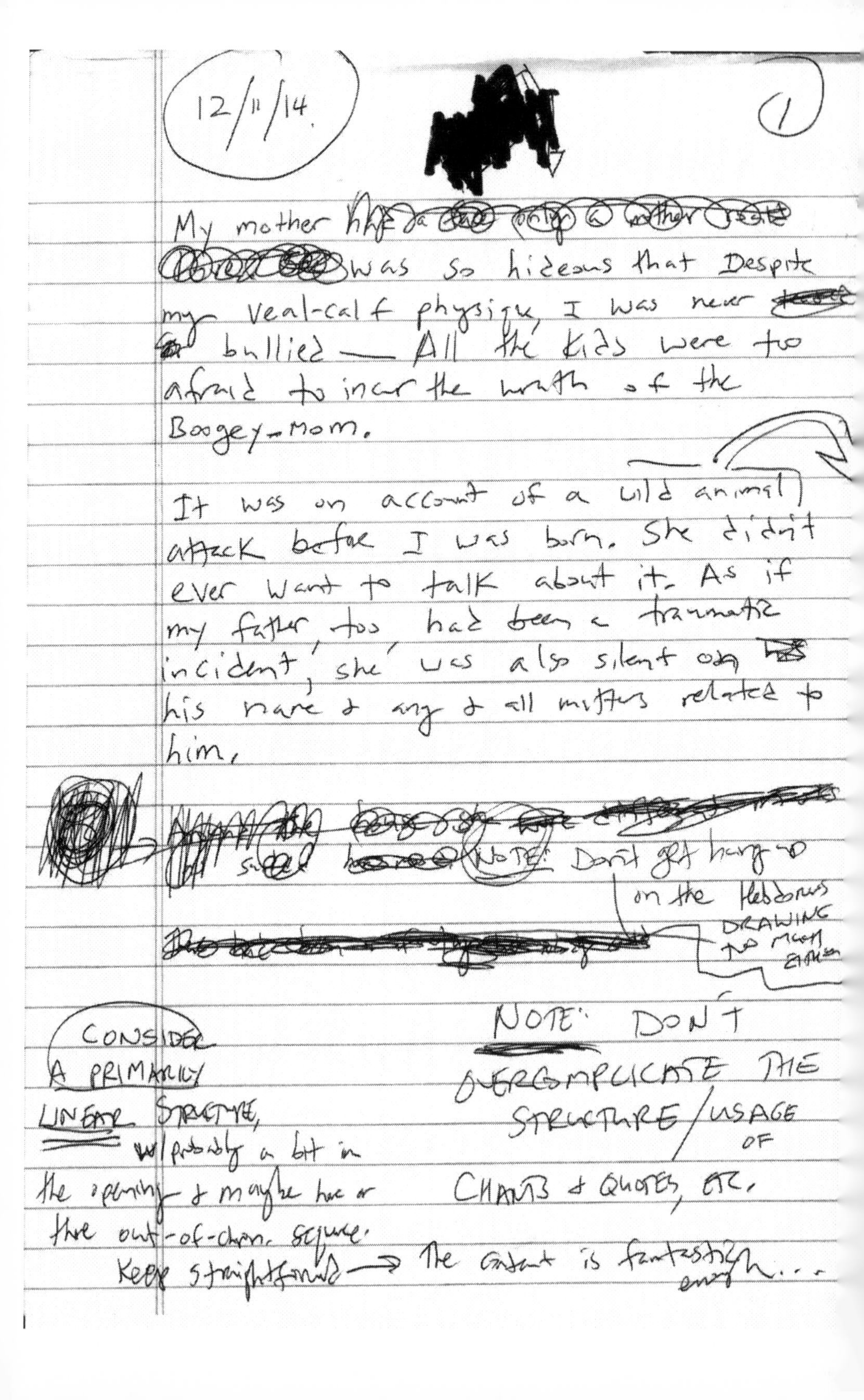
12/11/14.

1

My mother was so hideous that Despite my veal-calf physique, I was never bullied — All the kids were too afraid to incur the wrath of the Boogey-Mom.

It was on account of a wild animal attack before I was born. She didn't ever want to talk about it. As if my father, too, had been a traumatic incident, she was also silent on his name & any & all matters related to him.

NOTE: Don't get hung up on the Hideousness DRAWING NO MOM EITHER

CONSIDER A PRIMARILY LINEAR STRUCTURE, w/ probably a bit in the opening & maybe two or three out-of-chron. sequence.

NOTE: DON'T OVERCOMPLICATE THE STRUCTURE / USAGE OF CHANTS & QUOTES, ETC.

Keep straightforward → The content is fantastic enough...

SCISSORS SELDOM COME

PART #1
HEAVEN'S NOWHERE

"Just as what begins on earth goes nowhere, so what starts in heaven goes to earth; for earth is heaven's nowhere." – *The Dark Wintering*, Prologue (To my Unborn Grandson)

"The difficulty is to gain knowledge of the operations of secrecy while not knowing it; otherwise it should be other than itself." – *The Dark Wintering*, Chapter I.

ALWAYS OPEN WITH A JOKE

Knock-Knock.

Who's there?

Boo.

Boo Who?

Exactly…

One rainy night in 1888, a stranger calls on Dr. Nathaniel Fayteyant in The House Next to Nothing, urgently requesting assistance at the mansion of Harold Chapman and his family. Life and death are at stake. The moon is clear and the leeches ascendant.

And the doctor wonders:

Will I reap what I sow, or something I didn't?

EPILOGUE #1
TOO BLACK FOR BELIEVING

… A fast bonewhite something flows through the narrow murk between evergreens—can it finally be missing Ella-Rae—Didn't Mary Carson wrap her in a shawl of lace just before she ran off, covered in bloody chyle, her eyes like charred buboes? *What kind of world, after all, is this 1868? Who could be so evil as to do what he did to her? She may be a whore but that's no excuse. No doubt that Charlatan with his "I-M POSSIBLE" hokum … I didn't like him one stitch. When Sterling and the rest slandered me yellow that Quack even joined in, taunting "I'm Stanford Grost and I shake, I shake, I shake like the rattle on a snake…"*

But even trembling limbs can climb … a palsy is no pox. I'll bring Ella-Rae hearthside. I'll not be poltroon of New Toomes…

Whatever Stanford thinks he saw has dissolved into baroque trees of Connecticut forest. He calls out her name and the chill December air turns it to mist. He races up the hill to the wood's frayed perimeter, and pauses in the starsilty dark before stepping into the trees. His head wobbles yesyesyesyesyes; birth-hand and wooden both tremble; vibrating tuning forks, those bastards say, that only the dead can hear… The trees are rooted in cold shadow; but nothing white to be seen, not even the moonlight, which falls into weak spots of silvery gray.

That faint smell? Sickening, luxurious…

And where's Harper Noolan? He was supposed to meet Stanford by now. Two men would be safer than one.

Pine-needles crackle against the incomprehensible murmur of forest evenings, and out of time with his own, labored panting. He carefully trudges uphill through a restrictively inky trunkscape.

This earth is thorny, festooned with frozen tendrils; and patches of dead, knobby stalks steeply spike the slope and sally at the advance of his trespassing shins. The smell returns on an icy breeze: a delicious, sweetsalty formaldehyde aroma—a fine supper of chickens, pigs and woodcocks, prepared in a vivisected cadaver's newly embalmed chest cavity. Anticipation irrigates his tongue even as bile trickles throatward. He rubs tired eyes. When he lowers his real hand the darkness seems *inflicted*, less an absence of light than the cauterized blackness of a truncated appendage.

He calls her again.

His voice resounds, but the name crumbles as it leaves his mouth, the words "Ella-Rae" having been overshouted, eroded into useless scraps of cold, hoarse noise in ceaseless search for the good-hearted working girl…

Stanford hikes on, incomplete outlines of trees, bushes, vines, discrete woodland obscurities congealing into still, saltant obscurity. The further resistance of unseen flora scrapes through trouser to skin. *Every shape vague… why does this hour constrict?*

His ascent is peculiarly horizontal; he stops somewhere so black there can be no believing there—no sight—no proof… He trips on likely a root and stumbles into the flaking bark of a bumply tree. Stanford leans back and the trunk creaks.

Ella-Mae is gone forever, isn't she? Awful, but at least the anxious searching can be put to rest. He's experienced this sad/thankful certainty once before—just three years ago—while remaining miraculously standing in the brotherly gore and barely breathing the burning, groaning Appomattox air…

But wait—what small white figure emerges out of the night, desperately fast as a lost, little girl toward the safety of her mother's arms? His heart pumps hope and he smiles, kneels down, ready to receive her…

But how am I seeing her? There's no light…

Because her skin glistens with a gelid, fungal glow, just bright enough to let him perceive a brain-sized mass bursting from stumpen face; not a tumid, conjoined frothing twin, but a single rabid eyebulge that traps broken pupils roving like frightened spiders; to wonder how to distinguish between her chandelier arms and chandelier fingers; and to recognize the bonewhite flash of her flowing hem as her newly-sexed fleshskirt streaked with slushy pain. It undulates like a windblown shroud of tattered jellyfish.

Nearby, but beyond the woods, he hears Sterling's arrogant rasp: "Ella-Rae! Ella-Rae!"

The thing pauses in what appears to be a moment of forgetfulness. Its opposable somethings fumble about a torso of battlefield and baby flesh. What could it possibly have misplaced? What's that glint in its side—*God let it have been stabbed*—no, a handle, the fine gold crank of a music box … without turning its dead, spider-scrambling godlike eye from him, it turns the crank and a soft, slowgeared metallic *liebeslied* plinks, tin rain gently rusting a field of clocks—barely audible beneath the rotten sunrising skin.

She spreads closer with inexplicable waterfall locomotion, seems to arrive in Stanford's face even as she's still approaching. That's a brass doorknocker lodged under her eye, presumably to stop it from drooping off her bodyface … the mechanical song halts and again she tugs the crank, more violently … It's obvious that lacking a mouth, she's trying to use the toy to scream for her—it's clear she *remembers* screaming—that's the worst part, knowing this innervated fleshpile has memories—with each rough mishandling of the device she grows more frustrated at its preciously inarticulate tinkling. He's seen many a veteran thrash at a prosthetic leg just so.

Too far away, other voices call: "Ella-Rae!"

Back against the tree, Stanford slides down into a canopic-jar crouch, chin atop knees. The smell of rot and opulence is as overpowering and unexpected as opening your eyes in the morning to find the sun changed into a tidal wave. A gust of ovenly heat rushes over him. Her eye floats a few inches from his face; it oscillates, but it's not *looking* at him—it is *orienting itself* like an autonomous entity into a strategic position—as befits the *owner* of an eye.

Now she raises his alder hand and impales her eyesac on its chipped tip. He hasn't been healed but he can't move because this can't be real and if it can't be real then there can't be movement, fear or anything … there can't be shaking … but there cannot be cures for shaking either … there cannot be Stanford—a sick, poor man, an unloved man—a man nobody will miss—yet then how can it be that it is none other than Stanford who watches a twisted black pupil slop stillborn out of the punctured eye and stick to his flimsy face, leaking cold holes into his cheek, blinding icy blood dripping up and getting hotter as it ascends …

Her skirt rises over his head.

Now his falsetto whimpers echo and die in lubricated hollows.

i
BUNGHOLES OF BURDEN
EPITAPH #1

If it's true that those approaching death see their lives flash before their eyes, then Perceval's life has been but one giant horse-cock. For that's the only thing he can see now, while he's beating off a dead horse, clinging face-to-foreskin with the crystallized erection of a Clydesdale, the deceased steed sliding wildly down the snowy hill—they skid and foam over devious ground. As a desperate mariner hugs a sinking ship's mainmast Perceval fights not to lose hold of the petrified organ; with every jerk of the pillar he slips a little further toward the terrifying glans, beyond which nothing but white abyss. Letting go is out of the question—they're going too fast … he's about to rocket off like some grotesquely anthropomorphic, broken-necked ejaculate when the sole of his foot taps something mercifully unyielding as abattoir flooring. With relief he recalls the firm, naked cadaver at his feet, the fellow's dick clenched alone-at-last tightly inside the equine's asshole. Perceval tempers his embrace while his boots find purchase on the horsebanger's stiffened knees. But the worst isn't over—the three hurtle together, absurdly inextricable as Father—Son—Holy Shit Does Anyone

Really Believe That Crap? . . . bouncing now over wintersplit ravines —any second a hard crash will undoubtedly end their impromptu flight— . . .

—Perceval pictures a tombstone:

HERE LIES PERCEVAL RAPTUS
BORN UNDER THE SIGN OF YES TRESPASSING
? – DECEMBER 5, 1868
HE GAVE HIS LIFE FOR THE GREATER GOOD RIDDANCE

ii
see this frowzy creature

"There is something ghostly about a liar and nothing false about a ghost." – *The Dark Wintering*, Chapter II.

Perceval Raptus had been orphaned before memory and raised on the abuse and chilly broth of strangers. To the outside observer, he was no different than a million other hateful urchins in the stinking City—begging, thieving, lying, passed out on cobblestone beds—disease, assault ever-threatening and mere anogenital units away. Yet his was a deep and wide-ranging education. He learned that if there's a soul it's a beggar and if there's love it's not enough; the dead are like us—only more so; the world is a bottomless yet overflowing spittoon; starvation begins when the fast ends; the seasons switch back and forth like sluggish lycanthropes and their alter-egos; and the afterlife is the wet dream of bereaved voyeurs. O! And while necrophilia may be a victimless crime, it is *not* a topic appropriate for public conversation, &c.

When Perceval was about nine, he flopped now and then in a fleacloset with a fiery, indignant old woman who always let tramps sleep in her meager room. She gave them bread while she slept and ate dead pigeons on the roof . . . but what Perceval remembered most was her unending lamentations about "Voice."

She fancied herself a "Social Deformer." Every day Perceval

heard her going on about how all the poor suffering wretches needed a VOICE. *They* have no Voice—no Voice! Someone must give them a Voice. She'd point at Perceval and say "Even the insane should have a Voice!" *He* needs a Voice, *she* needs a Voice, *they* need a single giant VOICE to speak together as ONE.

This idea of handing out voices—even *consolidating* them—stimulated and became the organizing principle of his imagination. Bestowing Voice—what could be more esoteric and awe-inspiring?

Answer: *Receiving* Voice.

He knew that what she meant by "Voice" wasn't about talking or shouting; it might be related, somehow, but was infinitely greater. He wanted to be given *that* kind of voice. The closest Perceval could get to explaining it was a poor one—that it would be like finding a box in an abandoned attic. The lid is caked shut and doesn't budge on the first try; yet already you're fascinated by the way the detritus inside it has nothing to do with you. At the same time, your irresistible attraction to these mysterious effects implies just the opposite—they must have a great deal to do with you, perhaps deeply. You find a sunny, quiet place. It's important there's nobody else around to see you sifting through the contents of the box. Yet strangely, it is just when you are inspecting the remnants of a life with which you share no affiliation, that you feel the most urgent need for absolute, unbroken privacy. You cannot open this box—any box—without assuming the contents—though unknown—promise to reveal a coherent and possibly marvelous whole... this is the hubris of opening a box...

One quiet evening the old lady died peacefully in her sleep, moments after an etheromaniac bludgeoned her head with a horseshoe. Perceval returned to the street. It was too bad she was dead, but no shock—just the *Sickle of Life swinging sharp, relentlessly round and round*, as the ancient ballad whines...

But he was a loner among the tribe of bums for whom public congregation was second nature, even key to survival. It got around that he was "special-headed." He tended not to react when slapped; his face was blank as a dead man's visiting card; if given the choice, he'd turn down food or drink for useless books—having taught himself to read with a discarded copy of *Varney the Vampire.* But Perceval didn't care. On a rainy night in 1863, he even risked time in The Tombs for the sake of children's literacy.

Perceval was thirteen that night, wandering under a sky draping countless puppet-strings across Manhattan Island. Drizzled and dulled, he looked in the window of a hunch-backed dwarf's junk-shop in Gravelspitz Lane and thought he saw his reflection. But it was an English translation of the German children's book, *Struwwelpeter.* The cover featured *Struwwelpeter* himself against a white background, alone and open-eyed as a gaseous corpse afloat on a filthy milkpond.

Perceval was unaccountably, irreversibly enthralled:

This *Struwwelpeter* (The anonymous translator dubbed him *Peter Shit-Head*) was a boy about Perceval's age. He bore a numb, death-sentenced expression, blending immediate shock with the resignation of one long acquainted with their fate. Unaware of the long tear that clung like a strand of wet seaweed to his cheek, his reckless hair like the dry yellow weeds that memorialize unloved graves, prophet of meankind… Arms at his sides, empty palms facing outward, his freak-hands fanned ten long middle-fingers. As if wordlessly appealing to a threatening mob: "Look, I hold no weapons, mean no harm, I've stolen nothing. There's no need to hate me. All I've got are silly green stockings, a blousy red shirt, these disgraceful nails that twistingly dangle. These nails, they've gone too far for me to fix on my own, like long roots grown *up into me.* I'm like a tree or an abortion, condemned to its birthplace…"

The figure was too monstrous for men and too much of a man for the truly monstrous—yet he held onto his tiny dignity, like a mouse keeps his tail: behind his ass, maybe—but only to hold himself upright and balanced.

Perceval had to have it. He was hungry, but there was revelation hidden behind that cover—the gourmet nourishment of a last meal. The shop was closed; it had a flimsy side door that opened on a narrow alley. The lock was a joke. He pushed the door a teensy bit open, peered through the narrow brass-hinged space between door and frame. It was deserted.

Waiting...

Moonlight slowly flashed through the grimed window like sluggish bolts of lightning. Things were only partially intelligible by this cloud-toggled illumination, much as the scattered paragraphs of a letter torn to shreds. Perceval cautiously traversed a dull landscape of broken tools, rusty horseshoes, a buckled, keyless tin trumpet, a painting of an absurd arrangement of soldiers, stack of iron hotplates, false beard lying whitely on an obscurely purposed, old-fashioned coat with too many buttons, a bowl of befurred moth's wings, heaps of unstrung marionettes, and other evidence of unprosecuted crimes of boredom.

The book must've been propped in that window for many years—covered in dust. He was impatient to read the poem about the titular character, ignoring the other *"Funny Tales and Fucked-Up Pictures with 15 Brightly Colored Panels for Children 3 to 6."*

Page 11:

See this frowzy creature—
Fuck Me! It's Struwwelpeter!
To his fingers crusty,
Round his shit-head musty,
Scissors seldom come;
Lets his talons grow a year—
Never combs neglected hair—
Who loathes him? All and one!
Puke upon this Urban Satyr—
Disgusting pox—Struwwelpeter!

In the poem, *Peter Shit-Head* was cast as an exaggerated example of poor hygiene—a fairy-tale aberration. But Perceval had a more complex interpretation. On one level, *Struwwelpeter* was a triumph of realism. Any child who isn't taken care of—don't cut his hair, neglect the nails, wrap him in some stupid outfit—take away any chance of making his own future, why, he looks just like that, or worse ... Simultaneously, *Struwwelpeter* struck Perceval with sacred-ikon numinosity, the last day of a martyr's starvation, or even a burning, carny-barking bush.

Struwwelpeter regarded Perceval with an enigmatic expression that suggested this Jack-without-a-Box was just the type to guide him to one of those Voices that old Social Deformer never stopped going on about ... As Perceval padded away with the book tucked under his arm, a pallid hand swiped *through* his wrist. This was when he discovered that spirits are naturally eager to observe intruders at work. Perceval saw them literally forever trying to learn a trick or two about how to possess that to which they had no right. He often saw such illicit images after that evening—persons drowned, burned, poisoned, hacked or worse—quivering in the reflective surfaces of stolen objects. Their missing bodies strained at him with amputated limbs, decerebrated heads dim-lit with fiercely stupid hope. As if watching the displacement of a physical object from one location, one owner to another could demonstrate how, in like manner, they could steal existence.

These misty, floundering solicitations weren't frightening—the dead are like us, only more so—but he thought it one of the saddest things in the world that ghosts were never more or less than room-temperature.

They weren't cold at all.

Perceval brought *Struwwelpeter* to his current home, the disused, unfinished cellar of an Orange Alley tenement. The building shared two walls with an abattoir and a Soap, Toiletries, &c. factory. On even the driest days, the crude room sweated death and disinfectant; frightened chattel-blood and urine trilling through the dirt and loose stones of the eastern wall, and caustic residues of lye, dog fat and *Gentleman's Crotch Powder* westerly exuded. Rainy weather brought heavy seepage of cow, pig and chicken blood and piss on the one side, and stinging depurations opposite. They met in red and pink pools across the pocked ground. Bubbles of blood and piss would stink like murder-suicides when they popped. Then Perceval would sit atop a pile of crates with his chin resting on his knees, watching the cellar soak in its inability to contradict anything.

He'd created an archipelago of "crate islands" in the cellar, for use during stormy seasons when the runoff flooded and muddied the entire floor. The most prized of these spanned half the room and was topped with more crates full of stolen books, tallow candles, Scratchfyre Co. matches, and an unreliable spirit lamp: Papercut Island.

Perceval climbed atop creaky Shut-Eyeland. He rested the back of his head on a stack of pine and cork boards. Termite-holes in the ceiling like stars in a drop-down sky. He held the book close to his chest like a shield. He shut his eyes.

Perceval saw the inviting edge of a still forest, softly green-glowing like grass after sunshowers; and there was gold in the vision though he couldn't see it. He tried to imagine himself into the peaceful wood, but the edges curled away like oak shaved away by lathe, leaving a painfully white void. His head beating bangbang-bang like a chickenshit heart.

Suddenly it came to him: *If there's no way out, it doesn't mean you can't find a better corner to hide in…*

He must quit this hole and find a better corner—the one farthest away from an Orange Street alley tenement. Why not into the untamed wilderness? Unroll the edges of his vision flat, follow the map of it. Find whatever was golden.

It was a fever demanding strategic implementation.

…His first fervid tactic was to leave his archipelago of blood and soap, carpetbag empty but for a slim children's book. He wandered far, regularly almost starving to death, nearly bored, intermittently angry and consistently confused yet always somehow *led* without following.

Along the rotted line he got lost in Connecticut. His body was sore as if bedridden for months, though each day spanned long miles. He went gravy-eyed; seeing double, triple; quadruple—especially inconvenient, navigating dense woodland. Then one cold afternoon when the sky was all varicolored tufts of cloud like the coat of inbred cats, he fated upon Cirkle's Way.

Cirkle's Way couldn't be located on a map; but then, maps are made by people who want certainty, and will never account for the places about which we cannot be sure. To the west was a clock-tower; skewed steeple; the dark rectangle of the Scratchfyre Matchbox Mfg. factory, grand but frail like a structure left behind by a travelling carnival; red roofs and chimneys; a curlicue of river—porcelain silence; a single road thin as a fracture in tea-cup glazing.

Eastward the ground sloped steeply down at an angle that would make suicidal entertainment of dead-horse sledding; at the bottom was a solemn stone structure out of place in its modestly civilized surroundings. Standing apart from, yet close enough to be considered *among* the raddled clapboard buildings of Cirkle's Way, it rose four absurd stories from the bottom of the sharp-sloped road, with oriel windows large and heavy as iron lungs separated by angular, elaborate stained-glass panels. Behind it, a beetling wall of ugly wilderness, branches ampersanding, boughs and trunks blackly embrangled as Chickamauga dead; and the western, northern and southern sides cordoned by spears of noxious weeds. What purpose could such a majestically orchestrated building serve in *these* frowzy wilds?

He felt a flea's paw would strike him down . . . his eyes were dry like dead seas, arid and sorely red like the wafer-chapped assholes of devout Catholics, but he was too weak to rub them into tears. Just then: raddled, repurposed farm buildings juggled low to the ground a few stanzas away. He read four identically wiggly copies of a sign tacked over a wide porch:

THE LITHUANIAN ORPHAN ASYLUM FOR
WAYWARD YOUNG MEN IN NEED (WYMIN)
ST. FRANCIS OF ASSISI PROTECT US

Perceval walked up the short stair. The air blackened quicker than spit. He fell forward and his pate struck the door like a bill collector.

The snowmanly fellow who opened it knelt next to Perceval as the robed, bulky form of the Warden, Father Onderdonkalitis, appeared behind him in the doorway. Perceval's vision returned, impaired; he saw four sets of brown eyes above him and flinched as from straining assholes. No, *waitaminute*—they were 6teen killer's eyes, that would be hard and unflinching in the face of gore and yet uninterested in killing—for its own sake… cold eyes, but not evil.

Obviously a doctor…

"Father, would you mind helping me get this young man to the cot in my dispensary?"

"Of course doctor," Onderdonkalitis said, taking the thin, tow-headed boy's feet while the pale, portly physician slipped his hands beneath his armpits, thinking:

How strange that I myself arrived only a few days ago…

…The doctor had clearly known wealth and position, but he'd appeared on the orphanage doorstep rich only in tribulations, his sole possession one saddle-sized, blacktattered valise. His trousers and his coat, his shoes, scarf and all else were exceedingly fine; but his fabric had worn at the knees and elbows and the shoes cobbled with some cleverly improvised material. It was clear the portly doctor had been under a road of dark cloud for a long time.

He had a proposition for Onderdonkalitis.

They met in the chill austerity of the warden's office. The room was lit by one drafty window set in the wall behind the priest; an autumn morning flooded in, dogmatically transparent and all-pervasive. Onderdonkalitis began the interview by raising bushy eyebrows as if considering how to *answer* a delicate question. He was struck by the doctor's average-looking appearance. It was the man's most distinguishing feature. He had the suspicious anonymity of mail-order dildo packaging. The doctor's face, waist and features were gently round, suggesting moral benignancy or cannon-balls.

"I offer you, your brethren, and the orphans the immense benefit of my expertise in doctorcraft *gratis.* All I want is to serve your WYMIN—in return for nothing but food and lodging of the simplest kind."

"If only you had arrived a year earlier," the warden answered with a slight Lithuanian lilt. "Smallpox epidemic ended in '62."

"Overall duration?"

"About five years. So many died…"

"Is there a hospital hereabouts?"

Onderdonkalitis chuckled.

"We were forced to use the library, despite our Christian reservations. You probably saw this Moloch on the way into town—the adversarial structure that looks like it's marshalling the wilds at its back to sally up the hill.

"There was a wicked man who lived in Cirkle's Way, not very long ago really. His name was Otto Johngreatgrandson and he had the thing built for private use. To keep his personal library."

"Wicked? What did he do besides collect books?"

"The titles of the books alone—which shouldn't *ever* be read—speak loudly for his perfidy. Otherwise, it's not what he did or was, so much as what he did and was *not.* Cirkle's Way is a small place yet nobody knew him, what color his eyes were; there was much disagreement about his height and hair. However, all attested to his thin frame. Who else but a devil could leave such an impression without leaving the memory of it?

"He disappeared without warning soon before the pox. Possibly he was the cause, even. We had nowhere to bring the growing numbers of sick and expiring. We'd never been in the library before—had no right; we weren't even certain Johngreatgrandson was gone for good—or if an heir held claim to it—but the library was the only place big enough to safely exile a hundred patients at a time. We requisitioned it.

"Nothing but books—but what books. Wicked things. But the space was ample; we shifted the shelves we could move and brought in cots, improvised beds &c. as best we could…"

"And is the building currently in use?"

"No, Heaven protect us. It's an evil place, full of words of sin and so much death in the air. Besides, nobody wants to risk a renascent pox. It's hardly a salubrious environment."

The doctor smiled despite himself, managed to disguise it as a tic preliminary to a dry cough.

"It's good to speak with another man of learning after so long, but I must ask you directly, doctor: are you sure your motives are purely charitable?"

"Perhaps not, father," the visitor answered—too quickly? Too self-assured? "The truth goes beyond philanthropy. I believe God has called me to help your poor orphans. I have considerable expertise, and they carry considerable burdens which, you must admit, are too often impossible to relieve. Thankfully they have saints like yourself and the Church to heal their souls. Consider me a humble assistant, tending to their bodily salvation."

"You're from a big city. Yet you've traveled the rural ways far."

The doctor noticed that Onderdonkalitis' hands, formerly hid under the table, were constantly on the mysterious move—seemed to be practicing for a lame shadow-puppet performance.

"O I have, looking for somewhere I can make a difference."

"I am glad," Onderdonkalitis said. "Most people wouldn't come through here unless they were on the run from someone or something. We are not on any maps and I don't expect to host a cartographer in the near future. And especially a man of your background and learning. It is curious…"

His eyes had hardly any sclera and probed Dr. Chapman's face as he answered:

"On the run? O no, father. Say rather … on the walk, on the stroll. A pilgrim doesn't run, or he'll get too tired and expire before he reaches his destination."

"Can you put that less poetically?" the Lithuanian asked with gentle, sharp humor.

"I'm sorry?"

"Less like horseshit." He was waiting for him to reply with an almost maternal, encouraging patience and didacticism. "Please, go on."

Chapman flushed. He lowered his eyes and spoke haltingly, like a schoolboy reciting his Latin declensions:

"I'm a doctor. I became a doctor to be of use, and right now I am of no use to anyone. But here…"

Onderdonkalitis smiled; he believed Chapman.

"Father, would you mind telling me something else of this place? I came upon your Cirkle's Way quite by chance."

"Yes, our little town … I am wanted shortly for an inspection of the Onanist's Dormitory but I do have time for a synopsis."

"May I ask why there is such a large factory here, in this isolated, unmapped place?"

A grim smile rippled across Onderdonkalitis' face.

"I have also pondered that, doctor," he said, his large hands suddenly bursting open like pink-and-white fireworks in the air above his head before returning restively to the desktop.

"Your conclusion?"

"Because there are factories everywhere, in much the same way as smallpox, deceit, orphans, and vengeance. Actually, you may be able to help where that factory is concerned, as well. Many of the workers—most of the townspeople—have the phossy-jaw. Sickened from handling phosphorous at the Scratchfyre factory…

"While we're on the subject, I should also warn you about something in advance, so you don't get a fright at night: As more and more Cirkle's Way residents have contracted that disfiguring malady over the years, it's become common to see lambent green spots floating through the dark street as half-faced factory workers finish eighteen-hour shifts."

Chapman frowned.

"Did I say something wrong, doctor?"

"No, father. No. It's just… the devil is an accomplished devil."

"Yes. But one thing he's not, is an accomplished healer. So I'm glad you've offered your services. May you make a great difference here. And lucky for us all, we have many empty rooms. And I have piles."

iii
HERE COMES ETCETRACAINE!

> "The Dark Wintering was written to be read only by individuals on their death-beds who will either i) be unable to lucidly understand, and/or ii) act on its suggestions, such as: every straight line is the edge of sundial shadow; love is mutually unrequited guilt; that we live in a system of punishments eternally implemented, without reference to penal code. If you do not want to comprehend these and similar truths; if you do not want to make the world even worse; if you have more than a few days to live—then you must not read any further. After Chapter III there is no turning back." – *The Dark Wintering*, Chapter III.

JANUARY 1, 1864

Love at only sight is the only love.

Love at first sight, for example, can be re-created or at least approximated somehow—a 2nd, 3rd, 1,000th glimpse, &c. But love at only sight is pure.

Well. I couldn't save her—helped do the opposite, perhaps—and the gratitude I received that awful day ironic to its black core. Hard to imagine redemption after that day. Well I must try.

I suppose the next best thing would be to save the world. I only wish I could forget her sister's "thank you doctor, thank you." Sometimes it comes at me from nowhere, and reminds me of the evil I've done.

More irony: This place full of books not worth a snail's dowry is where I will lift Science Itself to undreamed of heights. First, I will complete my preliminary investigations.

After this, the hard part: Finding subjects to test the nostrum. I am finally ready to begin replacing the shaky foundation of *Materia Medica.*

JANUARY 2, 1864

This is the perfect site. Large, deserted, well-lit, many needed implements and compounds ready-to-hand. It's no surprise that while preparing the laboratory I found many ridiculous, superstitious books, but one caught my more serious attention. Although irrational and backwards as anything in Paracelsus or John Dee, certain passages turned my mind in a new and useful direction. I've found that when I become stuck on a problem of method or even substance, merely skimming a few pages engenders the little breakthroughs needed to continue my advance.

The book is called *The Dark Wintering* and written by that Otto Johngreatgrandson fellow I've heard both so much and so little about in Cirkle's Way. It is a bizarre text—easy enough to see that from the enigmatic symbol embossed on the cover:

▼

I hardly know how to classify it; I suppose it is occult in nature, though it claims otherwise:

Is this book a work of science, then? Not strictly speaking. Nor is it magic, as understood in the crude sense of the term. It is another discipline altogether. My teachers are beyond names, past recognition, impossible to refer to—they are not even "they," since that term is quantitative, and those of whom I speak cannot be numbered. For lack of more suitable words, say they are the Powers of &c. Better still, keep silent.

From this outré prolegomena, Johngreatgrandson grows a theory of what he calls the *&c. Principle.*

AUGUST 20, 1864

Thanks in part to *The Dark Wintering's* stimulating (if fanciful) influence (especially Chapters IV, VIII, VII and X), I've begun refining an unprecedented method—exciting myself to Apollonian over-exertion; I grow paler and thinner by the day (not thin enough!). It's as though I'm transforming into an entirely new species, living in a rare, inexplicable environment: air is my food, white phosphorous my sunrise and red for sunset—sleep, I call rumination—dreaming is deduction. Soon I must get some human rest.

Fortunately the orphanage doesn't occupy many hours. It's easy enough to escape on the pretense of a refreshing walk, or to say I'm studying the local flora for vulnerary properties. I know the orphans do not trust me and take pains to avoid my general area, which is excellent as far as free time goes. This may relate to my policy—once broken, O Lord!—of not looking my patients directly in the eyes. In any case, my interactions with them are quite brief. As long as I continue to treat Onderdonkalitis' flaring piles, I come and go like a ghost.

DECEMBER 6, 1867

Progress! The road ahead is long but I cannot help but put some of my findings onto the substantiality of journal-paper.

In short, I have discovered that because my anodyne is designed to cure ALL maladies, both existent and non-existent, I must never attempt to test its efficacy on empirical human subjects. This would be to introduce the particularities of each individual's reaction to the compound into my understanding of its effects; the completely wrong method to produce a drug designed to be universally effective.

In other words, the problem with the empirical method is that it is limited by empiricism. At the same time, however, I must not regress into some mediaeval, absurdly deductive system of investigation. The way I have discovered, with no little help from Otto Johngreatgrandson—is far too abstruse to explain in the context of this brief entry. Perhaps it can be distilled, however inadequately, into this motto:

DO NOT TEST IT—PERFECT IT.

Another advantage of this new approach to praxis, is that it keeps me at a far remove from touching, even peeping into anyone's wet secret places. It has taken away an ounce of my guilt, and that is far more than I ever dreamed possible.

JANUARY 4, 1868

Sometimes I've felt like a tin monkey with wind-up lifespan, tasked with a phantom's extratemporal errand. But I endured—and I am close. Soon I will secure a place among the Titans of History's Healers, next to Hippocrates and Galen, Jesus and Schnipesticles.

~~Anemia, angina, asthma, carcinoma, cholera, convulsive dyspepsia, cystitis, delirium tremens, gastric catarrh, insomnia, lumbago, neuralgia, nycaltopia, pericarditis, self-pollution, &c. &c~~ ... Ha! Hee! The list can never have enough *&c.* to suggest the infinite maladies of which it will be the destroyer, even those plagues not yet spread, an etcetera to include all future pestilences, applicable to every disease of which the human frame is subject, and also to the cure of disease in horses and cattle. I see now what Johngreatgrandson meant about the *&c. Principle.* It is absolutely needed to represent the wide reach of the solution, but nothing incarnate has ever encompassed infinity before—a new, infinitely grander conception of &c. is needed.

OCTOBER 7, 1868

ETCETRACAINE!

My impending miracle now properly dubbed:

How can I describe it?

&c. (Etcetera) is a self-contradictory glyph. Consider: 1) That which is limited can be fully enumerated and cataloged; 2) That which is infinite, cannot. But etcetera, disregarding all logic, proposes to 3) Represent both limitation and infinity. &c. is a dismissive gesture and infects all branches of knowledge and praxis—not only the medical.

Take, for example, the following list:

"Tortoise-shell; bovine horns and hoofs; twinning saw; bone; &c."

Anyone reading this suggestive inventory will immediately recognize that the etcetera here is meant to indicate any unstated items, limited to the class of "items related to the manufacture of hair-combs, such as hawk's-bill turtle shell; loggerhead turtle shell; wooden clamps; dye of Nicaragua . . ." At the same time, the &c. in this list—as in all lists—pretends to extend those very unnamed items to infinity.

In the context of medical diagnosis, etcetera might try to hoodwink us with a list of symptoms, such as: "fever, swelling, gastric pains, &c." What could be simpler to understand?

Yet I write as though it were real. I must remember always that until I have perfected the formula, it can be said to be little more than a vivid dream. Dreams—colorful nothingness, leviathans held at bay by the thinnest eyelid skin.

I only pray that Hextly's Brigade does not find me before then, and interrupt my Great Work before it can be accomplished. I am "Harold Chapman" here—I think this is my seventh or eighth alias; until now, I've made it my habit to invent a new one every three months, just to be safe. Why "Harold Chapman?" No idea. It's so innocuous. I know Hextly will not stop looking for me until he sees me tortured and dead. I wonder what manner of bog is on the menu tonight?

IV
THE POSSESSION OF PERCEVAL RAPTUS

> "Our sins, though enormous, must remain unnamable—and therefore inexculpable—because they are committed in a godless universe." – The Dark Wintering, Chapter IV.

On the night of December 5, 1868—five years after he collapsed on the orphanage steps—Perceval stood in the dinner line with his fellow WYMIN, listening to clinquant hail at the eaves. It was one week into that relentless blizzard that had made the violent, spring storm of 1861 seem like a cool mouse queef. Out beyond the thin asylum walls, men and mercury alike were freezing solid, snowfall breaking obscene records. In the cities, whores and cut-throats traipsed like angels over tree-tops bridged by icebroken boughs. Hundreds were perishing without coal, shelter, or bread. Skylines from Newport to Baltimore thickly faded into fossil moonscapes.

Perceval was in a weird mood, left brain daydreaming and the right blank. The priests liked him; he looked like a good person because he would've been one, if things had been different. And he was quiet and kept to himself.

Perceval didn't notice his turn had come until Thingstable's high whine spattered his cochlea:

"—he said next!"

At the serving table, Perceval held out his lunch bowl/dinner bowl/spittoon/bedpan/rat bath/roach lake, to receive a dollop of hot, graveolent mire.

The cavernous meal-room stunk of carbolic soap, through which wafted a vaguely rectal smell that could be plausibly described as Kraken farts. A spectacular, 1:1 scale replica of the cross and its hammered Nazarene overpowered the room like an eye-rattling EVERYTHING MUST GO sign.

A butcher-blocky rectangular table nearly bisected the chamber. It was an orderly accretion of surplus adult smallpox coffins; unmodified infant coffins served as seating for the WYMIN, and when they sat, their chins barely cleared the table's edge. Lunch and dinner, the boys on either side were able to watch a convincing illusion of decapitated heads slurping ooze opposite them, as they ate their own.

As was their ritual prior to meals, the WYMIN put down their bowls at their assigned spots and gathered in an ovoid formation round the table. Father Onderdonkalitis stood outside the perimeter of young men and beneath the crucifix; he waved a large hand that cast an all-enveloping hush. Perceval found the warden's hands so striking that they had a place of importance, recognition and identity normally reserved for faces. They never stopped dancing like mistrained elephants.

The bruise-faced lads stood quietly as lice-raided, pre- and post-sodomized bodyscratchers possibly can.

Perceval had rarely been able to distinguish between that which he hated from what he felt indifferent. But now the certainty of hate came upon him.

It had something to do with this priestly, externally-mandated silence.

Suddenly his right brain rose up from daydream to vision and his left was transfigured from blankness to limitless space ... Like anything you don't want to put into words, it was hard to find words for it ... To be forced to *feel* the same as others, to be sad or grateful with them, to believe, refute, suffer or celebrate *en masse*. In this imposed togetherness, Perceval was aware that he must do more than pretend—must pretend not to be pretending—he must deceive ... or something ... maybe he was just hungry ...

But no. Just as Father Onderdonkalitis was about to end the ritual with an "Amen"—an unheralded energy *flushed* through Perceval, administered thrilling enemas to every atom. He was *cleared* and resolute ... He'd never sung out loud before—was this an about-to-sing feeling? Vision merged with infinite, empty space. Perceval stared straight ahead, seeing nothing and not needing sight, like a figure on a prow ... You sit in a sunny, private place and the lid of the box comes off easily without hubris but revelation and surprise, surprise! Huge bright words dashed off his astronomical tongue like stars, each word was an earsplitting event:

> "WHO DIED AND MADE JESUS GOD EVEN IF YOU'RE SAVED IT DOESN'T MEAN YOU'RE SAFE GOD IS NOWHERE AT ONCE HIS SOLE FUNCTION IS TO PROVIDE THE MORAL SUPPORT NEEDED TO THOSE WHO HAVE JUST SNEEZED CAN YOU GET AN IMMACULATE DOSE OF THE CLAP GOD CAN GO TO HELL—AND YOU CAN ALL GO TO CHURCH ONLY 4-LETTERED WORDS ARE MADE INTO FLESH ... FUCK FUCKFUCK CAN WE

JUST EAT ALREADY SHIT GARDDAMN."

The episode ended as quickly as it had arrived. Perceval returned to his place in the ovoid of orphans and wondered why the WYMIN were looking at him with holy terror in their abandoned eyes. He vaguely thought it doesn't matter what you say … it's not the message, but the messaging … it was hard to explain.

The melodramatic writhings of the warden's hands broke Perceval's hypnostate. They travelled to his navel, where the thick fingers warped into threatening, interlocking gestures equal parts church-steeple, condor swoop, and creelful of snakes. His tall, thin form shook under his robes as though made from wild jets of air. Onderdonkalitis had flushed dog-dick puce and his lean face somehow projected the demonstrative quivering of a furious fat person.

"Wha …" Perceval said.

And then everything was suddenly wielding exclamation points like great cudgels, and not afraid to use them, either (e.g., Fisticuffs! Smack! Kick! Owtch! Scold! Kick! Kick! Slam! Throw! Good-Bye! Wait! Not Yet! Here's Your Stupid Cloak and Bag! Spit! Good-Bye! Forever!). And when the colored lights melted into midnight like sight into blindness, his brain slid across a ballroom floor of ice, twirling alone in the dark while beneath, cold-horned currents tried to stab waltzes through their ceiling … He was outside, on his knees. He wretched up some gutty blood, shook some splintered coffin cover out of his hair. Standing up and wiping some of his nosebleed with the back of his dry hand, he wrapped himself tightly in the cloak and shouldered his carpetbag. With relief he confirmed Peter Shit-Head was inside.

The world had grown a cold exoskeleton, the opaque, gleaming, relentlessly transparent colors of dreams about drowning, and still as an expired cephalopod. Weathervanes turned north in iron solidarity of beaks, hooves, heads, prows, the letter N, manes and arrows. And then the volleys of stinging hail started again, millions of subzero balls ripping Cirkle's Way entirely superfluous assholes.

After twenty minutes treading through the quickly accumulating snow, his legs ached stiffly as two priapatic willies. Huffing, face damp and uvula-red, wind on his eyes like cold pennies. Gradually, the phantom angles of a building in the fractured blur. A shop not far down the indiscernible road. The long, rectangular building boasted a narrow overhanging thatch—provisional shelter.

A sign on the door:

MANUFACTURER OF FERRULES &
DRAPER & SHEAR GRINDER &C.

He was exhausted but sleep = death.

The snow was piling up fast around him and the air was a curdled haze. Perceval needed a more acceptable enclosure. In this illogical night there was only one logical choice:

Otto Johngreatgrandson's library.

He'd have to risk the possibility of catching smallpox. As for all those rumors the library was haunted—they'd started circulating about a year after he'd first arrived in Cirkle's Way—that didn't scare him, of course. Since sometime in 1864 and ever since, strange red and blue lights had been reported coming from within, flashing across lifeless windows…

He plunged into the white shit again and soon lost all sense of direction.

After a while he stopped to catch his breath and the wind whirled *up* with tremendous force like a hump-back lunging its bulk to crest the sea; then fell just as fast. As the air cleared he could see a little better; the snow had descended into starry curves and piles in a bewildering range of shapes, and dramatically varied in height like the pipes of grand cathedral organs.

Then Perceval noticed a trinity of dim, greenish luminescences seeping through the gauzy air. The faint lights were spaced unevenly apart from each other, with two closer together on the right side—but all were the same size and set at the exact same level. It was this observation that told him he must head their way to reach the library.

The Daztgarham quadruplets lived in a house on the far eastern edge of Cirkle's Way. Once the four handsome identical brothers had formed a popular ventriloquist group, each with his own identical dummy reposed upon his lap. But when the biloquist rage passed in '64 they were penniless. They wound up in Cirkle's Way and took jobs at the Scratchfyre factory. They came down with the phossy jaw years ago, and their conditions had worsened considerably since. Not without humor, the Phossy four hacked up their dummies' faces into opisthognathous self-likenesses…

The green lights that Perceval descried through the frantic snow flared at the exact same level in the murk, like three lanterns set on a flat tabletop… it could only be ¾ of The Phossy four at their window.

Perceval headed their direction but as the crazy, black blizzard-magic started pulling lumps out of straight lines, he lost track of time and his way but didn't stop walking and the ground beneath his feet changed texture, gave spongy resistance. Buckled wood? Perceval knelt. Not wanting to take his hands out from the comparative warmth of his cloak, he lowered his face and probed with the tip of his nose… planks… a nail in the nostril. It must be pieces of the stable, not far behind the Daztgarhams' house. It meant he was still going toward the library, but he needed to tread carefully.

It would be a small relief to just crawl forward a while, partially sheltered from the wind by fallen stable walls. He numbly elbowed on… horseshoes? Frozen hay… pitchfork tines and shingles. Perceval's head knocked against something hard. Hairy? He wiped away icy integuments: the head of a corpse. It did not disturb him. The dead were like us, only more so. Intrigued, his fingers trawled around: The slight indentation where the ears take cartilaginous root… eminent cheekbone, leptorrhine nose… a frosty moustache, leading to the mucronated edge of a chipped incisor—and his hand suddenly dropped, striking the granite-hard Adam's apple of a very stiff neck.

The 4th Daztgarham.

He jerked away his hand, only to grab the hard mass of a horripilated buttock. What had this phossy-jawed fellow been doing out in the stable, under this sky of angel vomit—without pants?

Answer: The quadruplet had been sodomizing a stallion. The animal's horsehood like a fallen Doric column. Two lovers—worlds apart in life—yet, in dying, joined inextricably through the enormous lack of any world at all.

It was clear from the cadaver's face that he'd died ecstatically; this was the more disturbing because his jawless situation should've rendered such definite emotional expression impossible. Suddenly a snowy gust thwacked Perceval's head into the late ventriloquist's bony back. A sharp retort of cracking ice—the earth moved and the missing landscape, already an upside-down void, twisted in unnamable directions.

And Perceval was horse-sledding down the steep hill at incredible speed, toward the library … While in their shanty, the living 75% of the Daztgarhams wondered when their brother was coming back so they could get their turns. Why was he taking so long—Mr. four-second Phossy himself!?

V

THE BLANKET HORNPIPE

> "It's got my name, but I know that's not enough to prove its worth. After all, every dead liar's tombstone's got their name on it!" – Harold Chapman, 1868

There's one whorehouse in New Toomes, and there's a funny, wrestling pain in Harper Noolan's naked chest—an avian excitement and a man's fear of falling from a cathedral spire. There's longing and transformation in the musky, dim-flickered air. Ella-Rae has left the room for one adjacent, with faux smile of anticipation and the promise of quick return. Sitting at the foot of the greasy bed, Harper hears water splash in a basin, drip meek to bare boards. The lewd noise of neighboring business alternates with schoolboy fantasies of droplets striking, rolling off Ella-Mae's skin.

Try to relax. This is the only time you play the blanket hornpipe for the first time. But he's got nerves, his hands are starting to shake—what if she laughs at him like he's Stanford Grost? Hey—waitaminute—he's still got that nostrum in his pocket—that stuff he'd bought just today along with everyone else. The man with the green eyes said it would cure anything—even neuralgia—even obstacles to virile release...

Ella-Rae's soft voice:

"Be there in a second, hon."

"Take your time. Sure."

Harper quickly gets the packet from his coat where it hangs from the red chair where nobody had ever sat. He snorts a pinch of black powder up his nose.

Sneeze!

"Bless you," she says, wearing nothing but a chewed-up possum stole, and pushes him back on the bed.

He feels things change beneath her barely furry form. His head lightens. The hairs of her stole tremble lightly like cilia. Their tips lit in soft orange light from the candle beyond. The bristles sway with purpose. He's an idle parasite inside an organism.

Though her palms and his skin are touching naked he feels something separating the two. He wonders what, but it's pointless because really there's no word for this ignorance, the astounding depth of his not-knowing-her, far deeper than the rift between strangers passing on the street.

Maybe the Etcetracaine wasn't junk, because he's calm and steady now, and he's *almost* Harper Noolan. But not quite ... Her chest rises and falls. He seems to stand in a lake up to his eyes, peering at a wave about to cover his head...

Ella-Rae is on top, but he is inside?

Why doesn't it feel good yet, down there?

She's pulling her black hair tightly behind her ears. Her blue eyes are pretty like a lobster's that never close and can't see very far and always see too near.

Now Harper feels something down there—everywhere. Is that how it works? It's hot. His blood circulates with the river Nile. His blood gets lost in shadowy eddies. His saliva dammed, his tongue dry as shale quarries ... his blood laps in a gentle April way against the sides of his veins.

"You OK?" Ella-Rae says.

"I-M-POSSIBLE," he stutters, his body jelly.

His body cataleptic as knots in wood.

"Wha—"

Two dark, lidless eyes gleam at Ella-Rae. There is the slightest bit of humanity in them—that of an arsonist watching a churchful of children burn, finding the conflagration wasn't magnificent enough, the screams not as tormented as he'd hoped—but mostly they are ugly like lobster eyes...

"Hey. You sick? Are you OK..."

He's not. Ella-Rae springs backward and off the bed, hitting the floor with a slam and benumbed coccyx. He has no face, no face ... but the eyes grow, eager tumors from the flanks of a giant tongue. It writhes and twists and drowning spit froths over the eyes, black seas discharging poisoned tides.

He rears up to loll against and lick the ceiling tin, thicker at the eye-encysted tip, tapering to a wedding-band thin pink nub at its source in the mouth, which is also his tail and his feet. This mouth is the most horrible thing about the creature that was Harper Noolan: It's far too small to express the rage and satisfy the hunger which so clearly fills its tuberous host to bursting. It opens no more than mewing kitten jaws.

He has no body...his body has disappeared into itself.

Is that water spreading? Did she piss in terror?

She remembers there's no living without trying, springs up and runs through the sloshing famine. Halfway out the door the teeniest, most precious mouth nibbles an inch of skin off her heel. The bite immediately begins dancing or something. Now she's made it down the stairs and crumpled in a heap. Bassy questions, squeaky, nasal queries ... what happened? He cut you with a knife? She hears herself reply something like, can you just imagine how many terrible weeks it would take for that tiny mouth to chew you up, while you slowly went from fresh to rotten, conscious meat … A deep-throated, baritone question: What the hell does that mean?

Ella-Rae recognizes Mary Carson's voice cutting through the others. Mary's the kindest friend a girl could have: "Here, try this black powder I bought from that charming physician-man today. Maybe that will help the pain. Sniff it off my finger…"

Ella-Rae's pain is smiling or something in thrilling anticipation. Someone tumbles down the staircase in gray fractures and lands with his head next to hers; they could almost be lying back on the bed after an exhausting session. Ella-Rae's ribcage grins widely… and as the room swirls away she sees good-hearted Mary Carson giving the last of her *&c!* to the pale young man with the stare of a prosthetic head. She daubs it under his nostrils and he inhales deeply. Ella-Rae sees him smile too. No, wait—smiles are opening on everything, the floor, the wall, the air, he has no face…

Now she blacks out.

VI
CLEANLINESS IS NEXT TO GODLINESS GODLINESS IS THE GRANDEST FILTH

> "All things are poison, and nothing is without poison; Only the dose permits something not to be poisonous." – Philippus Aureolus Theophrastus Bombastus von Hohenheim (Paracelsus), as cited in *The Dark Wintering*, Chapter VI.

The autumn of 1861, so Fayteyant overhead a popular colleague quip, had come unwanted to New York, trees turning all the colors of immigrant flesh, red and yellow and brown, unloading swarthy leaves, flooding streets like the swarms of prognathous Italians daily shuttled from Castle Garden, overinfesting Manhattan Island's most pestilential zones.

At that time Doctor Nathaniel Fayteyant, M.D., D.D.S., F.R.S, K.T.S, Y.H.W.H., Fellow of the Chicago & New York & Hartford

& Massachusetts Academies of Medicine; Member of the Court of Examiners of the Royal College of Surgeons of England; Honorary Member of the Berlin Odontologischen Gesellschaft; Advisory Sexton Extraordinary to H.R.H. Edward VII &c., was practicing and serving as Chief Professor of Anatomy & Toxicology, Chemical Reactions & Productions, Department of the Taint, Left-Buttock & Uterus; as well as Special Lecturer in Surgery of the Extremities at Columbia University's College of Physicians and Surgeons, &c. &c. He'd also just published what became his most popular work: *When Pyaemia Supervenes Upon Shiv Gangrene in "The New York Halls of Justice and House of Detention," the Urine Assumes a Most Beautiful Pink Color, from the Great Destruction of the Colored Blood Corpuscles, Induced by the Presence of Pus in the Blood, & Sundry Other Observations &c. &c. Second Edition. Revised & Considerably Expanded.*

It was an exciting period. In addition to the ever-increasing esteem of his peers and rapidly growing list of surgical accomplishments, he was in the midst of working on a compound that, if perfected, would cure *all* diseases. Although Fayteyant would generally scoff at such a notion, certain happy mistakes made during recent toxicological experiments, had led him to believe it was possible—and that he was just the man to do it. Imagine how he could change the world...

One day that October, he was due at the College to demonstrate his pioneering methods of reducing the probability of systole in patients undergoing the *abdominal paracentesis* operation.

It was quite early in the morning, strawberry blonde light softening the city's edges. Not two paces out the door, Fayteyant ran right into the muscular chest of an enormous man dressed all in black. He didn't apologize, stepped silently backwards to let Fayteyant by.

The stranger had one lazy blue eye that made it impossible to determine his motives. His face overall was characterized by asymmetry wherever features come in pairs. One eye, for example, was exceedingly large, the other incongruously scrunched, like a hideous planet and its dissolute moon. His jug-handled ears stood close to 90-degree angles to his skull. ¾ of his stumpy nose were dyed a shade of claret. He had scarcely any lips and Fayteyant shivered when the man skull-grinned at him with mocking civility.

Standing to his right and stretching all down the block was a long line of men dressed identically to the ominous brute, suggesting a platoon of undertakers or bizarre dance troupe.

The giant nodded agreeably in a disagreeable way. Fayteyant rushed off to his surgical demonstration. Who was that fellow? And his little army? The whole business was incompre-hensible.

A young nurse greeted Fayteyant as he entered *The Horace Gravelspitz Hextly Theatre of Comparative Anatomy*. He saw no reason to reciprocate. Crowded in the observation stands above, 106 enraptured students waited to catch a glimpse of the magisterial surgeon at work.

In the center of the Olympian chamber was a wooden table; decumbent upon it an unconscious and naked octogenarian. He had a wild, holy-man aura about him, and in his dull, grey boiled-gooseberry eyes, one might learn to believe that Cleanliness is next to Godliness because Godliness is the Grandest Filth.

His abdomen was grossly distended as though a beaver curled upon his greater *omentum*. The surface was spotted with veins bullied by the peritoneal inflations of his cirrhosis. The engorged carmine *caput medusae* of serious ascites…

Now Fayteyant looked up to acknowledge the ambitious young men gathered like beggars in the gallery. He enjoyed their attention, the easy with which he thrilled them with a mere head-nod. It helped him shake off his h(a)unted feeling and remember how much he loved his work. In fact, it was an absolute fetish with him. He was fortunate that his own personal perversion could only be satisfied through socially celebrated acts of healing. He saved people from death while secretly enjoying himself with inexorable lewdness:

Inhaling air coughed and recoughed a million contagious times; feeling hideous parvenus with exophthalmic eyes blinking oblations at the Bedside Asclepius of him, brimming with begging for vulnerary grace; reading the Braille of skin maculated with cheloid suppurations; prodding cartilaginous intestines for belemnoid calcifications; lancing spitting pustules; embrocating the deep, rigid, redly strigose anal grooves of octogenarian piles…

Typically, Fayteyant was deadpan as aluminum. But today he was uncharacteristically distracted and vexed at himself for it. The inappropriately familiar grin of the asymmetrical stranger—irritated like an elusive strand of hair stuck to his sclera.

But it was nothing…

Now doctor approached patient with lighter step.

"Here before us, we see … what do you perceive? Not a pregnant female; but rather here is a man with acute abdominal dropsy in severe need of the *paracentesis abdominis* operation. First we will withdraw the fluid from his abdominal cavity…"

Fayteyant inserted the trocar, porting the old man's venous side. He suppressed his visceral delight; surgery was the pinnacle, the most invasive form of voyeurism—to pry into both the boggiest, friable and hardest parts of a person, places even they cannot reach. And to be able to indulge in this pleasure publically —while lesser voyeurs watch you satisfy the lurid urge! What perversion could excite more?

"Notice he makes no protest. Ether—and whiskey, no doubt! Now, let us see what ails our old Struwwelpeter…"

"—Shaft your Strudel-peppers!" a man barked and burst into the theatre, his sweaty face pink-flushed as an overvacuumed nipple, two blue eyes amphetagleaming, and a third, bright eye of green set in a ring on the middle-finger of his right hand. A pair of different rings flanked this finger-mounted, ocular prosthesis, each displaying perse, Grandidierite orbs with the circle/arrow/dot symbol for Uranus inlaid upon them in gold.

He was an imposing and gigantic man, and he strode up to Fayteyant and put his hands on his hips as though well-acquainted with supervising the labor of thousands:

Colonel Horace Gravelspitz Hextly: The Goat King of Madison Avenue.

The Colonel was a man to whom no doors were closed—he owned them all. Having first made his fortune in goats, he subsequently invested—like carbon itself—in practically everything—and everything practical. His daughter, Leta Hextly, was a rising star of the music world, a virtuoso pianist.

That the most powerful man in the City knew Fayteyant's name distended the doctor's pride as with acute abdominal dropsy. Whatever this Mammon wanted of him, to refuse Hextly's wishes = career suicide. He wiped the bloody, silver-plated cannulae of the trocar on his coat-tails, tossed it to the nurse, who caught it with a groan as it sliced her palm, a swift spurt of her blood baptizing Fayteyant across the surface of several anatomical systems. The doctor cried to her to finish the operation for him. As he rushed off to change, the Colonel said there was no time.

Raising his walking stick above his top hat like an Aquila, Hextly led them down the stairs so quickly that the old man's screams of agony in Fayteyant's ears died away much sooner than the patient. Next thing Fayteyant knew, the bright autumn day had been snuffed by Hextly's baize-curtained cab. They sat opposite each other. Only now did Fayteyant have a moment to take the measure of the man. Hextly wore a magnificent Ulster, immitigably solemn and alive, white hair dazzling—a Ziggurat with appetite. Fayteyant felt a growing sense of shame at his own dishabille state, nurse-blood exuding from his coat-tails and woolen thighs, and empurpling the Toile de Jouy cushions.

"Damn Indians," Hextly growled.

"O. What did they do now?"

"Nothing. That's just the problem. That's why I was down in Iquitos for the past eight months. Had to fire the whole lot from the plantation, lazy louts…"

"Rubber?"

"What else?"

"How tiresome for you. When did you return Stateside?"

"Why, just today, obviously! Why else would I be wearing these Wellington boots on Fifth Avenue?"

Fayteyant chuckled good-naturedly, not comprehending. However, the colonel's high leather boots *were* indeed crusty with what looked like dried mud—or something more pulverized and/or excremental.

"It's my daughter, Leta—if you were wondering," Hextly said.

"Leta Hextly! I am so very sorry your daughter is not well. I'm honored you called upon *me* with so many talented medical men in this city."

Hextly snorted violently.

His blue eyes were distant, travelling someplace nobody could hear a thing... the false green eye on his ring stared at the doctor, unblinking—smugly inanimate. Fayteyant noticed an identical ringband on Hextly's other hand, this one bereft of gemological adornment. It was strange that this powerful man should go about displaying unfinished jewelry on his finger ... the doctor's eyes returned to the muddied Wellingtons and he decided to speak about that which he knew before he went mad with all he didn't.

"May I ask the nature of her condition?"

"Run down. A mess. Pipes clogged, viscous. The stench!"

"Enemas? Enemas—have any been administered? Not tobacco-smoke enemas, I hope," Fayteyant said, sure of himself now—when *he* played the expert. "No matter how popular they may be at present, I must firmly declare such intervention as nothing but quackery—and of the most dangerous kind. I don't want to outrage but I *must* make my position clear on this treatment at the outset. Very dangerous and taken too lightly in the press. These health fads are no joke. No, there's nothing funny about what things should and should not go into your rectum, or what exits therefrom. Or even that which may be lodged in those quarters, howsoever and regardless of genesis, be it internal or external. And now that I think of it, in fact there's a fourth possible situation, in which—"

"—What? No, the *plantation* man. I had to bring my own men over for the plumbing. They cost more but that's how it is, I should know. Hard workers, Lithuanians, mostly... names like diseases to a man. *–itis* this and *–itis* that..."

Hextly reddened, grit perfect white teeth.

"The issue is *feminine* in nature, man," he said.

Fayteyant nodded.

"Uhm … I admire your daughter greatly—what exquisite virtuosity! Why I saw her not long ago, performing Liszt—*The Mephisto Waltz*, I believe. It was … very modern, but transporting—and it will be almost as much of an honor to meet her as it is to speak with you."

The Colonel breathed and sporadically snorted, exactly like an enraged centaur with transplanted cetacean lungs.

"Do right by me and I'll have you appointed Manhattan Island Commissioner of Lunacy. One of the most powerful positions in the city—did you know the C.O.L. can easily have his enemies committed to asylums of his choice? Within limits … you should see my balls, try to lift them."

Whenever Hextly spoke, Fayteyant could see Little Red Riding Hoods stuck between his teeth.

"Thank you, sir."

Hextly looked out his spotless window at his besotted city.

"Think before you thank," Hextly answered, adding without segue: "You should see my balls, doctor. They'd give you a hernia if you tried to lift them and make me cough. I do not cough for anyone. Am I understood?"

Fayteyant nodded. He decided it best to shut up.

"Hextly Headquarters" was a contrived and glacial structure, extravagating over Madison and 37th Street, a window-studded monolith with Asscher-cut corners. It was a diamond ring on the finger of Manhattan Island, proof she belonged to Hextly's alone.

Hextly manhandled Fayteyant through oak doors, the scale of which suggested the combined labor of a several thousand slaves. The scale of the place was such that even the foyer induced vertigo; Atlantean staircases sprawled up to halls historiated with the *lusus naturae* of medieval bestiaries: detailed engravings of bewildering caladrius and echeneis, kraken, manticore, leucrota and—most worrisome—herds of mighty centaurs with Hextly's shocking-white hair and determined features, pounding the other monsters into extinction…

The overpowering smell of animal fat was general throughout the house. They mounted a spiral staircase that spanned several stories top to bottom. Fayteyant's hand was about to alight on the banister, only to have Hextly smack it down.

"Goat fat, man. Don't you know goat fat?"

"In itself—yes, Colonel."

"Well, I suppose I wouldn't be the Goat King of Madison Avenue without my little secrets. I'm holding a ball here in two weeks' time—Leta will be performing a recital. Nothing gives these banisters a shine like the goat fat. My fellows brush it on thick and no one is to touch it for four weeks. Then they polish it off with silk and you should see them gleam—keep up, man!"

They were swallowed by high archways dressed in elaborate cambric portières; over leagues of marble—oriental smoking wing, three salons, velvet lamellated corridors where fantastic creatures seduced fluted columns; and then abruptly—like the tedious punch-line to an interminable jest—they reached Leta's bedroom.

It was a warm blizzard dream, ivory and polished horn and mother-of-pearl; there was a gorgeous dressing-table and much cheval-glass. The gold-fringed sarsenet drapes of a porphyrine canopy-bed were pulled half-aside; Leta sat propped up against pillows, half-buried beneath a landslide of white eiderdown, staring absorbedly at nothing and paying their entrance no mind.

"There she is," the Colonel said, not looking at her but the sky going nowhere outside a grand window. "I go away for eight months and this is what happens. You will fix this. She hasn't given a performance in almost a year—the public is fickle … Make sure she is right—and *looks* right—*before* the ball."

"Colonel, you said before that Leta was your eldest. How many other lovely daughters bless your life?"

"Just the one other. Vespertine."

"Well, I hope I have the pleasure to meet her too one day."

"That's easily arranged," Hextly said. "She's the top-notch secret agent preparing to wet herself behind that Japanese screen over there."

The ten toes of two small, bare feet faced the room from beneath the screen, pink and still as empty girl-slippers. The sunlight shifted through the window, and now Fayteyant noticed specks of broken glass, crystal, and modern Suhl porcelain littered across the floor in a fine, luxurious dust.

Disconcerted, Fayteyant remarked with sham buoyancy:

"O, but look over there. How unusual to have a piano in a bedroom. But of course when you are one of the finest musicians of the age, I suppose it makes sense!"

"It malconforms, doctor," Hextly said. "And it's nothing but fifth rate—just a Steinway & Sons…"

"Is it?"

"So I've commanded you to understand. Nonetheless it is good enough for Leta to practice upon when mandated."

An impressive oil painting of the famous Daztgarham Quadruplet Ventriloquists and their dummies hung over the piano.

"O and the Daztgarhams…amazing entertainers."

"There I must concur, doctor. I laugh myself to pieces every time I see their Knock-Knock routine. You know the one—Boo?"

"Boo…*Who*?" the doctor second-fiddled.

"Exactly!"

The Colonel grimaced in raucous approval, adding:

"Did you know they're horse-fuckers—every last four of them! Goats, too…I saw to that, of course!"

"Uhm. If I am to help I need my things, Colonel. I can examine Ms. Hextly, but then I must make arrangements to retrieve them from my lodgings. I can return posthaste."

"There's no need of that. Your tools of the trade are here already."

"I don't see how—"

"My man Bochkser and his men have taken care of it. They've been to your room, and everything's here already."

By this time Fayteyant had lost count of how many times he'd been confused into silence today. He stood rigidly, assuming an intense expression of diagnostic consideration.

"You know, Leta," Hextly said, acknowledging her for the first time," when the good doctor is done erasing your mistake I plan to make him Commissioner of Lunacy for Manhattan Island. That is, if anyone can find the poor man. I've heard *terrible* rumors..."

Leta continued to ignore him.

Hextly strode across the room to the Japanese screen and kicked it with a crusty Wellington boot—two dainty feet jumped out of sight, and they heard Vespertine slam into the wall behind her with a groan. Hextly spat at the fallen screen, striking the silky image of Mount Fuji.

"What do you think of that, Vespertine dear? Commissioner of Lunacy! Wouldn't *that* be splendid? The one currently in office isn't fit, is he? A real rat! Maybe he's gone missing in fact—run off with yet another whore. And don't think anyone would oppose me appointing Doctor Faint-at-heart here. I've got balls the size of Urānus!"

A rivulet of urine seeped out from beneath the screen, followed by another yet more urgently flowing. Hextly let it pool about his boots, laughed as grains of crystal and jade glinted in the faintly yellow translucence.

"*Now* do you understand why I wear these boots Doctor? What a relief it must be to you, finding out I'm not crazy after all."

Fayteyant whinnied in a manner beyond embarrassing.

The Goat King of Madison Avenue approached. He towered before the doctor like a horse proctologist raised on a surgical platform behind his patient. Hextly's eyes were colorless, perforations in a railway ticket.

"I promise you a most comfortable stay, doctor."

"I could not possibly—it's too magnanimous," Fayteyant stammered.

"Commissioner of Lunacy you say? It will be done! And look at this view! The prospect from your room is even more dazzling."

Fayteyant joined the billionaire to watch the nervous circulation of tiny figures on the streets below: An overcrowded tank of grasshoppers unwittingly waiting to fatten unsuspected snakes.

"I trust you doctor. You and I have enough in common for me to trust you."

"O sir, I cannot imagine..."

"We both love the dirtiest parts of our work, yes?" Hextly said with a leer. "O come now, doctor ... when I saw you poking holes in that old beggar today, I knew. Instead of roaring or calling out your Creator's name—instead of reckless release—*you* experience a state of control, unwavering confidence in the dexterous manipulation of your tools against strange flesh. Those innocent fools in the stands were unknowingly witnessing you in the throes of masterly prolonged orgasm—and you like to be watched, don't you?"

Fayteyant had no words.

"How could I tell? I'm the same way, man—I'm nearly always cumming my rich ass off—though unlike you, it's not easily hidden under the guise of benevolence. Don't worry. We're cut from the same stained cloth. I'm climaxing right now and I'm glad you are so dedicated a fetishist. It means you are the best at what you do. Because *I'm* the best at what I do. Your brain is a groin and your every thought licks it, yes? Your secret is safe with me. Your secret is why I trust you... O, and doctor?"

"Yes, Colonel?"

"Don't dare blow smoke up my man-hams."

There was a sharp rap at the door, at which sound Hextly grabbed a celadon vase and dropped it to the floor. The door opened immediately upon its shattering.

Fayteyant recognized the asymmetrical man.

"Your medical bag, doctor," he said, the voice quite ordinary. "Do let us know if you need anything else."

"Thank... you. That is fine for now."

"Now, I must go. Do attend her now—and do good work, by God. My man Bochkser here will attend to you. When you need him, simply look around and smash anything at all in this room—the more lovely, exquisite—the better. If he doesn't come right away, destroy something equally fine ... Balls like UrĀnus, doctor! Good-day to you."

Bochkser followed Hextly out of the room.

When the servant shut the door behind them, Fayteyant splashed over to the screen. Cowering beneath was a young woman in tears, a line of blood bisecting her smooth chin from where she was biting her lower lip. There was something extraordinarily beguiling about her, but he wasn't sure why. He was a generally disinterested amateur in this area. He supposed she was "beautiful," but he'd never been physically attracted to women or any other living creature—at least not in the *Biblical* way.

Fayteyant extended soft hands to help her stand. She smiled, releasing her lip from her penetrating teeth.

"Thank you, doctor. Thank you, thank you so much," she said, sweet and sincerely.

"There she goes again," Leta hissed. "Taking *everything* from me. Getting all the attention. Even *medical* attention!"

Standing at her bedside, Fayteyant took in the details of her appearance slowly, as though calling each back from memory. As was his steadfast practice with his patients, he took great care not to look her in the eyes (He *never* let his eyes truly meet with those of a patient unless it was surgically necessary. Otherwise it introduced too personal an element to the relationship). Leta's head drooped slightly down from a long neck streaked with blue veins. Her tangled blonde hair was fine as rat urine. Her blue nightdress was six times too large for her severe frame. She was tall, thin but for the second distended belly of his day. He was repelled by her lips, so dry like scorpion tails. Even such an amateur as he could tell Leta Hextly was quite as ugly as her idiot sister was not.

Money for the midwife.

Unmarried.

"Miss Hextly, this is a monumental honor. I am one of your most fervid admirers. Good afternoon. I am Doctor Nathaniel Fayteyant, M.D., D.D.S., F.R.S, K.T.S, Y.H.W.H., Fellow of the Chicago & New York & Hartford & Massachusetts Academies of Medicine; Member of the Court of Examiners of the Royal College of Surgeons of England; Honorary Member of—"

—O, just toss off."

"Uhm? O . . . O. How long have you been heavy with child?"

Seething silence.

"I'm only here to help..."

Fayteyant bent down to retrieve a vial of silvery, pea-sized pellets from his black bag. He held it up with a forced smile, keeping his eyes focused on the cranial region above her *glabella.*

"Don't fear; I'm a skilled obstetrician and apothecary. *This* is an abortifacient of my own creation—tested quite safe, for all stages of gestation. A variant of Diachylon, though more efficacious—I've replaced the litharge of gold fenugreek seed and gum ammoniac with, well... The *point* is we *will*... uhm, resolve your condition with minimal pain to your person—and your *person.*"

"Fucking exit."

"*Please.* You know I really am a devotee of your music, I think the world of you."

"O really? Well the world's a living hell..."

"Ah ... hardly my point, I'm afraid. But to proceed: is it six or seven? *Months*, I mean ... You are rather far along, which brings peculiar difficulties..."

She pulled some crystal bauble from canopied shadows, threw it across the room to a leopard chair, where it shattered over Vespertine's wincing head in a glassy spray.

Fayteyant's nerves flinched, and his buzzing fingers dropped the tube.

Vespertine shrieked as if slapped.

The door swung open.

"You rang?" Bochkser said.

Leta had disappeared beneath her silky white blankets.

"I... yes. Our initial consultation is over."

Bochkser graciously got his bag, and Fayteyant willingly let him escort him to his suite. It was filigree-gilt and mirror-paneled, with more velvet-carpeted sequestrations than all samovars in Russian literature. His apparatuses, chemical jars, books and other materials were arranged about the room. His recent universal cure-all experiments, his poisons. Somewhat disconcertingly, his wardrobe was there, too—his tobacco, his journals—literally *everything*...

Except his sense of control.

The situation was sticky as gleety pricks stuck in honey. This concatenation of mysteries wasn't medical and therefore out of his line. The sooner he could be done with Leta, the quicker could he return to his experiments toward a universal cure for the biological miseries of humankind ... the people had an uncouth and frankly scandalous attitude toward domestic valuables, Vespertine, a fearful, pissing refugee in her house, Leta's vulgar bellicosity; Hextly's planetary testicles, goat fat, green-eyed ring... the Commissioner of Lunacy. Fayteyant had met the man once, there was something extraordinary about him, but he couldn't quite recall—did the man have a ridiculous name? He couldn't place it, and fell asleep.

He woke in the middle of the night to a candle waving above him, portions of Vespertine's charming features bobbing in and out of its light, like face-fragments juggled in a tidal pool.

"What is it?" he groggled, clearing his throat.

She moved the candle so only her mouth was visible. Her lips arched like raised eyebrows and she pressed a vial of black and red pellets against them in a shushing finger gesture.

"Be careful! That's deadly poison. What were you doing in my bag? What's going on? Did you swallow any?"

"No, doctor... Thank you, doctor. Thank you... thank you."

Fayteyant felt her place the vial in his cold hand.

The candle went out; a kiss faintly wet his forehead; in the darkness he heard the door open and close again. He sat up and pulled his bag from under the bed and returned the toxin to its rightful compartment. He fell asleep again and dreamed there was no such thing as man-hams. He dreamed Leta Hextly hadn't told him to toss-off.

When he woke the next day, the only dream he recalled was one in which Vespertine shooshed him with a vial of toxins and kissed him. Such nonsense was easily shaken away and he soon regained his usual steely calm. After Bochkser brought him a delicious breakfast he enlisted the agreeably servile ogre in his scheme. That afternoon Fayteyant and Bochkser visited Leta's room. The doctor took his tube of abortifacient from his bag and pocketed the cork. Leta was mute and sullen and appeared unaware of their presence.

Enormous Bochkser straddled her body and pried her mouth wide open. A hoarsely prehistoric vocalization came out. This Fayteyant muffled by gently inserting a rubber funnel between her dry lips, which resembled the hardened corpses of earthworms who'd been squashed underfoot.

"I apologize. But I *must* do what your father wants," he said, addressing the funnel. "Now, I am going to pour the contents of this tube through here, but the abortifacient will dissolve as it greets your posterior pharynx. You are in no danger of asphyxiation. Ready…"

He tilted the glass and little silver beads of bromides, chloral hydrate, hyocyamine, physostigma, cannabis indica, amyl nitrate, conium, digitalis, ergot, pilocarpine, snailwallis root, &c. rolled down the rubber to pelt her throat.

"Thank you, Bochkser. Just a few left … stop moving your head—*stupid girl!*"

The very last pellets out to go down were red and black. He'd *never* be so incautious. Fayteyant couldn't help but look at her eyes, now. They were sharkly open, pupils dilating and constricting in time to her careening heartbeat. Without exception, every pellet in the dispensing vial should've been silver.

Had his dream about Vespertine and the toxins been actual? Krist, yes! And then Fayteyant remembered that he'd dropped the vial of abortifacient in Leta's bedroom yesterday, when Leta threw the crystal and Bochkser came to escort him to his suite … but he *hadn't* gone back to get it; yet it was in his bag this morning, exactly where it should've been—and he didn't think twice about it…

Fayteyant was stunned—and Bochkser had left the room before he knew it. Leta wasn't the only one about to die.

What followed happened fast: Fayteyant wanting to run but

morbidity fascinating him to the spot; Leta rising off the bed; the oscillation of her eyes between completely black ovals and dots small as printed-tabloid periods ... The way she reached the *Steinway & Sons* piano via a series of indescribable locomotive spasms ... How he must flee but couldn't stop watching like a peeping tom through the false security of boudoir closet-slats ... she fell to her knees. The dissonance when her purpling face collapsed into the keyboard, black eyes distended like oversatiated ticks ... clenching her teeth so hard they splintered and scattered like wedding rice ... her obese eyes *heaving* as a cord of coagulated blood and hair clots descended wriggling from her groin, entomological discharge thick as mooring rope ... the thing at the end of the rope resembling a humanoid, a diseased liver with twitching, deflating skeletal paws ... Leta's face leering over the keys, spewing bearded plasma as she began to play a ragged tarantella using her nose and a tongue that had sprouted cartilaginous, knuckle-sized nubs ... those jerky notes jabbed between Fayteyant's vertebrae like sharp needles, shocking him into action—grabbing his bag, opening the door—when a screeching behind him made him stop and turn around, against his will—she was singing while her mutated face hammered and flopped about the ivories:

"*You reap what you sow, doc and a lot of stuff you didn't ...*

It all adds up to nothing—the arithmetic of living!

Your madness gets madder, your cracked brain will shatter, roof sink into floor ...

In the House Next to Nothing you'll always be lost, the exits are never doors!"

At that point in the verse her face stopped playing the piano; it wagged like a tongue and Leta's ruined mouth belched gory foams festooned with silver pellets. The muck smothered the piano, rising so high as to completely censor the painted Daztgarham's lap dummies. It snuggled up to her bulbous waist where she knelt, corseting Leta in her own insides while churning toward a spanking-new Japanese screen—behind which Fayteyant glimpsed Vespertine's dainty feet rising on tiptoe in a dubious attempt to elude her sister's viscoid secretions ...

Then—*finally*—Fayteyant bolted as the expanding marble echoes of Hextly, Bochkser—and others—stampeded toward him down the corridor. He fled like a man in a dream and almost tottered down a mile of paralyzing stairs—the dizzying central staircase to the first floor. Without thought—as the scared skunk spritzes—he straddled the broad, adipocerous banister, squeezed his bag between his plump thighs, and slid down at the glistening velocity of goat fat.

With ten or so feet to go he flew off and landed harshly on his side as though tossed from a speeding locomotive, the blow cushioned somewhat by a six-ply *Thylacine* rug. He was in any case so adrenalized, he was unaware of any bodily sensations. Fayteyant sprung to his feet, panting. Identical black clouds of Bochksers were rapidly descending… His life was over in one way or another —if not by excruciating, slow death, then by slower, excruciating torture of new names, new assumed identities, new fugitive lives.

Hextly was like a roaring, objurgating Centaur God way up at the top of this many-storied nightmare… and then, skimming like one breath of air against another, bright like a ray of sun diving past his ear, came mad Vespertine's fragile exultation:

"Thank you doctor! Thank you! Thank you *so* much!"

And now all the troubling incidents of the past two days had been leading up to what happened next, the most profound, beautifully disturbing moment of Fayteyant's life: He looked up one last time before he escaped—why he took this unnecessary, time-wasting risk, he never knew—and saw that Hextly had thrown his dead daughter down to crush him, an act so desperate, so frighteningly pragmatic, that… that words failed…

She descended toward him wrapped in hushes that looked so awfully loud. Then her body missed him by mere inches, and it was midway through that thin but infinitely extended line between his possible death and the life that was to follow that her body seemed to slowly featherswoon past, as if gravity had a moment of indecision. Long fingernails tenderly sliced his face from cheek-bone to jawline. They looked into each other's eyes … Leta's no longer monstrous but sidereal and warm. Somehow, she was still alive.

Whatever hellish transformation she'd undergone, it was over. And while their eyes met, Fayteyant felt an unfamiliar sadness. A heart-ache that didn't know its own strength, as though rings of happy children seeking his attention were tugging on his trouser-cuffs, not understanding how easily their collective efforts to share their happiness with him could easily make him topple, unintentionally bring him to serious harm or even—

—Love at Only Sight.

Her skull split into a wide, screaming mouth. The rest of her followed her like an infant born off the edge of an unattended butcher-block. Fayteyant glimpsed a bolus with skeletal arms arc through the air. It started mewing.

Doused in goat fat, blood and ambiguous humors, he easily parted crowds across the full gamut of social classes down to the rowdiest. He looked like a newborn product of satanic magic, birthed clothed and fully-grown from Baphomet's cloaca. O, why had he looked in her eyes? He didn't slow down until the setting sun was a toxic orange, didn't stop running for hours until the darkness was continuous and inviolate as a moment of solemn memorial silence.

Fayteyant had miraculously eluded Hextly's brigade. Most likely the thing that had been Leta had somehow delayed them. But he was lost in the most subscrofulous quarter, in a narrow alley between a junk-shop and bakery. The world seemed worlds away. If only Leta had lived, if he could've been *her* hero—the wrong sister had been grateful to him, thanked him so effusively for such wrong reasons. His entire life must change. But it *had* been love at only sight. It must be real love, because he felt *guilty* when images of her gesticulating innards surfaced in his mind and he wanted to keep them there, to turn them over from all angles and examine her deepest gelatinous secrets … it was love because it was strong enough to chastise his fetish. To inculcate such intense shame. For the first time ever, he felt sickened over his constant preoccupation with biological revelation. Why, only a worm could think about such things while that precious woman lay murdered, cold as the cold marble floor that had opened her head…

But if he was going to learn to hate himself—and he desperately wanted to—he must leave Manhattan Island as quickly as possible. First, he had to determine where he was. The moon illuminated a sign nailed to the brick wall opposite:

GRAVELSPITZ LANE

PART #2

IS BLEEDING AN EXPLANATION?

VII

IF IT ENDS IN "-ITIS"

> "Far too much is made of faces, and especially eyes, which—if only because they are built without blueprint—lack the communally informative meaning of windows. The human face is a dead-end, painted into a theatrical illusion of expansive road. Look away from conjuring tricks; turn your face from the face if you would learn that time is of the putrescence." – *The Dark Wintering*, Chapter VII.

Perceval woke in hoary darkness dimly smudged by the faltering light of several lanterns dispersed throughout a vast space, set at varying heights and distances from each other. Instinctively, he reached for the safety of the petrified horse penis, but his hand touched nothing but hard wood . . . then his bag, *Struwwelpeter* intact. As his eyes began adjusting to the ill-lit room, he saw some lanterns were paned with colored glass; on a table or shelf nearby sat a squat jar of leeches in purple water, impaled by beams of blue and red light. It was likely a makeshift barometer; Doctor Chapman used leeches for that purpose in his office at the orphanage…

Gradually Perceval understood he was laying on a thin mattress, uniformly crusty as with stale elephant menses, and this on the floor of a cavernous space. It didn't smell like terrified blood or carbolic or the unsalted swamp of orphanage soup; the air here was laced with a unique, all-penetrating corruption much finer than smell-particles.

He sat up and all at once felt like an asskicked, see-sawing pile of shit, and couldn't stifle a groan. Suddenly a clear, bright lantern swung out of the darkness above him.

The man holding it was in his late twenties. His keen eyes were a difficult, screaming green. The right one was glass, and there was gold in it too, but Perceval couldn't tell where precisely. He smiled frequently; his mouth framed by parentheses indicating the many years over which he'd sustained this habit. He was thin as Egyptian papyrus god, erumpent hair the depthless black of ink-headed jackals. He wore black too, a chalkboard with inexhaustible capabilities to teach, deceive, praise, &c. He was funny ha-ha and he was funny strange. What had looked like a third eye glowing in his mouth turned out to be an expiring cigar; he exhaled smoke that brought tears to Perceval's eyes. Almost magic—smoke birthing water…

This man grinned at Perceval.

"Boo," he said.

Perceval was unmoved.

"Stolid! You look as though you've seen no ghosts at all—are you a ghost?"

"No. Perceval Raptus."

"You're from the orphan asylum?"

"How do you know?"

"You need a good scrubbing, man. Even your shadow stinks. What made you come out in this—to *this*?"

"Where are you from? There's nobody from round here who isn't from round here."

"Scratchfyre factory. Not long in town. I'm a bit of a nomad you might say. Decided to get the hell out before my jaw conflagrated and collapsed. The storm rolled in and I sheltered here."

"You don't look like a Scratchfyre worker. Too smooth."

"All right, you got me, I'm afraid. No, you might say this place is in my blood. By the way, I gander you're insane, but it suits you—like heat to *Cordyline*, or similar jungle flower. You see, I spent more than a decade overseeing the treatment of roughly 6,849 lunatics, 457 idiots, 148 epileptics, and approximately 11,349 wrongly-committed victims of revenge on an annual basis. There were approximately 699 homicidal cases yearly; of these lunacy induced by inebriation represented just over 28%. I instituted a system of balneal treatments especially for insane, idiot, epileptic, and wrongly-committed females; the data is as yet incomplete. I perfected institutional usage of the *Fayteyant Scale of Lunacy, Degeneracy and Dissolution, &c.* I'm a progressive. I saved the *polis* $12,565.34 by replacing 1,333 straw mattresses with hair repurposed from deceased inmates. I could bore you with more statistics and details—which only proves I'm an expert in my field. So I know Stark-Raving when I see it. That, and I found you outside the building... let's just say you rode into town, so to speak, via a contrivance such as rarely is employed by the mentally sound... Now, I'm going to poke around a bit more. Haven't been here long myself. Want a cigar? I've one left."

"You're sure your name is Harold Chapman?"

"No. I saw it written in one of those journals over there. Speaking of lunatics—no offense, man, but whoever wrote this has the grandest delusions of medical genius. Why do you ask?"

"The doctor at the orphanage is named Harold Chapman."

"O? But what *is* a *name*? You know how the click of your key locking your door behind you gives false security—a sound that guarantees nothing? Well, a name is just that sort of pancake, too."

"You're not him."

"No. But finders keepers. I've taken his name and I'm sticking to it. Who knows—maybe he's not him anymore anyway. I've seen that happen... Here, another good lantern for you, go ahead and snoop... Be right back," he said, disappearing into library shadows, whistling no tune.

Why didn't Perceval dislike this man? He supposed it was much the way some dogs simply accept each other after one fleeting exchange of butt-sniffs.

Perceval explored. Everywhere his light shone he found worm-eaten books strewn in piles of esoteric arrangement, some stacked high as snow banks. Meanwhile the bookshelves were crammed with a confusion of apparatuses, of which gallipots, glass cannulas, bellows, burette-stands, Swedish spring-steel, rubber-tubed brass tambours, retorts, capsules, graduated glasses, strainers, bell-metal mortars, wool and asbestos filtering media were merely a suggestion of the whole tangle of vulnerary items (and these jumbled together among a motley collection of containers of curdled asses' milk, sugar of Sargasso mosses, cherry laurel oil, adulterated iodine, green poppy-headed morphia, bitumens, extensive volatile oils, unclassified, mucopurulents, cochineal of ararat, &c.).

On a deep window-sill: alembics, beakers, a broad crucible and countless specialized vessels. There was a blue-banded, chipped ewer and basin. The water was fresh—melted ice. Perceval splashed some on his face, drank the rest like a dog.

"Gander what I found in these old Calomel boxes," the stranger called.

Five crates, each filled with neat stacks of wax-sealed, brown paper pouches roughly the size of hip flasks. The crates and their contents looked the same but different notes were tacked to the lids. 1st: *Precursor 1*; the 2nd *Prolegomena Factors (strychnine, aconite)*; *Batch 8 (no mercury)*, and two crates were distinguished by seemingly random numerals.

Perceval examined a packet, feeling a finely-ground, powdery substance contained within. Centered on both sides was a deep black pentagram, with the ligature *&c!* printed in white letters at the center. Beneath this emblem, a phrase:

ETCETRACAINE

"What's this?"

"Patent medicine! A cure-all, a nostrum... people are monsters, and monsters are miserable, and will buy anything they're told will turn them back into princes ... 190% pure quack ... gives me an idea though..."

Perceval saw ghosts shamble out the aubergine shadows. That could only mean his new companion was planning to steal something material, or had done so already...The smallpox victims, histories of their final days in the flickering of outstretched fingers:

They had gone cold, clammy, suffered through acute spasmodic eructation; cramps; extreme dehydration; prodigiously discharging their bowels while their ashy flesh shrunk three sizes too small. Cyanosis had cursed each pinched face, extremities livid. They looked poisoned by a monster out of Greek Mythology, with eyes sunk deep enough to catch rainwater.

They reminded Perceval just how tired he was. He felt he'd lost countless drams of blood.

He had to lie down soon. Even if this Harold Chapman (what else should he call him?) was planning to slit his throat, he nearly didn't care.

"We'll need a catchy slogan for it," Chapman said.

"What?"

"If we're going to sell it."

"Why?"

"Look, I can tell you're all right, and I need a right-hand man to do my grafting. There's got to be two. Only God and the Devil work alone, and as God-fearing a man I am, there's no mistaking me for the Creator. That leaves the possibility that I could be Saint Nick. But when's the last time you saw the devil with a sidekick? See, a salesman shouldn't ever work by himself—don't want your marks associating you with the forces of evil. You obviously have less than no cash, and you can't stay in this place—especially not with your doctor friend using it for his secret laboratory. He's obviously insane—no offense ... I've got to hit the road at sun-up. I've got a sweetheart meeting me in April in Rehobeth—that's only three towns from here, going east—New Toomes is the first and not far from Cirkle's Way. Come along. Get some cash and find yourself a sweetheart of your own."

"I thought you'd worked with … lunatics. What do you know about selling things?"

"Because it's about the same line of business. In fact, the best way to learn what the public wants is to observe the insane up close. And there can be no better training in salesmanship than to do the same—I've seen many a Moses or Heliogabalus I would've been willing to believe were the chosen of God or Emperor himself, if not for the context of our acquaintance-making—which was me locking them in cages.

"So, what do you think? No point dreaming with your eyes closed."

What the hell did that mean? Perceval had no idea. But faux Chapman had the confidence of the performer and the heckler in equal measure. He made you feel he was on your side and, at that same time *above* you, a privilege to watch him do his act.

"OK."

"I knew you were my man! Partners, eh. Wait, I've got it! *If it Ends in '-Itis' Why Not Try This?*"

"What if it ends in *pox*?"

"Doesn't matter. We'll convince them it does. People are just animals with money. They're so desperate to be happy monsters, you see. They just need to trust you and trust is nothing but wanting to trust somebody, and we'll make them want. We could even sell them the hokum in *that* over there."

Chapman nodded at a large, leather-bound book on a rusty operating table.

Perceval carefully removed the amber-corked bottle, a container of Kier's Rock Oil, some etidorpha spritzes and four entubed carminatives from the cover. He sat with the book and his lantern under the table.

The book creaked open. It stunk like tropical vivisection.

THE DARK WINTERING
BY OTTO JOHNGREATGRANDSON I

Perceval chose passages at random:

Read from right to left, we see embodied in the common typographic symbol for etcetera (&c.) an ontological sign illustrating three key stages of an alien evolution: A single point—an egg? Coal-chute to the underworld? Eye? The Void?—uncurls and rears up like a newly-hatched worm. This creature then stretches itself into a 3rd towering state—the infuriated lines and curves of its posture indicating a teleological design that is as highly specialized as it is ambiguous.

One must not tamper with &c. To do so could turn men and women into vicious Etceteracks. How would such metaphysically-immiscible lusus naturae appear?

They would each be absolutely unique, and yet simultaneously replicate each other precisely—like Leibniz's windowed monads perhaps, but with broken, filthy and rotting windows—each discrete and linked into an endless series of mistakes…

They would be the viscous, Dark Wintering of human kind. Let me elucidate the apt meaning of this phrase to describe the &c. Principle.

Observe snowfall. It is a cliché that no two snowflakes are alike. But looking deeper at this commonplace, our attention is drawn to the fact that once fallen en masse, these sui generis units of snow appear absolutely identical. What is this snowfall, so atomically divergent and mega-scopically self-identical? The case of Etcetera bears family resemblance. Snow is a list in which you get lost in depth while trying to find the length of it.

Who can know how many entities are implied in a given instance of etcetera? The question can also be formulated: Who can know how many flakes are fallen with a storm?

In any case, these Etceteracks would conflate human biology with the impossibility of the catalogued-yet-un-mentioned force of &c. Would such a thing even be alive?

Of course, the word "Alive" in fact means…

Perceval stopped reading Johngreatgrandson's text to examine handwritten notes filling the wide margins, written with the crude verticality of amorous confessions carved in tree-trunks:

> *&c! (Etcetracaine) makes an absolute commitment to the unstated. This includes a commitment to that which it Does Not and Can-Not include. For my present purposes, the Does-Not consists of the entire possible list of maladies worldwide, which are too numerous to completely inventory. The Can-Not is that which has not yet been discovered or produced, all unknown, future pestilences—and those which will never be.*
>
> *Etcetracaine does not suggest— but promises!*
>
> *In time, the &c! principle will be adopted by the other branches of knowledge and practical life. For it is a universal force and not limited to the realm of medicine; but its use must begin in some concrete form, and so it will first incarnate in my medicine. Maybe this isn't a merely contingent event. Indeed, the physician's art is applicable to more phenomena than suspected. Even natural forces, classified as inviolate and impervious to disease, are tainted with the same failures characterizing the organic kingdom. For example, who can deny that the wind that combs the wheat and haircut, the breezes who tambourinate the leaves of the trees, are epileptic events?*
>
> *I came to Cirkle's Way a physician without a practice. Had I been turned away from the orphanage, I doubt I'd be alive today for one reason or another. I was lucky to find shelter, let alone a place suitable to my experimentations in medicine, and penitence. If—but I must not write about myself—it's too painful. And who knows? Maybe I'm not myself anymore, anyway.*

There was no room left for doubt: the doctor *was* the library ghost—the perfect place for clandestine activities. Nobody in town would go near it, and besides, people were afraid of anything to do with Otto Johngreatgrandson. Perceval saw the genius of the doctor's scheme: The more he frequented the library and the *less* effort he made to conceal his presence, the greater his chances of *not* being discovered—the lights he needed for his experiments only served to strengthen local belief that it was haunted... He'd always liked the doctor, because he refused to look directly in your eyes when examining you...

Perceval suddenly felt a room-temperature presence reading *The Dark Wintering* through his shoulder. It was a pale girl, mercury-poisoned gums eternally suppurating, ashy rectum forever scorched by tobacco-smoke enema.

She was nodding in agreement with the weird passages, as if it wasn't nonsense.

Perceval returned to Johngreatgrandson's text:

Of course, the word "Alive" in fact means—

—"A man's got to do what a man doesn't have to do, right Percy?" Chapman confused things, giving him a friendly slap on the back. "Heading east, tomorrow we hit New Toomes."

Perceval wondered how they were supposed to do that in the middle of a record-breaking blizzard. Then he fell asleep beneath the table, *The Dark Wintering* on his lap. His mouth hung slack all night, and he drooled on the pages like a holy man spewing so much prayer, you just *know* he's lost the fucking thread.

VIII
FOR THE GREATER GOOD RIDDANCE

> "Things seek to be equally random and fated. They want to move into a completely unexpected and predetermined moment. Think of playing cards: Although every shuffle is fated, still the players shuffle again and again and again, cards flashing whitely before they assume clear forms in their hands. Each time it seems a little different, and it is easy to mistake the happening of different things for freedom. Fate is like several shadows that over-

lap each other on a white field—do they make one big shadow or are they a collection of intersecting shades?" – *The Dark Wintering*, Chapter VIII.

Perceval doesn't know why, but he's got a peculiar, burning-noose/rope-burn feeling time has started running backward since what happened this morning didn't yet transpire. It's too hot and weird to think about... Anyway, it's impressive watching Chapman speak to the New Toomes crowd—he has the confidence of a monsoon. They all want to see what his green lightning-eyes see, no matter the price. His tongue extends quick lies as a centipede strolls a wall—effortless and never tripping.

Nobody who notices pays any mind to Perceval as he quits Chapman's side. They're too hypnotized by the grafter, and Chapman's so swept away in his glitzy performance that he isn't aware of his right-hand man quietly stepping backwards to disappear behind a barn. Chapman's radiating in the throes of his bamboozle-gasm—*"WHETHER OR NOT IT ENDS IN -ITIS, WHY NOT TRY THIS?"* Their eyes are moistened with hopes that just a pinch of Etcetracaine powder is needed for their piles, catarrh, dyspepsia, consumption, self-pollution, neuralgia, ague, &c. to be forever cast out of their bodies...

Now Perceval's about two streets away. The crowd's started chanting some raucous shanty about a rattle-snake... the song ends in schadenfreude chortling. Coming up on his right he spots the:

NEW TOOMES WHOREHOUSE

Perceval walks up a short flight of rickety stairs. It's seems too quiet for a bordello, but a note tacked to the wall explains that today there's a special Two-for-One on Gaggings, illustrated by crude renditions of a variety of voluntary esophageal-obstructive acts. Two men are playing cards, sitting on barstools too high for the round table between them. They're constantly bending down to put hands down and choose new ones, and every time either one sits up straight again he groans.

"Do you have a room?"

They don't look up. The impatient sound of shuffling cards.

"All girls are occupied," the thinner one says. "On account of the Two-fer-One."

"And that snake-oil hawker," fatty spits more than mutters.

"You can wait outside, on the steps if you want. When a sweaty fella who ain't me or him comes out the front door, it's your turn."

"No it ain't," the fatter says. "You gotta go."

"Not talking to you. The fella newly arrived."

"What?"

"Not talking to you," the sour thin one repeats.

"I don't want a girl," Perceval says. "I'll pay—double—for a room. Just to sleep."

Neither has bothered to glance Perceval's way. The game continues, spines folding and straightening, the soft friction of the cards punctuated by grunts … Perceval stays where he's standing, awkward and blank-faced. This goes on for ten, fifteen minutes, maybe more. Skinny finally breaks the silence:

"Two dollars and third room on the left up those stairs."

"And nobody'll bother me."

"If you're gone tomorrow morn."

"And if anyone asks if you've seen me—you haven't. Deal?"

"Ain't you been payin' any attention," says Fatty, shuffling. "We haven't even tried."

Perceval reaches into his gray cloak. He tosses three or four dollars on the table. This is just a small portion of the cash he'd stolen from Chapman's carpetbag this morning, which Chapman had entrusted to Perceval's care while he went to take a troubled, knollside shit. Of course, he did so while facing Perceval and their stuff; but the combination of cold wind in his eyes and the strain of evacuation forced Chapman's face into a squinty grimace, sustained mask-like over the considerable duration of his trial. Perceval recognized his chance. It had been five years since he'd pulled off this kind of brazen theft, but the required legerdemain came back easy. Like remembering how to fall off a bicycle.

The reason being that Perceval had changed his mind about Chapman when they set off from Johngreatgrandson's library this morning. This Etcetracaine racket wasn't for him, and neither were travelling companions. Chapman would just get in the way to Voice... It was difficult to explain; it was like when you risked falling through rotten floorboards, catching tetanus from upturned nails, to retrieve that sealed box from a shadowy corner of an abandoned house... You don't want anyone else there with you to stress the floorboards under you, or the rungs of the splintering ladder, and most importantly you must be alone when you pry the lid off... Anyway Perceval left Chapman about half of his cash. He did owe him something.

The room is seasonless with dust. Sepia-grained light struggles down from a high window... a bed, 3.5-legged table, a tall stool like downstairs, and a spirit-lamp. Perceval doesn't even consider the bed. He guesses the safest corner, lies down and spoons his carpetbag. Sleep comes fast.

After the Two-for-One period of the day is over, the passionless caterwauling of empty men and women doesn't wake him—nothing he hasn't heard a million times in the streets, among the WYMIN—it's an unrecognizable sound that jolts him awake in uneven blackness. It's an undefined but very late hour.

Perceval presses his ear to the thin wall: The unmistakably smooth, irrigated scrape of tongue licking against it, magnified tenfold. Something trickles into his ear through the plank: Calid, steaming saliva, spiced with eyelashes or arachnid prosthetics ... suddenly the wall bursts open like a bladder in an Inquisitorial vice. Perceval falls backwards, shuts his eyes, but the fluid crowds into his mouth. It tastes like sour tidal waves. The spit rises to his Adam's apple. It's full of rumors. Each drop whispers *pass it on* to the next ... by the time Perceval gets the message it's been distorted from *"I am wet"* to *"No voice without spit, but much spit without voice . . ."* Perceval dives beneath the surface to find his carpetbag. It opens as he swims upward, and *Struwwelpeter* drifts out into the humid backwash. He grasps at the spine and the pages turn to little plankton-sized bits of pulp.

Now he blacks out . . .

. . . And now he regains consciousness. He's just a tad soaked and lying flat on his back. The ground beneath him wobbles between mass and incorporeality. He sort of remembers tumbling down a flight of stairs, and getting his nose picked by a pretty finger with black grains resembling roach-turds under its painted nail. His head feels like an untethered bathysphere . . . Everything is more rumor than real, yet more message than murmur. The thin and fat card players are there, only they're upside-down and making really funny faces, and swaying as though strung up like slaughterhouse hogs.

First, Perceval wonders why they're hanging upside-down.

Next, he thinks: *Waitaminute—I'm the one upside-down* . . . his back is pressed against the ceiling—then he falls from the grip of a pungent adhesive that had maybe leaked from his spine and glued him up there; his chin kicks the edge of the round cardplayers' table. His neck almost snaps off as he hits the swilly, sawdusty, tobacco-stained floor . . .

Somehow, Perceval stands up/down/in/out/back/nowhere. His veins buckle and writhe like sodomized worms, burrow deep until he feels them shiver refugee-knotted in his most xenophobic places . . . A vertical, foot-wide slit rises groggily to the surface of his abdomen, wakes up and yawns to greet the night . . . He collapses back to the floor, cold hemorrhages spume, and then he's up again, the slit vomiting his intestines, his wound sickened by whatever in him isn't damaged. A long strand hangs down from his belly to the misshapen thing that echoes a mishandled brain. Streams of bleeding gut just about everywhere. He loses balance again, slips falls into an increasingly hermetic mess . . . Krist, this up-and-down shit has got to stop already!

He's surprised to realize that nothing's being taken away from him. He feels fervid—no room-temperature sensation = no ghosts, which means *no theft in progress*—just maybe, even, some invaluable moment is being *given* to him in this unwrapping … opening a box without hubris … And then you find a good spot where you can be all alone. Your blood rushes—enough hesitation already—the lid pops off and …

A rifle fires point-blank in Perceval's face.

A patch of black blood overtakes one eye, while the other gazes at whatever faraway place is brought into focus through the telescope of a Winchester barrel.

One half of his head is gone and the other doesn't look remotely face-like. *Maybe* like a fucked-up shellfish. A twitchy Perceval-eye swings across his new mouth, dribbling incontinent cerebrospinal fluid that sizzles, evaporates on his burnt tongue. Like he's feeding himself with a dropper.

"Got him," someone says.

"He's standing again," says another.

"What in God's name …"

Perceval's chest and abdomen open wide.

The men gathered in the New Toomes Whorehouse are startled to see the organs remaining within him have rearranged themselves, architecturalized into rickety steps that lead up into an abandoned attic.

Now they are running the wrong way.

IX
THE ETCETERACKS ARE COMING!

> "The universe is organized according to a rational and harmonious principle: Things go from bad to worse, as well as worse to bad; these opposing forces ultimately balance so that one does not gain undue influence on our lives." – *The Dark Wintering*, Chapter IX.

"Ready to make a fortune?"

Uhm? Perceval opened his eyes, lifted his head, knocked the crown of his skull on the underside of the library table.

"Careful!" Chapman said good-naturedly. "Food's up there."

Perceval had the oddest sense that time was running backward and all this was happening *after* what was yet to transpire. It was too weird to hold onto. *The Dark Wintering* slipped from his lap; he crawled past, stood and drowsily nodded at Faux Harold Chapman, who was insultingly well-rested.

Something smelled edible.

"Breakfast, Perceval. Help yourself—we've a long walk ahead."

Atop the table was a goblet of hot barley meal porridge, hot cornmeal pudding, one goblet of hot cocoa, a bowl of warm milk and cracked wheat, and two eggs. How Chapman had made this come to pass was a trifling mystery. Perceval wolfed it down and his body began to rejuvenate. He stretched sore legs, ambled to an oversized oriel window that faced the dead and living Datzgarhams, the Lithuanian Orphanage, the ruinous Scratchfyre factory and the rest of Cirkle's Way.

The sky was blatantly missing, and beneath its disappearance an endless continent of snow seemed to deny the existence of human history.

"I found some good, leather bags in the back of the Library with wide straps," Chapman chirped behind him. "Easy to carry. I've loaded them up with Etcetracaine packets. Two for each of us—they weigh almost nothing."

"How?" Perceval asked.

"Ah! Just follow me—You've got to think outside the coffin."

Chapman led Perceval through a maze of disorderly bookshelf corridors. Cots, stained sheets. He tripped over a masticated dolly. An alcove of burnt bibles, a clearing loaded with leather bags. Some were open; here and there a little eyesocket or skeletal gesture jutted into the pale light now pouring through the lofty windows.

"That's where I found ours," Chapman said.

"Here—go ahead, open that door."

Perceval turned the brass knob and saw the thinnest carpet of frost extending a mere twenty feet or so from the library, like a white shadow ending where a clear forest path of twigs and pine needles began.

"How?"

"I've seen this 1,000 times making the rounds of lunatic asylums. Inside, it's Babel and Babylon. Step through an everyday door in the wall and—bang!—it's Brooklyn. Everything needs a limit, even a blizzard. That path right there leads east to New Toomes. And you'll be fox-fucked if it isn't *exactly* where the snow stopped falling, am I right?"

They made good progress. By afternoon the sky had come back, shallow blue. Here and there white cumuli hung in discrete, unmoving clumps. The air was crisp, the trees were spindly, the old, narrow road had been trodden into a dead riverbed. They stopped only twice—once to eat, and again to deal with the consequences. They otherwise journeyed in silence. It seemed only a few chilly hours had passed when a flock of tilted houses spiked the horizon with belemnoid rooftops...

New Toomes was the kind of place pessimists went for reassurance and confirmation of their worst fears. The houses were gray-brown, gray-yellow, or gray-black, all maculated with lime-white bird-droppings. There were more narrow, deadweedy alleys between buildings than there were buildings. The New Toomies were a grum, squabby bunch. Half were drunks and the other half too melancholic or bored to drink. Nothing changed, perhaps because degeneration has an absolute pinnacle. God knows how this kind of thing goes on decade after decade ... So when the two strangers came into town with their curious sacks of powdery pouches, people were mighty interested. It was the first novelty many could recall in forever...

A small crowd gathered in the ovoid town square to hear the travelling man with the screaming green eyes. Bland as any other congregation of anonymassholes, but for the clonic, fully-body spasms of a man holding a cane it would've benefited him to use. Chapman lured the New Toomies in like a psychopomp leading eager shades to Elysian fields. A few feet behind him, Perceval stood expressionless, exceedingly Perceval-like, with the two full bags of *&c!* at his side like a pair of well-trained, heeled mastiffs.

&c!

"...And so good people, a pinch of my powder puts that new *Coca-Cola* nonsense to shame. Etcetracaine curse neuralgia, hysteric melancholia, self-enervation, dwarfism, systole, quinsy, exophthamalia, Saint Anthony's Fire, hyperkeratosis, tenesmus, furuncluar conditions—and of course, catarrh and peritonitis! Even demonomania! It is a guaranteed product for any medical problem whatsoever and conducive to your neverending eucrasy—that's happiness...

"Now you might say, Dr. Chapman, I *know* happiness is not a product. You might say you know happiness is not a product and you would be right—you're smart folk, and if you weren't I wouldn't be talking to you on the level like this. On a high, scientific level. I'm explaining things because I know you are smart and smart people want explanations before they can accept something as true—or hokum. So you could come up to me and say I know you're a doctor but happiness is not some product like a lathe or a sack of flour. And we would say you are absolutely 115% right. Happiness is not a product. But it is a byproduct of this product here—*Chapman's Etcetracaine, A.K.A. Chapman's Omni-Cure Powder or Food or Solvent, &c.* It's got my name, but I know that's not enough to prove its worth. After all, every dead liar's tombstone's got their name on it! You're laughing because you got the joke—I can't tell you how many folks are too dim to figure that doozy out—but consider this, now: You might say to me, OK Doctor Why-Trust-You, it's impossible for happiness to be a byproduct of a product. That's shrewd, that's a good question. I'm glad you asked it. I could be a quack. It's OK; I know you're thinking that, too. Well if you want to call me a quack that's fine with me because I'm the goose that lays the golden eggs—you could say the golden-star eggs. But I shouldn't jest too much. This is serious; it's about your life and the lives of your children and all the generations to come. So let me ask you if you ever noticed something about the word Impossible. Let's think about that. Let's see what's hiding in there, in plain sight, like all good things—the Lord God Above and sunshine and fruitful crops, and you there—yes *you*, lovely little girl—my but that's a darling music box—O no, m'am let her play, it's lovely. I was saying, this is a town with fine blood. What is the word IMPOSSIBLE? You're right to point out that most of all it's made up of POSSIBLE. That's true. So people think that if you take the POSSIBLE out, well, that's called IMPOSSIBLE. In fact look closely now—can you all see this sign? The letters are magnetic—I slide POSSIBLE a little bit over there and we're left with what looks like two letters. Son, can you say them for me? That's right but a tiny louder please. You hear him? I-M. What's that sound like? 'I AM.' What did God say in the Bible—that's just it, 'I AM.' So where's that leave us? Just here: IMPOSSIBLE really means: I AM POSSIBLE. You might say, but you're just foolin' with words. 'I A-M' is not 'I-M,' it only sounds like it. But consider this: Does an accordion look like music, or does it sound like it? Does a fiddle look like an accordion? Does a fiddle look like music? Not until they are played. What I'm doing here is playing the IMPOSSIBLE the way it should be, so you can hear the music of the truth. So, who will be first? Whether or not it ends in -itis . . . *why not try this?*"

The crowd threw back faces punctured with howling mouths and knowing, *wink-wink* laughter. In the palm of his sleight-of-hand.

"I know you're just itching to scratch your itches with this, but I just got three quick questions for you:

"You'd trust a good chap, right?"

"YEAH!"

"And you'd trust a good man?"

"YEAH!"

"So you can double-trust a good Chap-man, am I right?"

"YEAH! YEAH!"

"All right, then!" he said, laughing. "Come on down and get it, cheap! Chatty Percy over here will hand out the packets…"

Some of the crowd chuckled, others puzzled or peered. Chapman turned round to find Perceval gone…

Chapman wasn't confused for more than a second before he realized the gullible-looking orphan had fucked him, and good.

But there was no time to admire Perceval for this daring accomplishment. A half-assed line of New Toomies had formed.

The first one up was the shaky man, probably younger than the sixty-five winters he seemed, stunted as though he'd lived his best years stuffed in a snuffbox. He had difficulty getting the cash from his pocket with his quivering "good" hand—the other being an alder prosthetic…

Some men behind him began to laugh and sing (to the tune of the ancient *Ballad of the Sickle of Life*):

"I'm Stanford Grost and I shake, I shake, I shake like the rattle on a snake…"

One by one the others joined in, and before long Chapman himself was leading them through chorus after triumphant chorus.

The House Next to Nothing

> "Indeed, by the end of this chapter you should know in your marrow that there is no greater analogue for life than a cemetery; it encompasses both spheres of the human experiment. One half of it, built of stone and inerasable inscriptions, consists of the regularly expanding world of superstitious, solid and enduring objects; and beneath this hard, unyielding display lies the truer half of our lives—the objective, time-eaten world of decomposing reality." – *The Dark Wintering*, Chapter X.

> "*You are here.*" – Blumenkrank's Condemnation.

The Sinking Season, 1888

I am nearly seventy years old. How is it that for the past 27 years I've been so completely empty and so full of guilt at the same time? Are these identical feelings, or am I multiple, or is there no such thing as simultaneity? Does the arithmetic of life really add up to nothing? These questions alone animate the dusty air of this new home:

The House Next to Nothing.

This place has been erected on the outskirts of not much, on the worst soil the south has to offer. It doesn't rise so much as peep above the rim of an extreme concavity of earth. When I first approached, I mistook the top floor for first story, puzzlestruck as to the purpose of such a squat structure. Then I found only a house after all; howsoever it reminded me of a bird stuck headfirst in an upended trumpet, a feathered gag blocking brass throat. But since moving in I've discovered the ground beneath is vaginal in elasticity, the house a mass stretching it toward the center of the earth, down toward an abyss over which it's more tarp than top. This place grows heavier with its own disappearance.

Why would I choose to live here? Because there is something that oh-so-perfectly should not be in this house: It is a fearsome, solid ghost—a real rhinoceros of a phantom. Yet I am afraid to touch it lest it vanish. That would mean it wasn't real.

When I saw it, I said to the owner—man named Shiel—how in God's name did that get in here? Who lived here? Why depart without this piano? He answered: Don't Know—Some Quiet Folk—What Piano?—just like that, the first consonant of each spoken word capitalized in a weird dialect; but he had the meek and downcast eyes of a horticulturist.

I know this improbable piano. It is a Steinway & Sons Carved Rosewood Square grand. It belonged to Leta Hextly. Somehow it has followed me through a maze *stretching nearly three decades and forty-eight states long: From The Goat King's Headquarters, his balls the size of Uranus and one finger knuckled with unblinking green eye, where I fell in love while Leta fell, to the fugitive's shameful road, to false names (I still don't know why I picked Harold Chapman), an orphanage in Cirkle's Way, where I thought I could hide in a library and change the world—atone for the death of my beloved—curse Otto Johngreat-grandson (I'd rather not wonder what became of him)—where all my unfinished &c! was stolen, where I finally gave up—*DO NOT TEST IT—REJECT IT*—back to the road, just after reports of those monstrous deaths across Connecticut. And now, sunk down to Kentucky—this South—urinal of the Yankee States.*

I haven't changed the world for the better. Committed Etcetricity never defeated Dismissive Etcetricity. Nobody has thanked me in years, not a soul has needed me. But at least I did uncover a hitherto unknown species, in the mirror: I am a creature sui generis—the 7-Sided Animal, or Belua Septfariam. You can easily identify Septfariam by taking the following inventory of dimensions: inside; outside; left side; right side; top side; bottom side; and homicide. Ha! Ha. I suppose I should've gone into cryptozoology.

But I don't feel sorry for myself. I'm not even capable. Over the decades of running, my self-pity has metastasized from within to the people and whole world to whom and which I am so helplessly adjacent, until it's become an unbounded condolence without locus.

Piano, piano.

This ivory-grinned monster is my accuser and judge. And when the House Next to Nothing collapses at last, it will be my psychopomp, and then—who knows?

For the past week, Fayteyant had spent each day sitting by a dirty window, exhausted, resigned to ugly things, listening to sloppy, cymbal-shaped sounds of rain. Thus was he occupied the night the storm ended. Now and then he'd consult his improvised barometer, a bottle of leeches in ditchwater kept on the sill; well past midnight, they began convulsing, black tongues cunnilicting to their swampy world's surface—storm's peroration at hand. The rain wore thin; the final leech ascended while brindled skies fled, leaving muddied roads and flooded tarns and pools of quiet inside and out of his two-story clapboard. A practical-joke moon appeared unexpectedly and overbright, as if to mislead the wind and tides, confuse veins and seasons.

He quit the casement, entered the ill-lit study, sat on a wobbly chair of moldy, red silk brocade, facing the piano. As if it were real as a crime scene, as if his touch would tamper with crucial evidence, he simply stared at the bone keys in the dusty silence—

——*Knock-Knock*——

They were contrived woody-tolled blows, so unexpected as to seem hoax deliveries from other worlds—like the March 31, 1847 Wayne County, New York spirit-rappings with which the Fox sisters and their dining room table ushered in the modern Spiritualism nonsense...

——*Knock-Knock*——

The sound was an uneasy mix of *demand*, the firmly repeated striking of knuckle on wood, and an undermining of that urge to mandate a response—a palpably uncertain *hope*—heavily expressed in the hush that set one strike apart from its fellows. Someone was at the door.

The floors sagged severely, approaching the infundibuliform of a Calla Lily, and Fayteyant navigated the dark, funneling declivities of the floor with arthritic forbearance, holding aloft ha hissing lamp dimmer than a firefly's ass.

——*Knock-Knock! Knock-Knock*——

"Who's there?" he called, pulling the door inwards.

...*Boo.*

A slight, soaking breathless man from some dark-skinned, exploited land stood under the portico. His vague dark clothes were mud-drenched from boot to head. He looked shamed, dragged, dunked; disguised as his very own battered soul.

Boo Who?

Fayteyant immediately diagnosed the visitor as falling somewhere between the general classifications of Simpleton and Mongolian Idiot, with secondary Imbecilic and Religious traits, a tertiary Feeble-Minded marker, as per his own *Fayteyant Scale of Lunacy, Degeneracy and Dissolution, &c.* The stranger was harmless, possibly good-natured. Definitely moronic.

"Well?" Fayteyant demanded.

"You . . . are . . . a doctor," he panted.

Exactly . . .

"What's this? No, you are mistaken. What do you want?"

"Shiel told me you are a doctor . . . please help. My master is dying . . . His family, his beloved family is in danger . . ."

"And why did Shiel think me a medical man? The subject of my profession was never discussed during our short business transaction. Why, can't you see I'm just a retired piano de-tuner?"

Was that a gout of blood running down one side of the stranger's face? Or only slickening mud?

"He said you looked like a man who had watched many die in his day, but your eyes were too cold for a murderer, or a soldier."

Exactly . . .

Fayteyant was too tired to continue being foxy.

". . . Where?"

"It is an estate over the hill, less than half a mile from here. Along the road to Fandango Camp Commons, past Palindrome Satyr Point. You know, near a Scratchfyre factory . . ."

The doctor's eyes telescoped remote. He gazed past the servant into the rustling night. It was run wild with leaves and grass and gusts in cold twiggy darkness, yet strangely hollow, very lonesome. A wave of nostalgic frustration washed over Fayteyant; it was like remembering an old, long-forgotten song and humming the melody perfectly—while being unable to recall the title or a single lyric.

"I'll go with you. Wait here."

Fayteyant felt the galvanizing thrill of a resurgent fetish: A visceral and chimerical emotion of danger and escape, distance and penetration. No need to dress; he hadn't changed his clothing in a week. His medical bag sat on a steamer trunk adjacent to the door, having faithfully waited two decades for its renascent necessity.

It was a bulky, tattered, leathery gallimaufry of items he'd managed to scrape together from the Otto Johngreatgrandson Library and here-and-there: phosphorous tablets, pouches of lobelia, tortoiseshell lancets and related venesectional cups, ampoules of *Tinctura Antiperiodica*, cyanide gauze, relatively unsullied scalpels, calomel bottles—better leave those behind—woolen strips, Tasmanian Tigerfur-threaded straight needles, diminutive ointment pots, graduated instruments, a flask of evaporating turpentine with ether, and troves of dust for inducing The Sneeze. No Etcetracaine. That had all been stolen from the smallpoxed nooks of Otto Johngreatgrandson's library.

The 7-Sided Animal gave the empty room a purposeless glance. The leeches were sinking again through the turbid moonlight.

The rain would soon return.

"Thank you sir," the man spluttered. Was he crying? "I am Mendasico, forever in your debt. Now please, *please* ... This way ... my master is dying ..."

"Think before you thank—but lead on. By the way, who is my patient?"

"O! Harold Chapman—he is a great doctor, too. Perhaps you have heard of him?"

Fayteyant gripped one of Mendasico's arms and carried the old man's bag in the other. Under the bright moon the doctor noticed a long sliver of mirror embedded in the side of his visitor's face.

They trudged up the wet incline to the road, feet sinking inches with each step. They paused at the top for Fayteyant to catch his breath.

"Your employer—what's his name again?"

"Harold Chapman. Please let's hurry, now ... I'll help you, the whole way. Doctor, why are you so pale?"

"What are the chances? I am ... do you know my name?"

"No, doctor. Tell me."

"It's a funny thing ... terrible, perhaps ... and a long story. If I tell you, it will be after our mission of mercy is over ..."

*c!

They rushed along the landslide of a road. The Chapman Estate came into view as the rain began. The building towered over acres of unbroken woodland with the peaks and valleys of a natural landscape. To the east rose a fascicle of towers like taut nerves. Moving westward was a low country of widow's peaks and flat stone roof. Windows seemed flung randomly into the face of the house—triangles, decahedrons, squares, rhomboids, rectangles and circles of clear and stained glass, each darker and dustier than the last as things buried under things buried under things in cellars.

The tracks of an indeterminate number and size of footsteps ascended, descended and obliterated each other across the porch steps … As he tore up the stair, Fayteyant realized he hadn't even asked just why he was needed … carried away by what was either a gigantic, urgent moment or compilation of inextricable urgencies—is a fire made of flame or flames?—Mendasico violently pushed the neo-Grecian front doors open.

"Just to the left here, doctor … the parlor …"

Several black kidskinned chairs, a ponderous rosewood table, and an étagère were strewn violently across the room. All were claw-footed, so that the overturned furniture resembled a scene of big-game slaughter more than any domestic chaos. A standing pier mirror had been shattered as though by a team of pugilists, flinging miniature, topsy-turvy parlor-views across the bewildering, sixty-seven-color oriental carpet … and no doubt, a wicked piece into Mendasico's face … Next to a massy, disarmed grandfather clock, a Parian bust of Heliogabalus had tumbled and rolled into the cold fireplace. It seemed to bleed from its decapitated neck, but Fayteyant soon saw the source of the sticky red pool: A man lay face-down on the glazed hearth tiles. Phalanxes of blood straight as sundial shadows reached out from beneath his body. It looked like ancient evidence; perhaps all blood, once spilled, has been spilled for centuries …

Was this Harold Chapman?

"How did this happen?" Fayteyant demanded.

"He is dying," Mendasico repeated, smiling nervously.

A muffled voice rose up from the wounded:

"Is bleeding an explanation?"

Fayteyant knelt down next to him.

"I suppose it is . . . Not a good one."

"Good *enough*?"

"Not really."

"O, can you really be so cuntdescending to a dying man?"

"Please," Mendasico begged. "You are both Harold Chapman, you are both doctors—you said yourself sir, *what are the chances?* It must mean something—you must help him as you would help yourself . . ."

Suddenly, from the next room came an excessively masculine groan or the sound of a monument being dragged across flat rock.

"What was that?" Fayteyant asked.

"You say your name is Harold Chapman—Doctor Harold Chapman?" said the bleeding man, mostly into the Chinese rug.

"Who are you?" Fayteyant said, and yanked the man roughly onto his back.

The younger Harold Chapman, who had cheated the world with Etcetracaine, knew the flabby-faced man swaying above him was the one who'd wanted to save the world with it. Below him, the older Harold Chapman saw a bruised, pulp-nosed man with brilliant green eyes—one animal—one of glass. The prosthetic was severely cracked, anthracitic pupil cleft by some vicious assault; chandelier light scintillated in the crystalline fissures, bringing it to uncanny, overly-alive life—the real eye comatose in comparison . . . he was almost familiar . . . Suddenly:

Another enraged groan or monolithic displacement—

—Then the loud attack of a large slab of flesh against an unhinging door—

Silence.

Mendasico's dusky face paled with anxiety. He picked up a fireplace poker and stood facing the noise, trembling a little.

"What is that?"

"What are you referring to?" slurred the wounded man.

"That babelcrashing in the next room! What's going on here?"

"O, that. I spent so much time, you know, around lunatics—in another life, believe it or not, I was Commissioner of Lunacy, my dear Doctor Chapman. One slept through such maniacal outbursts ... ugh my head. Dizzy..."

"Please doctor, can you save him now?" Mendasico asked—meek, irritated.

"Wha—O him? He's not dying. Just concussed, confused—but wait, Commissioner of Lunacy? Was this in New York City, by chance?"

"Yes, yes. Of course it was New York City. Didn't I just tell you that? Since you won't take bleeding as an explanation, will love do? Is love reason enough for all this?"

"Don't you mean Leta?" Fayteyant said coldly.

"Love. Yes, didn't I just say that? Wait, no, no, *no* ... no *Leta*. She was *there*, pretty damn ugly, though that didn't stop me from knocking her upside the womb—they all look the same when they're crying. But Leta wasn't the one I loved, you know ... could you hurry up and stanch the blood, doctor? I believe it's exuding from this Heliogabalus-nose-sized hole in my crown—"

"—Wait. Mr. Mendasico, you mentioned that Mr. Chapman's family was in danger, too—where are they, then?

"I only meant, they will be in danger if my master dies ... they are not hurt of themselves."

"That doesn't answer my question."

In a corner across the parlor, something damp and heavy fell to the floor, followed by the metallic discord of worried chains. Fayteyant whirled round to see a Japanese screen faintly vibrating ... the room became unaccountably hot and humid.

"What the devil's that?" he said.

Nearby, a splintery complaint was followed by a crashing door.

Fayteyant stood, swiped a brass candlestick from the hearth, clutched it tight with a brave, liver-spotted hand.

Mendasico scrambled against his nerves to his wounded master, and dragged him behind the an upset settee. Chapman's head nodded, blood rilling down his forehead, off his nose ... he was becoming increasingly intoxicated with its drainage. At a loss, Fayteyant grabbed his medical bag and joined them on the mock-sheltering side of the settee, standing a few feet behind. The doorway on the opposite side of the room filled with seething blackness.

It was an exaggerated man in a kind of mourning uniform. One eye exceedingly large, the other scrunched, like a comparative anatomical display which shows the vagina crowning with infant's bulging head on the left, and its contracted, postpartum aspect on the right. His ears jug-handled, nose nubbed... The face sliced into crimson reticules of longitude and latitudes. One hand was clenched into a massive fist, mirror-punching knuckles torn to the bone and caked in tinseled blood. One of his knees was shattered and he shambled forward slowly. It was unbelievable he could move at all, and without a wince.

"Bochkser?" Fayteyant disbelieved. The doctor's heartbeats had gone *strigendo*, coalescing like an ominous drum roll.

"O, you know him too?" Younger Chapman said, upright and leaning against Mendasico, who held him so in a bear hug. He laughed, heckling, mirthless.

"I don't believe it," Bochkser said. "Doctor Nathaniel Fayteyant? Two birds."

"This is *not* Doctor Fay—whoever!" Mendasico snapped, as though personally offended. "That gentle man over there is Doctor Harold Chapman—just as *this* man in my arms is Doctor Harold Chapman. Don't you see, assassin? It is a sign. Try to kill *one* Dr. Harold Chapman, and *two* appear. Understand?"

"Dr. Fayteyant?" the master of the house said, chin on chest and eye still on Bochkser. "It is an honor! I just *love* your scale..."

Bochkser was momently confused. Then he giggled.

At his back Fayteyant heard an intestinal, poisonous, voiceless howl thrashing, choking throatless against chained confinement. He turned—nothing but the Japanese screen ... Sweat flooded his wrinkled brow... the air almost tropical.

Bochkser unblocked the doorway, revealing The Goat King of Madison Avenue. He hadn't aged a greedy day, posed gloriously firm and free, as though urinating off a terrace.

"Ah, there you are, Eyeball! Did you really think you could keep my man and I trapped behind a mere closet door? Who's that Geriatric Queefsniffer back there—wait, it can't. Is it?"

"They're both Harold Chapman, sir."

"What? That is rich," Hextly said with jolly snort.

"O God," Fayteyant said.

"God is just the oldest asshole in the room," Hextly said, "though you're a close second. But what are the chances, Doctor Faint-at-heart? I feared we'd lost your trail decades ago—you'd be dead in some gutter not worth owning. But we kept on after *this* one. Bochkser here determined he was snaking about under the alias Harold Chapman, and tracked him to this miserable pit. And now it turns out that you too are masquerading about as a Doctor Harold Chapman!"

Hextly walked over to the bar and poured two whiskeys. He brought one to Bochkser and straddled the only unmolested chair, sipping his own.

"Take your time, Bochkser. After twenty-seven years, what's a few minutes—hours? We're in no rush. Marshall your strength..."

"Listen, Father-in-law. How could I help it if Vespertine and I loved each other? So she ran away from you—why, I told you that just a moment ago—but she's happier here than on Madison Avenue. By the way you are welcome to stay for dinner... I can tell you all about my latest money-making venture. *You* inspired it and I want to thank you, and offer you a stake in the business. It's a cologne—distilled from goat fat! Smells like shit. I call it: *Sodomist*..."

"Shut up, Johngreatgrandson!" Hextly said, his blue eyes stinging Fayteyant. "Old man, you could've had this anonymasshole's job, man, if you hadn't let my Leta die... not to mention what you did to her career."

"The Commissioner of Lunacy," Fayteyant said. "*He's* Johngreatgrandson?"

"Otto Johngreatgrandson the Third, to *you*, my good doctor," Fayteyant's host said. "My grandfather was 300% mad-raving—but the library he'd built in Cirkle's Way was a good, out-of-the-way place to hole up, what with awful Bochkser on my trail."

"The library? You took my name—stole my life's work, my Etcetracaine…"

"But it wasn't your name, was it? Besides, I did you a favor, you walking corpse. You should've seen the side effects! I admit it helped me build my fortune, but I barely escaped New Toomes alive. You should see what it did to my wife! I kept one as a memento. She mistook it for pepper…she always was a ninny, eh…"

"Where's my lovely daughter, hmn? Where's Vespertine now? I want to make up for disowning her. I'm going to disembowel her."

"I know you're going to kill me," Fayteyant said. "So be it. But you should know that you murdered Leta. She was *alive* when you dropped her like a bag of rocks."

Hextly snorted. "Both my daughters were idiots, both thought they loved this idiot here. We're going to kill you, man, yes. But first I have to see an eyesocket about an empty ring…"

"My eye," Johngreatgrandson said, somehow more lucid. "I haven't seen that since you and the Bochkser Brigade corned me in Gravelspitz Lane…"

"You had amazing luck, last time, getting away before I could finish. Time for me to complete this pair of rings—see, asshole? And, I have a lovely glass locket too, just the right size for your seeing orb. I'll fill it with formaldehyde, wear it round my neck. I'll have all *three* of your eyes."

"Leave my Master alone," Mendasico said, saintly, imbecilic.

Hextly finished his whiskey in one gulp and drew a pistol from his coat. He put it in his mouth, then took it out and frowned, deliberating. Then he nodded to himself and shoved the barrel into one nostril. Holding the other closed with his finger, he blew his nose into the revolver.

"Greetings from my excretings," Hextly said, and fired it into Mendasico's face. The servant fell backwards, taking Johngreatgrandson down with him.

"I want to do this right so we will take our time, right, man?" Hextly said to Bochkser.

Johngreatgrandson III was whimpering, cruelly conscious.

"I feel much better," Bochkser said, adjusting the erection in his pants to a more comfortable, midnight angle. Just need to steady myself."

Hextly joined his servant in scanning the room.

"Don't see any canes, man."

"No need, sir," Bochkser said. He hobbled over to the étagère and sat on it. He gripped his leg with shattered knee and twisted it until it came off at the joint. Without a grimace, he tied the end of his trousers tightly round the stump and, reaching to the floor with a long arm, collected the exenterated pendulum of a grandfather clock. Bochkser then set his disconnected leg on the floor so that it stood by itself. He shoved the pendulum into the marrow of it until it was securely in place. Then he got up, and took a few steps. His amputated limb served as a perfect cane.

"Good, man!" Hextly said. "I must say, it really is you, Bochkser. Attend to the doctor while I finalize my transaction with the triops." Bochkser hobbled forward on his legs, a deadly cripple.

He approached Fayteyant with terrible slowness. The doctor stepped back, candlestick in hand, watching Hextly rifling through his medical bag for a surgical instrument, when a loud crash and something like a moan slathered in grave-wax turned his head to see the Japanese Screen on the floor; it buckled up and down as though a family of six was trapped and asphyxiating beneath.

Johngreatgrandson III began to cry in agony.

Bochsker's heavy, unsyncopated tread … Fayteyant ran to the screen, pulled it aside.

The brass candlestick dropped from his hand. Behind him, Hextly was pontificating about testicles and Magellan. Beneath him, a writhing Etceterack, adult-sized abortion tugging on umbilical cord of chain, one end staked to the floor by a railroad spike, the other affixed in a hole burned through its mid-section.

He recognized Vespertine at once. Even though her hair had fallen out, head to pubis, and her nails grown incredibly calcinated, piercing tips hanging down to what were either knees or labia … Her front teeth protruded past lower lip, which was disturbingly human, full and feminine. Her mouth opened wide, tongue a blackish-blue. Her eyes had caved into her head and slipped to the back of her mouth, vibrating with the uvula. Like her mouth, her eyes had remained strikingly unchanged from the last time he'd seen her.

Fayteyant caught a glimpse of blackness at the end of his tunnel, thrown into relief against the rest of the dark like red fire at the center of a rose.

Bochkser was a minute or so away now…

He couldn't flee this time and drew strength from the miraculously limited options available to him. Without hesitation he used up the last of his feeble strength to yank at the tethering spike, falling to his knees with the effort. He managed to loosen it a little, and Vespertine did the rest. She uncurled and reared up like a newly-hatched worm, stretching itself into its final towering state—the odd lines and curves of her limbs and hips designed for terrible, highly-specialized ends … the doctor looked up, seeing only Vespertine, arched over all like a rabid firmament, like a December 5th, 1868 blizzard-sky … Fayteyant felt the unusual heat disperse as a wave of room temperature air enveloped him and her gorgeous, human lips descended on insect strings to swing fish-luring before his old eyes.

She dripped closer. She said:

"*Thank you, doctor. Thank you … thank you …*"

"My child!" Fayteyant said, his voice cracking with emotion. "You are welcome. You're so very, very welcome…"

And even as his sight ebbed away into darkness, Fayteyant's eyes misted. They filled with tears of gratitude, because he'd given someone a second chance. It didn't matter *who*; there was no time left for that. And he cried because it didn't matter who *he* was, either—only that someone had given a defeated old man this precious gift, to choose his last words, and he'd gotten them right … He'd made them beautiful—

—*Perfect!*

Because they were true.

Because there was no time left to think otherwise.

EPITAPH #2
EPILOGUE #2
FUCK ME! IT'S—

> "... and so I must conclude that there is indeed life after death—the worms live richly on the corpse ... And perhaps by now you have figured out that all this time you have been reading my suicide note. I apologize for the great length. Since you must have read past Chapter III, I hope you too were already on your way to Oblivion; otherwise I am sorry—All I can say is you're headed somewhere much worse—a place so terrible, there are no words for it." – *The Dark Wintering*, Epilogue & Good-Bye.

I apologize for startling you—I'm not used to seeing anyone round these parts. Not any longer. What do you have there, that smells so good? O, cold sausages? Florida oranges and a goblet of cornmeal mush? No, thank you I ate—it seems I'm always eating. I couldn't. Such kindness is exceedingly rare. What? No, I'm sure we haven't met before. It's just that I look like several different ugly people at once, so I'm bound to remind you of some hideous acquaintance.

What's that book next to you? I see! Be careful ... well, I only mean that books can inflict wounds far worse than papercuts ... May I ask if you are feeling all right? I'm sorry if it's not my business but you appear burdened, under a dark cloud. No, I don't know if it's that obvious really, but I've done many things wrong in my life and know what it is to be troubled by regrets that send you to the road. So I've got more insight into your condition than most. Cheer up; things may always go from worse to bad. May I? Thank you, these legs do need a rest now and then ... there. What was I saying? Yes: You seem to have been forever sitting, nibbling and thinking last thoughts in this obscure grove—indifferent and tense, waiting a turn that will either never come or arrive too soon. A grain of wondering sand on an hourglass floor.

May I ask where you're headed? No, don't go that way. Yes, it's true. New Toomes is a ghost town—literally and figuratively. What do I mean? There is something ocean-floor about the desolation, or like it's at the bottom of an alien vertical world. You feel you shouldn't even be able to *get* here. The idea you might ever be able to leave seems doubly ludicrous...

The gray buildings sway together like lynched men neck-hung off the great boughs of a single tree; the wind carries a curious salty, rotten stench that sets the brain against itself: Do you smell blood-drained corpses, their hard veins embalmed with purulent urine—or the sweet/formaldehyde aroma of chickens, pigs and woodcocks boiled in the cauldron of a cadaver's dissected chest cavity? And in that same wind lurk vivid approximations of things you've never heard before, faint but horribly imaginable: the unjust sodomy of velvet alphabet blocks on ruptured accordions; the increasingly compressed panting of a dog chained to the misaligned pistons of a machine, crushing its windpipe while running deranged circles round the faulty device; pneumatically triggered face-clacks; fork tines and dry beautymarks waltzing off East River bridges ... Weird words, eh? Weird times...

Even the natural landscape has changed since those creatures came and went—if went they did. *Etceteracks* they called them round here—they say they were all wracked with pain and their eyes cried black powders. Their pupils scrambling around, like ghostly thought through the bizarre grooves, fissures and cul-de-sacs of the human brain ... the ataxic trampling and prancing of monsters through the small world, stumpies dragged, the coffin-headed scraping wallpaper and bark off trees, knocking portraits from hallways and wasp nests from boughs, hoofed genitals moving forward through a series of failed attempts at masturbation—whispery garment-sounds of oleaginous facecreepers, whose every misstep exuded alien vocabularies...living, killing mistakes.

That's what I've heard...

If you go that way, you'll see the trees have grown—not up—but into obscene togetherness. Intertwined like severed fingers reassembling into some forbidden gesture. People say they leak sticky shadows, independent of the sun's movements in the sky. And the ground is softer; what was rocky is spongy and hard dirt is turning into a seeping mess. Perhaps that's why the buildings sway so. Or maybe, like the more fanciful say, those things eventually merged together and into the land itself. That New Toomes and its vicinity is one great living organism now, a beast part human, part world, part something worse—but that's just speculation, and we'll never know.

Why?

O, because a dozen-or-so self-styled "Monster Hunters" went to catch them some Etceteracks—the toughest old salts I'd ever seen and all loaded up with rifles and sabers and knives and bravado. Only one ever came back from the vicinity of New Toomes. To him we owe the only description of what might still be darkening that accursed land and maybe even now spreading beneath the rind of that orange. And as for him, when he first returned he told them a bit:

All day he'd been lying on his belly in the mud at the edge of a field, waiting for something. He'd been hearing things: In the wind, indecipherable lamentations; laughter jagged and fast as lightning; the growling of empty-stomached brains; senescent musical gears tinkling, exactly like two streams of piss crossing over tambourines. But nothing he could see. No heads to mount on a wall ... Night was near and he was close to giving up, when he saw a creature silhouetted against the depressing sun.

It was the size of a smallish man and roughly so-shaped. As it moved away from him into the west it held its arms out on either side. His fingernails were long, curved and indurate as obstetric specula, caked with sediments human, canine, and porcine; red ribbons of flesh tied round each as though it had ten things to remember. The hair on its head was grotesquely extended in every direction and seemed to hover over him like a saint with a dense cloud of flies for halo. This mane was moldy, sheathed in browns, dun, bistre, whites, ochres, greens, fuscous hues—of the entire spectrum of mammalian dung-hues. It was obvious that no water, no scissors had approached that musty mop for many years.

The hunter set his sights on the back of the thing's head. He was prepared to fire when it abruptly stopped moving; he was curious as to why…And at that point in the story he'd stop talking and just sit in the corner rocking himself to and fro. He'd jam his fingers in his ears, like trying to block out the sound of an explosion. And they stopped asking him to go on after that part, because he'd never tell and it only made him more agitated, the poor sod. He'd bury his face in his hands, like the muzzle of a starving hyena into deepest carrion.

Well, he started trying other things. In his ears, I mean. The fingers weren't enough to keep out whatever message only he could hear. He put sticks in there, forced in slugs with spoon handles. Eventually he moved on to screwdrivers.

He's dead these days.

Now you tell me, what in the name of Krist ought you make of that?

I know. Questions are crippled thoughts, aren't they? But I've got a theory. I think that Etceterack said something.

I think its voice was so monstrous, so overwhelming, that it drove him insane…

But it's getting late; I must be going. When you're done with your meal, take care to head west—through, believe it or not—yet *another* abandoned town. They used to call it Cirkle's Way. You can't miss it; you'll pass a great stone building on the way to the main road—a library. You might see a single old tombstone in the back with the curious epitaph:

DON'T GO

No idea. This library, it's decrepit but impassive and enduring as the sphinx. It'll be dark by the time you get there, and even I must own that at night it looks like a haunted charnel house…

I advise you to ignore these, keep your wits about you and don't stop until you see the road past the caved-in factory and clocktower. And even though it's so cold, if you see lights flickering back and forth across the library windows—don't be tempted to look there for lodging.

You just keep going.

You just keep going faster than you can…

What? O, never mind—I was mumbling to myself, hermit that I am. Of course! Yes, I was quite serious. You can unburden yourself to me without fear of judgment.

I'm listening…

My but that is a very sad story, my friend. And afterwards, did you quit her body or hold vigil? No, of course … you had to get away. They'd have snapped your neck damn quick. And the blood? The *glomerulus*? How did you manage without anyone noticing? But then where exactly had the breasts been misplaced? I see … O, so that was the *second* one. The third? I apologize if I lost track … but the details aren't so important anymore, are they?

I'm glad you told me. I hope our meeting has been of some help to you. At least know you are not alone. I've done far worse things than you, my poor friend…

Me? You're right, that's only fair. O no—I can answer that in a heartbeat. I don't need to think about it… I can tell you, with dead certainty that, looking back on my long life, the thing I regret most of all is that I read far too much.

AFTERWORD

"Thank you very much to the person who threw this glass bottle at my head; it nearly killed me but you missed again so you have to keep trying next week."

– Iggy Pop, following The Stooges' closing performance of "Louie, Louie" at the Michigan Palace in Detroit, on February 9, 1974

www.eriktjohnson.net

@YES_TRESPASSING

You have read too much.

THOUGHT I'D CHECK IN, IF YOU ARE STILL INTERESTED IN PUTTING OUT A COLLECTION OF MY STORIES. I THINK WE LAST SPOKE ABOUT THIS SIX MONTHS AGO OR SO, NOT SURE, TIME FLIES AND I SLEEP THROUGH IT, SO NO IDEA EXACTLY WHEN IT WAS... I HAVE THE EMAIL CHAIN SOMEWHERE...

IF SO, WHAT WOULD BE OUR NEXT STEPS? YOU ASKED ME TO SEND YOU SOME ROUGH DRAFTS WITH NOTES WRITTEN ON THEM THAT WE WERE THINKING FOR AESTHETIC PURPOSES, BUT I NEVER DID GET THOSE TO YOU. DO YOU STILL WANT THOSE?

HELLO FROM BROOKLYN, NYC, HOME OF SATURDAY NIGHT FEVER AND HUBERT SELBY...

FOR YOUR FICTION COLLECTION, HAVE YOU THOUGHT OF A TITLE IF WE DECIDE TO INCLUDE EITHER TWO OR THREE OF THE SECTIONS? I LIKE THE IDEA OF HAVING SEPARATE SECTIONS WITHIN A SINGLE COLLECTION: BLUMENKRANK AND OTHER HORRORS, THE LEAF AND OTHER FANTASIES, ETC., BUT I WAS WONDERING IF YOU WANTED "SOMETHING &C!" AS A TITLE FOR THE ENTIRE PROJECT, WITH "SOMETHING" REPLACED WITH A BETTER WORD OF YOUR CHOOSING. I'M NOT SURE WHY, BUT I'M DRAWN TO HAVING "&C!" SOMEWHERE IN THE TITLE. I WOULD EVEN CONSIDER JUST &C!, BUT I'M NOT YET SURE IF WE CAN INCLUDE SPECIAL CHARACTERS IN THE TITLE, OR IF IT WOULD MAKE THINGS DIFFICULT FOR FINDING THE TITLE ONLINE

I'M SENDING YOU SOME SCANS OF MANUSCRIPTS WITH DOODLES AND SOME DRAWINGS I WORKED ON DURING VARIOUS COMPOSITION PROCESSES... WILL CONTINUE TO SEND MORE WHEN I GET TIME. THERE SHOULD BE 19 PDFS ATTACHED.

JUST AN IDEA, NEEDS FINESSING IF IT WERE TO BE ANYTHING AT ALL...

HERE'S ANOTHER CONCEPTION... THERE COULD ALSO BE A CONCEPTUAL JOKE IN HERE ABOUT HOW DURER DID ALL THAT WORK AND I AM TRESPASSING ON IT, TAKING IT AS MY OWN, ETC.

here's an idea on how to get the #c! symbol in there nice and clear... the concept is the one with the background being a marked up manuscript; marks would be in red, the #c! could be a kind of exclamation written in the corner

here's another one, which matches more closely with your cover sketch from a previous email.

we can even jot something down on the polaroid...

i think everything on the front and using back for text looks best, at least out of these 3 concepts... but, i think the picture is creepier if you can see just how enormous the woods are in relation to the 2 children. they look more lost when the picture takes up more of the cover... whatcha thoughts?

i had a dream about the cover last night, so i woke up this morning and made it.

i don't know why i'm on this blank polaroid thing, but there's something strange about a blank one, as if anticipating for it to develop, or perhaps there's nothing there at all... it's a simple front cover, and this keeps the image of the kids intact on the back cover.

it could be the cover is mainly the photo with the looming woods, but then the yes trespassing and the part with my name, etc. look like pieces of paper taped on a white background over the picture. or duct taped there... or pinned

just shooting ideas...

actually, i like that a lot! and the kids on the back work well with that on the front... very cool.

#c!

or put everything on the front and leave room on the back for text...

i just brainstormed out 2 possible options for the toc of yes trespassing. i pasted and attached it as a word document, since the pasted text might show up funky on your computer...

here is a sketch of how a book of my stuff might be organized.

just hit me today. anyway take a look. see if stews and juices.

because the stories are so off-kilter and occasionally hard to pin down, one idea is to divide them thematically, whether they are horror or fantasy or whatever. i think it needs to be a little more high-concept than tales of fantasy and horror or that kind of thing.

this is more mysterious but i think seems like a better way to have different types of stories instead of like stories about inventions, stories about doom, etc.

oh, i came up with this erik t [sic] johnson idea as a way to differentiate me from the 8 million erik t. johnsons out there. also i like the lowercase t; and like that "sic" follows it in a way consistent with typographical usage. what do you think? i don't want to confuse people, but on the other hand i would still be called erik t. johnson basically.